MW01122375

Patricia Wentworth

# A Marriage Under the Terror

e-artnow 2020

*Patricia Wentworth*
# A Marriage Under the Terror

**Romance in the Shadows of the French Revolution**

e-artnow, 2020
Contact: info@e-artnow.org

ISBN 978-80-273-4004-0

## Contents

CHAPTER I A PURLOINED CIPHER 11
CHAPTER II A FORCED ENTRANCE 15
CHAPTER III SHUT OUT BY A PRISON WALL 19
CHAPTER IV THE TERROR LET LOOSE 24
CHAPTER V A CARNIVAL OF BLOOD 30
CHAPTER VI A DOUBTFUL SAFETY 37
CHAPTER VII THE INNER CONFLICT 43
CHAPTER VIII AN OFFER OF FRIENDSHIP 48
CHAPTER IX THE OLD IDEAL AND THE NEW 52
CHAPTER X THE FATE OF A KING 56
CHAPTER XI THE IRREVOCABLE VOTE 62
CHAPTER XII SEPARATION 65
CHAPTER XIII DISTURBING INSINUATIONS 72
CHAPTER XIV A DANGEROUS ACQUAINTANCE 76
CHAPTER XVI AN UNWELCOME VISITOR 91
CHAPTER XVII DISTRESSING NEWS 96
CHAPTER XVIII A TRIAL AND A WEDDING 100
CHAPTER XIX THE BARRIER 106
CHAPTER XX A ROYALIST PLOT 111
CHAPTER XXI A NEW ENVIRONMENT 116
CHAPTER XXII AT HOME AND AFIELD 125
CHAPTER XXIII RETURN OF TWO FUGITIVES 130
CHAPTER XXIV BURNING OF THE CHÂTEAU 140
CHAPTER XXV ESCAPE OF TWO MADCAPS 146
CHAPTER XXVI A DYING WOMAN 153
CHAPTER XXVII BETRAYAL 156
CHAPTER XXVIII INMATES OF THE PRISON 164
CHAPTER XXIX THROUGH DARKNESS TO LIGHT 170

## CHAPTER I
## A PURLOINED CIPHER

It was high noon on a mid-August morning of the year 1792, but Jeanne, the waiting-maid, had only just set the coffee down on the small table within the ruelle of Mme. de Montargis' magnificent bed. Great ladies did not trouble themselves to rise too early in those days, and a beauty who has been a beauty for twenty years was not more anxious then than now to face the unflattering freshness of the morning air. Laure de Montargis stirred in the shadow of her brocaded curtains, put out a white hand for the cup, sipped from it, murmured that the coffee was cold, and pushed it from her with a fretful exclamation that made Jeanne frown as she drew the tan-coloured curtains and let in the mid-day glare. Madame had been up late, Madame had lost at faro, and her servants would have to put up with Heaven alone knew how many megrims in consequence.

"Madame suffers?" inquired Jeanne obsequiously, but with pursed lips.

The lady closed her eyes. Laying her head back against the delicately embroidered pillows, she indicated by a gesture that her sufferings might be taken for granted.

"Madame has the migraine?" suggested the soft, rather false-sounding voice. "Madame will not receive?"

"Heavens! girl, how you pester me," said the Marquise sharply.

Then, falling again to a languid tone, "Is there any one there?"

Jeanne smiled with malicious, averted face as she poured rose-water from a silver ewer into a Sévres bowl, and watched it rise, dimpling, to the flower-wreathed brim.

"There is M. le Vicomte as usual, Madame, and Mme. la Comtesse de Maillé, who, learning that Madame was but now awakened, told me that she would wait whilst I inquired if Madame would see her."

"Good Heavens! what an hour to come," said the lady, with a peevish air.

"Madame la Comtesse seemed much moved. One would say something had occurred," said Jeanne.

The Marquise raised her head sharply.

"—And you stand chattering there? Just Heaven! The trial that it is to have an imbecile about one! The glass quickly, and the rouge, and the lace for my head. No, not that rouge-the new sort that Isidore brought yesterday;—arrange these two curls-now a little powder. Fool! what powder is this?"

"Madame's own," submitted Jeanne meekly.

The suffering lady raised herself and dealt the girl a sounding box on the ear.

"Idiot! did I not tell you I had tired of the perfume, and that in future the white lilac powder was the only one I would use? Did I not tell you?"

"Yes, Madame"—but there was a spark beneath the waiting-maid's discreetly dropped lids.

The Marquise de Montargis sat bolt upright, and contemplated her reflection in the wide silver mirror which Jeanne was steadying. Her passion had brought a little flush to her cheeks, and she noted approvingly that the colour became her.

"Put the rouge just here, and here, Jeanne," she ordered, her anger subsiding;—then, with a fresh outburst—"Imbécile, not so much! One does not have the complexion of a milkmaid when one is in bed with the migraine; just a shade here now, a nuance. That will do; go and bring them in."

She drew a rose-coloured satin wrap about her, and posed her head, in its cloud of delicate lace, carefully. Her bed was as gorgeous as it well might be. Long curtains of rosy brocade fell about it, and a coverlid of finest needlework, embroidered with bunches of red and white roses on a white satin ground, was thrown across it. The carved pillars showed cupids pelting one another with flowers plucked from the garlands that wreathed their naked chubbiness.

Madame de Montargis herself had been a beauty for twenty years, but a life of light pleasures, and a heart incapable of experiencing more than a momentary emotion had combined to leave her face as unlined and almost as lovely as when Paris first proclaimed her its reigning queen of beauty.

She was eminently satisfied with her own looks as she turned languidly on her soft pillows to greet her friends.

Mme. de Maillé bent and embraced her; M. le Vicomte Sélincourt stooped and kissed her gracefully extended hand. Jeanne brought seats, and after a few polite inquiries Mme. de Maillé plunged into her news.

"Ma chère amie!" she exclaimed, "I come to tell you the good news. My daughter and her husband have reached England in safety." Tears filled her soft blue eyes, and she raised them to the ceiling with a gesture that would have been affected had her emotion been less evidently sincere.

"Ah! chère Comtesse, a thousand felicitations!"

"My dear, I have been on thorns, I have not slept, I have not eaten, I have wept rivers, I have said more prayers in a month than my confessor has ever before induced me to say in a year. First I thought they would be stopped at the barriers, and then-then I pictured to myself a hundred misfortunes, a thousand inconveniences! I saw my Adèle ill, fainting from the fatigues of the road; I imagined assaults of brigands, shipwrecks, storms-in short, everything of the most unfortunate-ah! my dear friends, you do not know what a mother suffers-and now I have the happiness of receiving a letter from my dearest Adèle-she is well; she is contented. They have been received with the greatest amiability, and, my friends, I am too happy."

"And your happiness is that of your friends," bowed the Vicomte.

Mme. de Montargis' congratulations were polite, if a trifle perfunctory. The convenances demanded that one should simulate an interest in the affairs of one's acquaintances, but in reality, and at this hour of the day, how they did bore one! And Marie de Maillé, with her soft airs, and that insufferable Adèle of hers, whom she had always spoilt so abominably. It was a little too much! One had affairs of one's own. With the fretful expression of half an hour before she drew a letter from beneath her pillow.

"I too have news to impart," she said, with rather a pinched smile. "News that concerns you very closely, M. le Vicomte," and she fixed her eyes on Sélincourt.

"That concerns me?"

"But yes, Monsieur, since what concerns Mademoiselle your betrothed must concern you, and closely, as I said."

"Mademoiselle my betrothed, Mlle. de Rochambeau!" he cried quickly. "Is she then ill?"

Mme. de Montargis smiled maliciously.

"Hark to the anxious lover! But calm yourself, my friend, she is certainly not ill, or she would not now be on her way to Paris."

"To Paris?"

"That, Monsieur, is, I believe, her destination."

"What? She is coming to Paris now?" inquired Mme. de Maillé with concern.

The Marquise shrugged her shoulders.

"It is very inconvenient, but what would you?" she said lightly; "as you know, dear friend, she was betrothed to M. le Vicomte when she was a child. Then my good cousin, the Comte de Rochambeau, takes it into his virtuous head that this world, even in his rural retreat, is no longer good enough for him, and follows Madame, his equally virtuous wife, to Paradise, where they are no doubt extremely happy. Until yesterday I pictured Mademoiselle almost as saintly and contented with the holy Sisters of the Grace Dieu Convent, who have looked after her for the last ten years or so. Then comes this letter; it seems there have been riots, a château burned, an intendant or two murdered, and the good nuns take advantage of the fact that the steward of Rochambeau and his wife are making a journey to Paris to confide Mademoiselle to their care, and mine. It seems," she concluded, with a little laugh, "that they think Paris is safe, these good nuns."

"Poor child, poor child!" exclaimed Mme. de Maillé in a distressed voice; "can you not stop her, turn her back?"

The Marquise laughed again.

"Dear friend, she is probably arriving at this minute. The Sisters are women of energy."

"At least M. de Sélincourt is to be congratulated," said Mme. de Maillé after a pause; "that is if Mademoiselle resembles her parents. I remember her mother very well-how charming, how spirituelle, how amiable! I knew her for only too short a time, and yet, looking back, it seems to me that I never had a friend I valued more."

"My cousin De Rochambeau was crazy about her," reflected Mme. de Montargis; "he might have married anybody, and he chose an Irish girl without a sou. It was the talk of Paris at the time. He was the handsomest man at Court."

"And Aileen Desmond the loveliest girl," put in Mme. de Maillé thoughtlessly; then, observing her hostess's change of expression, she coloured, but continued —"They were not so badly matched, and," with a little sigh, "they were very happy. It was a real romance."

Mme. de Montargis' eyes flashed. Twenty years ago beautiful Aileen Desmond had been her rival at Court. Now that for quite a dozen years gossip had coupled her name with that of the Vicomte de Sélincourt, was Aileen Desmond's daughter to take her mother's place in that bygone rivalry?

Mme. de Maillé, catching her glance, wondered how it would fare with any defenceless girl who came between Laure de Montargis and her lover. She was still wondering whilst she made her farewells.

When M. le Vicomte had bowed her out he came moodily back to his place.

"It is very inconvenient, Madame," he said pettishly.

"You say so," returned the lady.

"Pardon, Madame, it was you who said so."

The Marquise laughed. It was not a pleasant laugh.

"Of course it was I," she cried. "Who else? It is hardly likely that M. le Vicomte finds a rich bride inconvenient."

Sélincourt's face changed a little, but he waved the words away.

"Mademoiselle is nothing to me," he asserted. "Chère amie, do you suspect, do you doubt the faithful heart which for years has beaten only for one beloved object?"

The lady pouted, but her eyes ceased to sparkle.

"And that object?" she inquired, with a practised glance.

"Angel of my life-need you ask?"

It was indeed unnecessary, since a very short acquaintance with this fervid lover was sufficient to assure any one that his devotion to himself was indeed his ruling and unalterable passion; perhaps the Marquise was aware of this, and was content to take the second, but not the third place, in his affections. She looked at him coquettishly.

"Ah," she said, "you mean it now, now perhaps, Monsieur, but when she comes, when you are married?"

"Eh, ma foi," and the Vicomte waved away his prospective marriage vows as lightly as if they were thistle-down, "one does not marry for love; the heart must be free, not bound-and where will the free heart turn except to the magnet that has drawn it for so long?"

Madame extended a white, languid hand, and Monsieur kissed it with more elegance than fervour. As he was raising his head she whispered sharply:

"The new cipher, have you got it?"

He bent lower, and kissed the fair hand again, lingeringly.

"It is here, and I have drafted the letter we spoke of; it must go this week."

"The Queen is well?"

"Well, but impatient for news. There is an Austrian medicine that she longs for."

"Chut! Enough, one is never safe."

"Adieu, then, m'amie."

"Adieu, M. le Vicomte."

Monsieur took his leave with an exquisite bow, and all the forms that elegance prescribed, and Madame lay back against her pillows with closed eyes, and the frown which she never permitted to appear in society. Jeanne threw a sharp glance at her as she returned from closing the door upon Sélincourt. Her ears had made her aware of whispering, and now her eyes showed her a small crumpled scrap of paper, just inside the ruelle of Madame's bed. A love-letter? Perhaps, or perhaps not. In any case the correspondence of the mistress is the perquisite of the maid, and as Jeanne came softly to the bedside she covered the little twisted note with a dexterous foot, and, bending to adjust the rose-embroidered coverlid, secured and hid her prize. In a moment she had passed behind the heavy curtains and was scanning it with a practised eye-an eye that saw more than the innocent-seeming figures with which the white paper was dotted. Jeanne had seen ciphers before, and a glance sufficed to show her the nature of this one, for at the foot of the draft was a row of signs and figures, mysterious no longer in the light of the key that stood beneath them. Apparently Jeanne knew something about secret correspondence too, for there in the shadow behind the curtain she nodded and smiled, and once even shook her fist towards the unconscious Marquise. Next moment she was again in evidence, and but for that paper tucked away inside her bodice she would have found her morning a hard one. Madame wished this, Madame wished that; Madame would have her forehead bathed, her feet rubbed, a thousand whims complied with and a thousand fancies gratified. Soft-voiced and deft, Jeanne moved incessantly to and fro on those small, neatly-shod feet, which she sometimes compared not uncomplacently with those of her mistress, until, at last, at the latter end of all conceivable fancies there came one for repose-the rosy curtains were drawn, and Jeanne was free.

Half an hour later a deftly-cloaked figure stood before a table at which a dark-faced man wrote busily—a paper was handed over, a password asked and given.

"Is it enough now?" asked Jeanne the waiting-maid. And the dark-faced man answered, without looking up, "It is enough-the cup is full."

## CHAPTER II
## A FORCED ENTRANCE

Mademoiselle de Rochambeau had been a week in Paris, but as yet she had tasted none of its gaieties-for gaieties there were still, even in these clouding days when the wind of destiny blew up the storm of the Terror. The King and Queen were prisoners in the Temple, many of the noblesse had emigrated, but what remained of the Court circles still met and talked, laughed, gamed, and flirted, as if there were no deluge to come. To-day Mme. de Montargis received, and Mlle. de Rochambeau, dressed by a Parisian milliner for the first time, was to be presented to her cousin's friends.

She had not even seen her betrothed as yet-that dim figure which she had contemplated for so many years of cloistered monotony, until it had become the model upon which her dreams and hopes were hung. Now that the opening of the door might at any moment reveal him in the flesh, the dreams wore suddenly thin, and she was conscious of an overpowering suspense. She hoped for so much, and all at once she was afraid. Husbands, to be sure, were not romantic, not the least in the world, and, according to the nuns, it would be the height of impropriety to wish that they should be. One married because it was the convenable thing to do, but to fall in love-fi donc, Mademoiselle, the idea! Aline laughed, for she remembered Sister Séraphine's face, all soft and shocked and wrinkled, and then in a minute she was grave again. Dreams may be forbidden, but when one is nineteen they have a way of recurring, and it is certain that Mlle. de Rochambeau's heart beat faster than Sister Séraphine would have approved, as she stood by Mme. de Montargis' gilded chair and heard the servant announce "M. le Vicomte de Sélincourt."

He kissed Madame's hand; and then hers. A sensation that was almost terror caught the colour from her face. Was this little, dark, bowing fop the dream hero? His eyes were like a squirrel's—black, restless, shallow-and his mouth displeased her. Something about its puckered outline made her recoil from the touch of it upon her hand, and the Marquise, glancing at her, saw all the young face pale and distressed. She smiled maliciously, and reflected on the folly of youth and the kind connivance of Fate.

Sélincourt, for his part, was well enough satisfied. Mademoiselle was too tall for his taste, it was true; her beautifully shaped shoulders and bust too thin; but of those dark grey Irish eyes there could be no two opinions, and his quick glance approved her on the whole. She would play her part as Mme. la Vicomtesse very creditably when a little modish polish had softened her convent stateliness, and for the rest he had no notion of being in love with his bride. It was long, in fact, since his small, jaded heart had beaten the faster for any woman, and his eyes left her face with a genuine indifference which did not escape either woman.

"Mademoiselle, I felicitate Paris, and myself," he said, with a formal bow. Mademoiselle made him a stately reverence, and the long-dreamed-of meeting was over.

He turned at once to her cousin.

"You have written to our friend, Madame?"

"I wrote immediately, M. le Vicomte."

He lowered his voice.

"The paper with the cipher on it, did I give you my copy as well as your own?"

"But no, mon ami. Why, have you not got it?"

Sélincourt raised his shoulders.

"Certainly not, since I ask if you have it," he returned.

Madame's delicate chin lifted a little.

"And when did you find this out?" she asked.

"I had no occasion to use the code until yesterday, and then... " the lift of his shoulders merged into a decided shrug.

The Marquise turned away with a slight frown. It was annoying, but then the Vicomte was always careless, and no doubt the paper would be found; it must be somewhere, and her guests were assembling.

Of such stuff were the conspirators of those days-triflers, fops, and flirts; men who mislaid the papers which meant life and death to them and to a hundred more; women who chattered secrets in the hearing of their lackeys and serving-maids, unable to realise that these were listeners more dangerous than the chairs and tables of their gaily furnished salons. What wonder that of all the aristocratic plots and counterplots of the Revolution there was not one but perished immature? Powdered nobles and painted dames, they played at conspiracy as they played at love and hate, played with gilded counters instead of sterling gold, and in the end they paid the reckoning in blood.

Meanwhile Madame received.

The gay, softly lighted salon filled apace. Day was still warm outside, but the curtains were drawn, and clusters of wax candles, set in glittering chandeliers, threw their becoming light upon the bare shoulders of the ladies and lent the rouge a more natural air.

Play was the order of the day, the one real passion which held that world. Life and death were trifles, birth and marriage a jest, love and hate the flicker of shadow and sunshine over shallow waters; but the gambler could still feel joy of gain or rage of loss, and the faro table demanded an earnestness which religion was powerless to evoke. Mlle. de Rochambeau stood behind her cousin's chair. The scene fascinated, interested, excited her. The swiftly passing cards, the heaps of gold, the flushed faces, the half-checked ejaculations, all drew and enchained her attention; for this was the great world, and these her future friends.

At first the game itself was a mystery, but by degrees her quick wits grasped the principle, and she watched with a breathless interest. Madame de Montargis won and won. As the rouleaux of gold grew beside her, she slid them into an embroidered bag, where her monogram shone in pearls and silver and was wreathed by clustering forget-me-nots.

Now she was not in such good luck. She knit her brows, set her teeth into the full lower lip, pouted ominously-and cheated. Quite distinctly Mademoiselle saw her change a card, and play on smilingly, as the change brought fickle fortune to her side once more. Aline de Rochambeau's hand went up to her throat with a nervous gesture. She wore around it a single string of pearls-milk-white, and of great value. In her surprise and agitation she caught sharply at the necklet, and in a moment the thread snapped, and the pearls rolled here and there over the polished floor. Aileen Desmond had worn them last, a dozen years before, and the silken string had had time to rot since then.

The players took no notice, but Mademoiselle de Rochambeau gave a soft little cry and went down on her knees to pick up her pearls. The greater number were to her hand, but a few had rolled away to the corner of the room. Mademoiselle put what she had picked up into her muslin handkerchief, and slipped it into her bosom. Then she went timidly forward, casting her looks here, there, and everywhere in search of the three pearls which she still missed. She found one under the fold of a heavy curtain, and as she bent to pick it up she heard voices in the alcove it screened, and caught her own name.

"The little Rochambeau"—just like that.

It was a woman's voice, very clear, and a little shrill, and then a man said:

"She is not bad-she has eyes, and a fine shape, and a delicate skin. Laure de Montargis will be green with jealousy."

The woman laughed, a high, tinkling laugh, like the trill of a guitar.

"The faithful Sélincourt will be straining at his leash," pursued the same voice. "It is time he ranged himself; and, after all, he has given her twelve years."

Another ripple of laughter.

"What a gift! Heaven protect me from the like. He is tedious enough for an hour, and twelve years!—that poor Laure!"

"Chère Duchesse, she has permitted herself distractions." Here the voice dropped, but Aline caught names and shuddered. She rose, bewildered and confused, and as she crossed the room and took her station near Madame again, her eyes looked very dark amidst the pallour of her face. The hand that knotted the fine handkerchief over the last of her pearls shook more than a little, and at a sudden glance of Sélincourt's she looked down, trembling in every limb. M. de Sélincourt, her betrothed, and Laure de Montargis, her cousin-lovers. But Laure was married. M. de Montargis was with the Princes-his wife had spoken of him only that day. Oh, kind saints, what wickedness was this?

Aline's brain was in a whirl, but through her shocked bewilderment emerged a very definite horror of the sallow-faced, shifty-eyed gentleman whom she had been taught to regard as her future husband. She shuddered when she remembered that he had kissed her hand, and furtively she rubbed the place, as if to efface a stain. If she had been less taken up with her own thoughts, she would have noticed that whereas the room appeared to have grown curiously quiet, there was a strange sound of trampling, and a confused buzz of speech outside. Suddenly, however, the door was burst open, and a frightened lackey ran in, followed by another and another.

"Madame —a Commissioner-and a Guard-oh, Madame!" stammered one and another.

Mme. de Montargis raised her arched eyebrows and stared at the foremost man in displeased silence. He fell back muttering incoherently, and she turned her attention to the game once more. But her guests hesitated, and ceased to play, for behind the lackey came a little procession of three, and with it some of the desperate reality of life seemed to enter that salon of the artificial. A Commissioner of the Commune walked first, with broad tri-coloured sash above an attire sufficiently rough and disordered to bear witness to his ardent patriotism. His lank black hair hung unpowdered to his shoulders, and his fat, sallow face wore an expression of mingled dislike and complacency. He was followed by two blue-coated National Guards, who looked curiously about them and smelled horribly of garlic.

Madame's gaze dwelt on them with a surprised resentment that did not at all distinguish between the officer and his subordinates.

"Messieurs, this intrusion—" she began, and on the instant the Commissioner was by her side.

"Ci-devant Marquise de Montargis, you are my prisoner," and rough as his voice came his hand upon her shoulder. With a fashionable oath Sélincourt drew his sword, and a woman screamed.

("It was the La Rivière," said Mme. de Montargis afterwards. "I always knew she had no breeding.")

M. le Commissionaire had a fine dramatic sense. He experienced a most pleasing conviction of being in his element as he signed to the nearest of his underlings, and the man, without a word, drew back the heavy crimson curtains which screened the window towards the street.

The afternoon sun poured in, turning the candle-light to a cheap tawdry yellow, and with it came a sound which I suppose no one has yet heard unmoved-the voice of an angry crowd. Oaths flew, foul words rose, and above the din sounded a shrill scream of—"The Austrian spy, bring out the Austrian spy!" and with a roar the crowd took up the word, "To the lantern, to the lantern, to the lantern!"

There was no uncertainty about that voice, and at that, and the Commissioner's meaning gesture, Sélincourt's sword-arm dropped to his side again. If Madame turned pale her rouge hid it, and her manner continued calm to the verge of indifference. When the shouting outside had died down a little she turned politely to the man beside her.

"Monsieur, your hand incommodes me; if you would have the kindness to remove it"; and under her eye, and the faint, stinging sarcasm which flavoured its glance, he coloured heavily and withdrew a pace. Then he produced a paper, drawing from its rustling folds fresh confidence and a return to his official bearing.

"The ci-devant Vicomte de Sélincourt," he said in loud, harsh tones; and, as Sélincourt made a movement, "You, too, are arrested."

"But this is an outrage," stammered the Vicomte, "an outrage, fellow, for which you shall suffer. On what charge-by what authority?"

The man shrugged fat shoulders across which lay the tri-colour scarf.

"Charge of treasonable correspondence with Austria," he said shortly; "and as to authority, I am the Commune's delegate. But, ma foi, Citizen, there is authority for you if you don't like mine," and, with a gesture which he admired a good deal, he waved an arm towards the street, where the clamour raged unchecked. As he spoke a stone came flying through the glass, and a sharp splinter struck Sélincourt upon the cheek, drawing blood, and an oath.

"You had best come with me before those outside break in to ask why we delay," said the delegate meaningly.

Madame de Montargis surveyed her guests. She was too well-bred to smile at their dismay, but something of amusement, and something of scorn, lurked in her hazel eyes. Then, with her usual slow grace, she took Sélincourt's arm, and walked towards the door, smiling, nodding, curtsying, speaking here a few words and there a mere farewell, whilst the Commissioner followed awkwardly, spitting now and then to relieve his embarrassment, and decidedly of the opinion that these aristocrats built rooms far too long.

"Chère Adèle, 't is au revoir."

"Marquise, I cannot express my regrets."

"Nay, Duchesse, mine is the discourtesy, though a most unintentional one. I must rely upon the kindness of my friends to forgive it me."

Aline de Rochambeau walked after her cousin, but participated in none of the farewells. She felt cold and very bewildered; her only instinct to keep close to the one protector she knew. To stay behind never occurred to her. In the vestibule Madame de Montargis paused.

"Dupont!" she called sharply, and the stout major-domo of the establishment emerged from a group of frightened servants.

"Madame —" Dupont's knees were shaking, but he contrived a presentable bow.

Madame's eyes had lost their smile, but the scorn remained. She spoke aloud.

"Discharge those three fools who ran in just now, and see that in future I have lackeys who know their place," and with that she walked on again. All the way down the grand staircase the noise of the mob pursued them. In the vestibule more of the Guard waited with an officer, and yet another Commissioner. The three men in authority conferred for a moment, and then the Commissioners hurried their prisoners to a side door where a fiacre stood waiting. They passed out, and behind them the door was shut and locked. Then, for the first time, Madame seemed to be aware of her cousin's presence.

"Aline-little fool! —go back-but on the instant —"

"Ma cousine — —"

"Go back, I say. Mon Dieu, Mademoiselle, what folly!"

The girl put her hand on the door, tried it, and said, in a low, shaking voice:

"But it is locked — —"

"Decidedly, since those were my orders," growled the second Commissioner. "What's all this to-do? Who 's this, Renard? Send her back."

"But I ask you how?" demanded Renard, "since the door is locked inside, and-Heavens, man, they are coming this way!"

Lenoir uttered an imprecation.

"Here, get in, get in!" he shouted, pushing the girl as he spoke. "It is the less matter since the house and all effects are to be sealed up. Get in, I say, or the mob will be down on us!"

Madame gave him a furious glance, and took her seat beside her trembling cousin. Sélincourt and Renard followed. Lenoir swung himself to the box-seat, and the fiacre drove off noisily, the sound of its wheels on the rough cobble-stones drowning by degrees the lessening outcries of the furious crowd behind.

## CHAPTER III
## SHUT OUT BY A PRISON WALL

The fiacre drew up at the gate of La Force. M. le Vicomte de Sélincourt got down, bowed politely, and assisted Madame de Montargis to alight. He then gave his hand to her cousin, and the little party entered the prison. Mme. la Marquise walked delicately, with an exaggeration of that graceful, mincing step which was considered so elegant by her admirers. She fanned herself, and raised a scented pomander ball to her nostrils.

"Fi donc! What an air!" she observed with petulant disgust.

Renard of the dramatic soul shrugged his shoulders. It was vexing not to be ready with a biting repartee, but he was consoled by the conviction that a gesture from him was worth more than many words from some lesser soul. His colleague Lenoir—a rough, coarse-faced hulk-scowled fiercely, and growled out:

"Eh, Mme. l'Aristocrate, it has been a good enough air for many a poor devil of a patriot, as the citizen gaoler here can tell you, and turn and turn about's fair play." And with that he spat contemptuously in Madame's path, and scowled again as she lifted her dainty petticoats a trifle higher but crossed the inner threshold without so much as a glance in his direction.

Bault, the head gaoler of La Force, motioned the prisoners into a dull room, used at this time as an office, but devoted at a later date to a more sinister purpose, for it was here in days to come-days whose shadow already rested palpably upon the thick air-that the hair of the condemned was cut, and their arms pinioned for the last fatal journey which ended in the embraces of Mme. Guillotine.

Bault opened the great register with a clap of the leaves that betokened impatience. He was a nervous man, and the times frightened him; he slept ill at nights, and was irritable enough by day.

"Your names?" he demanded abruptly.

Mme. de Montargis drew herself up and raised her arched eyebrows, slightly, but quite perceptibly.

"I am the Marquise de Montargis, my good fellow," she observed, with something of indulgence in her tone.

"First name, or names?" pursued Citizen Bault, unmoved.

"Laure Marie Josèphe."

"And you?" turning without ceremony to the Vicomte.

"Jean Christophe de Sélincourt, at your service, Monsieur. Quelle comédie!" he added, turning to Mme. de Montargis, who permitted a slight, insolent smile to lift her vermilion upper lip. Meanwhile the Commissioners were handing over their papers.

"Quite correct, Citizens." Then, with a glance around, "But what of this demoiselle? There is no mention of her that I can see."

Lenoir laughed and swore.

"Eh," he said, "she was all for coming, and I dare say a whiff of the prison air, which the old Citoyenne found so trying, will do her no harm."

Bault shook a doubtful head, and Renard threw himself with zeal into the role of patriot, animated at once by devotion to the principles of liberty, and loyalty to law and order.

"No, no, Lenoir; no, no, my friend. Everything must be done in order. The Citoyenne sees now what comes of treason and plots. Let her be warned in time, or she will be coming back for good. For this time there is no accusation against her."

He spoke loudly, hand in vest, and felt himself every inch a Roman; but his magniloquence was entirely lost on Mademoiselle, for, with a cry of dismay, she caught her cousin's hand.

"Oh, Messieurs, let me stop! Madame is my guardian, my place is with her!"

Mme. de Montargis looked surprised, but she interrupted the girl with energy.

"Silence then, Aline! What should a young girl do in La Force? Fi donc, Mademoiselle!"—as the soft, distressed murmur threatened to break out again—"you will do as I tell you. Mme. de

Maillé will receive you; go straight to her at the Hotel de Maillé. Present my apologies for not writing to her, and —

"Sacrebleu!" thundered Lenoir furiously, "this is not Versailles, where a pack of wanton women may chatter themselves hoarse. Send the young one packing, Bault, and lock these people up. Are the Deputies of the Commune to stand here till nightfall listening to a pair of magpies? Silence, I say, and march! The old woman and the young one, both of you march, march!"

He laid a large dirty hand on Mlle. de Rochambeau's shoulder as he spoke, and pushed her towards the door. As she passed through it she saw her cousin delicately accepting M. de Sélincourt's proffered arm, whilst her left hand, flashing with its array of rings, still held the sweet pomander to her face. Next moment she was in the street.

Her first thought was for the fiacre which had conveyed them to the prison, but to her despair it had disappeared, and there was no other vehicle in sight.

As she stood in hesitating bewilderment, she was aware of the sound of approaching wheels, and looking up she saw three carriages coming, one behind the other, at a brisk pace. There were three priests in the first, one of them so old that all the solicitous assistance of the two younger men was required to get him safely down the high step and through the gate. In the second were two ladies, whose faces seemed vaguely familiar. Was it a year or only an hour ago that they had laughed and jested at Mme. de Montargis' brilliant gathering? They looked at her in the same half uncomprehending manner, and passed on. The last carriage bore the De Maillé crest, but a National Guard occupied the box-seat in place of the magnificent coachman Aline had seen the day before, when Mme. de Maillé had taken her old friend's daughter for a drive through Paris.

The door of the chariot opened, and Mme. De Maillé, pale, almost fainting, was helped out. She looked neither to right nor left, and when Aline started forward and would have spoken, the National Guard pushed her roughly back.

"Go home, go home!" he said, not unkindly; "if you are not arrested, thank the saints for it, for there are precious few aristocrats as lucky to-day"; and Aline shrank against the wall, dumb with perturbation and dismay.

As in a dream she listened to the clang of the prison gate, the roll of departing wheels, and it was only when the last echo died away that the mist which hung about her seemed to clear, and she realised that she was alone in the deserted street.

Alone! In all her nineteen years she had never been really alone before. As a child in her father's château, as a girl in her aristocratic convent, she had always been guarded, sheltered, guided, watched. She had certainly never walked a yard in the open street, or been touched by a man's hand, as the Commissioner Lenoir had touched her a few minutes since. She felt her shoulder burn through the thin muslin fichu that veiled it so discreetly, and the blood ran up, under her delicate skin, to the roots of the curling hair, where gold tints showed here and there through the lightly sprinkled powder.

It was still very hot, though so late in the afternoon, and the sun, though near its setting, shot out a level ray or two that seemed to make palpable the strong, brooding heat of the evening.

Aline felt dazed, and so faint that she was glad to support herself against the rough prison wall. When she could control her trembling thoughts a little, she began to wonder what she should do. She had only been a week in Paris, she knew no one except her cousin, the Vicomte, and Mme. de Maillé, and they were in prison-they and many, many more. For the moment these frowning walls stood to her for home, or all that she possessed of home, and she was shut outside, in a dreadful world, full of unknown dangers, peopled perhaps with persons who would speak to her as Lenoir had done, touch her even-and at that she flushed again, shuddered and looked wildly round.

A very fat woman was coming down the street-the fattest woman Mlle. de Rochambeau had ever seen, yes, fatter even than Sister Josèphe, she considered, with that mechanical detachment of thought which is so often the accompaniment of great mental distress.

She wore a striped petticoat and a gaily flowered gown, the sleeves of which were rolled up to display a pair of huge brown arms. She had a very broad, sallow face, and little pig's eyes sunk deep in rolls of crinkled flesh. Aline gazed at her, fascinated, and the woman returned the look. In truth, Mlle. de Rochambeau, with her rose-wreathed hair, her delicate muslin dress, her fichu trimmed with the finest Valenciennes lace, her thin stockings and modish white silk shoes, was a sufficiently arresting figure, when one considered the hour and the place. The fat woman hesitated a moment, and in that moment Mademoiselle spoke.

"Madame — —"

It was the most hesitating essay at speech, but the woman stopped and swung her immense body round until she faced the girl.

"Eh bien, Ma'mselle," she said in a thick, drawling voice.

Mademoiselle moistened her dry lips and tried again.

"Madame —I do not know-can you tell me-oh! you look kind, can you tell me what to do?"

"What to do, Ma'mselle?"

"Oh yes, Madame, and-and where to go?"

"Where to go, Ma'mselle?"

"Yes, Madame."

"But why, Ma'mselle?"

When anything terrible happens to the very young, they are unable to realise that the whole world does not know of their misfortune. Thus to Mlle. de Rochambeau it appeared inconceivable that this woman should be in ignorance of so important an event as the arrest of the Marquise de Montargis and her friends. It was only when, to a puzzled expression, the woman added a significant tap of the gnarled forefinger upon the heavy forehead, and, with a shrug of voluminous shoulders, prepared to pass on, that it dawned upon her that here perhaps was help, and that it was slipping away from her for want of a little explanation.

"Oh, Madame," she exclaimed desperately, "do listen to me. I am Mlle. de Rochambeau, and it is only a week since I came to Paris to be with my cousin, the Marquise de Montargis, and now they have arrested her, and I have nowhere to go."

A sound of voices came from behind the great gate of the prison.

"Walk a little way with me," said the fat woman abruptly. "There will be more than you and me in this conversation if we loiter here like this. Continue, then, Ma'mselle-you have nowhere to go? But why not to your cousin's hotel then?"

"My cousin would have had me do so, but the Commissioners would not permit it. Everything must be sealed up they said, the servants all driven out, and no one to come and go until they had finished their search for treasonable papers. My cousin is accused of corresponding with Austria on behalf of the Queen," Mlle. de Rochambeau remarked innocently, but something in her companion's change of expression convicted her of her imprudence, and she was silent, colouring deeply.

The fat woman frowned.

"Madame, your cousin, had a large society; her friends would protect you."

Aline shook her head.

"I don't know who they are, Madame. Mme. de Maillé, to whom my cousin commended me, is also in prison, and others too-many others, the driver of the carriage said. I have nowhere to go, nowhere to go, nowhere at all, Madame."

"Sainte Vierge!" exclaimed the fat woman. The ejaculation burst from her with great suddenness, and she then closed her lips very tightly and walked on for some moments in silence.

"Have you any money?" was her next contribution to the conversation, and Mademoiselle started and put her hand to her bosom. Until this moment she had forgotten it, but the embroidered bag containing her cousin's winnings reposed there safely enough, neighboured by her broken string of pearls. She drew out the bag now and showed it to her companion, who gave a sort of grunt, and permitted a new crease, expressive of satisfaction, to appear upon her broad countenance.

"Eh bien!" she exclaimed. "All is easy. Money is a good key—a very good key, Ma'mselle. There are very few doors it won't unlock, and mine is not one-besides the coincidence! Figure to yourself that I was but now on my way to ask my sister, who is the wife of Bault, the head gaoler of La Force, whether she could recommend me some respectable young woman who required a lodging. I did not look, it is true, for a noble demoiselle,"—here the smooth voice took a tone which caused Mademoiselle to glance up quickly, but all she saw was a narrowing of the eyes above a huge impassive smile, and the flow of words continued—"la, la, it is all one to me, if the money is safe. There is nothing to be done without money."

Mlle. de Rochambeau drew a little away from her companion. She was unaccustomed to so familiar a mode of speech, and it offended her.

The little, sharp eyes flashed upon her as she averted her face, and the voice dropped back into its first tone.

"Well then, Ma'mselle, it is easily settled, and I need not go to my sister at all to-night. It grows dark so early now, and I have no fancy for being abroad in the dark; but one thing and another kept me, and I said to myself, 'Put a thing off often enough, and you'll never do it at all.' My cousin Thérèse was with me, the baggage, and she laughed; but I was a match for her. 'That's what you've done about marriage, Thérèse,' I said, and out of the shop she bounced in as fine a temper as you'd see any day. She's a light thing, Thérèse is; and, bless me, if I warned her once I warned her a hundred times! Always gadding abroad-and her ribbons-and her fal-lals—and the fine young men who were ready to cut one another's throats for her sake! No, no, that's not the way to get a husband and settle oneself in life. Look at me. Was I beautiful? But certainly not. Had I a large dot? Not at all. But respectable-Mon Dieu, yes! No one in all Paris can say that Rosalie Leboeuf is not respectable; and when Madame, your cousin, comes out of prison and hears you have been under my roof, I tell you she will be satisfied, Ma'mselle. No one has ever had a word to say against me. I keep my shop, and I pay my way, even though times are bad. Regular money coming in is not to be despised, so I take a lodger or two. I have one now, a man. A man did I say? An angel, a patriot, a true patriot; none of your swearing, drinking, hiccupping, lolloping loafers, who think if they consume enough strong liquor that the reign of liberty will come floating down their throats of itself. He is a worker this one; sober and industrious is our Citizen Dangeau, and a Deputy of the Commune, too, no less."

Mlle. de Rochambeau, slightly dazed by this flow of conversation, felt a cold chill pass over her. Commissioners of the Commune, Deputies of the Commune! Was Paris full of them? And till this morning she had never heard of the Commune; it had always been the King, the Court; and now, to her faint senses, this new word brought a suggestion of fear, and she seemed for a moment to catch a glimpse of a black curtain vibrating as if to rise. Behind it, what? She reeled a little, gasped, and caught at her companion's solid arm. In a moment it was round her.

"Courage, Ma'mselle, courage then! See, we are arrived. It is better now, eh?"

Mademoiselle drew a long breath, and felt her feet again. They were in an alley crowded with small third-rate shops, and so closely set were the houses that it was almost dark in the narrow street. Mme. Leboeuf led the way into one of the dim entrances, where a strong mingled odour of cabbages, onions, and apples proclaimed the nature of the commodities disposed of.

"Above, it will be light enough still," asserted Rosalie between her panting breaths. "This way, Ma'mselle; one small step, turn to the left, and now up."

They ascended gradually into a sort of twilight, until suddenly a sharp turn in the stair brought them on to a landing with a fair-sized window. Opposite was a gap in the dingy line of houses, and through this gap shone the strong red of the setting sun.

Mlle. de Rochambeau looked out, first at the gorgeous pageant in the sky, and then, curiously, at the strangeness of her new surroundings. She saw a tangle of mean slums, streets nearly all gutter, from which rose sounds of children squabbling, cats fighting, and men swearing. Suddenly a woman shrieked, and she turned, terrified, to realise that a man was passing them on his way down the stair.

She caught a momentary but very vivid impression of a tall figure carried easily, a small head covered with short, dark, curling hair, and a pair of eyes so blue and piercing that her own hung on them for an instant in surprise before they fell in confusion. The owner of the eyes bowed slightly, but with courtesy, and passed on. Madame Leboeuf was smiling and nodding.

"Good evening, Citizen Dangeau," she said, and broke, as he passed, into renewed panegyrics.

## CHAPTER IV
## THE TERROR LET LOOSE

Jacques Dangeau was at this time about eight-and-twenty years of age. He was a successful lawyer, and an ardent Republican, a friend of Danton, and a fairly prominent member of the Cordeliers' Club.

Under a handsome, well-controlled exterior he concealed an unbounded enthusiasm and a passionate devotion to the cause of liberty. When Dangeau spoke, his section listened. He carried always in his mind a vision of the ideal State, in the service of which a race should be trained from infancy to the civic virtues, inflamed with a pure ambition to spend themselves for humanity. He saw mankind, shedding brutishness and self, become sober, law-abiding, just; — in a word, he possessed those qualities of vision and faith without which neither prophet nor reformer can influence his generation. Dangeau had the gift of speech, and, carried on a flood of burning words, some perception of the ultimate Ideal would rise upon the hearts of even the most degraded among his hearers. For the moment they too felt the glow of a reflected altruism, and forgot that to them, and to their fellows, the Revolution meant unpunished pillage, theft recognised, and murder winked at.

As Dangeau walked through the darkening streets his heart burned in him. The events of the last month had brought the ideal almost within grasp. The grapes of liberty had been trodden long enough in the vats of oppression. Now the long ferment was nearing its close, and the time approached when the wine of life should be free to all; and that glorious moment of anticipation held no dread of intoxication or excess. Truly a patriot might be hopeful at this juncture. Capet and his family, sometime unapproachable, lay prisoners now, in the firm grip of the Commune, and the possession of such hostages enabled Paris to laugh at the threats of foreign interference. The proclamation of the Republic was only a matter of weeks, and then-renewed visions of a saturnian reign-peace and plenty coupled with the rigid virtues of old Rome-rose glowingly before his eyes.

As he entered the Temple gates he came down to earth with a sigh. He was on his way to take his turn of a duty eminently distasteful to him-that of guarding the imprisoned King and his family. As a patriot he detested Louis the Tyrant, as a man he despised Louis the man; but the spectacle of fallen greatness was disagreeable to his really generous mind, and he was of sufficiently gentle habits to revolt from the position of intrusive familiarity into which he was forced with regard to the women of the party.

The Tower of the Temple, where the unfortunate Royal Family of France were at this time confined, was to be reached only by traversing the Palace of the same name, and crossing the court and garden where the work of demolishing a mass of old houses, which encroached too nearly upon Capet's prison, was still proceeding. Patriotic ardour had seen a spy behind every window, a concealed courtier in every niche; so the buildings were doomed, and falling fast, whilst from the debris arose a strong enclosing wall pierced by a couple of guarded entries. Broken masonry lay everywhere, and Dangeau stumbled precariously as he made his way over the rubble. The workmen had been gone this half-hour, but as he halted and called out, a man with a lantern advanced and piloted him to the Tower.

The Commune was responsible for the prisoners of the Temple, and the actual guarding of them was delegated to eight of its Deputies. These were on duty for forty-eight hours at a stretch, and were relieved by fours every twenty-four hours.

As Dangeau entered the Council-room, those whose term of duty was finished were already leaving. The office of gaoler was an unpopular one, and most men, having once satisfied their curiosity about the prisoners, were very unwilling to approach them again. The sight of misfortune is only pleasing to a mind completely debased, and most of these Deputies were worthy men enough.

Dangeau was met almost on the threshold by a fair-haired, eager-looking youth, who hailed him warmly as Jacques, and, linking his arm in his, led him, unresisting, into the deep embrasure of the window.

"What is it, Edmond?" inquired Dangeau, an unusually attractive smile lighting up his rather grave features. It was plain that this young man roused in him an amused affection.

"Nothing," said Edmond aloud, "but it is so long since I saw you. Have you been dead, buried, or out of Paris?"

"Since the arm you pinched just now is reasonably solid flesh and blood, you may conclude that during the past fortnight Paris has been rendered inconsolable by my absence," said Dangeau, laughing a little.

Edmond Cléry threw an imperceptible glance at his fellow-Commissioners. Two being always with the prisoners, there remained four others, and of these a couple were playing cards at the wine-stained table, and two more lounged on the doorstep smoking a villanously rank tobacco and talking loudly.

Certainly no one was in the least interested in the conversation of Citizens Dangeau and Cléry. Yet for all that Edmond dropped his voice, not to a whisper, but to that smooth monotone which hardly carries a yard, and yet is distinctly audible to the person addressed. In this voice he asked:

"You have not been to the Club?"

Dangeau shook his head.

"Nor seen Hébert, Marat, Jules Dupuis?"

An expression of distaste lifted Dangeau's finely cut lip.

"I have existed without that felicity," he observed, with a slightly sarcastic inflexion.

"Then you have been told-have heard-nothing?"

"My dear Edmond, what mysteries are these?"

Edmond Cléry leaned a little closer, and dropped his voice until it was a mere tenuous thread.

"They have decided on a massacre," he said.

"A massacre?"

"Yes, of the prisoners."

"Just Heaven! No!"

"It is true. Things have fallen from Hébert once or twice. He and Marat have been closeted for hours-the devil's own alliance that-and the plan is of their hatching. Two days ago Hébert spoke at the Club. It was late, Danton was not there. They say—" Cléry hesitated, and stole a glance at his companion's set face—"they say he wishes to know nothing."

"A lie," said Dangeau very quietly.

"I don't know. There, Jacques, don't look at me like that! How can I tell? I tell you my brain reels at the thought of the thing."

"What did Hébert say? He spoke?"

"Yes; said the people must be fleshed-there was not sufficient enthusiasm. Paris as a whole was quiescent, apathetic. This must be changed, an elixir was needed. What? Blood-blood of traitors-blood of aristocrats-oppressors of the people. Bah!—you can fancy the rest well enough."

"Did any one else speak?"

"Marat said the Jacobins were with us."

"Robespierre?"

"In it, of course, but would n't dirty those white hands for the world," said Cléry, sneering.

"No one opposed it?"

"Oh, yes, but hooted down almost at once. You know Dupuis's bull voice? It did his friends a good turn, bellowing slackness, lack of patriotism, and so on. I wish you had been there."

Dangeau shook his head.

"I could have done nothing."

"Ah, but you could; there 's no one like you, Jacques. Danton thunders, and Marat spits out venom, and Hébert panders to the vile in us, but you really make us see an ideal, and wish to be more worthy of it. I said to Barrassin, 'If only Dangeau were here we should be spared this shame.'"

The boy's face flushed as he spoke, but Dangeau looked down moodily.

"I could have done nothing," he repeated. "If they spoke as openly as that it is because their plans are completed. Did you hear any more?"

Edmond looked a little confused.

"Not there-but-well, I was told—a friend told me-it was for to-morrow," and he looked up to find Dangeau's eyes fixed steadily on him.

"A friend, Edmond? Who? Thérèse?"

Cléry coloured hotly.

"Why not Thérèse, Jacques?"

"Oh, if you like to play with gunpowder it's no business of mine, Edmond; but the girl is Hébert's mistress, and as dangerous as the devil, that's all. And so she told you that?"

Cléry nodded, a trifle defiantly.

"To-morrow," said Dangeau slowly; "where?"

"At all the prisons. One or two of the gaolers are warned, but I do not believe they will be able to do anything."

Dangeau was thinking hard.

"They sent me away on purpose," he said at last.

"Curse them!" said Cléry in a shaking voice.

Dangeau did not swear, but he nodded his head as who should say Amen, and his face was bitter hard.

"Is anything intended here?" he asked sharply.

"No, not from head-quarters; but Heaven knows what may happen when the mob tastes blood."

Dangeau gave a short laugh.

"Why, Jacques?" said Cléry, surprised.

"Why, Edmond," repeated Dangeau sardonically, "I was thinking that it would be a queer turn for Fate to play if you and I were to die to-morrow, fighting in defence of Capet against the people."

"You would do that?" asked Edmond.

"But naturally, my friend, since we are responsible for him."

He had been leaning carelessly against the wall, but as he spoke he straightened himself.

"Our friends upstairs will be getting impatient," he said aloud. "Who takes the night duty with me?"

Cléry was about to speak, but received a warning pressure of the arm. He was silent, and Legros, one of the loungers, came forward.

Dangeau and he went out together. Upstairs silence reigned. The two Commissioners on duty rose with an air of relief, and passed out. The light of a badly trimmed oil-lamp showed that the little party of prisoners were all present, and Dangeau saluted them with a grave inclination of the head that was hardly a bow. His companion, clumsily embarrassed, shuffled with his feet, spat on the floor, and lounged to a seat.

The Queen raised her eyebrows at him, and, turning slightly, smiled and nodded to Dangeau. Mme. Elizabeth bowed abstractedly and turned again to the chessboard which stood between her and her brother. Mme. Royale curtsied, but the little Dauphin did not raise his head from some childish game which occupied his whole attention. His mother, after waiting a moment, called him to her and, laying one of her long delicate hands on his petulantly twitching shoulder, observed gently:

"Fi donc, my son; did you not see these gentlemen enter? Bid them good evening!"

The child tossed his head, but as his father's gaze met him, he hung it down again, saying in a clear childish voice, "Good evening, Citizens."

Mme. Elizabeth's colour rose perceptibly at the form of address, but the Queen smiled, and, giving the boy's shoulder a little tap of dismissal, she turned to Dangeau.

"We forget our manners in this solitude, Monsieur," she said in her peculiarly soft and agreeable voice. Then after a pause, during which Dangeau, to his annoyance, felt that his face was flushing, "It is Monsieur Dangeau, is it not?"

"Citizen Dangeau, at your service."

Marie Antoinette laughed; the sound was pleasing but disturbing. "Oh, my good Monsieur, I am too old to learn these new forms of address. My son, you see, is quicker"; the arch eyes clouded, the laugh dropped to a sigh, then rippled back again into merriment. "Only figure to yourself, Monsieur, that I have had already to learn one new language, for when I came to France as a bride, all was strange-oh, but so strange-to me. I had hard work, I do assure you; and that good Mme. de Noailles was a famous task-mistress!"

"Should it be harder to learn simplicity?" said Dangeau, a faint tinge of bitterness in his pleasant voice.

"Why, no, Monsieur," returned the Queen, "it should not be. My liking has always been for simplicity. Good bread to eat, fresh water to drink, and a clean white dress to wear-with these things I could be very well content. But, alas! Monsieur, the last at least is lacking us; and simplicity, though a cardinal virtue now, does not of itself afford an occupation. Pray, Monsieur Dangeau, could you not ask that my sister and I should be permitted the consolation of needlework?"

Dangeau coloured.

"The Commune has already decided against needle-work," he said rather curtly.

"But why then, Monsieur?"

"Because we all know that the needle may be used instead of the pen, and that it is as easy to embroider treason on a piece of stuff as to write it on paper," he replied, with some annoyance.

The Queen gave a little light laugh.

"Oh, de grace! Monsieur," she said, "my sister and I are not so clever! But may we not at least knit? There is nothing treasonable in a few pins and a little wool, is there, M. le Député?"

Dangeau shook his head doubtfully. Consciousness of the Queen's fascination rendered his outward aspect austere, and even ungracious.

"I will ask the Council," was all he permitted himself to say, but was thanked as charmingly as though he had promised some great concession. This did not diminish his discomfort, and he was acutely conscious of Mme. Elizabeth's frown, and of a coarse grunt from Legros.

The prisoners did not keep late hours. Punctually at ten the King rose, embraced Mme. Royale, kissed his sister's forehead and the Queen's hand, and retired to his own apartment, accompanied by M. le Dauphin, his valet, and the Deputy Legros. The Queen, Mme. Elizabeth, and Mme. Royale busied themselves for a moment with putting away the chessmen, and a book or two that lay about. They then proceeded to their own quarters, which consisted of two small rooms opening from an ante-chamber. There Marie Antoinette embraced her sister and daughter, and they separated for the night. Dangeau was obliged to enter each apartment in turn, in order to satisfy himself that all was in order, after which he locked both doors, and drew a pallet-bed across that which led to the Queen's room. Here he stretched himself, but it was long ere he slept, and his thoughts were very bitter. No Jacobin of them all could go as far as he in Republican principles. To him the Republic was not only the best form of government, but the only one under which the civic virtues could flourish. It was his faith, his ardent religion, the inspiration of his life and labours, and it was this faith which he was to see clouded, this religion defiled, this inspiration befouled-and at the hands of his co-devotees, Hébert, Marat, and their crew. They worshipped at the same altar, but they brought to it blood-stained hands, lives foul with license, and the smoking blood of tortured sacrifices.

Paris let loose on the prisoners! He shuddered at the thought. Once the tiger had tasted blood, who could assuage his thirst? There would be victims enough and to spare. Curled fops of the salons; scented exquisites of the Court; indolent, luxurious priests; smooth-skinned, bright-eyed women; children foolish and unthinking. He saw the sea of blood rise and rise till it engulfed them all.

Strange that he should think of the girl he had seen for an instant on Rosalie's stairway. How uneasily she had looked at him, and with what a rising colour. How young she seemed, how delicately proud. Her face stayed with him as he sank into a sleep, vexed by prophetic dreams.

The next morning passed uneasily. It was a hot, cloudless day, and the small room in which the prisoners were confined became very oppressive. The King spent a part of the time in superintending the education of his son, and whilst thus engaged certainly appeared to greater advantage than at any other time. The child was wayward, wilful, and hard to teach; but the father's patience appeared inexhaustible, and his method of imparting information was not only painstaking, but attractive.

The Princesses read or conversed. Presently the King got up and began pacing the room. It was a habit of his, and, after glancing at him once or twice, Mme. Elizabeth rose and joined him. Now and then they stood at the window and looked out. The last few houses to be demolished were falling fast, and the King amused himself by speculating on the direction likely to be taken by each crashing mass of masonry. He made little wagers with his sister, was chagrined when he lost, and pleased out of all reason when he won. Dangeau's lip curled a little as he watched the trivial scene, and perhaps the Queen read his thought, for she said smilingly:

"Prisoners learn to take pleasure in small things, Monsieur"; and Dangeau bit his lip. The quick intuition, the arch glance, confused him.

"All things are comparative," continued Marie Antoinette. "When I had many amusements and occupations, I would not have turned my head to remark what now constitutes an event in my monotonous day. Yesterday a workman hurt his foot, and I assure you, Monsieur, that we all regarded him with as much interest as if he had been a dear friend. Trifles have ceased to be trifles, and soon I shall look out for a mouse or a spider to tame, as I have heard of prisoners doing."

"I cannot imagine even the loneliest of unfortunates caring for a spider," said Dangeau, with a smile.

"No, Monsieur, nor I," returned the Queen. She seemed about to speak again, and, indeed, her lips had already opened, when, above the crash of the falling masonry, there came the heavy boom of a gun. Dangeau started up. It came again, and yet a third time.

"It is the alarm," said Legros stolidly.

Immediately there was a confused noise of voices, shouting, footsteps. Dangeau and his colleague pressed forward to the window. The workmen were throwing down their tools; here a group stood talking, gesticulating, there half a dozen were running-all was confusion.

Louis had recoiled from the window. His great face was a sickly yellow, and the sweat stood in large beads upon the skin.

"Is there danger? What is it?" he stammered, and caught at the table for support.

Mme. Royale sat still, her long, mournful features steadily composed. She neither moved nor cried out, but Dangeau saw the thin, unchildish shoulders tremble. Mme. Elizabeth embraced first her brother, and then her sister, demanding protection for them in agitated accents. Only the Queen appeared unmoved. She had risen and, passing her arm through that of her husband, rapidly addressed a few words to him in an undertone. Inaudible to others, they had an immediate effect upon him, for he retired to the back of the room, sat down, and drew his little son upon his knee.

The Queen then turned to the Commissioners.

"What is it, Messieurs?" she asked. "Is there danger?"

"I don't know," answered Legros bluntly.

Dangeau threw her a reassuring glance.

"It is a street riot, I think," he said calmly. "It is probably of no consequence; and in any case, Madame, we are here to protect you, with our lives if necessary. You may be perfectly assured of that."

The Queen thanked him with an earnest look and resumed her seat. The noise outside decreased, and presently the routine of the day fell heavily about them once more.

If Dangeau were disturbed in mind his face showed nothing, and if he found the day of an interminable length he did not say so. When the evening brought him relief, he found the Council in considerable excitement. The prisons had been raided, "hundreds killed," said one. "Bah! only one or two, nothing to speak of," maintained another.

Edmond Cléry looked agitated.

"It is only the beginning," he whispered, as he passed his friend. He was on duty with the prisoners, so further conversation was impossible; but Dangeau's sleep in the Council-room was not much sounder than that of the night before in the Queen's ante-chamber.

## CHAPTER V
## A CARNIVAL OF BLOOD

September the third dawned heavy with murky clouds, out of which climbed a sun all red, like a ball of fire. The mists of the autumn morning caught the tinge, but no omens could add to the tense foreboding which wrapt the city. It needed no signs in the sky to prophesy a day of terror.

At La Force a crowded court-yard held those of the prisoners who had escaped the previous day's massacre. They had been driven from their cells at dawn, and, after an hour or two of strained anticipation, had gathered into their accustomed coteries. Mme. de Lamballe, who had heard the mob howling for her blood, sat placidly beautiful. Now and then she spoke to a friend, but for the most part she kept her eyes on the tiny copy of *The Imitation of Christ* which was found in her blood-stained clothes later on in that frightful day. Others, less devout, or less alarmed, were gossipping, chattering, even laughing, or playing cards, as if La Force were Versailles, and the hands on the clock of Time had never moved for the last four years.

Mme. de Maillé was gone. Her hacked corpse still lay in its pool of blood, her dead eyes stared unburied at the lowering sky; but Mme. de Montargis sat in her old place, her attendant Vicomte at her side. If her face was pale the rouge hid it, and at least her smile was as ready, her voice as careless, as ever. Bault, the gaoler, stared as he passed her.

"These aristocrats!" he muttered; "any honest woman would be half-dead of fright after yesterday, and what to-day will bring, Heaven knows! I myself, mille diables! I myself, I shake, my hand trembles, I am in the devil's own sweat-and there she sits, that light woman, and laughs!"

As he passed into his own room, his wife caught him by the arm — —

"Jean, Jean, mon Dieu, Jean! They are coming back!" He strained his ears, listening, gripping his wife, as she gripped him.

"It is true," he murmured hoarsely.

A sullen, heavy drone burdened the air. It was like the sound of the rising tide on a day of storm-far off, but nearer, every moment nearer, nearer, until it drowned the thumping of the frightened pulses which beat so loudly at his ears. A buzz as of infernal bees-its component parts, laughter of hell, audible lust of cruelty, just retribution clamorous, and the cry of innocent blood shed long ago. All this, blent with the howl of the beast who scents blood, made up a sound so awful, that it was small wonder that the sweat dripped heavily from the brow of Bault, the gaoler, or that his wife clung to his arm, praying him to think of their children.

To his honour be it said that he risked his life, and more than his life, to save some two hundred of his prisoners, but for the rest-their doom was sealed.

It had been written long ago, in letters of cumulative anguish, when the father of Mme. de Montargis had torn that shrieking peasant bride from her husband's side on their marriage-day, when her grandfather hanged at his gates the starving wretches who clamoured over-loudly for release from the gabelle-hardly a noble family in France but had some such record at their backs, signs in an alphabet that was to spell "The Terror." At the hands of the fathers was sown the seed of hate, and the doom of the reaping came fast upon their children.

King Mob was at his revels, but he must needs play a ghastly comedy with the victims. There should be a trial for each, a really side-splitting affair. "A table, Bault," and up with the judges, three of them, wrapped in a drunken dignity, a chair apiece, a bonnet rouge on each august head; and prisoner after prisoner hurried up, and interrogated. A look was enough for some, a word too much for others. Here and there a lucky answer drew applause, and won a life, but for the most part came the sentence, "A l'Abbaye,"—and straightway off went the condemned to the inviolable cloisters of death.

Mme. de Montargis came up trippingly upon the Vicomte de Sélincourt's arm. Their names were enough-both stank in the nostrils of the crowd. There was a shout of "Austrians, Austrian spies! take them away, take them out!"

"To the Abbaye," bawled the reverend judges, and Madame made them a little curtsey. This was better than she expected.

"I thank you, Messieurs," she murmured; and then to the Vicomte: "Mon ami, we are in luck. The Abbaye can hardly be more incommodious than La Force."

"Quelle comédie!" responded Sélincourt, with a shrug, and with that the door before them opened.

Let us give them the credit of their qualities. That open door gave straight into hell-an inferno of tossing pikes which dripped with blood, dripped to a pavement red and slippery as a shambles, whilst a hoarse, wild-beast roar, full of oaths, and lust, and savage violence, broke upon their ears.

If Mme. de Montargis hesitated, it was for the hundredth part of a second only. Then she raised her scent-ball carelessly to her nostrils, and the hand that held it did not shake.

"Tiens, mon ami," she said, "your comedy becomes tragedy. I never thought it my rôle, but it seems le bon Dieu thinks otherwise"; and with that she stepped daintily out on to the reeking cobble-stones. One is glad to think that the first pike-thrust was well aimed, and that it was an unconscious form that went down to the mire and blood below.

The beautiful Lamballe was just behind. They say she knew she was going to her death. There is a tale of a dream-God! what a dream!—an augury, what not? Heaven knows no great degree of prescience was required. She turned very pale, her eyes on her book until the last moment, when she slipped it into her pocket, with one of those unconscious movements dictated by a brain too numb to work otherwise than by habit. She met the horror with dilated eyes-eyes that glazed to a faint before death struck her. Nature was merciful, and death a boon, for over her corpse began a carnival of lust and blood so hideous that imagination staggers at it, and history veils it in shuddering generalities. No need to dwell upon its details.

What concerns us is that, having her head upon a pike, and the mutilated body trailing by the heels, the whole mad mob set off to the Temple, to show Marie Antoinette her friend, and to serve the Queen as they had served the Princess.

It was between twelve and one in the day that news of what was passing came to the Temple. It was the fat Butin who brought it. He came in on the Council panting, gasping, dripping with the moisture of heat and fear. All his broad, scarlet face was drawn, and his lips, under the bristling moustache, were pale—a thing very strange and arresting. It was plain that he had news of the first importance, but it was some time before he could speak. When his voice came it was all out of key, and his whole portly body quivered with the effort to control it.

"Hell is out, Citizens!" were his first connected words. Then—"Oh! they are mad, they are mad, and they are just behind me. Close the gates quickly, or they 'll be through!"

A bewildered group emitted Dangeau.

"What has happened, Citizen?" he asked steadily. "A riot? Like yesterday?"

"Like yesterday? No, ma foi, Citizen! Yesterday was child's play, a mere nothing; to-day they murder every one, and when they have murdered they tear in pieces. They have assassinated the Lamballe, and they are coming here for Capet's wife!"

"How many?" asked Dangeau sharply.

"How do I know!" and fat Butin wrung his hands. "The streets are full of them, leaping, and howling, and shouting like devils. Does the Citizen suppose I stayed to count them?—I, the father of a family!"

The Citizen supposed nothing so unlikely; in fact, his questions asked, he was not thinking of Butin at all. His brain was working quickly, clearly. Already he saw his course marked out, and, as a consequence, he assumed that command of the situation which is always ceded to the man who sees his way before him whilst his fellows walk befogged.

He sat at the table and wrote two notes, despatching one to the President of the Legislative Council and the other to the General Council of the Commune.

Then he announced their contents, speaking briefly and with complete assurance.

"I have written asking for six members of the Assembly and six of the Council, popular men who will assist us to control the mob. We shall, of course, defend the prisoners with our lives if necessary, but there must be no fighting unless as a last recourse. Where is the captain of the Guard?"

The officer came forward, saluting.

"You have-how many men?"

"Four hundred, Citizen."

"You can answer for them-their discipline, their nerve?"

"With my life!"

"Very well, attend to your instructions. Both sides of the great gates are to be opened."

"Opened, Citizen?" stammered the captain, whilst a murmur of dissatisfaction ran through the room.

Dangeau's brows made a dangerous straight line.

"Opened," he repeated emphatically. "Between the outer and inner doors you will draw up a double line of your steadiest men-unarmed."

It was only the officer's look which protested this time, but it quailed before Dangeau's glance of steel.

"You will place a strong guard beyond, out of sight. These men will be fully armed. All corridors, passages, and courts leading to the Tower will be held in sufficient force, but not a man is to make so much as a threatening gesture without orders. You will be so good as to carry out these instructions without delay. I shall join you at the gate."

The captain swung away, and Dangeau turned to his colleagues.

"I propose to try to bring the people to reason," he said; "if they will hear me, I will speak to them. If not-we can only die. The prisoners are a sacred trust, but to have to use violence in defending them would be fatal in the extreme, and every means must be taken to obviate the necessity. Legros, you are a popular man, and you, Meunier; meet the mob, fraternise with the leaders, promote a feeling of confidence. They must be led to feel that it is our patriotism which denies them, and not any sentiment of sympathy with tyrants."

There was a low murmur of applause as Dangeau concluded. He had acted so rapidly that these slow-thinking bourgeois had scarcely grasped the necessity for action before his plan was laid before them, finished to the last detail.

As he left the room, he had a last order to give: "Tell Cléry and Renault to keep the prisoners away from the windows"; and with that was on his way to the gates.

His instructions were being carried out expeditiously enough. The great gates stood wide, and he passed towards them through a double row of the National Guard. A sharp, scrutinising glance appeared to satisfy him. These were what he wanted-men who could face a mob, unarmed, as coolly as if they were on parade; men who would obey orders without thought or question. They stood, a solid embodiment of law and order, discipline, and decorum.

Dangeau took off his tri-coloured sash, borrowed a couple more, knotted them together, suspended them across the unbarred entrance, and, having requisitioned a chair, sat down on it, and awaited the arrival of the mob.

He had not long to wait.

They came, heralded by a dull, hideous roar: no longer the tiger howl of the unfleshed beast, but the devilish mirth of the same beast, full fed, but not yet sated, and of mood wanton as well as murderous. It would still kill, but with a refinement of cruelty. The pike-thrust was not enough. It would not suffice them to butcher the Queen-she must first kiss the livid lips of their other victim; she must be stripped, insulted, dragged alive through the Paris streets.

In this new mood they had stopped on their way to the Temple, broken into the trembling Clermont's shop, and forced that skilful barber to dress the Princesse de Lamballe's exquisite hair and rouge the bloodless cheeks.

The hair was piled high, and wreathed with roses; roses bloomed in the dead cheeks, beneath the lifeless violet of the loveliest eyes in France. Only the mouth drooped livid, ghastly, drained of delight. Clermont had done what he could. Even terror could not rob his fingers of their skill, but, as he muttered to himself, with shaking lips, "Am I, le bon Dieu, to make the dead live?" Rouge and rose-wreathed hair made Death more ghastly still, but the mob was satisfied, and tossing him a diamond buckle for his pains, they swung off again, the head before them.

It was thus that Dangeau saw them come. For a moment the blood ran thick and turgid through his brain, the next it cleared, and, though his heart beat fast, it was with the greatest appearance of calm that he mounted his improvised rostrum, and held up his hand in a gesture demanding silence.

The mob swept on unheeding; nearer, nearer, right on without check or pause, to the fragile ribbon that alone barred their way. Had Dangeau changed colour, had his eye flickered, or that outstretched arm quivered ever so little, they would have been on him-over him, and another massacre would have been written on the stained pages of History.

But Dangeau stood motionless; an unbearable tension held him rigid. His steady eyes-like steel with the sun on it-fixed the leader of the mob;—fixed him, held him, stopped him. A bare yard from the gates, the man who held the head aloft slackened speed, hesitated, and finally came to a standstill so close to Dangeau that a little of the scented powder in the Princess's hair fell down and whitened the sleeve of his outstretched arm. Like sheep, the silly crowd behind checked as their leader checked, and stopped as he had stopped.

Dangeau and he stood looking at one another. The man was a giant, black and hairy, stripped to the waist and a-reek with blood. Under a villainous, low brow his hot, small eyes winked and glared, shifted, and fell at last before the steadier gaze.

Dangeau turned a little, beckoning with his hand, and there was a momentary lull in the chorus of shouts, oaths, and obscene songs.

"What do you want?" he shouted.

The mob renewed its wild-beast howl.

Dangeau beckoned again.

"Let your leader speak," he called; and as the ruffian with the head was pleased to second his suggestion, he obtained a second interval in the storm.

"What do you want?" he asked again, and received this time an answer, couched in language too explicit to be transcribed, but the substance of which was that the Capet woman was to kiss her precious friend.

"And then?" Dangeau's speech fell cold and clear as ice upon the heated words of the demagogue.

"And then, aha! then—" She was to be taught what the people's vengeance meant. For how many years had they toiled that she might have her sport? Now she should make sport for them, and then they would tear her limb from limb, show her traitorous heart to Paris, where she had lived so wantonly; burn her vile body to ashes.

Again that high, cool voice——

"And then?"

The ruffian scowled, spat viciously, and swore.

"Then, then—a thousand devils! What did the Citizen mean with his 'and then'? He supposed that they should go home until there was another tyrant to kill."

"And then-shall I tell you what then?—will you hear me, Dangeau? Some of you know me," and his eye lit on a wizened creature who danced horribly about the headless corpse.

"Antoine, have you forgotten the February of two years ago?"

The ghastly object ceased its strange rhythmic movements, stared a moment, and broke into voluble speech.

"'T is a patriot, this Dangeau, I say it—I whom he saved from prison. Listen to him. He has good, strong words. Tell us then, Citizen, tell us what we're to do," and he capered nearer, catching at Dangeau's chair with fingers horribly smeared.

Silence fell, and, after a very slight pause, Dangeau leaned forward and began to speak in a low, confidential tone.

"All here are patriots, are they not? Not a traitor amongst you, citizens all, proved and true. You have struck down the enemies of France, and now you ask what next?" His voice rose suddenly and thrilled over the vast concourse.

"Citizens of Paris, the whole world looks to you-the nations of Europe stand waiting. They look to France because it is the cradle of the new religion-the religion of humanity. France, revolted from under the hand of her tyrants, rises to give the law to all future generations. With us is the rising sun, whose beams shed liberty, justice, equality; and on this splendid dawn all eyes are fixed."

"They shall see us crush the tyrants!" bellowed the crowd.

"They shall see it," repeated Dangeau, and the words rang like an oath. "Europe shall see it, the World shall see it. But, friends, shall we not give them a spectacle worthy of their attention, read them a lesson that shall stand on the page of History for ever? Shall we not take a little time in devising how this lesson may be most plainly taught? Shall a few patriots-earnest, sincere, passionately devoted to liberty it is true, but unauthorised by France, or by the duly delegated authority of the people-shall a few weak men, in an outburst of virtuous indignation putting a tyrant to death, shall this impress the waiting peoples? Will they not say, 'France did not will it-the people did not will it-it was the work of a few'? Will they not say this? On the other side, see—a crowded hall, the hall of the people's delegates. They judge and they condemn, and Justice draws her sword. In the eye of the day, in the face of the world, before the whole people, there falls the tyrant's head. Then would not Europe tremble? Then would not thrones based on iniquity totter, tyrants fall, and the universal reign of liberty begin?"

The crowd swayed, hypnotised by the rolling voice, for Dangeau had the tones that thrill, that stir, that soothe. We do not always understand the fame of dead-and-gone orators. Their periods leave us cold, their arguments do not move us, their words seem no more eloquent than another's; and yet, in their day, these men swept a whirlwind of emotion, colour, life, conviction, into their hearers' hearts. Theirs was the gift of temperament and tone. As the inspired musician plays upon his instrument, so they on theirs-that oldest and most sensitive instruments of all, the human heart.

Dangeau's voice pealed out above the throng. He took the biggest words, the most extravagant phrases, the cheapest catchwords of the day, and blended them with the magic of his voice to an irresistible spell. Suddenly he changed his key. The mob was listening, their attention gained-he could give them something more than a vague magniloquence.

"Frenchmen!" he said earnestly, "do we oppose you with arms? Do we threaten, do we resist you? No, for I am most certain that there is not a man among you who would be turned from his purpose by fear-Frenchmen do not feel so mean a sentiment-but is there a Frenchman here who is not always ready to listen to the sacred dictates of reason? Hear me then."

Somewhere inside Dangeau's brain a little mocking devil laughed, but the crowd applauded—a fine appetite for flattery characterises the monster Demos-it was pleased, and through its thousand mouths it clamorously demanded more.

"I stand here to make that appeal to your reason, which I am assured cannot fail. First, I would point out to you that these prisoners are not only prisoners of ours, but hostages of France. Look at our frontiers: England threatens from the sea, Austria and Spain from the south; but their hands are tied, Citizens, their hands are tied. They can threaten and bluster, but they dare take no steps which would lead to the sacrifice of the tyrant and his brood. Wait a little, my friends; wait a little until our brave Dumouriez has won us a battle or two, and then the day of justice may dawn."

He paused a moment, and, gauging his audience, cried quickly:

"Vive Dumouriez! Vive l'armée!"

Half a dozen voices echoed him at first, but in a minute the cry was taken up on the outskirts of the crowd, and came rolling to the front in a storm of cheers.

Dangeau let it have its course, then motioned for silence, and got it.

"France owes much to Dumouriez," he said. "We are a nation of soldiers, and we can appreciate his work. Let us support him, then, and do nothing to embarrass him in his absence. Let him first drive the invaders of France back across her insulted frontiers, and then —" He was interrupted by a howl of applause, but he got the word again directly.

"Citizens of Paris," he called, "your good name is in your own keeping. They are some who would be glad to see it lost. There are some, I will name no names, who are jealous of the pre-eminence of our beautiful Paris. They would be glad of an excuse for moving the seat of government. I name no names, I make no accusations, but I know what I know."

"Name them, name them! —down with the traitors!" shouted the mob.

"They are those who bid you destroy the prisoners," returned Dangeau boldly. "They are those who urge you to lay violent hands on a trust which is sacred, because we have received it from the hands of the people. They are those who wish to represent you to the world as incapable of governing, blind with passion. Shall this be said?"

A shout of denial went up.

"Citizens of Paris, you have elected us your representatives. You have reposed in us this sacred trust. If we abuse it, you have your remedy. The Nation which elected can degrade; the men who have placed in us their confidence can withdraw that confidence; but whilst we hold it, we will deserve it, and will die in its defence."

The crowd shook with applause, but there were dissenting voices. One or two of the leaders showed dark, ominous faces; the huge man with the head scowled deepest, he seemed about to speak, and eyed Dangeau's chair as if he contemplated annexing it.

None knew better than Dangeau how fickle a thing is a crowd's verdict, or how easily it might yet turn against him. He laid his hand on the grimy shoulder beside him.

"To show the confidence that we repose in you, I suggest that this citizen, and five of his colleagues, shall be admitted into the garden; you shall march round the Tower if you will, and it will be seen that it is only your own patriotism and self-control that safeguards the prisoners, and not any force opposed to you."

This proposal aroused great enthusiasm. Dangeau, who was fully aware of the risks he ran in making it, hastily whispered to two of the Commissioners sent him in response to his appeal to the Commune, bidding them remain at the gate and keep the mob in a good temper, whilst he himself accompanied the ringleaders.

It was a strange and horrifying procession that took its way through palace rooms which had looked upon many scenes of vice but none so awful as this.

Dangeau, a guard or two, six filthy, reeking creatures, drawn from the lowest slums, steeped in wickedness as in blood; the exquisite head, lovely to the last, set on a dripping pike; the white, insulted body, stripped to the dust and mire of Paris; the frightful odour of gore diffused by all, made up a total effect of horror unparalleled in any age.

To the last day of Dangeau's life it remained a recurrent nightmare. He was young, he had lived a clean, honest life, he had respected women, nourished his soul on ideals, and now — —

At the time he felt nothing-neither disgust nor horror, nausea nor shame. It was afterwards that two things contended for possession of his being-sheer physical sickness, and a torment of outraged sensibility. He had vowed himself to the service of Humanity, and he had seen Humanity desecrate its own altar, offering upon it a shameful and bloody sacrifice. Just now it was fortunate that feeling was in abeyance, and that it was the brain in Dangeau, and not the conscience, that held sway. All of him, except that lucid brain, lay torpid, stunned, asleep; but in its cells thought flashed on thought, seizing here an impulse, there an instinct, bending them to the will, absorbing them in its designs.

All the way the butchers talked. One of them fancied himself a wit. Fortunately for posterity his jests have not been preserved. Another gave a detailed and succinct account of every person murdered by him. A third sang filthy songs. Dangeau's brain ordered him not to offend these bestial companions, and in obedience to it he nodded, questioned, appeared to commend.

Arrived at the garden, the whole company took up the chorus of the song, and began to march round the Tower, holding the head aloft and calling on the Queen to come and look at it.

Those of the workmen who still remained at their posts came gaping forward-some of them joined the tune; the excitement rose, and cries of "The Austrian, the Austrian; give us the Austrian!" began to be heard.

Within there was a dead silence. The little group of prisoners were huddled together at the farther side of the room. Mme. Elizabeth held her rosary, and her pale lips moved incessantly. One of the Commissioners, Renault, a strong, heavy-featured man, stood impassively by the window watching the progress of events, whilst Cléry, his eager young face flushed with excitement, was trying to keep up a conversation with the Princesses in order to prevent the terrifying voices from without reaching their ears. Although no one could be ignorant of what was passing, they seconded his attempts bravely. Marie Antoinette was the most successful. She preserved that social instinct which covers under an airy web the grimmest and most evident facts. Death was such a fact-vastly impolite, entirely to be ignored; and so the Queen conversed smilingly, even whilst the mother's eye rested in anguish upon her children.

Suddenly even her composure was shattered.

There was a loud shout of "Come out, Austrian! Look, Austrian!" and a shape appeared at the window—a head, omen of imminent tragedy. That head had shared the Queen's pillow, those drawn lips had smiled for her, those heavy lids closed over eyes whose beauty to her had been the lovely, frank affection which beamed from them. Thus, in this fearful shape, came the intimation of that friendship's close.

Cléry sprang up with a cry of "Don't look!" but he was too late. With a hoarse sound, half cry, half strained release of breath too frantically held, the Queen shrank back.

In that moment her face went grey and hollow, her death-mask showed prophetic, but after that one movement, that one cry, she sat quite still and made no sound. Mme. Royale had fainted, and Elizabeth knelt beside her shuddering and weeping.

Renault's great shoulders blocked the window, and even as he pressed forward the head was withdrawn.

Down below a second crisis was being fought through. Dangeau began to feel the strain of that scene by the Temple gates; his nervous energy was diminished, and the dreadful six were straining at the leash. They howled for the Austrian, they bellowed forth threats, they vociferated. One of them caught Dangeau by the shoulder and levelled a red pike at his head; but for a moment the steely composure of the eyes held him, and the next a friendly hand struck down the weapon.

"It is Dangeau, our Dangeau, the people's friend!" shouted his rescuer, a powerful workman. "I am of his section," and he squeezed him in a grimy embrace.

Dangeau, released, sprang on a heap of rubble, and made his final effort.

"Hé, mes braves!" he cried, "it is growing late; half Paris knows your deeds, it is true, but how many are still ignorant? Will you let darkness overtake you with your trophies yet undisplayed? Away, let the other quarters hear of your triumphs. Vaunt them before the Palais Royal, and let the Tuileries, so often defiled by the Tyrant's presence, be purified now by these relics, evidence of the people's power!"

As he ceased, his words were taken up by all present.

"To the Palais Royal! To the Tuileries!" they howled.

Dangeau, not only saved, but a hero-so fickle a thing is the mood of the sovereign people-was cheered, embraced, carried across the court-yard, and with difficulty permitted to remain behind; whilst the whole mob, singing, shouting, and dancing, took its frenzied course towards the royal palaces.

## CHAPTER VI
## A DOUBTFUL SAFETY

Mlle. de Rochambeau knelt by her open window. She had been praying, but for a long time her lips had not moved, and now it seemed as if their numbness had invaded her heart, and lay there deadening fear, emotion, sorrow, all-all except that heavy beating, to which she listened half unconsciously, as though it were a sound from some world which hardly concerned her.

She had not left the little room at all. On the first day she had been put off civilly enough. "Rest a little, Ma'mselle, rest a little; to-morrow I will make my sister a little visit, and you shall accompany me. To-day I am busy, and without me you would not be admitted to the prison."

But when to-morrow came, there were at first black looks, then impatient words, and finally the key turned in the lock and hours of terrifying solitude. The one small window overlooked a dark and squalid street where the refuse of the neighbourhood festered. It was noisy and malodorous, and she sickened at every sense. The sounds, the smells, the sight of the wizened, wicked-looking children, who fought, and swore, and scrabbled in the noisome gutter below, all added to her growing apprehension.

Closing the cracked pane she retreated to the farther corner of the attic, and again slow hours went by.

About noon a distant roar startled her to the window once more. Nothing was to be seen, but the sound came again, and yet again; increasing each time in violence, and becoming at last a heavy, continuous boom.

There is scarcely anything so immediately terrifying as that dull mutter of a city in tumult. Mlle. de Rochambeau's smooth years supplied her with no experience by which to measure the threat of that far uproar, and yet every nerve in her body thrilled to it and cried danger! It was then that she began to pray. The afternoon wore on, and she grew faint as well as frightened. Rosalie Leboeuf had set coffee and coarse bread before her in the early morning, but that was now many hours since.

The sun was near to setting when a loud shouting arose in the street below, shocking her from the dizzy quiescence into which she had fallen. Looking out, she saw that the children had scattered, pushed aside by rapidly gathering groups of their elders. Every house appeared to be disgorging an incredible number of people, and in their midst swayed a very large man, extremely drunk, and half naked. Such clothes as he possessed appeared to have been torn and rent in a most amazing manner, and scraps of them depended fantastically from naked shoulders and battered belt. His swarthy head retained its bonnet rouge, whose original colour was dyed, here and there, a deeper and more portentous crimson.

He waved great windmills of arms, and talked loudly in a thick guttural voice, adding strange gestures and stranger oaths. A sort of fascination kept Mademoiselle's eyes riveted upon him, and presently she began to catch words-phrases.

"Dear holy Virgin! what was he saying?—Impossible impossible, impossible!" And then quite suddenly her shocked brain yielded to the truth. There had been a massacre of the prisoners-this man had been there; he was recounting his exploits, boasting of the number he had killed.

"Mother most merciful, protect! save!—" But the ghastly catalogue ran on. They say that in those days many claimed the murderer's praise who had never acted the murderer's part. Men with hands innocent of blood daubed themselves horribly, and went home boasting of unimaginable horrors, guiltless the while as the children who hung eagerly on the tale. There was a madness abroad—a fearful, epidemic madness that seized its thousands, and time and again set Paris reeking like a shambles and laughing wantonly in the face of outraged Europe.

Whether Jean Michel were innocent or not, his conversation was equally horrifying. Mlle. de Rochambeau listened to it, shaking. The things said were inconceivable, and mercifully some of them passed over her innocence leaving it unbruised, save for a gradually accumulating weight of horror.

Suddenly she caught her cousin's name—"that wanton, the Montargis, damned Austrian spy," the man called her, and added Sélincourt's name to hers with a foul oath.

"I struck them, I! My pike was the first!" he shouted. Then drawing a scrap of reeking linen from his belt he waved it aloft, proclaiming, "This is her blood!" and looked around him for applause.

It was too much. A gasp broke from the girl's rigid lips, a damp dew from her brow. The twilight quivered-turned to darkness-then broke into a million sparks of flame, and a merciful oblivion overtook her.

Jean Michel may be left to the tender mercies of Louison his wife, a little woman and a venomous, having that command over her husband which one sees in the small wives of large men. Having haled him home, she burned his precious trophy, and poured much cold water on his hot and muddled head. Afterwards she gave her tongue free course, and we may consider that Jean Michel had his deserts.

When Mlle. de Rochambeau shuddered back again to consciousness, the room was dark. Outside, quiet reigned, and a beautiful blue dusk, just tinged with starlight. She dragged herself up into a half-sitting, half-kneeling position, and looked long and tremblingly into the tranquil depths above. All was peace and a cool purity, after the red horror of the day. The lights of the city looked friendly; they spoke of homes, of children, of decent comfort and ordered lives, and over all brooded the great sapphire glooms of the darkening ether and the lights of the houses of God. A strange calm slid into her soul-the hour held her-life and death were twin points in a fathomless, endless stretch of peace eternal.

The flesh no longer enchained her-weak with shock and fasting, it released its grip, and the freer spirit peered forth into the immensities.

Aline's body lay motionless, but her soul floated in a calm sea of light.

How long this lasted she did not know, but presently she became aware that she was listening to some rather distant sound. It came slowly nearer, and resolved itself into a man's heavy step, which mounted the narrow stairway, and paused ominously beside her door. Some of the strange calm from which she came still wrapped her, but her heart began to beat piteously. Her hearing seemed preternaturally acute, and she was aware of a pause, of one or two quickly drawn breaths, and then the dull sound of a groan-such a sound as may come from a man utterly weary and forespent when he imagines himself alone. The pause, the groan were over even as she listened, and the door opposite hers closed sharply upon Jacques Dangeau.

A throb of relief shook her back into normal humanity. It was, of course, the man she had seen on the stairs, and all at once she was conscious of immense fatigue; her head sank lower and lower, the darkness closed upon her, and she slept.

Rosalie stumbled over her an hour later, and took fright when the girl just stirred, and no more. She had intended her young aristocrat to pass a chastening day. Fasting was good for the soul, it rendered young girls amenable, and Rosalie wished to come to terms with this friendless but not unmoneyed demoiselle whom chance, luck, or some other god of her rather mixed beliefs had thrown her way. She had not, however, meant to leave the girl quite so long without food, but sallying out in quest of news she had been detained by her trembling sister, whose timid soul saw no safety anywhere in all red, raving Paris.

Rosalie set down her light and bent over the sleeping girl. A shrewd glance showed her a drawn fatigue of feature and a collapsed discomfort of attitude beyond anything she was prepared for.

"Tett, tett!" she grunted; "that Michel-could she have heard him? It is certainly possible. Well, well, there will be no talk to-night, that 's a sure thing. Here, Ma'mselle! Ma'mselle!"

Mlle. de Rochambeau opened her eyes, but only to close them again. The lids hung half shut, and under them lay heavy violet streaks. This was slumber that was half a swoon, and with a shrug of her vast shoulders, and a mental objurgation of the tenderness of aristocrats, Rosalie set herself to getting a cup of strong hot broth down the girl's throat.

Mademoiselle moaned and gasped, but when a sip or two had been chokingly swallowed, she raised her head and took the warm drink eagerly. She was about to sink back again into her old position when she felt strong arms about her, and capable hands loosened her dress and pulled off shoes and stockings. With a sigh of content, she felt herself laid down on the bed, her head touched a pillow, some one covered her, and she fell again upon a deep, deep, dreamless sleep.

It was high noon before she awoke, and then it was to a sense of bewildered fatigue beyond anything she had ever experienced. She lay quite still, and watched the little patch of sky which showed above the roofs of the houses opposite. It was very blue, and small glittering clouds raced quickly across it. Slowly, slowly as she looked, yesterday came back to her, but with a strange remoteness, as if it had all happened too long ago to weep for. A great shock takes us out of time and space. Emotion crystallises and ceases to flow along its accustomed channels. Aline de Rochambeau was never to forget the experience she had just passed through, but for the time being it seemed too far away to pierce the numbness round her heart.

A cry in the street did something; her cheek paled, and Rosalie coming noisily in found her sitting up in bed with wide, frightened eyes. She caught at the woman's arm and spoke in a sort of hurried whisper.

"Ah, Madame, is it true? For Heaven's love tell me! Or have I had some terrible dream?" and her voice sank, as if the sound of it terrified her.

Rosalie's fat shoulders went shrugging up to Rosalie's thick, red ears.

"Is what true?" she asked. "It is certainly true that you have slept fourteen hours, no less; long enough to dream anything. They called it laziness when I was young, my girl."

Mlle. de Rochambeau joined both hands about her wrist. "Tell me-only tell me, Madame —I heard-oh, God! —I heard a man in the street-he said" —shuddering —"he said the prisoners were all murdered-and my cousin-oh, my poor cousin!" Words brought her tears, and she covered her face from Rosalie's convincing nod.

"As to all the prisoners, for that I cannot answer, but certainly there are some hundreds less of the pestilent aristocrats than there were. As to your cousin, the ci-devant Marquise de Montargis, she 's as dead as mutton."

Aline looked up-she was not stupid, and this woman's altered tone was confirmation enough without any further words. Two days ago, it had been "Ma'mselle," and the respectful demeanour of a servant, smiles and smooth words had met her, and now that rough "my girl" and these brutal words! Rosalie Leboeuf was no pioneer. Had some terrible change not taken place, she would never have dared to speak and look as she was looking and speaking now.

Mademoiselle had not the Rochambeau blood for nothing. She drew herself up, looked gravely in the woman's face, and said in a fine, cold voice:

"I understand, Madame. Is it permitted to ask what you propose to do with me?"

Rosalie stared insolently. Then planting herself deliberately on a chair, she observed:

"It is certainly permitted to ask, my little aristocrat-certainly; but I should advise fewer airs and graces to a woman who has saved your life twice over, and that at the risk of her own."

Mademoiselle was silent, and Rosalie took up her parable. "Where would you have been by now, if I had not brought you home with me? There 's many a citizen who would have been glad to find a cage for a pretty stray bird like you, and how would that have suited you-eh? Better rough words from respectable Rosalie Leboeuf than shameful kisses from Citizen Such-a-one. And yesterday-if I had whispered yesterday, 'Montargis is dead, but there's a chick of the breed roosting in my upper room,' as I might very well have done, very well indeed, and kept your money into the bargain-what then, Miss Mealy-mouth? Have you a fancy for being stripped and dragged at a cart's tail through Paris, or would you relish being made to drink success to the Revolution in a brimming mug of aristocrats' blood? Eh! I could tell you tales, my girl, such tales that you 'd never sleep again, and that's what I 've saved you from, and do I get thanks-gratitude? Tush! was that ever the nobles' way?"

"Madame—I am-grateful," said Mademoiselle faintly. Her lips were ashen, and the breath came with a gasp between every word.

"Grateful-yes, indeed, I should think you were grateful," responded Rosalie, her keen eyes on the girl's ghastly face. With a little nod, she decided that she had frightened her enough. "I want more than your 'Madame, I'm grateful,'" and as she mimicked the faltering tones the blood ran back into Mademoiselle's white cheeks. "So far we have talked sentiment," she continued, with a complete change of manner. Her brutality slipped from her, and she became the bargaining bourgeoise.

"Let us come to business."

"With all my heart, Madame."

"Tut-no Madame-Citoyenne, or Rosalie. Madame smells of treason, disaffection, what not. What money have you?"

"Only what I showed you yesterday."

"But you could get more?"

"I do not think so, I know nothing of my affairs-but there was a good deal in that bag. I put it-yes, I 'm sure I did-under the pillow. Oh, Madame, my money 's not here! The bag is gone!"

"Té! té! té!" went Rosalie's tongue against the roof of her mouth; "gone it is, and for a very good reason, my little cabbage, because Rosalie Leboeuf took it!"

"Madame!"

"Ma'mselle!" mimicked the rough voice. "It is the little present that Ma'mselle makes me-the token of her gratitude. Hein! do you say anything against that?"

Mademoiselle was silent. She was reflecting that she still had her pearls, and she put a timid hand to her bosom. A moment later, she sank back trembling upon her pillow. The pearls were gone. It was not for nothing that Rosalie had undressed her the night before. She bit her lip, constraining herself to silence; and Rosalie, twinkling maliciously, maintained the same reserve. She was neither a cruel nor a brutal woman, though she could appear both, if she had an end to gain, as she had now.

She meant Mlle. de Rochambeau no harm, and honestly considered that she had earned both gold and pearls. Indeed, who shall say that she had not? Girls had to be managed, and were much easier to deal with when they had been well frightened. When she was well in hand, Rosalie would be kind enough, but just now, a touch of the spur, a flick of the whip, was what was required-and yet not too much, for times changed so rapidly, and who knew how long the reign of Liberty would last? She must not overdo it.

"Well now, Citoyenne," she said suddenly, "let us see where we are. You came to Paris ten days ago. Who brought you?"

"The Intendant and his wife," said Mademoiselle.

"And they are still in Paris?" (The devil take this Intendant!)

"No; they returned after two days. I think now that they were frightened."

"Very likely. Worthy, sensible people!" said Rosalie, with a puff of relief. "And you came to the Montargis? Well, she 's dead. Are you betrothed?"

Aline turned a shade paler. How far away seemed that betrothal kiss which she had rubbed impatiently from her reluctant hand!

"I was fiancée to M. de Sélincourt."

"That one? Well, he's dead, and damned too, if he has his deserts," commented Rosalie. "Hm, hm-and you knew no one else in Paris?"

"Only Mme. de Maillé-she remembered my mother."

"An old story that-she is dead too," said Rosalie composedly. "In effect, it appears that you have no friends; they are all dead."

Aline shrank a little, but did not exclaim. In this nightmare-existence upon which she had entered, it was as natural that dreadful things should happen as until two days ago it had seemed to her young optimism impossible.

Rosalie pursued the conversation.

"Yes, they are all dead. I gave myself the trouble of going to see my sister this morning on purpose to find out. Marie is a poor soft creature; she cried and sobbed as if she had lost her dearest friends, and Bault, the great hulk, looked as white as chalk. I always say I should make a better gaoler myself-not that I 'm not sorry for them, mind you, with all that place to get clean again, and blood, as every one knows, the work of the world to get out of things."

Mademoiselle shuddered.

"Oh!" she breathed protestingly, and then added in haste, "They are all dead, Madame, all my friends, and what am I to do?"

Rosalie crossed her arms and swayed approvingly. Here was a suitable frame of mind at last-very different from the hoity-toity airs of the beginning.

"Hein! that is the question, and I answer it this way. You can stay here, under my respectable roof, until your friends come forward; but of course you must work, or how will my rent be paid? A mere trifle, it is true, but still something; and besides the rent there will be your ménage to make. For one week I will feed you, but after that it is your affair, and not mine. Even a white slip of a girl like you requires food. The question is, what can you do to earn it?"

Mademoiselle de Rochambeau coloured.

"I can embroider," she said hesitatingly. "I helped to work an altar cloth for the Convent chapel last year."

Rosalie gave a coarse laugh.

"Eh-altar cloths! What is the good of that? Soon there will be no altars to put them on!"

"I learned to embroider muslin too," said Mademoiselle hastily. "I could work fine stuffs, for fichus, or caps, or handkerchiefs, perhaps."

Rosalie considered.

"Well, that's better, though you 'll find it hard to fill even your pinched stomach out of such work; but we can see how it goes. I will bring you muslin and thread, and you shall work a piece for me to see. I know a woman who would buy on my recommendation, if it were well done."

"They said I did it well," said Mademoiselle meekly. Her eyes smarted suddenly, and she thought with a desperate yearning of comfortable Sister Marie Madeleine, or even the severe Soeur Marie Mediatrice. How far away the Convent stillness seemed, and how desirable!

"Good," said Rosalie; "then that is settled. For the rest, I cannot have Mlle. de Rochambeau lodging with me. That will not go now. What is your Christian name?"

"Aline Marie."

"Aline, but no-that would give every donkey something to bray over. Marie is better-any one may be Marie. It is my sister's name, and my niece's, and was my mother's. It is a good name. Well, then, you are the Citoyenne Marie Roche."

Mademoiselle repeated it, her lip curling a little.

"Fi donc-you must not be proud," remarked Rosalie the observant. "You are Marie Roche, you understand, a simple country girl, and Marie Roche must not be proud. Neither must she wear a fine muslin robe and a silk petticoat or a fichu trimmed with lace from Valenciennes. I have brought you a bundle of clothes, and you may be glad you had Rosalie Leboeuf to drive the bargain for you. Two shifts, these good warm stockings, a neat gown, with stuff for another, to say nothing of comb and brush, and for it all you need not pay a sou! Your own clothes in exchange, that is all. That is what I call a bargain! Brush the powder from your hair and put on these clothes, and I 'll warrant you 'll be safe enough, as long as you keep a still tongue and do as I bid you."

"Thank you," said Mademoiselle, with an effort. Even her inexperience was aware that she was being cheated, but she had sufficient intelligence to know herself completely in the woman's power, and enough self-control to bridle her tongue.

Rosalie, watching her, saw the struggle, inwardly commended the victory, and with a final panegyric on her own skill at a bargain she departed, and was to be heard stumping heavily down the creaking stair.

As soon as she was alone Aline sprang out of bed. Most of her own clothes had been removed, she found, and she turned up her nose a little at the coarse substitutes. There was no help for it, however, and on they went. Then came a great brushing of hair, which was left at last powderless and glossy, and twisted into a simple knot. Finally she put on the petticoat, of dark blue striped stuff, and the clean calico gown. There was a tiny square of looking-glass in the room, cracked relic of some former occupant, and Aline peeped curiously into it when her toilette was completed. A young girl's interest in her own appearance dies very hard, and it must be confessed that the discovery that her new dress was far from unbecoming cheered her not a little. She even smiled as she put on the coarse white cap, and turned her head this way and that to catch the side view; but the smile faded suddenly, and the next moment she was on her knees, reproaching herself for a hard heart, and praying with all dutiful earnestness for the repose of her cousin's soul.

## CHAPTER VII
## THE INNER CONFLICT

September passed on its eventful way. Dangeau was very busy; there were many meetings, much to be discussed, written, arranged, and on the twenty-first the Assembly was dissolved, and the National Convention proclaimed the Republic.

Dangeau as an elected member of the Convention had his hands full enough, and there was a great deal of writing done in the little room under the roof. Sometimes, as he came and went, he passed his pale fellow-lodger, and noted half unconsciously that as the days went on she grew paler still. Her gaze, proud yet timid, as she stood aside on the little landing, or passed him on the narrow stair, appealed to a heart which was really tender.

"She is only a child, and she looks as if she had not enough to eat," he muttered to himself once or twice, and then found to his half-shamed annoyance that the child's face was between him and his work.

"You are a fool, my good friend," he remarked, and plunged again into his papers.

He burned a good deal of midnight oil in those days, and Rosalie Leboeuf, whose tough heart really kept a soft corner for him, upbraided him for it.

"Tiens!" she said one day, about the middle of October, "tiens! The Citizen is killing himself."

Dangeau, sitting on the counter, between two piles of apples, laughed and shook his head.

"But no, my good Rosalie-you will not be rid of me so easily, I can assure you."

"H'm —you are as white as a girl-as white as your neighbour upstairs, and she looks more like snow than honest flesh and blood."

Dangeau, who had been wondering how he should introduce this very subject, swung his legs nonchalantly and whistled a stave before replying. The girl's change of dress had not escaped him, and he was conscious, and half ashamed of, his curiosity. Rosalie plainly knew all, and with a little encouragement would tell what she knew.

"Who is she, then, Citoyenne?" he asked lightly.

"Eh! the Citizen has seen her—a slip of a white girl. Her name is Marie Roche, and she earns just enough to keep body and soul together by embroidery."

Dangeau nodded his head. He did not understand why he wished to gossip with Rosalie about this girl, but an idle mood was on him, and he let it carry him whither it would.

"Why, yes, Citoyenne, I know all that, but that does n't answer my question at all. Who *is* Marie Roche?"

Rosalie glanced round. Indiscretion was as dear to her soul as to another woman's, and it was not every day that one had the chance of talking scandal with a Deputy. To do her justice, she was aware that Dangeau was a safe enough recipient of her confidences, so after assuring herself that there was no one within earshot, she abandoned herself to the enjoyment of the moment.

"Aha! The Citizen is clever, he is not to be taken in! Only figure to yourself, then, Citizen, that I find this girl, a veritable aristocrat, weeping at the gates of La Force, weeping, mon Dieu, because they will not keep her there with her friends! Singular, is it not? I bring her home, I am a mother to her, and next day, pff-all her friends are massacred, and what can I do? I have a charitable heart, I keep her-the marmot does not eat much."

Dangeau enjoyed his Rosalie.

"She earns nothing, then?" he observed, with a subdued twinkle in his eye.

"Oh, a bagatelle. I assure you it does not suffice for the rent; but I have a good heart, I do not let her starve"; and Rosalie regarded the Deputy with an air of modest virtue that sat oddly upon her large, creased face.

"Excellent Rosalie!" he said, with a soft, half-mocking inflection.

She bridled a little.

"Ah, if the Citizen knew!" she said, with a toss of the head, which, aiming at the arch, merely achieved the elephantine.

"If it is a question of the Citoyenne's virtues, who does not know them?" said Dangeau. He made her a little bow, and kept the sarcasm out of his voice this time. He was thinking of his little neighbour's look of starved endurance, and contrasting her mentally with the well-fed Rosalie. He had not much confidence in the promptings of the latter's heart if they countered the interests of her pocket. Suddenly a plan came into his head, and before he had time to consider its possible drawbacks, he found himself saying:

"Tell me, then, Citoyenne, does this Marie Roche write a good hand?"

"H'm —well, I suppose the nuns in that Convent of hers taught her something, and as it was neither baking nor brewing, it may have been reading and writing," said Rosalie sharply. "Does the Citizen wish her to write him a billet-doux?"

To Dangeau's annoyed surprise he felt the colour rise to his cheeks as he answered:

"Du tout, Citoyenne, but I do require an amanuensis, and I thought your protégée might earn my money as well as another. I imagine that much fine embroidery cannot be done in the evenings, and it would be then that I should require her services."

"The girl is an aristocrat," said Rosalie suspiciously.

Dangeau laughed.

"Are you afraid she will contaminate me?" he asked gaily. "I shall set her to copy my book on the principles of Liberty. Desmoulins says that every child in France should get it by heart, and though I do not quite look for that, I hope there will be some to whom it means what it has meant for me. Your little aristocrat shall write it out fair for the press, and we shall see if it will not convert her."

"It will take too much of her time," said Rosalie sulkily.

"A few hours in the evening. It will save her eyes and pay better than that embroidery of hers, which as you say barely keeps body and soul together. I hope we shall be able to knit them a little more closely, for at present there seems to be a likelihood of a permanent divorce between them."

Rosalie looked a little alarmed.

"Yes, she looks ill," she muttered; "and as you say it would be only for an hour or two."

"Yes, for the present. I am out all day, and it is necessary that I should be there. I write so badly, you see; your little friend would soon get lost amongst my blots if she were alone, but if I am there, she asks a question, I answer it-and so the work goes on."

"H'm —" said Rosalie; "and the pay, Citizen?"

Dangeau got down from the counter, laughing.

"Citoyenne Roche and I will settle that," he said, a little maliciously; "but perhaps, my good Rosalie, you would speak to her and tell her what I want? It would perhaps be better than if I, a stranger, approached her on the subject. She looks timid-it would come better from you."

Rosalie nodded, and caught up her knitting, as Dangeau went out. On the whole, it was a good plan. The girl was too thin-she did not wish her to die. This would make more food possible, and at the same time entail no fresh expense to herself. Yes, it was decidedly a good plan.

"It is true, I have a charitable disposition," sighed Rosalie.

Dangeau went on his way humming a tune. The lightness of his spirits surprised him. The times were anxious. New Constitutions are not born without travail. He had an arduous part to play, heavy responsible work to do, and yet he felt the irrational exhilaration of a schoolboy, the flow of animal spirits which is induced by the sudden turn of the tide in spring, and the uplifted heart of him who walks in dreams. All this because a girl whom he had seen some half-dozen times, with whom he had never spoken, whose real name he did not know, was going to sit for an hour or two where he could look at her, copy some pages of his, which she would certainly find dull, and take money, which he could ill spare, to bring a little more colour into cheeks whose pallor was beginning to haunt his sleep.

Dangeau bit his lip impatiently. He did not at all understand his own mood, and suddenly it angered him.

"The girl is an aristocrat-nourished on blind superstition, cradled in tyranny," said his brain.

"She is only a child, and starved," said his heart; and he quickened his steps, almost to a run, as if to escape from the two voices. Once at the Convention business claimed him altogether, Marie Roche was forgotten, and it was Dangeau the patriot who spoke and listened, took notes and made suggestions. It was late when he returned, and he climbed the stair somewhat wearily. He was aware of a reaction from the unreasoning gaiety of the morning. It seemed cold and cheerless to come back night after night to an empty room and an uncompanioned evening, and yet he could remember the time, not so long ago, when that dear solitude was the birthplace of burning dreams, and thoughts dearer than any friend.

He had not felt so dull and dreary since the year of his mother's death, his first year alone in life, and once or twice he sighed as he lighted a lamp and bent to the heaped-up papers which littered his table. Half an hour later, a low knocking at the door made him pause.

"Enter!" he called out, expecting to see Rosalie.

The door opened rather slowly, and Mlle. de Rochambeau stood hesitating on the threshold. Her eyes were wide and dark with shyness, but her manner was prettily composed as she said in her low, clear tones:

"The Citizen desires my services as a secretary? Rosalie told me you had asked her to speak to me——"

Dangeau sprang up. His theory of universal equality, based upon universal citizenship, was slipping from him, and he found himself saying:

"If Mademoiselle will do me so much honour."

Mademoiselle's beautifully arched eyebrows rose a little. What manner of Deputy was this? She had observed and liked the gravity of his face and the distant courtesy of his manner, or utmost privation would not have brought her to accept his offer; but she had not expected expressions of the Court, or a bow that might have passed at Versailles.

"I am ready, Citizen," she said, with a faint smile and a fainter emphasis on the form of address.

For the second time that day Dangeau flushed like a boy. He was glad that a table had to be drawn nearer the lamp, a chair pushed into position, ink and paper fetched. The interval sufficed to restore him to composure, and Mademoiselle being seated, he returned to his papers and to silence.

When the first page had been transcribed, Mademoiselle brought it over to him.

"Is that clear, and as you wish it, Citizen?"

"It is very good indeed, Citoyenne"; and this time his tongue remembered that it belonged to a Republican Deputy. If Mademoiselle smiled, he did not see it, and again the silence fell. At ten o'clock she rose.

"I cannot give you more time than this, I fear, Citizen," she said, and unconsciously her manner indicated that an audience was terminated. "My embroidery is still my 'cheval de bataille,' and I fear it would suffer if my eyes keep too late hours."

Her low "Good-night," her scarcely hinted curtsey passed, even whilst Dangeau rose, and before he could reach and open the door, she had passed out, and closed it behind her. Dangeau wrote late that night, and waked later still. His thoughts were very busy.

After some evenings of silent work, he asked her abruptly:

"What is your name?"

Mademoiselle gave a slight start, and answered without raising her head:

"Marie Roche, Citizen."

"I mean your real name."

"But yes, Citizen"; and she wrote a word that had to be erased.

Dangeau pushed his chair back, and paced the room. "Marie Roche neither walks, speaks, nor writes as you do. Heavens! Am I blind or deaf?"

"I have not remarked it," said Mademoiselle demurely. Her head was bent to hide a smile, which, if a little tremulous, still betokened genuine amusement-amusement which it certainly would not do for the Citizen to perceive.

"Then do you believe that I am stupid, or"—with a change of tone—"not to be trusted?"

Mademoiselle de Rochambeau looked up at that.

"Monsieur," she said in measured tones, "why should I trust you?"

"Why should you trust Rosalie Leboeuf?" asked Dangeau, with a spice of anger in his voice. "Do you not consider me as trustworthy as she?"

"As trustworthy?" she said, a little bitterly. "That may very easily be; but, Monsieur, if I trusted her, it was of necessity, and what law does necessity know?"

"You are right," said Dangeau, after a brief pause; "I had no right to ask-to expect you to answer."

He sat down again as he spoke, and something in his tone made Mademoiselle look quickly from her papers to his face. She found it stern and rather white, and was surprised to feel herself impelled towards confidence, as if by some overwhelming force.

"I was jesting, Monsieur," she said quickly; "my name is Aline de Rochambeau, and I am a very friendless young girl. I am sure that Monsieur would do nothing that might harm me."

Dangeau scarcely looked up.

"I thank you, Citoyenne," he said in a cold, constrained voice; "your confidence shall be respected."

Perhaps Mademoiselle was surprised at the formality of the reply-perhaps she expected a shade more response. It had been a condescension after all, and if one condescended, one expected gratitude. She frowned the least little bit, and caught her lower lip between her white, even teeth for a moment, before she bent again to her writing.

Dangeau's pen moved, but he was ignorant of what characters it traced. There is in every heart a moment when the still pool becomes a living fountain, because an angel has descended and the waters are divinely troubled. To Jacques Dangeau such a moment came when he felt that Aline de Rochambeau distrusted him, and by the stabbing pain that knowledge caused him, knew also that he loved her. When he heard her speak her name, those troubled waters leapt towards her, and he constrained his voice, lest it should call her by the sweet name she herself had just spoken-lest it should terrify her with the resonance of this new emotion, or break treacherously and leave her wondering if he were gone suddenly mad.

He forced his eyes upon the page that he could not see, lest the new light in them should drive her from her place. He kept his hand clenched close above the pen, lest it should catch at her dress-her hand-the white, fine hand which wrote with such clear grace, such maidenly quiet, and all the while his heart beat so hard that he could scarcely believe she did not hear it.

Ten o'clock struck solemnly, and Mademoiselle began to put away her writing materials in her usual orderly fashion.

"You are going?" he stammered.

"Since it is the hour, Citizen," she answered, in some surprise.

He held the door, and bowed low as she passed him.

"Good-night, Citizen."

"Good-night, Citoyenne."

Mlle. de Rochambeau passed lightly out. He heard her door close, and shut his own. He was alone. A torrent as of emotion sublimed into fire swept over him, and soul and body flamed to it. He paced the room angrily. Where was his self-control, his patriotism, his determination to live for one only Mistress, the Republic of his ardent dreams? A shocked consciousness that this aristocrat, this child of the enemy, was more to him than the most ardent of them, assaulted his mind, but he repulsed it indignantly. This was a madness, a fever, and it would pass. He had led too solitary a life, hence this girl's power to disturb him. Had he mixed more with women he would have been safe-and suddenly he recalled Rosalie's handsome cousin, the Thérèse of his warning to young Cléry. She had made unmistakable advances to him more than once, but he had presented a front of immovable courtesy to her inviting smiles and glances. Certainly an affair with her would have been a liberal education, he reflected half scornfully, half whimsically disgusted, and no doubt it would have left him less susceptible. Fool that he was!

Far into the night he paced his room, and continued the mental struggle. Love comes hardly to some natures, and those not the least noble. A man trained to self-control, master of his own soul and all its passions, does not without a struggle yield up the innermost fortress of his being. He will not abdicate, and love will brook no second place. The strong man armed keepeth his house, but when a stronger than he cometh-All that night Dangeau wrestled with that stronger than he!

It was some days before the evening task was interrupted again. If Dangeau could not speak to her without a thousand follies clamouring in him for utterance, he could at least hold his tongue. Once or twice the pen in those resolute fingers flagged, and his eyes rested on his secretary longer than he knew. Heavy shadows begirt her. The low roof sloped to the gloom of the unlighted angles in the wall. Outside the lamp-light's contracted circle, all seemed strange, unformed, grotesque. Weird shadows hovered in the dusk background, and curious flickers of light shot here and there, as the ill-trimmed flame flared up, or suddenly sank. The yellow light turned Mademoiselle's hair to burnished gold, and laid heavy shadows under her dark blue eyes. Its wan glow stole the natural faint rose from her cheeks and lips, giving her an unearthly look, and waking in Dangeau a poignant feeling, part spiritual awe, part tender compassion for her whiteness and her youth, that sometimes merged into the wholly human longing to touch, hold, and comfort.

Once she looked up and caught that gaze upon her. Her face whitened a little more, and she bent rather lower over her writing, but afterwards, in her own room, she blushed angrily, and wondered at herself, and him.

What a look! How dared he? And yet, and yet-there was nothing in it to scare the most sensitive maidenliness, not a hint of passion or desire.

Out of the far-away memories of her childhood, Aline caught the reflection of that same look in other eyes-the eyes of her beautiful mother, haunted as she gazed by the knowledge that the little much-loved daughter must be left to walk the path of life alone, unguarded by the tender mother's love. Those eyes had closed in death ten years before, but at the recollection Aline broke into a passionate weeping, which would not be stilled. One of her long-drawn sobs reached waking ears across the way, and Dangeau caught his own breath, and listened. Yes, again-it came again. Oh God! she was weeping! The unfamiliar word came to his lips as it comes to those most unaccustomed in moments of heart strain.

"O God, she is in trouble, and I cannot help her!" he groaned, and in that moment he ceased to fight against his love. To himself he ceased to matter. It was of her, of the beloved, of the dear sadness in her voice, of the sweet loneliness in her eyes that he thought, and something like a prayer went up that night from the heart of a man who had pronounced prayer to be a degrading superstition. Long after Aline lay sleeping, her wet lashes folded peacefully over dreaming eyes, he waked, and thought of her with a passion of tenderness.

## CHAPTER VIII
## AN OFFER OF FRIENDSHIP

It was some nights later that Mlle. de Rochambeau, copying serenely according to her wont, came across something which made her eyes flash and her cheeks burn. So far she had written on without paying much heed to the matter before her, her pen pursuing a mechanical task, whilst her thought merely followed its clear, external form, gracing it with fine script and due punctuation. At first, too, the strangeness of her situation had had its share in absorbing her mind, but now she was more at her ease, and began, as babies do, to take notice. Custom had set its tranquillising seal upon her occupation, and perhaps a waking interest in Dangeau set her wondering about his work. Certain it is that, having written as the heading of a chapter "Sins against Liberty," she fell to considering the nature of Liberty and wondering what might be these sins against it, which were treated of, as she began to perceive, in language theological in its fervour of denunciation. Dangeau had written the chapter a year ago, in a white heat of fury against certain facts which had come to his knowledge; and it breathed a very ardent hatred towards tyrants and their rule, towards a hereditary aristocracy and its oppression. Mlle. de Rochambeau turned the leaf, and read—"a race unfit to live, since it produces men without honour and justice, and women devoid of virtue and pity." She dropped the sheet as if it burned, and Dangeau, looking up, found her eyes fixed on him with an expression of proud resentment, which stung him keenly.

"What is it?" he asked quickly.

She read the words aloud, with a slow scorn, which went home.

"And Monsieur believes that?" she said, with her eyes still on his.

Dangeau was vexed. He had forgotten the chapter. It must read like an insult. So far had love taken him, but he would not deny what he had written, and after all was it not well she should know the truth, she who had been snatched like some pure pearl from the rottenness and corruption of her order?

"It is the truth," he said; "before Heaven it is the truth."

"The truth-this?" she said, smiling. "Ah no, Monsieur, I think not."

The smile pricked him, and his words broke out hotly.

"You are young, Citoyenne, too young to have known and seen the shameless wickedness, the crushing tyranny, of this aristocracy of France. I tell you the country has bled at every pore that vampires might suck the blood, and fatten on it, they and their children. Do you claim honour for the man who does not shame to dishonour the hearths of the poor, or pity for the woman who will see children starving at her gate that she may buy herself another string of diamonds-hard and cold as her most unpitiful heart?"

"Oh!" said Mademoiselle faintly.

"It is the truth-the truth. I have seen it-and more, much, much more. Tales not fit for innocent girls' ears like yours, and yet innocent girls have suffered the things I dare not name to you. This is a race that must be purged from among us, with sweat of blood, and tears if needs be, and then-let the land enjoy her increase. Those who toiled as brutes, oppressed and ground down below the very cattle they tended, shall work, each man for his own wife and children, and the prosperity of the family shall make the prosperity of France."

Mlle. de Rochambeau listened impatiently, her finely cut mouth quivering with anger, and her eyes darkening and deepening from blue to grey. They were those Irish eyes, of all eyes the most changeable: blue under a blue sky, grey in anger, and violet when the soul looked out of them-the beautiful eyes of beautiful Aileen Desmond. They were very dark with her daughter's resentment now.

"Monsieur says I am young," she cried, "but he forgets that I have lived all my life in the country amongst those who, he says, are so oppressed, so enslaved. I have not seen it. Before my parents died and I went to the Convent, I used to visit the peasants with my mother. She was an angel, and they worshipped her. I have seen women kiss the fold of her dress as she passed, and the children would flock to her, like chickens at feeding-time. Then, my father-he was so good, so just. In his youth, I have heard he was the handsomest man at Court; he had the royal favour, the King wished for his friendship, but he chose rather to live on his estates, and rule them justly and wisely. The meanest man in his Marquisate could come to him with his grievance and be sure it would be redressed, and the poorest knew that M. le Marquis would be as scrupulous in defence of his rights as in defence of his own honour. And there were many, many who did the same. They lived on their lands, they feared God, they honoured the King. They did justly and loved mercy."

Dangeau watched her face as it kindled, and felt the flame in her rouse all the smouldering fires of his own heart. The opposition of their natures struck sparks from both. But he controlled himself.

"It is the power," he said in a sombre voice; "they had too much power-might be angel or devil at will. Too many were devil, and brought hell's torments with them. You honour your parents, and it is well, for if they were as you speak of them, all would honour them. Do you not think Liberty would have spoken to them too? But for every seigneur who dealt equal justice, there were hundreds who crushed the poor because they were defenceless. For every woman who fostered the tender lives around her, there were thousands who saw a baby die of starvation at its starving mother's breast with as little concern as if it had been a she-wolf perishing with her whelps, and less than if it were a case of one of my lord's hounds and her litter."

Mademoiselle felt the angry tears come sharply to her eyes. Why should this man move her thus? What, after all, did his opinions matter to her? She chid her own imprudence in having lent herself to this unseemly argument. She had already trusted him too much. A little tremour crept over her heart-she remembered the September madness, the horror, and the blood-and the colour ebbed slowly from her cheeks as she bent forward and took her pen again.

Dangeau saw her whiten, and in an instant his mood changed. Her hand shook, and he guessed the cause. He had frightened her; she did not trust him. The thought stabbed very deep, but he too fell silent, and resumed his work, though with a heavy heart. When she rose to go, he looked up, hesitated a moment, and then said:

"Citoyenne."

"Yes, Citizen."

"Citoyenne, it would be wiser not to express to others the sentiments you have avowed to-night. They are not safe-for Marie Roche."

"No, Citizen."

Mademoiselle's back was towards him, and he had no means of discovering how she took his warning.

"That process of purging, of which I spoke, goes forward apace," he continued slowly; "those who have sinned against the people must expiate their sins, it may be in blood."

"Yes, Citizen."

Something drove him on-that subtle instinct which drives us all at times, the desire to probe deeply, to try to the uttermost.

"They and their innocent children, perhaps," he said gloomily, and her own case was in his mind. "What do your priests say-is it not 'to the third and fourth generation'?"

She turned and faced him then, very pale, but quite composed. There was no coward blood in her.

"You are trying to tell me that you will denounce me," she said quietly.

The words fell like a thunderbolt. All the blood in Dangeau's body seemed to rush violently to his head, and for a moment he lost himself. He was by her side, his hands catching at her shoulders, where they lay heavy, shaking.

"Look me in the face and say that again!" he thundered in the voice his section knew.

"Ah!" cried Mademoiselle —"what do you mean, Monsieur? This is an outrage, release me!"

His hands fell, but his eyes held hers. They blazed upon her like heated steel, and the anger in them burned her.

"Ah! you dare not say it again," he said very low.

"Monsieur, I dare." Her gaze met his, and a strange excitement possessed her. She would have been less than woman had she not felt her power-more than woman had she not used it.

Dangeau spoke again, his voice muffled with passion. "You dare say I, Jacques Dangeau, am a spy, an informer, a betrayer of trust?"

Mademoiselle's composure began to return. This man shook when he touched her; she was stronger than he. There was no danger.

"Not quite that, Citizen," she said quietly. "But I did not know what a patriot might consider his duty."

He turned away, and bent over his table, arranging a paper here, closing a drawer there. After a few moments he came to where she stood, and looked fixedly at her for a short time. His former look she had met, but before this her eyes dropped.

"Citoyenne," he said slowly, "I ask your pardon. I had hoped that —" He paused, and began again. "I am no informer-you may have reliance on my honour and my friendship. I warned you because I saw you friendless and inexperienced. These are dangerous times-times of change and development. I believe with all my heart in the goal towards which we are striving, but many will fall by the way-some from weakness, some by the sword. I was but offering a hand to one whom I saw in danger of stumbling."

His altered tone and grave manner softened Aline's mood. "Indeed, Citizen," she cried on the impulse, "you have been very kind to me. I am not ungrateful —I have too few friends for that."

"Do you count me a friend, Citoyenne?"

Mademoiselle drew back a shade.

"What is a friend-what is friendship?" she said more lightly.

And Dangeau sought for cool and temperate words.

"Friendship is mutual help, mutual good-will —a bond which is rooted in honour, confidence, and esteem. A friend is one who will neither be oppressive in prosperity nor faithless in adversity," he said.

"And are you such a friend, Citizen?"

"If you will accept my friendship, you will learn whether I am such a friend or not."

The measured words, the carefully controlled voice, emboldened Mademoiselle. She threw a searching glance at the dark, downcast features above her, and her youth went out to his.

"I will try this friendship of yours, Citizen," she said, with a little smile, and she held out her hand to him.

Dangeau flushed deeply. His self-control shook, but only for a moment. Then he raised the slim hand, and, bending to meet it, kissed it as if it had been the Queen's, and he a devout Loyalist.

It was Aline's turn to wake and wonder that night, acting out the little scene a hundred times. Why that flame of sudden anger-that tempest which had so shaken her? What was this power which drew her on to experiment, to play, with forces beyond her understanding? She felt again the weight of his hands upon her, her flesh tingled, and she blushed hotly in the darkness. No one had ever touched her so before. Wild anger woke in her, and wilder tears came burning to her burning cheeks. Truly a girl's heart is a strange thing. The shyest maid will weave dream-tales of passionate love, in which she plays the heroine to every gallant hero history holds or romance presents. Their dream kisses leave her modesty untouched, their fervent speeches bring no faintest flush to her virgin cheeks. Comes then an actual lover, and all at once is changed. The garment of her dreams falls from her, and leaves her naked and ashamed. A look affronts, a word offends, and a touch goes near to make her swoon.

Aline lay trembling at her thoughts. He had touched, had held her. His strong hands had bruised the tender flesh. She had seen a man in wrath-had known that it was for her to raise or quell the storm. And then that kiss-it tingled yet, and she threw out her hand in protest. All her pride rose armed. She, a Rochambeau, daughter of as haughty a house as any France nourished, to lie here dreaming because a bourgeois had kissed her hand! —this was a scourge to bring blood. It certainly brought many tears, and at the last she knelt for a long while praying. The waters of her soul stilled at the familiar words of peace, and settled back into a virgin calm. As yet only the surface had been ruffled by the first breath which heralded the approaching storm. It had rippled under the touch, tossed for an hour, flung up a drop or two of salt, indignant spray, and sunk again to sleep and silence. Below, the deeps lay all untroubled, but in them strange things were moving. For when she slept she dreamed a strange dream, and disquieting. She thought she was at Rochambeau once more, and she wondered why her heart did not leap for joy, instead of being heavy and troubled, beyond anything she could remember.

The sun was sinking, and all the fields lay golden in the glory, but she was too weary to heed. Her feet were bare and bleeding, her garments torn and scanty, and on her breast lay a little moaning babe. It stretched slow, groping hands to her and wailed for food, and her heart grew heavier and darker with every step she took. Suddenly Dangeau stood by her side. He was angry, his voice thundered, his look was flame, and in loud, terrible tones he cried, "You have starved my child, and it is dead!" Then she thought he took the baby from her arms, and an angel with a flaming sword flew out of the sun, and drew her down-down-down....

She woke terrified, bathed in tears. What a dream! "Holy Mary, Mother and Virgin, shield me!" she prayed, as she crouched breathless in the gloom. "The powers of darkness-the powers of evil! Let dreams be far and phantoms of the night-bind thou the foe. His look, his fearful look, and his deep threatening voice like the trump of the Angel of Judgment! Mary, Virgin, save!"

Thoughts wild and incoherent; prayers softening to a sob, sobs melting again into a prayer! Loneliness and the midnight had their way with her, and it was not until the tranquillising moon shot a silver ray into the small dark room that the haunting agony was calmed, and she sank into a dreamless sleep.

## CHAPTER IX
## THE OLD IDEAL AND THE NEW

It was really only on four evenings of the week that Dangeau was able to avail himself of Mlle. de Rochambeau's services.

On Sundays she took a holiday both from embroidery and copying, and on Mondays and Thursdays he spent the evening at the Cordeliers' Club.

It was on a Saturday that Dangeau had stormed, proffered friendship, and kissed Mademoiselle's hand, so that during the two days that followed both had time to calm down, to experience a slight revulsion of feeling, and finally to feel some embarrassment at the thought of their next meeting.

On Tuesday Dangeau was in his room all the afternoon. He had some important papers to read through, and when he had finished them, felt restless, yet disinclined to go out again.

It was still light, but the winter dark would fall in half an hour, and the evening promised to be wet and stormy. A gust of wind beat upon the window now and again, leaving it sprayed with moisture. Dangeau stood awhile looking out, his mood grey as the weather. Some one not far off was singing, and he opened his window, and leaned idly out to see if the singer were visible. The sound at once grew faint, almost to extinction, and latching the casement he fell to pacing his room. By the door he paused, for the sound was surely clearer. He turned the handle and stood listening, for Mademoiselle's door was ajar, and from within her voice came sweetly and low. He had an instant vision of how she would look, sitting close to the dull window, grey twilight on the shining head bent over the fine white work as she sang to keep the silence and the loneliness from her heart. The song was one of those soft interminable cradle songs which mothers sing in every country place, rocking the full cradle with patient rhythmic foot, the while they spin or knit, and every word came clear to a lilting air:

"She sat beneath the wayside tree,
Et lon, lon, lon, et la, la, la—
She heard the birds sing wide and free,

Hail Mary, full of grace!
"She had no shelter for her head,
Et lon, lon, lon, et la, la, la,
Except the leaves that God had spread—

Hail Mary, full of grace!
"Down flew the Angel Gabriel,
Et lon, lon, lon, et la, la, la,
He said, 'Maid Mary, greet thee well!'

Hail Mary, full of grace!"

The song was interrupted for a moment, but he heard her hum the tune. To the lonely man came a swift, holy thought of what it would be to see her rock a child to that soft air in a happy twilight, no longer solitary. He heard her move her chair and sigh a little as she sat down again. The daylight died as if with gasps for breath palpably withdrawn:

"She laid her Son in the oxen's stall,

Et lon, lon, lon, et la, la, la—

Herself she did not rest at all,

Hail Mary, full of grace!"

Another pause, another sigh, and then the sound of steps moving about the room. Then the door was shut, and with a little smile half tender, half impatient, Dangeau turned to his work again.

When the evening was come, and Mademoiselle was in her place, he asked her suddenly:

"What do you do with yourself on Sunday?"

"I take a holiday, Citizen," she answered demurely, and without looking up.

"But what do you do with your holiday, Citoyenne," said Dangeau, persistent.

Mademoiselle smiled a little and blushed a little, smile and blush alike reproving his curiosity, but after a slight hesitation she said:

"I go to one of the great churches."

"And when you are there?"

"Is it the Catechism?" ventured Mademoiselle, and then went on hastily, "I say my prayers, Citizen."

"And could you not say them at home?"

"Why, yes, and I do, Citizen, but I go to hear the Mass; and then the church is so solemn, and big, and beautiful. Others are praying round me, and I feel my prayers are heard."

Dangeau frowned and then broke out impatiently:

"That idea of prayer-it is so selfish-each one asking, asking, asking. I do not find that ennobling!"

"Is it so selfish to ask for patience and courage, then, Citizen?"

"And is that what you pray for?" he asked, arrested by something in her tone.

Aline's colour rose high under his softened look, and she inclined her head without speaking.

"That might pass," said Dangeau reflectively. "I do not believe in priests, or an organised religion, but I have my own creed. I believe in one Supreme Being from whom flows that tide which we call Life when it rises in us, and Death when it ebbs again to Him. If the creature could, by straining towards the Creator, draw the life-tide more strongly into his own soul, that would be worthy prayer; but to most men, what is religion?—a mere ignoble system of reward or punishment, fit perhaps for children, or slaves, but no free man's creed."

"What would you give them instead, Citizen?" asked Mademoiselle seriously.

"Reason," cried Dangeau; "pure reason. Teach man to reason, and you lift him above such degrading considerations. Even the child should not be punished, it should be reasoned with; but there—" He paused, for Mademoiselle was laughing a soft, irrepressible laugh, that filled the small, low room.

"Oh, Citizen, forgive me," she cried; "but you reminded me of something that happened when I was a child. I do not quite know whether the story fits your theory or mine, but I will tell it you, if you like."

"If it fits my theory, I shall annex it unscrupulously, of that I give you fair warning," said Dangeau, laughing. "But tell it to me first, and we will dispute about it afterwards."

Aline leaned back in her upright chair, and a little remembering smile came into her eyes.

"Well, Citizen, you must know that I was only nine years old when I went to the Convent, and I was a spoilt child, and gave the good nuns a great deal of trouble, I am afraid.

"The sister in charge of us was Sister Marie Josèphe, and we were very fond of her; but when we were naughty, out came a birch rod, and we were soundly punished.

"Now Sister Marie Josèphe was not strong; she suffered much from pain in her head, and sometimes it was so bad that she was obliged to be alone, and in the dark. When this happened,

Sister Géneviève took her place, and Sister Géneviève was like you, Citizen; she believed in the efficacy of pure reason! If under her regime there was a crime to be punished, then there was no birch rod forthcoming, but instead, a very long, dreary sermon-an hour by the clock, at least-and at the end a very limp, discouraged sinner, usually in tears. But, Citizen, it was ennuyant, most terrible ennuyant, and much, much worse than being whipped; for that only lasted a minute, and then there were tears, kisses, promises of amendment, and a grand reconciliation. Well, I must tell you that I had a great desire to see the moon rise over the hill behind us. Our windows looked the other way, and as it was winter time we were all locked in very early. Adèle de Matignon dared me to get out. I declared I would, and I watched my time. I am sure Sister Marie Josèphe must have been very much surprised by my frequent and tender inquiries after her health at that time.

"'Always a little suffering, my child,' she would say, and then I would whisper to Adèle, 'We must wait.'

"At last, however, a day came when the good sister answered, 'Ah, it goes better, thanks to the Virgin,' and I told Adèle that it would be for that evening. Well, I got out. I climbed through a window, and down a pear tree. I scratched my hands, and fell into some bushes, and after all there was no moon! The night was cloudy and presently it began to rain. I assure you, Citizen, I was very well punished before I came up for judgment. Of course I was discovered, and, to my horror, found myself in the hands of Sister Géneviève. 'But where is Sister Marie Josèphe?' I sobbed. 'Ah, my child!' said Sister Géneviève mildly, 'this wickedness of yours has brought on one of her worst attacks, and she is suffering too much to come to you.' I cried dreadfully, for I was very much discouraged, and felt that one of Sister Géneviève's sermons would remove my last hope in this world. She did not know what to make of me, I am sure, but I had to listen to more pure reason than I had ever done before, and I assure you, Citizen, that it gave me a headache almost as bad as poor Sister Marie Josèphe's."

Mademoiselle laughed again as she finished her tale, and looked at Dangeau with arch, malicious eyes. He joined her laughter, but would have the last word; for,

"See, Citoyenne," he said, "see how your tale supports my theory, and how fine a deterrent was the pure reason of Sister Géneviève as compared with the birch rod of Sister Marie Josèphe!"

"But if it is a punishment, then your theory falls to the ground, since you were to do away with all reward and punishment!" objected Aline.

Dangeau's eyes twinkled.

"You are too quick," he said in mock surrender.

Mademoiselle took up her pen.

"I am very slow over my work," she answered, smiling. "See how I waste my time! You should scold me, Citizen."

They wrote for awhile, but Dangeau's pen halted, the merriment died out of his face, leaving it stern and gloomy. These were no times to foster even an innocent gaiety. Abruptly he began to speak again.

"You see only flowers and innocence upon your altars, but I have seen them served by cruelty, blood, and lust."

Aline looked up, startled.

"I could not tell you the tales I know-they are not fit." His brow clouded. "My mother was a good woman, good and religious. I have still a reverence for what she reverenced; I can still worship the spirit of her worship, though I have travelled far enough since she taught me at her knee. I have seen too many crimes committed in the name of Religion," and he broke off, leaning his head upon his hand.

Mlle. de Rochambeau's eyes flashed.

"And in the name of Liberty, none?" she asked with a sudden ring in her voice.

A vision of blood and horror swept between them. Dangeau saw in memory the gutters of Paris awash with the crimson of massacre. Dead, violet eyes in a severed head pike-lifted stared at him from the gloom, and under his gaze he thought they changed, turned greyer, darker, and took the form and hue of those which Aline raised to his. He shuddered violently, and answered in a voice scarcely audible:

"Yes, there have been crimes."

Then he looked up again, snatching his thoughts back to control.

"Liberty is only a name, as yet," he said; "we have taken away the visible chain which manacled the body, but an invisible one lies deep, and corroded, fettering the heart and will, and as it rusts into decay it breeds a deadly poison there. The work of healing cannot be done in a day. There can be no true liberty until our children are cradled in it, educated in it, taught to hold it as the air, without which they cannot breathe. That time is to come, but first there will be much bitterness, much suffering, much that is to be deplored. You may well pray for strength and patience," he continued, after a momentary pause, "for we shall all need them in the times that are coming."

Slowly, but surely, the spirit of the two great Republican Clubs was turning to violence and lust of power. Hébert, Marat, and Fouquier Tinville were rising into prominence-fatal, evil stars, driven on an orbit of mad passion.

Robespierre's name still stood for moderation, but there was, at times, an expression on his livid face, a spark in his haggard eyes, which left a more ominous impression than Marat's flood of vituperation or Tinville's calculating cruelty.

Dangeau's heart was very heavy. The splendid dawn was here-the dawn longed for, looked for, hoped for through so many hours of blackest night-and behold, it came up redly threatening, precursor, not of the full, still day of peace, but of some Armageddon of wrath and fury. The day of peace would come, must come, but who could say that he would live to see it? There were times when it seemed unutterably far away.

A dark mood was upon him. He could not write, but stared gloomily before him. That anxiety, that quickened sense of all life's sadness and dangers which comes over us at times when we love, possessed him now. How long would this young life, which meant he was afraid to gauge how much to him, be safe in the midst of this fermenting city? Her innocence stabbed his soul, her delicate pride caught at his heart-strings. How long could the one endure? How soon might not the other be dragged in the dust? Rosalie he knew only too well. She would not betray the girl, but neither would she go out of her own safe way to protect her; and she was venal, narrow, and hard.

He did not kiss Mademoiselle's hand to-night, but he took it for a moment as she passed, and stood looking down at it as he said:

"If God is, He will bless you."

Mademoiselle's heart beat violently.

"And you too, Citizen," she murmured, with an involuntary catch of the breath.

"Do you pray for me?" he asked, filled with a new emotion.

"Yes, Citizen," she said, in a very low voice.

Dangeau was about to speak again-to say he knew not what-but with her last words she drew her hand gently away, and was gone. He stood where she had left him, breathing deeply. Suddenly the gloom that lay upon him became shot with light, and hope rose trembling in his heart. He felt himself strong—a giant. What harm could touch her under the shield of his love? Who would dare threaten what he would cherish to the death? In this new exultation he flung the window wide, and leaned out. A little snow had fallen, and the heaviness of the air was relieved. Now it came crisp and vigorous against his cheek. Far above, the clouds made a wide ring about the moon. Serenely tranquil she floated in the space of clear, dark sky, and all the night was irradiated as if by thoughts of peace.

## CHAPTER X
## THE FATE OF A KING

December was a month of turmoil and raging dissensions. Faction fought faction, party abused party, and all was confusion and clamour. In the great Hall of the Convention, speaker succeeded speaker, Deputy after Deputy rose, and thundered, rose, and declaimed, rose, and vituperated. Nothing was done, and in every department of the State there reigned a chaos indescribable. "Moderation and delay," clamoured the Girondins, smooth, narrow Roland at their head, mouthpiece, as rumour had it, of that beautiful philosopher, his wife. "To work and have done with it," shouted the men of the Mountain, driving their words home with sharp accusations of lack of patriotism and a desire to favour Monarchy.

On the 11th of the month, the Hall had echoed to the Nation's indictment of Louis Capet, sometime King of France.

On the 26th, Louis, still King in his own eyes, made answer to the Nation's accusation by the mouth of his advocate, the young Désèze.

For three hours that brave man spoke, manfully striving against the inevitable, and, having finished a most eloquent speech, threw his whole energies into obtaining what was the best hope of the King's friends-delay, delay, delay, and yet again delay.

The matter dragged on and on. Every mouthing Deputy had his epoch-making remarks to make, and would make them, though distracted Departments waited until the Citizen Deputies should have finished judging their King, and have time to spare for the business of doing the work they had taken out of his hands; whilst outside, a carefully stage-managed crowd howled all day for bread, and for the Traitor Veto's head, which they somehow imagined, or were led to imagine, would do as well.

The Mountain languished a little without its leader, who was absent on a mission to the Low Countries, and, Danton's tremendous personality removed, it tended to froth of accusation and counter-accusation, by which matters were not at all advanced. At the head of his Jacobins sat Robespierre, as yet coldly inscrutable, but amongst the Cordeliers there was none to replace Danton.

In the early days of January, the Netherlands gave him back again, and the Mountain met in conclave-its two parties blended by the only man who could so blend them. The long Committee-room was dark, and though it was not late, the lamps had been lighted for some time. Under one of them a man sat writing. His straight, unnaturally sleek hair was brushed carefully back from a forehead of spectral pallor. His narrow lips pressed each other closely, and he wrote with an absorbed concentration which was somehow not agreeable to witness.

Every now and then he glanced up, and there was a hinted gleam of red —a mere spark not yet fanned into flame-behind the shallows of his eyes. The lamp-light showed every detail of his almost foppish dress, which was in marked contrast to his unpleasing features, and to the custom of his company; for those were days when careful attire was the aristocrat's prerogative, and clean linen rendered a patriot gravely suspect.

By the fire two men were talking in low voices-Hébert, sensual, swollen of body, flat and pale of face; and Marat, a misshapen, stunted creature with short, black, curling hair, pinched mouth, and dark, malignant gaze.

"We get no further," complained Hébert, in a dull, oily voice, devoid of ring.

Marat shrugged his crooked shoulders.

"We are so ideal, so virtuous," he remarked viciously. "We were so shocked in September, my friend; you should remember that. Blood was shed-actually people were killed-fie then! it turns our weak stomachs. We look askance at our hands, and call for rose-water to wash them in."

"Very pretty," drawled Hébert, pushing the fire with his foot. "There are fools in the world, and some here, no doubt; but after all, we all want the same thing in the end, though some make a boggle at the price. I want power, you want power, Danton wants it, Camille wants it, and so does even your piece of Incorruptibility yonder, if he would come out of his infernal pose and acknowledge it."

Robespierre looked up, and down again. No one could have said he heard. It was in fact not possible, but Hébert grew a faint shade yellower, and Marat's eyes glittered maliciously.

"Ah," he said, "that's just it-just the trouble. We all want the same thing, and we are all afraid to move, for fear of giving it to some one else. So we all sit twiddling our thumbs, and the Gironde calls the tune."

Hébert swore, and spat into the fire.

"Now Danton is back, he will not twiddle his thumbs for long," he said; "that is not at all his idea of amusing himself. He is turning things over-chewing the cud. Presently, you will see, the bull will bellow, and the whole herd will trot after him."

"Which way?" asked Marat sarcastically.

"H'm—that is just what I should like to know."

"And our Maximilian?"

"What does he mean? What does he want?" Hébert broke out uneasily, low-voiced. "He is all for mildness and temperance, justice and sobriety; but under it-under it, Marat?"

Marat's pointed brows rose abruptly.

"The devil knows," said he, "but I don't believe Maximilian does."

Robespierre looked up again with calm, dispassionate gaze. His eye dwelt on the two for a moment, and dropped to the page before him. He wrote the words, "Above all things the State"—and deep within him the imperishable ego cried prophetic, "L'État, c'est moi!"

The room began to fill. Men came in, cursing the cold, shaking snow from their coats, stamping icy fragments from their frozen feet. The fire was popular. Hébert and Marat were crowded from the place they had occupied, and a buzz of voices rose from every quarter. Here and there a group declaimed or argued, but for the most part men stood in twos and threes discussing the situation in confidential tones.

If intellect was less conspicuous than in the ranks of the Gironde, it was by no means absent, and many faces there bore its stamp, and that of ardent sincerity. For the most part they were young, these men whose meeting was to make History, and they carried into politics the excesses and the violence of youth.

Here leaned Hérault de Séchelles, one of the handsomest men in France; there, declaiming eagerly, to as eager a circle of listeners, was St. Just with that curious pallor which made his face seem a mere translucent mask behind which there burned a seven-times-heated flame.

"I say that Louis can claim no rights as a citizen. We are fighting, not trying him. The law's delays are fatal here. One day posterity will be amazed that we have advanced so little since Cæsar's day. What-patriots were found then to immolate the tyrant in open Senate, and to-day we fear to lift our hands! There is no citizen to-day who has not the right that Brutus had, and like Brutus he might claim to be his country's saviour! Louis has fought against the people, and is now no longer a Frenchman, but a stranger, a traitor, and a criminal! Strike, then, that the tocsin of liberty may sound the birth hour of the Nation and the death hour of the Tyrant!"

"It is all delay, delay," said Hérault gloomily to young Cléry. "Désèze works hard. Time is what he wants-and for what? To hatch new treasons; to get behind us, and stab in the dark; to allow Austria to advance, and Spain and England to threaten us! No, they have had time enough for these things. It is the reckoning day. Thirty-eight years has Louis lived and now he must give an account of them."

"My faith," growled Jean Bon, shaking his shaggy head, to which the winter moisture clung, "My faith, there are citizens in this room who will take matters into their own hands if the Convention does not come to the point very shortly."

"The Convention deliberates," said Hérault gloomily, and Jean Bon interrupted him with a brutal laugh—

"Thunder of Heaven, yes; talk, talk, talk, and nothing done. We want a clear policy. We want Danton to declare himself, and Robespierre to stop playing the humanitarian, and say what he means. There has been enough of turning phrases and lawyers' tricks. Louis alive is Louis dangerous, and Louis dead is Louis dust; that's the plain truth of it."

"He is of more use to us alive than dead, I should say," cried Edmund Cléry impetuously. "Are we in so strong a position as to be able with impunity to destroy our hostages?"

Hébert, who had joined the group, turned a cold, remembering eye upon him.

"Austria does not care for Capet," he said scornfully; "Antoinette and the boy are all the hostages we require. Austria does not even care about them very much; but such as they are they will serve. Capet must die," and he sprang on a bench and raised his voice:

"Capet must die!—I demand his blood as the seal of Republican liberty. If he lives, there will be endless plots and intrigues. I tell you it is his life now, or ours before long. The people is a hard master to serve, my friends. To-day they want a Republic, but to-morrow they may take a fancy to their old plaything again. 'Limited Monarchy!' cries some fool, and forthwith on goes Capet's crown, and off go our heads! A smiling prospect, hein, mes amis?"

There was a murmur, part protest, part encouragement.

Hébert went on:

"Some one says deport him; he can do no more harm than the Princes are doing already. Do you perhaps imagine that a man fights as well for his brother's crown as for his own? The Princes are half-hearted—they are in no danger, the crown is none of theirs, their wives and children are at liberty; but put Capet in their place, and he has everything to gain by effort and all to lose by quiescence. I say that the man who says 'Send Capet out of France' is a traitor to the Republic, and a Monarchist at heart! Another citizen says, 'Imprison him, keep him shut up out of harm's way.' Out of harm's way-that sounds well enough, but for my part I have no fancy for living over a powder magazine. They plot and conspire, these aristocrats. They do it foolishly enough, I grant you, and we find them out, and clap them in prison. Now and then there is a little blood-letting. Not enough for me, but a little. Then what? More of the breed at the same game, and encore, and encore. Some day, my friends, we shall wake up and find that one of the plots has succeeded. Pretty fools we should look if one fine morning they were all flown, our hostages-Capet, the Austrian, the proud jade Elizabeth, and the promising youth. Shall I tell you what would be the next thing? Why, our immaculate generals would feel it their duty to conclude a peace with profits. There would be an embracing, a fraternising, a reconciliation on our frontiers, and hand in hand would come Austria and our army, conducting Capet to his faithful town of Paris. It is only Citizen Robespierre who is incorruptible-meaner mortals do not pretend to it. In our generals' place, I myself, I do not say that I should not do the same, for I should certainly conclude that I was being governed by a parcel of fools, and that I should do well to prove my own sanity by saving my head."

Danton had entered as Hébert sprang up. His loose shirt displayed the powerful bull-neck; his broad, rugged forehead and deep-set passionate eyes bespoke the rough power and magnetism of his personality. He came in quietly, nodding to a friend here and there, his arm through that of Camille Desmoulins, who, with dark hair tossed loosely from his beautiful brow, and strange eyes glittering with a visionary light, made an arresting figure even under Danton's shadow.

In happier days the one might have been prophet, ruler, or statesman; the other poet, priest, or dreamer of ardent dreams; but in the storm of the Red Terror they rose, they passed, they fell; for even Danton's thunder failed him in the face of a tempest elemental as the crash of worlds evolving from chaos.

He listened now, but did not speak, and Camille, at his side, flung out an eager arm.

"The man must die!" he shouted in a clear, ringing voice. "The people call for his blood, France calls for his blood, the Convention calls for his blood. I demand it in the sacred name of Liberty. Let the scaffold of a King become the throne of an enduring Republic!"

Robespierre looked up with an expression of calm curiosity. These wild enthusiasms, this hot-blooded ardour, how strange, how inexplicable, and yet at times how useful. He leaned across the table and began to speak in a thin, colourless voice that somehow made itself heard, and enforced attention.

"Capet has had a fair trial at the hands of a righteous and representative Assembly. If the Convention is satisfied that he is innocent, maligned perhaps by men of interested motives"—there was a slight murmur of dissent—"or influenced to unworthy deeds by those around him, or merely ignorant-strangely, stupidly ignorant-the Convention will judge him. But if he has sinned against the Nation, if he has oppressed the people, if he has given them stone for bread, and starvation for prosperity-if he has conspired with Austria against the integrity of France in order to bolster up a tottering tyranny, why, then"—he paused whilst a voice cried, "Shall the people oppressed through the ages not take their revenge of a day?" and an excited chorus of oaths and execrations followed the words—"why, then," said the thin voice coldly, "still I say, the Convention will judge him."

Maximilian Robespierre took up his pen and wrote on. Something in his words had fanned the scattered embers into flame, and strife ran high. Jules Dupuis, foul-mouthed and blasphemous, screamed out an edged tirade. Jean Bon boomed some commonplace of corroboration. Marat spat forth a venomous word or two. Robespierre folded the paper on which he wrote, and passed the note to Danton at his elbow. The great head bent, the deep eyes read, and lifting, fixed themselves on Robespierre's pale face. It was a face as strange as pale. Below the receding brow the green, unwinking eyes held steady. The red spark trembled in them and smouldered to a blaze.

Danton looked strangely at him for a moment, and then, throwing back his great shoulders and raising his right hand high above the crowd, he thundered:

"Citizens, Capet must die!"

A roar of applause shook the room, and drowned the reverberations of that mighty voice-Danton's voice, which shook not only the Mountain on which he stood, and from which he fell, but France beyond and Europe across her frontiers. It echoes still, and comes to us across the years with all the man's audacious force, his pride of patriotism, and overwhelming energy! raised it now, and beckoning for silence——

"We are all agreed," he cried, "Louis is guilty, and Louis must die. If he lives, there is not a life safe in all France. The man is an open sore on the flesh of the Constitution, and it must be cut away, lest gangrene seize the whole. Above all there must be no delay. Delay means disintegration; delay means a people without bread, and a country without government. Neither can wait. Away with Louis, and our hands are free to do all that waits to be done."

"The frontiers-Europe-are we strong enough?" shouted a voice from the back.

Danton's eyes blazed.

"Let Europe look to herself. Let Spain, Austria, and England look to themselves. The rot of centuries is ripe at last. Other thrones may totter, and other tyrants fall. Let them threaten-let them threaten, but we will dash a gage of battle at their feet-the bloody head of the King!"

At that the clamour swallowed everything. Men cheered and embraced. There was shouting and high applause.

Danton turned from the riot and fell into earnest talk with Robespierre. In Hébert's ear Marat whispered:

"As you said. The bull has roared, and we all follow."

"All?" asked Hébert significantly.

"Some people have an inexplicable taste for being in the minority," said Marat, shrugging.

"As, for instance?"

"Our young friend Dangeau."

"Ah, that Dangeau," cursed Hébert, "I have a grudge against him."

"Very ungrateful of you, then," said Marat briskly; "he saved Capet and his family at a time when it suited none of us that they should die. We want a spectacle-something imposing, public, solemn; something of a fête, not just a roaring crowd, a pike-thrust or two, and pff! it is all over."

"It is true."

"See you, Hébert, when we have closed the churches, and swept away the whole machinery of superstition, what are we going to give the people instead of them? I say La République must have her fêtes, her holidays, her processions, and her altars, with St. Guillotine as patron saint, and the good Citizen Sanson as officiating priest. We want Capet's blood, but can we stop there? No, a thousand times! Paris will be drunk, and then, in a trice, Paris will be thirsty again. And the oftener Paris is drunk, the thirstier she will be, until — —"

"Well, my friend?" Hébert was a little pale; had he any premonition of the day when he too should kneel at that Republican altar?

Marat's face was convulsed for a moment.

"I don't know," he said, in sombre tones.

"But Dangeau," said Hébert after a pause, "the fellow sticks in my gorge. He is one of your moral idealists, who want to cross the river without wetting their feet. He has not common-sense."

"Danton is his friend," said Marat with intention.

"And it's 'ware bull.' "

"I know that. See now if Danton does not pack him off out of Paris somewhere until this business is settled."

"He might give trouble-yes, he might give trouble," said Marat slowly.

"He is altogether too popular," grunted Hébert.

Marat shrugged his shoulders.

"Oh, popularity," he said, "it's here to-day and gone to-morrow; and when to-morrow comes — —"

"Well?"

"Our young friend will have to choose between his precious scruples and his head!"

Marat strolled off, and Jules Dupuis took his place. He came up in his short puce coat, guffawing, and purple-faced, his loose skin all creased with amusement.

"Hé, Hébert," he chuckled, "here 's something for the Père Duchesne," and plunged forthwith into a scurrilous story. As he did so, the door opened and Dangeau came in. He looked pale and very tired, and was evidently cold, for he made his way to the fireplace, and stood leaning against it looking into the flame, without appearing to notice what was passing. Presently, however, he raised his head, recognising the two men beside him with a curt nod.

Hébert appeared to be well amused by Dupuis' tale. Its putrescent scintillations stimulated his jaded fancy, and its repulsive dénouement evoked his oily laugh.

Dangeau, after listening for a moment or two, moved farther off, a slight expression of disgust upon his face.

Hébert's light eyes followed him.

"The Citizen does not like your taste in wit, my friend," he observed in a voice carefully pitched to reach Dangeau's ear.

Dupuis laughed grossly.

"More fool he, then," he chuckled.

"You and I, mon cher, are too coarse for him," continued Hébert in the same tone. "The Citizen is modest. Tiens! How beautiful a virtue is modesty! And then, you see, the Citizen's sympathies are with these sacrés aristocrats."

Dangeau looked up with a glance like the flash of steel.

"You said, Citizen —?" he asked smoothly.

Hébert shrugged his loosely-hung shoulders.

"If I said the Citizen Deputy had a tender heart, should I be incorrect? Or, perhaps, a weak stomach would be nearer to the truth. Blood is such a distressing sight, is it not?"

Dangeau looked at him steadily.

"A patriot should hold his own life as lightly as he should hold that of every other citizen sacred until the State has condemned it," he said with a certain quiet disgust; "but if the Citizen says that I sympathise with what has been condemned by the State, the Citizen lies!"

Hébert's eyes shifted from the blue danger gleam. Bully and coward, he had the weakness of all his type when faced. He preferred the unresisting victim and could not afford an open quarrel with Dangeau. Danton was in the room, and he did not wish to offend Danton yet. He moved away with a sneer and a mocking whisper in the ear of Jules Dupuis.

Dangeau stood warming himself. His back was straighter, his eye less tired. The little interchange of hostilities had roused the fire in his veins again, and for the moment the cloud of misgiving which had shadowed him for the last few days was lifted. When Danton came across and clapped him on the shoulder, he looked up with the smile to which he owed more than one of his friends, since to a certain noble gravity of aspect it lent a very human, almost boyish, warmth and glow.

"Back again, and busy again?" he said, turning.

"Busier than ever," said Danton, with a frown. He raised his shoulders as if he felt a weight upon them. "Once this business of Capet's is arranged, we can work; at present it's just chaos all round."

Dangeau leaned closer and spoke low.

"I was detained-have only just come. Has anything been done-decided?"

"We are unanimous, I think. I spoke, they all agreed. Robespierre is with us, and his party is well in hand. Death is the only thing, and the sooner the better."

Dangeau did not speak, and Danton's eye rested on him with a certain impatience.

"Sentiment will serve neither France nor us at this juncture," he said on a deep note, rough with irritation. "He has conspired with Austria, and would bring in foreign troops upon us without a single scruple. What is one man's life? He must die."

Dangeau looked down.

"Yes, he must die," he said in a low, grave voice, and there was a momentary silence. He stared into the fire, and saw the falling embers totter like a mimic throne, and fall into the sea of flame below. A cloud of sparks flew up, and were lost in blackness.

"Life is like that," he said, half to himself.

Danton walked away, his big head bent, the veins of his throat swollen.

## CHAPTER XI
## THE IRREVOCABLE VOTE

Danton returned was Danton in action. Force possessed the party once more and drove it resistless to its goal. Permanent Session was moved, and carried-permanent Session of the National Convention-until its near five hundred members had voted one by one on the three all-important questions: Louis Capet, is he guilty, or not guilty? Shall the Convention judge him, or shall there be a further delay, an appeal to the people of France? If the Convention judges, what is its judgment-imprisonment, banishment, or death?

Forthwith began the days of the Three Votings, stirring and dramatic days seen through the mist of years and the dust-clouds raised by groping historians. What must they have been to live through?

It was Wednesday evening, January 16, and lamps were lit in the Hall of the Convention, but their glow shone chiefly on the tribune, and beyond there crowded the shadows, densely mysterious. Vergniaud, the President, wore a haggard face-his eyes were hot and weary, for he was of the Gironde, and the Gironde began to know that the day was lost. He called the names sonorously, with a voice that had found its pitch and kept it in spite of fatigue; and as he called, the long procession of members rose, passed for an instant to the lighted tribune, and voted audibly in the hearing of the whole Convention. Each man voted, and passed again into the shadow. So we see them-between the dark past and the dark future-caught for an instant by that one flash which brands them on history's film for ever.

Loud Jacobin voices boomed "Death," and ranted of treason; epigrams were made to the applause of the packed galleries. For the people of Paris had crowded in, and every available inch of room was packed. Here were the *tricoteuses* —those knitting women of the Revolution, whose steel needles were to flash before the eyes of so many of the guillotine's waiting victims, before the eyes indeed of many and many an honourable Deputy voting here to-night. Here were swart men of St. Antoine's quarter-brewers, bakers, oilmen, butchers, all the trades-whispering, listening, leaning over the rail, now applauding to the echo, now hissing indignantly, as the vote pleased or displeased them. Death demanded with a spice of wit pleased the most —a voice faltering on a timorous recommendation to mercy evoked the loudest jeers.

Dangeau sat in his place and heard the long, reverberating roll of names, until his own struck strangely on his ear. He rose and mounted into the smoky, yellow glare of the lamps that swung above the tribune. Vergniaud faced him, dignified and calm.

"Your vote, Citizen?" and Dangeau, in clear, grave reply:

"Death, Citizen President."

Here there was nothing to tickle the waiting ears above, and he passed down the steps again in silence, whilst another succeeded him, and to that other another yet. All that long night, and all the next long day, the voices never ceased. Now they rang loud and full, now low and hesitating; and after each vote came the people's comment of applause, dissent, or silence.

Dangeau passed into one of the lower galleries reserved for members and their friends. His limbs were cramped with the long session, and his throat was parched and dry; coffee was to be had, he knew, and he was in quest of it. As he got clear of the thronged entrance, a strange sight met his eye, for the gallery resembled a box at the opera, infinitely extended.

Bare-necked women flashed their diamonds and their wit, chattering, laughing, and exchanging sallies with their friends.

Refreshments were being passed round, and Deputies who were at leisure bowed, and smiled, and did the honours, as if it were a place of amusement, and not a hall of judgment.

A bold, brown-faced woman, with magnificent black eyes, her full figure much accentuated by a flaring tricolour sash, swept to the front of the gallery, and looked down. In her wake came a sleepy, white-fleshed blonde, mincing as she walked. She too wore the tricolour, and Dangeau's lips curled at the desecration.

"Philippe is voting," cried the brown woman loudly. "See, Jeanne, there he comes!"

Dangeau looked down, and saw Philippe Égalité, sometime Philippe d'Orleans, prince of the blood and cousin of the King, pass up the tribune steps. Under the lamps his face showed red and blotched, his eyes unsteady; but he walked jauntily, twisting a seal at his fob. His attire bespoke the dandy, his manner the poseur. Opposite to Vergniaud he bowed with elegance, and cried in a voice of loud effrontery, "I vote for Death."

Through the Assembly ran a shudder of recoil. Natural feeling was not yet brayed to dust in the mortar of the Revolution, and it thrilled and quickened to the spectacle of kinsman rising against kinsman, and the old blood royal of France turning from its ruined head publicly, and in the sight of all men.

"It is good that Louis should die, but it is not good that Philippe should vote for his death. Has the man no decency?" growled Danton at Dangeau's ear.

Long after, when his own hour was striking, Philippe d'Orleans protested that he had voted upon his soul and conscience-the soul whose existence he denied, and the conscience whose voice he had stifled for forty years. Be that between him and that soul and conscience, but, as he descended the tribune steps, Girondin, Jacobin, and Cordelier alike drew back from him, and men who would have cried death to the King's cousin, cried none the less, "Shame on Égalité!"

Only the bold brown woman and her companion laughed. The former even leaned across the bar and kissed her hand, waving, and beckoning him.

Dangeau's gaze, half sardonically curious, half disgusted, rested upon the scene.

"All posterity will gaze upon what is done this day," he said in a low voice to Danton —"and they will see this."

"The grapes are trodden, the wine ferments, and the scum rises," returned Danton on a deep, growling note.

"Such scum as this?"

"Just such scum as this!"

Below, one of the Girondins voted for imprisonment, and the upper galleries hissed and rocked.

"Death, death, death!" cried the next in order.

"Death, and not so much talk about it!"

"Death, by all means death!"

The blonde woman, Jeanne Fresnay, was pricking off the votes on a card.

"Ah-at last!" she laughed. "I thought I should never get the hundred. Now we have one for banishment, ten for imprisonment, and a hundred for death."

The brown Marguerite Didier produced her own card —a dainty trifle tied with a narrow tricolour ribbon.

"You are wrong," she said —"it is but eight for imprisonment. You give him two more chances of life than there is any need to."

"That's because I love him so well. Is he not Philippe's cousin?" drawled the other, making the correction.

Philippe himself leaned suddenly between them.

"I should be jealous, it appears," he said smoothly. "Who is it that you love so much?"

The bare white shoulders were lifted a little farther out of their very scanty drapery.

"Eh-that charming cousin Veto of yours. Since you love him so well, I am sure I may love him too. May I not?"

Philippe's laugh was a little hoarse, though ready enough.

"But certainly, chère amie," he said. "Have I not just proved my affection to the whole world?"

Mademoiselle Didier laughed noisily and caught him by the arm.

"There, let him go," she said with impatience. "At the last he bores one, your good cousin. We want more bonbons, and I should like coffee. It is cold enough to freeze one, with so much coming and going."

Again Dangeau turned to his companion.

"An edifying spectacle, is it not?" he asked.

Danton shrugged his great shoulders.

"Mere scum and froth," he said. "Let it pass. I want to speak to you. You are to be sent on mission."

"On mission?"

"Why, yes. You can be useful, or I am much mistaken. It is this way. The South is unsatisfactory. There is a regular campaign of newspaper calumny going on, and something must be done, or we shall have trouble. I thought of sending you and Bonnet. You are to make a tour of the cities, see the principal men, hold public meetings, explain our aims, our motives. It is work which should suit you, and more important than any you could do in Paris at present."

Dangeau's eyes sparkled; a longing for action flared suddenly up in him.

"I will do my best," he said in a new, eager voice.

"You should start as soon as this business is over." Danton's heavy brow clouded. "Faugh! It stops us at every turn. I have a thousand things to do, and Louis blocks the way to every one. Wait till my hands are free, and you shall see what we will make of France!"

"I will be ready," said Dangeau.

Danton had called for coffee, and stood gulping it as he talked. Now, as he set the cup down, he laid his hand on Dangeau's shoulder a moment, and then moved off muttering to himself:

"This place is stifling-the scent, the rouge. What do women do in an affair of State?"

In Dangeau's mind rose a vision of Aline de Rochambeau, cool, delicate, and virginal, and the air of the gallery became intolerable. As he went out in Danton's wake, he passed a handsome, dark-eyed girl who stared at him with an inviting smile. Lost in thought, he bowed very slightly and was gone. His mind was all at once obsessed with the vision he had evoked. It came upon him very poignantly and sweetly, and yet-yet-that vote of his, that irrevocable vote. What would she say to that?

Duty led men by strange ways in those strange days. Only of one thing could a man take heed-that he should be faithful to his ideals, and constant in the path which he had chosen, even though across it lay the shadows of disillusion and bitterness darkening to the final abyss. There could be no turning back.

The dark girl flushed and bit an angrily twitching lip as she stared after Dangeau's retreating figure. When Hébert joined her, she turned her shoulder on him, and threw him a black look.

"Why did you leave me?" she cried hotly. "Am I to stand here alone, for any beast to insult?"

"Poor, fluttered dove," said Hébert, sneering. He slid an easy arm about her waist. "Come then, Thérèse, no sulks. Look over and watch that fool Girondin yonder. He 's dying, they say, but must needs be carried here to vote for mercy."

As he spoke he drew her forward, and still with a dark glow upon her cheeks she yielded.

## CHAPTER XII
## SEPARATION

Rosalie Leboeuf sat behind her counter knitting. Even on this cold January day the exertion seemed to heat her. She paused at intervals, and waved the huge, half-completed stocking before her face, to produce a current of air. Swinging her legs from the counter, and munching an apple noisily, was a handsome, heavy-browed young woman, whose fine high colour and bold black eyes were sufficiently well known and admired amongst a certain set. An atmosphere of vigour and perfect health appeared to surround her, and she had that pose and air which come from superb vitality and complete self-satisfaction. If the strait-laced drew their skirts aside and stuck virtuous noses in the air when Thérèse Marcel was mentioned, it was very little that that young woman cared.

She and Rosalie were first cousins, and the respectable widow Leboeuf winked at Thérèse's escapades, in consideration of the excellent and spicy gossip which she could often retail.

Rosalie was nothing if not curious; and just now there was a very savoury subject to hand, for Paris had seen her King strip to the headsman, and his blood flow in the midst of his capital town.

"You should have been there, ma cousine," said Thérèse between two bites of her apple.

"I?" said Rosalie in her thick, drawling way. "I am no longer young enough, nor slim enough, to push and struggle for a place. But tell me then, Thérèse, was he pale?"

Thérèse threw away the apple core, and showed all her splendid teeth in a curious feline mixture of laugh and yawn.

"Well, so-so," she said lazily; "but he was calm enough. I have heard it said that he was all of a sweat and a tremble on the tenth of August, but he did n't show it yesterday. I was well in front-Heaven be praised, I have good friends-and his face did not even twitch when he saw the steel. He looked at it for a moment or two-one would have said he was curious-and then he began to speak."

Rosalie gave a little shudder, but her face was full of enjoyment.

"Ah," she breathed, leaning forward a little.

"He declared that he died innocent, and wishing France-nobody knows what; for Santerre ordered the drums to be beaten, and we could not hear the rest. I owe him a grudge, that Santerre, for cutting the spectacle short. What, I ask you, does he imagine one goes to the play in order to miss the finest part, and I with a front place, too! But they say he was afraid there would be a rescue. I could have told him better. We are not fools!"

"And then——?"

"Well, thanks to the drums, you couldn't hear; but there was a whispering with the Abbé, and Sanson hesitating and shivering like a cat with a wet paw and the gutter to cross. Everything was ready, but it seems he had qualms-that Sanson. The National Guards were muttering, and the good Mère Garnet next to me began to shout, 'Death to the Tyrant,' only no one heard her because of Santerre's drums, when suddenly he bellowed, 'Executioner, do your duty!' and Citizen Sanson seemed to wake up. It was all over in a flash then; the Abbé whispered once, called out loudly, and pchtt! down came the knife, and off came the head. Rose Lacour fainted just at my elbow, the silly baggage; but for me, I found it exciting-more exciting than the theatre. I should have liked to clap and call 'Encore!'"

Rosalie leaned back, fanning, her broad face a shade paler, whilst the girl went on:

"His eyes were still open when Sanson held up the head, and the blood went drip, drip, drip. We were all so quiet then that you could hear it. I tell you that gave one a sensation, my cousin!"

"Blood-ouf!" said Rosalie; "I do not like to see blood. I cannot digest my food after it."

"For me, I am a better patriot than you," laughed Thérèse; "and if it is a tyrant's blood that I see, it warms my heart and does it good."

A shudder ran through Rosalie's fat mass. She lifted her bulky knitting and fanned assiduously with it.

Her companion burst into a loud laugh.

"Eh, ma cousine, if you could see yourself!" she cried.

"It is true," said Rosalie, with composure, "I grow stouter; but at your age, Thérèse, I was slighter than you. It is the same with us all-at twenty we are thin, at thirty we are plump, and at forty—" She waved a fat hand over her expansive form and shrugged an explanatory shoulder, whilst her small eyes dwelt with a malicious expression on Thérèse's frowning face.

The girl lifted the handsomest shoulders in Paris. "I am not a stick," she observed, with that ready flush of hers; "it is these thin girls, whom one cannot see if one looks at them sideways, who grow so stout later on. I shall stay as I am, or maybe get scraggy-quel horreur!"—and she shuddered a little—"but it will not be yet awhile."

Rosalie nodded.

"You are not thirty yet," she said comfortably, "and you are a fine figure of a woman. 'T is a pity Citizen Dangeau cannot be made to see it!"

Up went Thérèse's head in a trice, and her bold colour mounted.

"Hé!"—she snorted contemptuously—"is he the world? Others are not so blind."

There was a pause. Rosalie knitted, smiling broadly, whilst Thérèse caught a second apple from a piled basket, and began to play with it.

"He is going away," said Rosalie abruptly, and Thérèse dropped the apple, which rolled away into a corner.

"Tctt, tctt," clicked Rosalie, "you have an open hand with other folk's goods, my girl! Yes, certainly Citizen Dangeau is going away, and why not? There is nothing to keep him here that I know of."

"For how long?" asked Thérèse, staring out of the window.

"One month, two, three-how do I know, my cabbage? It is business of the State, and in such matters, you should know more than I."

"When does he go?"

"To-morrow," said Rosalie cheerfully, for to torment Thérèse was a most exhilarating employment, and one that she much enjoyed. It vindicated her own virtue, and at the same time indulged her taste for gossip.

Thérèse sprang up, and paced the small shop with something wild in her gait.

"Why does he go?" she asked excitedly. "He used to smile at me, to look when he passed, and now he goes another way; he turns his head, he elbows me aside. Does he think I am one of those tame milk-and-water misses, who can be taken up one minute and dropped the next? If he thinks that, he is very much mistaken. Who has taken him from me? I insist on knowing; I insist that you tell me!"

"Chut," said Rosalie, with placid pleasure, "he never was yours to take, and that you know as well as I."

"He looked at me," and Thérèse's coarse contralto thrilled tragically over the words.

"Half Paris does that." Rosalie paused and counted her stitches. "One, two, three, four, knit two together. Why not? you are good to look at. No one has denied it that I know of."

"He smiled." Her eyes glared under the close-drawn brows, but Rosalie laughed.

"Not if you looked at him like that, I 'll warrant; but as to smiling-he smiles at me too, dear cousin."

Thérèse flung herself into a chair, with a sharp-caught breath.

"And at whom else? Tell me that, tell me that, for there is some one-some one. He thinks of her, he dreams of her, and pushes past other people as if they were posts. If I knew, if I only knew who it was——"

"Well?" said Rosalie curiously.

"I 'd twist her neck for her, or get Mme. Guillotine to save me the trouble," said Thérèse viciously.

As she spoke, the door swung open, and Mlle. de Rochambeau came in. She had been out to make some trifling purchase, and, nervous of the streets, she had hurried a good deal. Haste and the cold air had brought a bright colour to her cheeks, her eyes shone, and her breath came more quickly than usual.

Thérèse started rudely, and seeing her pass through the shop with the air of one at home, she started up, and with a quick spring placed herself between Mademoiselle and the inner door.

For a moment Aline hesitated, and then, with a murmured "Pardon," advanced a step.

"Who are you?" demanded Thérèse, in her roughest voice.

Rosalie looked up with an expression of annoyance. Really Thérèse and her scenes were past bearing, though they were amusing, for a little.

"I am Marie Roche," said Mademoiselle quietly. "I lodge here, and work for my living. Is there anything else you would like to ask me?"

Thérèse's eyes flashed, and she gave a loud, angry laugh.

"Eh-listen to her," she cried, "only listen. Yes, there is a good deal I should like to ask-amongst other things, where you got that face, and those hands, if your name is Marie Roche. Aristocrat, that is what you are-aristocrat!" and she pushed her flushed face close to Mademoiselle's rapidly paling one.

"Chut, Thérèse!" commanded Rosalie angrily.

"I say she is an aristocrat," shouted Thérèse, swinging round upon her cousin.

"Fiddlesticks," said Rosalie; "the girl's harmless, and her name's her own, right enough."

"With that face, those hands? Am I an imbecile?"

"Do I know, I?" and Rosalie shrugged her mountainous shoulders. "Bah, Thérèse, what a fuss about nothing. Is it the girl's fault if her mother was pretty enough to take the seigneur's fancy?"

The scarlet colour leapt into Mademoiselle's face. The rough tones, the coarse laugh with which Rosalie ended, and which Thérèse echoed, offended her immeasurably, and she was far from feeling grateful for the former's interference. She pushed past her opponent, and ran up the stairs without pausing to take breath.

Meanwhile Thérèse turned violently upon her cousin.

"Aristocrat or not, she has taken Dangeau from me," she screamed, with the sudden passion which makes her type so dangerous. "Why did you not tell me you had a girl in the house?—though what he can see in such a pinched, mincing creature passes me. Why did you not tell me, I say? Why? Why?"

"Eh, ma foi! because you fatigue me, you and your tempers," said Rosalie crossly. "Is this your house, par exemple, that I must ask you before I take any one to live in it? If the man likes you, take him, and welcome. I am not preventing you. And if he does n't like you, what can I do, I? Am I to say to him, 'Pray, Citizen Dangeau, be careful you do not speak to any girl, except my cousin Thérèse?' It is your own fault, not mine. Why did n't you marry like a respectable girl, instead of taking Heaven knows how many lovers? Is it a secret? Bah! all Paris knows it; and do you think Dangeau is ignorant? There was Bonnet, and Hébert, and young Cléry, and who knows how many since. Ciel! you tire me," and Rosalie bent over her knitting, muttering to herself, and picking fiercely at dropped stitches.

Thérèse picked up an apple and swung it from one hand to another, her brows level, the eyes beneath them dangerously veiled. Some day she would give herself the pleasure of paying her cousin Rosalie out for that little speech. Some day, but not to-day, she would tear those fat, creased cheeks with her nails, wrench out a few of the sleek black braids above, sink strangling fingers into the soft, fleshy rolls below. She gritted her teeth, and slipped the apple deftly to and fro. Presently she spoke in a tolerably natural voice:

"It is not every one who is so blind, voyez-vous, ma cousine."

As she spoke, Dangeau came through the shop door. He was in a hurry-these were days of hurry-and he hardly noticed that Rosalie was not alone, until he found Thérèse in his path. She was all bold smiles, and a glitter of black eyes, in a moment.

"The Citizen forgets an old friend."

"But no," he returned, smiling.

"It is so long since we met, that I thought the Citizen might have forgotten me."

"Is it so long?" asked Dangeau innocently; "surely I saw you somewhere lately. Ah, I have it-at the trial?"

"Ah, then you remember," cried Thérèse, clapping her hands.

Dangeau nodded, rather puzzled by her manner, and Rosalie permitted herself an audible chuckle. Thérèse turned on her with a flash, and as she did so Dangeau bowed, murmured an excuse, and passed on. This time Rosalie laughed outright, and the sound was like a spark in a powder-magazine. Red rage, violent, uncontrollable, flared in Thérèse's brain, and, all considerations of prudence forgotten, she launched herself with a tigress's bound straight at her cousin's ponderous form.

She had reckoned without her host.

Inside those fat arms reposed muscles of steel, behind those small pig's eyes lay a very cool, ruthless, and determined brain, and Thérèse felt herself caught, held, propelled across the floor, and launched into the street, all before she could send a second rending shriek after her first scream of fury.

Rosalie closed and latched the door, and sank panting, perspiring, but triumphant, into her seat again.

"Be calm," she observed, between her gasps; "be wise, and go home. For me, I bear no malice, but for you, my poor Thérèse, you will certainly die in an apoplexy some fine day if you excite yourself so much. Ouf-how out of breath I am!"

Thérèse stood rigid, her face convulsed with fury, her heart a black whirlpool of all the passions; but when Rosalie looked up again, after a vigorous bout of fanning, she was gone, and, with a sigh of relief, the widow Leboeuf settled once more to her placid morning's work.

The past fortnight had gone heavily for Mlle. de Rochambeau. Since the days of the votings she had not seen Dangeau, for he had only returned late at night to snatch a few hours' sleep before the earliest daylight called him to his work again. She heard his step upon the stair, and turned from it, with something like a shudder. What times! what times! For the inconceivable was happening-the impossible had come to pass. What, was the King to die, and no one lift a hand to help? In open day, in his own capital? Surely there would be a sign, a wonder, and God would save the King. But now-God had not saved him-he was dead. All the previous day she had knelt, fasting, praying, and weeping, one of many hundreds who did likewise; but the knife had fallen, the blood royal was no longer inviolate-it flowed like common water, and was swallowed by the common earth. A sort of numb terror possessed Aline's very soul, and the little encounter with Thérèse gave it a personal edge.

As she sat, late into the evening, making good her yesterday's stint of embroidery, there came a footstep and a knocking at her door, and she rose to open it, trembling a little, and yet not knowing why she trembled since the step was a familiar one.

Dangeau stood without, his face worn and tired, but an eager light in his eyes.

"Will you spare me a moment?" he asked, motioning to his open door.

"Is it about the copying?" she said, hesitating.

"The copying, and another matter," he replied, and stood aside, holding the door for her to pass. She folded her work neatly, laid it down, and came silently into his room, where she remained standing, and close to the door.

Dangeau crossed to his table, asked her a trifling question or two about the numbering of the thickly written pages before him, and then paused for so long a space that the constraint which lay on Mademoiselle extended itself to him also, and rested heavily upon them both.

"I am going away to-morrow," he said at last.

"Yes, Citizen." It was her first word to him for many days, and he was struck by the altered quality of the soft tones.

They seemed to set him infinitely far away from her and her concerns, and it was surprising how much that hurt him.

Nevertheless he stumbled on:

"I am obliged to go; you believe that, do you not?"

"But, yes, Citizen." More distant still the voice that had rung friendly once, but behind the distance a weariness that spurred him.

"You are very friendless," he said abruptly. "You said that I might be your friend, and the first thing that I do is to desert you. If I had been given a choice-but one has obligations-it is a trust I cannot shirk."

"Monsieur is very good to trouble himself about me," said Mademoiselle softly. "I shall be safe. I am not afraid. See then, Citizen, who would hurt me? I live quietly, I earn my bread, I harm no one. What has any one so insignificant and poor as I to be afraid of? Would any one trouble to harm me?"

"God forbid!" said Dangeau earnestly. "Indeed, I think you are safe, or I would not go. In a month or six weeks, I shall hope to be back again. I do not know why I should be uneasy." He hesitated. "If there were a woman you could turn to, but there-my mother died ten years ago, and I know of no one else. But if a man's help would be of any use to you, you could rely on Edmond Cléry-see, I will give you his direction. He is young, but very much my friend, and you could trust him. Show him this"—he held out a small, folded note—"and I know he will do what he can."

Mademoiselle's colour was a little tremulous. His manner had taken suddenly so intimate, so possessive, a shade. Only half-conscious that she had grown to depend on him for companionship and safety, she was alarmed at discovering that his talk of her being alone, and friendless, could bring a lump into her throat, and set her heart beating.

"Indeed, Monsieur, there is no need," she protested, answering her own misgivings as much as his words. "I shall be safe. There is no one to harm me."

He put the note into her hand, and returned to the table, where he paused, looking strangely at her.

"So young, so friendless," beat his heart, "so alone, so unprotected. If I spoke now, should I lose all? Is she old enough to have learned their accursed lesson of the gulf between man and man-between loving man and the woman beloved? Surely she is too lonely not to yearn towards shelter." He made a half step towards her, and then checked himself, turning his head aside.

"Mademoiselle," he said earnestly, "you are very much alone in the world. Your order is doomed-it passes unregretted, for it was an evil thing. I do not say that every noble was bad, but every noble was nourished in a system that set hatred between class and class, and the outcome of that antagonism has been hundreds of years' oppression, lust, starvation, a peasantry crushed into bestiality by iniquitous taxes, and an aristocracy, relieved of responsibility, grown callous to suffering, sunk in effeteness and vice. There is a future now for the peasant, since the weight is off his back, and his children can walk erect, but what future is there for the aristocrat? I can see none. Those who would survive, must out from their camp, and set themselves to other ways of thought, and other modes of life." He paused, and glanced at her with a dawning hope in his eyes.

Mademoiselle de Rochambeau raised her head a little, proudly.

"Monsieur, I am of this order of which you speak," she said, and her voice was cold and still.

"You were of them, but now, where are they? The links that held you to them have been wrenched away. All is changed and you are free-the daughter of the new day of Liberty."

"Monsieur, one cannot change one's blood, one's race. I am of them."

"But one can change one's heart, one's faith," he cried hotly; and at that Mademoiselle's hand went to her bosom, as if the pressure of it could check the quick fluttering within.

"Not if one is Rochambeau," she said very low.

There was an instant's pause, whilst she drew a long breath, and then words came to her.

"Do you know, Monsieur, that for seven hundred years my people have kept their faith, and served the King and their order? In all those years there have been many men whom you would call bad men—I do not defend them-there have been cruel deeds done, and I shudder at them, but the worst man of them all would have died in torments before he would have accepted life at the price of honour, or come out from his order because it was doomed. That I think is what you ask me to do. I am a Rochambeau, Monsieur."

Her voice was icy with pride, and behind its soft curves, and the delicate colour excitement painted there, her face was inexorably set. The individuality of it became as it were a transparent veil, through which stared the inevitable attributes of the race, the hoarded instinct of centuries.

Dangeau's heart beat heavily. For a moment passion flared hot within him, only to fall again before her defenceless youth. But the breath of it beat upon her soul, and troubled it to the depths. She stood waiting, not knowing how to break the spell that held her motionless. Something warned her that a touch, a movement, might unchain some force unknown, but dreadful. It was as if she watched a rising sea-the long, long heaving stretch, as yet unflecked with foam, where wave after wave towered up as if about to break, yet fell again unbroken. The room was gone in a mist-there was neither past nor future. Only an eternal moment, and that steadily rising sea.

Suddenly broke the seventh wave, the wave of Fate.

In the mist Dangeau made an abrupt movement.

"Aline!" he said, lifting his eyes to her white face. "Aline!"

Mademoiselle de Rochambeau felt a tremor pass over her; she was conscious of a mastering, overwhelming fear. Like something outside herself, it caught her heart, and wrung it.

"No, no," said her trembling lips; "no, no."

With that he was beside her, catching her unresisting hand. Cold as ice it lay in his, and he felt it quiver.

"Oh, mon Dieu, are you afraid of me-of me?" he cried, in a hoarse whisper.

She tried to speak, but could not; something choked the sound, and she only stood there, mechanically focussing all her energies in an effort to stop the shivering, which threatened to become unbearable.

"Aline," he said again, "Aline, look at me."

He bent above her, nearer, till his face was on a level with her own, and his eyes drew hers to meet them. And his were full of all sweet and poignant things-love and home, and trust, and protection-they were warm and kind, and she so cold, and so afraid. It seemed as if her soul must go out to him, or be torn in two. Suddenly her fear of him had changed into fear of her own self. Did a Rochambeau mate thus? She saw the red steel, wet with the King's life, the steel weighted by the word of this man, and his fellows. She saw the blood gush out and flow between them in a river of separation. To pass it she must stain her feet-must stain her soul, with an uncleansable rust. It could not be-Noblesse oblige.

She caught her hand from his and put it quickly over her eyes.

"No, no, no-oh no, Monsieur," she cried, in a trembling whisper.

He recoiled at once, the light in his face dying out.

"It is no, for always?" he asked slowly.

She bent her head.

"For always, and always, and always?" he said again. "All the years, all the ways wanting you-never reaching you? Think again, Aline."

She rested her hand against the door and took a step away. It was more than she could bear, and a blind instinct of escape was upon her, but he was beside her before she could pass out.

"Is it because I am what I am, Jacques Dangeau, and not of your order?" he asked, in a sharp voice.

The change helped her, and she looked up steadily.

"Monsieur, one has obligations-you said it just now."

"Obligations?"

"And loyalties-to one's order, to one's King."

"Louis Capet is dead," he said heavily.

"And you voted for his death," she flashed at him, voice and eye like a rapier thrust.

He raised his head with pride.

"Yes, Mademoiselle, I voted for his death."

"That is a chasm no human power can bridge," she said, in a level voice. "It lies between us-the King's death, the King's blood. You cannot pass to come to me —I may not pass to come to you."

There was an infinite troubled loneliness behind the pride in her eyes, and it smote him through his anger.

"Adieu, Mademoiselle," he said in a low, constrained voice. He neither touched her hand, nor kissed it, but he bowed with as much proud courtesy as if he had been her equal in pride of race. "Adieu, Mademoiselle."

"Adieu, Monsieur."

She passed out, and heard the door close harshly behind her. It shut away-ah, what? The Might-have-been —the Forbidden-Eden perhaps? She could not tell. Bewildered, and exhausted, she fell on her knees in the dark by her narrow bed, and sobbed out all the wild confusion of her heart.

## CHAPTER XIII
## DISTURBING INSINUATIONS

February came in dreary, and bleak, and went out in torrents of rain. For Aline de Rochambeau a time of dull loneliness, and reaction, of hard grinding work, and insufficient food. She had to rise early, and stand in a line with other women, before she could receive the meagre dole of bread, which was all that the Republic One and Indivisible would guarantee its starving citizens. Then home again, faint and weary, to sit long hours, bent to catch the last, ultimate ray of dreary light, working fingers sore, and tired eyes red, over the fine embroidery for which she was so thankful still to find a sale.

All these wasted morning hours had to be made up for in the dusk and dark of the still wintry evenings. With hands stiff and blue, she must thread the fine needle, and hold the delicate fabric, working on, and on, and on. She did not sing at her work now, and the silence lay mournfully upon her heart.

> "No tread on the stair, no passing step across the way.
>
> What slow, long days-what empty, halting evenings."

Rosalie eyed her with a half-contemptuous pity in those days, but times were too hard for the pity to be more than a passing indulgence, and she turned to her own comfortable meals without a pang. Times were hard, and many suffered-what could one do?

"For me, I do not see that things are changed so wonderfully," sighed brown little Madeleine Rousse, Rosalie's neighbour.

Mlle. de Rochambeau and she were standing elbow to elbow, waiting for the baker to open his doors, and begin the daily distribution.

"We were hungry before, and we are hungry now. Bread is as scarce, and the only difference is that there are more mouths to feed."

Her small face was pinched and drawn, and she sighed heavily, thinking of five clamouring children at home.

"Eh, Madeleine," cried Louison Michel, wife of that redoubtable Septembrist, Jean, the butcher. "Eh, be thankful that your last was not twins, as mine was. There was a misfortune, if you like, and I with six already! And what does that great stupid oaf of mine say but, 'Hé, Louison, what a pity it was not three!' 'Pity,' said I, and if I had been up and about, I warrant you I 'd have clouted him well; 'pity, indeed, and why?' Well, and what do you think-you 'd never guess. 'Oh,' says he, with a great sheep's grin on his face, 'we might have called them Liberty, Equality, and Fraternity.' And there he stood as if he had said something clever. My word! If I was angry! 'The charming idea, my friend,' I said. 'I who have to work for them, whilst you make speeches at your section, what of me? Take that, and that,' said I, and I threw what was handy at him-Liberty, Equality, and Fraternity, indeed!"

Madeleine sighed again, but an impudent-faced girl behind Aline whispered in her ear, "Jean Michel has one tyrant from whom the Republic cannot free him!"

Louison's sharp ears caught the words, or a part of them, and she turned with a swing that brought her hand in a resounding slap upon the girl's plump cheek, which promptly flamed with the marks of five bony fingers.

"Eh-Ma'mselle Impudence, so a wife mayn't keep her own husband in order? Perhaps you 'd like to come interfering? Best put your fingers in some one else's pies, and leave mine alone."

The girl sobbed angrily, and Louison emitted a vicious little snort, pushing on a pace as the distribution began, and the queue moved slowly forward.

A month before Mlle. de Rochambeau would have shrunk and caught her breath, but now she only looked, and looked away.

At first these hours in the open street were a torture to the sensitive, gently-bred girl. Every eye that lighted upon her seemed to be stripping off her disguise, and she expected the tongue of every passer-by to proclaim and denounce her.

After the shock of the September massacres, it was impossible for her to realise that the greater part of those she encountered were plain, hungry, fellow-creatures, who cared little about politics, and much about their daily bread, but after a while she found she was one of a crowd—a speck, a dust mote, and that courage of the crowd, that sloughing of the individual, began to reassure her. She lost the sensation of being alone, the centre of observing eyes, and took her place as one of the great city's humble workers, waiting for her share of its fostering; and she began to find interest in the scenes of tragedy and comedy which those hours of waiting brought before her. The long standing was fatiguing, but without the fresh air and enforced companionship of these morning hours, she would have fared worse than she did. Brains of coarser fibre than hers gave way in those days, and the cells of the Salpêtrière could tell a sadder tale than even the prisons of Paris.

One day of drenching rain, as she stood shivering, her thin dress soaked, her hair wet and dripping, a heavy-looking, harpy-eyed creature stared long and curiously at her. The wind had caught Aline's hair, and she put up her slim hand smoothing it again. As she did so, the woman's eyes took a dull glare and she muttered:

"Aristocrat."

Terror teaches the least experienced to dissemble, and Mademoiselle had learned its lesson by now. Her heart bounded, but she managed a tolerably natural shrug of the shoulders, and answered in accents modelled on those of Rosalie:

"My good mother, I? The idea! I—but that amuses me," and she laughed; but the woman gave a sort of growl, shook her dripping head, and repeated hoarsely:

"Aristocrat, aristocrat," in a sort of chant, whilst the rain, following the furrows of the grimy, wrinkled cheeks, gave her an expression at once bleared and malignant.

"It is Mère Rabotin," said the woman at Mademoiselle's side. "She is a little mad. They shot her son last tenth of August, and since then she sees aristocrats and tyrants everywhere."

The old woman threw her a wicked glance.

"In you, I see nothing but a fat cow, whose husband beats her," she remarked venomously, and a laugh ran down the line, for the woman crimsoned, and held her tongue, being a rather stupid, garrulous creature destined to be put out of action at once by a sharp retort.

"But this"—pursued Mère Rabotin, fingering Mademoiselle's shrinking hand—"this is an aristocrat's hand. Fine and white, white and fine, and why, because it has never worked, never worked as honest hands do, and every night it has bathed in blood-ah, that is a famous whiteness, mes amis!"

Mademoiselle drew her hand away with a shudder, but recovering her self-possession, she held it up, still with that careful laugh.

"Why, Mère Rabotin," she cried, "see how it is pricked and worn. I work it to the bone, I can tell you, and get little enough even then."

"Aristocrat, aristocrat," repeated the hag, watching her all the time. "Fine white hands, and a black heart-blue blood, and a light name-no mercy or pity. Aristocrat!"

All the way it kept up, that half-mad drone. The women in front and behind shrugged impatient shoulders, staring a little, but not caring greatly.

Mademoiselle kept up her pose, played the poor seamstress, and played it well, with a sigh here, and a laugh there, and all the time in her ears the one refrain:

"Aristocrat, aristocrat!"

She came home panting, and lay on her bed listening for she knew not what, for quite an hour, before she could force her trembling fingers to their work again. Next day she stayed indoors, and starved, but the following morning hunger drove her out, and she went shaking to her place in the line of waiting citizens. The woman was not there, and she never saw her again. After awhile she ceased to feel alarmed. The feeling of being watched and stared at, wore off, and life settled down into a dull monotony of work, and waiting.

It was in these days that Rosalie made up her quarrel with Thérèse Marcel; and upon the reconciliation began a gradual alteration in the elder woman's habits. There were long absences from the shop, after which she would return flushed, and queer-eyed, to sit muttering over her knitting, and these absences became more and more frequent.

Mlle. de Rochambeau, returning with her daily dole of bread, met her one day about to sally forth.

Thérèse was with her, and saluted Mademoiselle with a contemptuous laugh.

"Are you coming with us, Mlle. White-face?" she called.

Aline shook her head with a civil smile.

"There are two women in to-day's batch—I have been telling Rosalie. She did n't mean to come, but that fetched her. She has n't seen a woman kiss Madame Guillotine yet, but the men find her very attractive, eh, Rosalie?"

Rosalie's broad face took on a dull flush, and her eyes became suddenly restless.

"Eh, Marie," she said, in a queer, thick voice. "Come along then-you sit and work all day, and in the end you will be ill. Every one must take a holiday some time, and it is exciting, this spectacle; I can tell you it is exciting. The first time I was like you, I said no, I can't, I can't; but see you, I could think of nothing else, and at last, Thérèse persuaded me. Then I sat, and shivered-yes, like a jelly-and saw ten knives, and ten heads, and half a dozen Citizen Sansons-but after that it went better, and better. Come, then, and see for yourself, Marie," and she put a heavy hand on the girl's shrinking shoulder.

White-faced, Aline recoiled.

"Oh, Citoyenne," she breathed, and shrank away.

Thérèse laughed loud.

"Oh, Citoyenne, Citoyenne," she mimicked. "Tender flower, pretty lamb, but the lamb's throat comes to the butcher's knife all the same," and her eyes were wicked behind their mockery.

"Have you heard any news of that fine lover of yours, since he rode away," she went on.

"I have no lover," answered Mademoiselle, the blood flaming into her thin cheeks.

"You are too modest, perhaps?" sneered Thérèse.

"I have not thought of such things."

"Such things-just hear her! What? you have not thought of Citizen Dangeau, handsome Citizen Dangeau, and he living in the same house, and closeted with you evening after evening, as our good Rosalie tells me? Does one do such things without thinking?"

Mademoiselle's flush had faded almost as it had risen, leaving her white and proud.

"Citoyenne, you are in error," she said quietly. "I am a poor girl with my bread to earn. The Citizen employed me to copy a book he had written. He paid well, and I was glad of the money."

"I dare say you were"—and Thérèse's coarse laugh rang out—"so he paid you well, and for copying, for copying-that was it, my pious Ste. Nitouche. Copying? Haha—I never heard it called that before!"

Mademoiselle turned haughtily away, only a deepening of her pallor showed that the insult had reached her, but Rosalie caught her cousin's arm with an impatient—"Tiens, Thérèse, we shall be late, we shall not get good places," and they went out, Thérèse still laughing noisily.

"Vile, vile, shameless woman," thought Aline, as she stood drawing long breaths before her open window.

The strong March wind blew in and seemed to fan her hot anger and shame into a blaze. "How dare she-how dare she!"

Woman-like, she laid the insult to Dangeau's account. It was another stone added to the wall which she set herself night and day to build between them. It rose apace, and this was the coping-stone. Now, surely, she was safe. Behind such a wall, so strong, so high, how could he reach her? And yet she was afraid, for something moved in the citadel, behind the bastion of defence-something that fluttered at his name, that ached in loneliness, and cried in the night—a traitor, but her very heart, inalienable flesh and blood of her. She covered her face, and wrestled, as many a time before, and after awhile she told herself—"It is conquered," and with a smile of self-scorn sat down again to her task too long delayed.

Outside, Paris went its way. Thousands were born, and died, and married, and betrothed, in spite of scarce bread, war on the frontiers, and prisons full to bursting.

The Mountain and the Gironde were only held from one another's throats by Danton's strong hand; but though their bickerings fill the historian's page, under the surface agitation of politics, the vast majority of the population went its own way, a way that varies very little under successive forms of government, since the real life of a people consists chiefly of those things about which historians do not write.

Tragedy had come down and stalked the streets of Paris, but there were thousands of eyes which did not see her. Those who did, talked loudly of it, and so it comes that we see the times through their eyes, and not through those of the silent and the blind.

In the south Dangeau made speech after speech. He wrote to Danton from Lyons:

"This place smoulders. Words are apt to prove oil on the embers. There are 900 prisoners, and constant talk of massacre. Chalier is a firebrand, the Mayor one of those moderate persons who provoke immoderate irritation in others. We are doing our best."

Danton frowned heavily over the curt sentences, drawing those black brows of his into a wrathful line. He turned to other letters from other Deputies, all telling the same weary tale of jangle and discord, strife and clamour of parties unappeased and unappeasable. Soon he would be at death-grips with the Gironde-force opposed to philosophy, action to eloquence, and philosophic eloquence would go to the guillotine shouting the Marseillaise.

His feet were set upon a bloody path, and one from which there was no returning. All Fate's force was in him and behind him, and he drove before it to his doom.

## CHAPTER XIV
## A DANGEROUS ACQUAINTANCE

It was in April that Fate began to concern herself with Mlle. de Rochambeau once more. It was a day of spring's first exquisite sweetness-air like new-born life sparkling with wayward smiles, as the hurrying sunbeams glanced between one white cloud and the next; scent of all budding blossoms, and that good smell of young leafage and the wet, fecund earth.

On such a day, any heart, not crushed quite dumb and dry, must needs sparkle a little too, tremble a little with the renewal of youth, and sing a little because earth's myriad voices call for an echo.

Aline put on her worn print gown with a smile, and twisted her hair with a little more care than usual. After all, she was young, time passed, and life held sunshine, and the spring. She sang a little country air as she passed to and fro in the narrow room.

Outside it was delicious. Even in the dull street where she took her place in the queue the air smelled of young flowering things, and touched her cheeks with a soft, kissing breath, that brought the tender colour into them. Under the bright cerulean sky her eyes took the shade of dark forget-me-nots.

It was thus that Hébert saw her for the first time-one of Fate's tricks-for had he passed on a dull, rainy, day, he would have seen nothing but a pale, weary girl, and would have gone his way unnoticing, and unremembered, but to-day that spring bloom in the girl's heart seemed to have overflowed, and to sweeten all the air around her. The sparkle of the deep, sweet, Irish eyes met his cold, roving glance, and of a sudden changed it to an ugly, intent glitter. He passed slowly by, then paused, turned, and passed again.

When he went by for the second time, Aline became aware of his presence. Before, he had been one of the crowd, and she an unnoticed unit in it, but now, all at once, his glance seemed to isolate her from the women about her, and to set her in an insulting proximity to himself.

She looked down, coldly, and pressed slowly forward. After what seemed like a very long time, she raised her eyes for a moment, only to encounter the same fixed, insolent stare, the same pale smile of thick, unlovely lips.

With an inward shudder she turned her head, feeling thankful that the queue was moving at a good rate, and that the time of waiting was nearly over. It was not until she had secured her portion that she ventured to look round again, and, to her infinite relief, the coast was clear. With a sigh of thankfulness she turned homewards, plunging her thoughts for cleansing into the fresh loveliness of the day.

Suddenly in her ear a smooth, hateful voice:

"Why do you hurry so, Citoyenne?"

She did not look up, but quickened her pace.

"But, Citoyenne, a word—a look?"

Hébert's smile broadened, and he slipped a dexterous arm about the slim waist, and bent to catch the blue glance of her eyes. Experience taught him that she would look up at that. She did, with a flame of contempt that he thought very becoming. Blue eyes were apt to prove insipid when raised, but the critic in him acknowledged these as free from fault.

"Citizen!" she exclaimed, freeing herself with an unexpectedly strong movement. "How dare you! Oh, help me, Louison, help me!"

In the moment that he caught her again she had seen the small, wiry figure of Jean Michel's wife turn the corner.

"Louison, Louison Michel!" she called desperately.

Next moment Hébert was aware of some one, under-sized and shrivelled looking, who whirled tempestuously upon him, with an amazing flow of words.

"Oh, my Ste. Géneviève! And is a young girl not to walk unmolested to her home. Bandit! assassin! tyrant! pig! devil! species of animal, go then-but on the instant-and take that, and that, to remember an honest woman by,"—the first "that" being a piece of his hair torn forcibly out, and thrown into his perspiring face, and the second, a most superlative slap on the opposite cheek.

He was left gasping for breath and choking with fury, whilst the whirlwind departed with as much suddenness as it had come, covering the girl's retreat with shaken fist, and shrill vituperation.

After a moment he sent a volley of curses in her wake. "Fury! Magaera!" he muttered. "So that is Jean Michel's wife! If she were mine, I 'd wring her neck."

He thought of his meek wife at home, and laughed unpleasantly.

"For the rest, she has done the girl no good by interfering." This was unfortunately the case. Hébert's eye had been pleased, his fancy taken; but a few passing words, a struggle may be, ending in a kiss, had been all that was in his thought. Now the bully in him lifted its head, urging his jaded appetite, and he walked slowly after the women until he saw Mademoiselle leave her companion, and enter Rosalie's shop. An ugly gleam came into his eyes-so this was where she lived! He knew Rosalie Leboeuf by sight and name; knew, too, of her cousinship with his former mistress, Thérèse Marcel, and he congratulated himself venomously as he strolled forward and read the list of occupants which, as the law demanded, was fixed on the front of the house at a distance of not more than five feet from the ground:

"Rosalie Leboeuf, widow, vegetable seller, aged forty-six. Marie Roche, single, seamstress, aged nineteen. Jacques Dangeau, single, avocat, aged twenty-eight,"—and after the last name an additional notice—"absent on business of the Convention."

Hébert struck his coarse hands together with an oath. Dangeau-Dangeau, now it came back to him. Dangeau was infatuated with some girl, Thérèse had said so. He laughed softly, for Thérèse had gone into one of her passions, and that always amused him. If it were this girl? If it were-if it only were, why, what a pleasure to cut Dangeau out, and to let him find on his return that the bird had flown to a nest of Hébert's feathering.

There might be even more in it than that. The girl was no common seamstress; pooh-he was not stupid-he could see as far into a brick wall as others. Even at the first glance he had seen that she was different, and when her eyes blazed, and she drew herself from his grasp, why, the aristocrat stood confessed. Anger is the greatest revealer of all.

Madame la Roturière may dress her smiling face in the mode of Mme. l'Aristocrate; may tune her company voice to the same rhythm; but put her in a passion, and see how the mud comes boiling up from the depths, and how the voice so smooth and suave just now, rings out in its native bourgeois tones.

Hébert knew the difference as well as another, and his thoughts were busy. Aristocrat disguised, spelled aristocrat conspiring, and a conspiring aristocrat under the same roof as Jacques Dangeau, what did that spell?

He rubbed his pale fat hands, where the reddish hair showed sickly, and strolled away thinking wicked thoughts. Plots were the obsession of the day, and, to speak the truth, there were enough and to spare, but patriot eyes were apt to see double, and treble, when drunk with enthusiasm, and to detect a conspirator when there was only a victim. Plots which had never existed gave hundreds to the knife, and the populace shouted themselves into a wilder delirium.

Did the price of bread go up? Machinations of Pitt in England. Did two men quarrel, and blows pass? "Monarchist!" shouted the defeated one, and presently denounced the other.

Had a woman an inconvenient husband, why, a cry of "Austrian Spy!" and she might be comfortably rid of him for ever.

Evil times for a beautiful, friendless girl upon whom gross Hébert cast a wishful eye!

He walked into the shop next day, and accosted Rosalie with Republican sternness of manner.

"Good-day, Citoyenne Leboeuf."

Rosalie was fluttered. Her nerves were no longer quite so reliable as they had been. Madame Guillotine's receptions were disturbing them, and in the night she would dream horribly, and wake panting, with her hands at her fat throat.

"Citizen Hébert," she murmured.

He bent a cold eye upon her, noting a beaded brow.

"You have a girl lodging here-Marie Roche?"

"Assuredly, Citizen."

"I must speak to her alone."

Rosalie rallied a little, for Hébert had a certain reputation, and Louison had not held her tongue.

"I will call her down," she said, heaving her bulky form from its place.

"No, I will go up," said Hébert, still with magisterial dignity.

"Pardon me, Citizen Deputy, she shall come down."

"It is an affair of State. I must speak privately with her," he blustered.

Rosalie's eyes twinkled; her nerves were steadying. They had begun to require constant stimulation, and this answered as well as anything else.

"Bah," she said. "I shall not listen to your State secrets. Am I an eavesdropper, or inquisitive? Ask any one. That is not my character. You may take her to the farther end of the shop, and speak as low as you please, but, she is a young girl, this is a respectable house, and see her alone in her room you shall not, not whilst she is under my care."

"That privilege being reserved for my colleague, Citizen Dangeau," sneered Hébert.

"Tchtt," said Rosalie, humping a billowy shoulder—"the girl is virtuous and hard-working, too virtuous, I dare say, to please some people. Yes, that I can very well believe," and her gaze became unpleasantly pointed—"Well, I will call her down."

She moved to the inner door as she spoke, and called up the stair: "Marie! Marie Roche! Descend then; you are wanted."

Hébert stood aside with an ill grace, but he was quite well aware that to insist might, after yesterday's scene, bring the whole quarter about his ears, and effectually spoil the ingenious plans he was revolving in his mind.

He moved impatiently as Mademoiselle delayed, and, at the sound of her footstep, started eagerly to meet her.

She came in quite unsuspiciously, looking at Rosalie, and at first seeing no one else. When Hébert's movements brought him before her, she turned deadly white, and a faintness swept over her. She caught the door, fighting it back, till it showed only in that change of colour, and a rather fixed look in the dark blue eyes.

Hébert checked a smile, and entrenched himself behind his office.

"You are Marie Roche, seamstress?"

"Certainly, Citizen."

"Father's and mother's names?"

"By what right do you question me?" the voice was icy with offence, and Rosalie stirred uneasily.

"It is the Citizen Deputy Hébert; answer him," she growled-and Hébert commended her with a look.

Really this was amusing-the girl had spirit as well as beauty. Decidedly she was worth pursuing.

"Father's and mother's names?" he repeated.

Mademoiselle bit her lip, and gave the names she had already given when she took out her certificate of Citizenship.

They were those of her foster-parents, and had she not had that rehearsal, she might have faltered, and hesitated. As it was, her answer came clear and prompt.

Hébert scowled.

"You are not telling the truth," he observed in offensive tones, expecting an outburst, but Mlle. de Rochambeau merely looked past him with an air of weary indifference.

"I am not satisfied," he burst out. "If you had been frank and open, you would have found me a good friend, but I do not like lies, and you are telling them. Now I am not a safe person to tell lies to, not at all-remember that. My friendship is worth having, and you may choose between it and my enmity, my virtuous Citoyenne."

Mademoiselle raised her delicate eyebrows very slightly.

"The Citizen does me altogether too much honour," she observed, her voice in direct contradiction to her words.

"Tiens," he said, losing self-control, "you are a proud minx, and pride goes before a fall. Are you not afraid? Come," dropping his voice, as he caught Rosalie's ironical eye —"Come, be a sensible girl, and you shall not find me hard to deal with. I am a slave to beauty—a smile, a pleasant look or two, and I am your friend. Come then, Citoyenne Marie."

Mademoiselle remained silent. She looked past Hébert, at the street. Rosalie got up exasperated, and pulled her aside.

"Little fool," she whispered, "can't you make yourself agreeable, like any other girl. Smile, and keep him off. No one wants you to do more. The man 's dangerous, I tell you so, I—— You 'll ruin us all with your airs and graces, as if he were the mud under your feet."

Aline turned from her in a sudden despair.

"I am a poor, honest girl, Citizen," she said imploringly. "I have no time for friendship. I have to work very hard, I harm nobody."

"But a friend," suggested Hébert, coming a little closer, "a friend would feel it a privilege to do away with that necessity for hard work."

Mademoiselle's pallor flamed. She turned sharply away, feeling as if she had been struck.

"Good-day, Citizen," she said proudly; "you have made a mistake," and she passed from Rosalie's detaining hand.

Hébert sent an oath after her. He was most unmagisterially angry. "Fool," he said, under his breath —"Damned fool."

Rosalie caught him up.

"He is a fool who wastes his time trying to pick the apple at the top of the tree, when there are plenty to his hand," she observed pointedly.

He swore at her then, and went out without replying.

From that day a period of terror and humiliation beyond words set in for Mlle. de Rochambeau. Hebert's shadow lay across her path, and she feared him, with a sickening, daily augmenting fear, that woke her gasping in the night, and lay on her like a black nightmare by day.

Sometimes she did not see him for days, sometimes every day brought him along the waiting queue, until he reached her side, and stood there whispering hatefully, amusing himself by alternately calling the indignant colour to her cheeks, and replacing it by a yet more indignant pallor.

The strain told on her visibly, the thin cheeks were thinner, the dark eyes looked darker, and showed unnaturally large and bright, whilst the violet stains beneath them came to stay.

There was no one to whom she could appeal. Rosalie was furious with her and her fine-lady ways. Louison, and the other neighbours, who could have interfered to protect her from open insult, saw no reason to meddle so long as the girl's admirer confined himself to words, and after the first day Hébert had not laid hands on her again.

The torture of the man's companionship, the insult of his look, were beyond their comprehension.

Meanwhile, Hébert's passing fancy for her beauty had changed into a dull, malignant resolve to bend, or break her, and through her to injure Dangeau, if it could possibly be contrived.

Women had their price, he reflected. Hers might not be money, but it would perhaps be peace of mind, relief from persecution, or even life-bare life.

After the first few days he gave up the idea of bringing any set accusation against Dangeau. The man was away, his room locked, and Rosalie would certainly not give up the key unless a domiciliary visit were paid —a thing involving a little too much publicity for Hébert's taste. Besides, he knew very well that rummage as he might, he would find no evidence of conspiracy. Dangeau was an honest man, as he was very well aware, and he hated him a good deal the more for the inconvenient fact. No, it would not do to denounce Dangeau without some very plain evidence to go upon. The accuser of Danton's friend might find himself in an uncommonly tight place if his accusations could not be proved. It would not do-it was not good enough, Hébert decided regretfully; but the girl remained, and that way amusement beckoned as well as revenge. If she remained obstinate, and if Dangeau were really infatuated, and returned to find her in prison, he might easily be tempted to commit some imprudence, out of which capital might be made. That was a safer game, and might prove just as well worth playing in the end. Meanwhile, was the girl Marie Roche, and nothing more? Did that arresting look of nobility go for nothing, or was she playing a part? If Rosalie knew, Thérèse might help. Now how fortunate that he had always kept on good terms with Thérèse.

He took her a pair of gold ear-rings that evening, and whilst she set them dangling in her ears, he slipped an arm about her, and kissed her smooth red cheek.

"Morbleu!" he swore, "you 're a handsome creature, Thérèse; there 's no one to touch you."

"What do you want?" asked Thérèse, with a shrewd glance into his would-be amorous eyes.

"What, ma belle? What should I want? A kiss, if you 'll give it me. Ah! the old days were the best."

Thus Hébert, disclaiming an ulterior motive.

Thérèse frowned, and twitched away from him.

"Ma foi, Hébert, am I a fool?" she returned, with a shrug. "You 've forgotten a lot about those same old days if you think that. I 'll help you if I can, but don't try and throw sand in my eyes, or you 'll get some of it back, in a way that will annoy you"; and her black eyes flared at him in the fashion he always admired. He thought her at her best like that, and said so now.

"Chut!" she said impatiently. "What is it that you want?"

Hébert considered.

"You see your cousin sometimes, the widow Leboeuf, who has the shop in the rue des Lanternes?"

"I see her often enough, twice-three times a week at present."

"Could you get something out of her?"

"Not if she knew I wanted to. Close as a miser's fist, that's what Rosalie is, if she thinks she can spite you; but just now we are very good friends-and, well, I dare say it might be done. Depends what it is you want to know."

Hébert looked at her keenly.

"Perhaps you can tell me," he said, watching her face. "That girl who lodges there, who is she? What is her name-her real name?"

In a flash Thérèse was crimson to the hair, and he had her by the wrist, swinging her round to face him.

"Oho!" she cried, laughing till the new ear-rings tinkled, "so that's it-that's the game? Well, if you can give that stuck-up aristocrat the setting-down I 've promised her ever since I first saw her, I 'm with you."

Hébert pounced on one word, like a cat.

"Aristocrat? Ah! I thought so," he said, his breathing quickening a little. "Who is she, then, ma mie?"

Thérèse regarded him with a little scorn. She did not care who got Hébert, since she had done with him herself, but what, *par exemple*, did he see in a pale stick like that-and after having admired her, Thérèse? Certainly men were past understanding.

She lolled easily on the arm of the chair.

"I 've not an idea, but I dare say I could find out-that is, if Rosalie knows."

"Well, when you do, there 'll be a chain to match the ear-rings," said Hébert, his arm round her waist again.

All the same, April had passed into May before Thérèse won her chain.

It was in the time between that Hébert haunted Mlle. de Rochambeau's footsteps, and employed what he considered his most seductive arts, producing only a sensation of shuddering defilement from which neither prayer nor effort could free her thoughts. One day, goaded past endurance, she left Dangeau's folded note at the door of Cléry's lodging. When it had left her hand, she would have given the world to have it back. How could she speak to a man of this shameful pursuit of Hébert? How, having put Dangeau out of her life, could she use his help, and appeal to his friend? And yet, how endure the daily shame, the nightly agony of remembering those smooth, poisonous whispers, that pale, dreadful smile? She cried her eyes red and swollen, and Edmond Cléry, looking up from a bantering exchange of compliments with Rosalie, wondered as she came in, first if this could be she, and then at his friend's taste. He permitted himself a complacent memory of Thérèse's glowing cheeks and supple curves, and commended his own choice. Rosalie's needles clicked amiably. She liked young men, and this was a personable one. What a goose this girl was, to be sure!—like a frightened rabbit with Hébert, and now with this amiable young man, shrinking, white-faced! Bah! she had no patience with her.

Edmond bowed smilingly.

"My homage, Citoyenne," he said.

Aline forced a "Bonjour, Citizen," and then fell silent again. Ah! why had she left the note-why, why, why?

Cléry began to pity her plight, for there was something chivalrous in him which rose at the sight of her obvious unhappiness, and he gave the impulse rein.

"Will you not tell me how I can serve you?" he said in his gentlest voice. "It will be both a pleasure and an honour."

Aline raised her tired eyes to his, and read kindness in the open glance.

"You are very good," she said slowly, and looked past him with a hesitating air.

Rosalie was busy serving at the moment, and a shrill argument over the price of cabbage was in process. She stepped closer, and spoke very low.

"Citizen Dangeau said I might trust you, Citizen."

"Indeed you may; I am his friend and yours."

Even then the colour rose a little at this linking of their names. The impulse towards confidence increased.

"I am in trouble, Citizen, or I should not have asked your help. There is a man who follows, insults me, threatens even, and I am without a protector."

"Not if you will confide that honour to me," said Cléry quickly.

She smiled faintly.

"You are very good."

"But who is it? Tell me his name, and I will see that you are not molested in future."

"It is the Citizen Deputy Hébert," faltered Aline, all her terror returning as she pronounced the hateful name.

Clary's brows drew close, and a long whistle escaped his lips.

"Oho, Hébert," he said—"Hébert; but there, Citoyenne, do not be alarmed, I beg of you. Leave it to me"; after which he made his adieux without conspicuous haste, leaving Rosalie much annoyed at having missed most of the conversation.

Two days later, Hébert came foaming in on Thérèse. When he could speak, he swore at her.

"See here, Thérèse, if you 've a hand in setting Cléry at me, let me warn you. I 'll take foul play from no woman alive, without giving as good as I get, and if there 's any of your damned jealousy at work, you she-devil, I 'll choke you as soon as look at you, and with a great deal more pleasure!"

Thérèse stepped up to him and fixed her great black eyes on his pale, twitching ones.

"Don't be so silly, Hébert," she said steadily, though her colour rose. "What is it all about? What has young Cléry done to you? It 's rather late in the day for you to start quarrelling."

"Did you flatter yourself it was about you?" said Hébert brutally. "Not much, my girl; I've fresher fish to fry. But he came up to me an hour ago, and informed me he had been looking for me everywhere to tell me my pursuit of that pattern of virtue, our good Dangeau's mistress, must cease, or I 'd have him to reckon with, and what I want to know is, have you a hand in this, or not?"

Thérèse was heavily flushed, and her eyes curiously veiled.

"What! Cléry too?" she said in a deep whisper. "Dangeau, and you, and Cléry. Eh! I wish her joy of my cast-off clouts. But she shall pay-Holy Virgin, she shall pay!"

Hébert caught her by the shoulder and shook it.

"What are you muttering? I ask you a plain question, and you don't answer it. What about Cléry-did you set him on?"

She threw back her head at that, and gave a long, wild laugh.

"Imbécile!" she screamed. "I? Do you hate him? Well, think how I must love him when he too goes after this girl-goes to her from me, from swearing I am his goddess, his inspiration? Ah!"—she caught at her throat—"but at least I can give you his head. The fool-the fool to betray a woman who holds his life in her hands! Here is what the imbecile wrote me only a week ago. Read, and say if it 's not enough to give him to the embraces of the Guillotine?"

The paper she thrust at Hébert came from her bosom, and when he had read it his dull eyes glittered.

"'The King's death a crime-perhaps time not ripe for a Republic.' Thérèse, you 're worth your weight in gold. I don't think Edmond Cléry will write you any more love-letters."

Thérèse drew gloomily away.

"And the girl?" she asked, with a shiver.

"That, my dear, was to depend on what you could find out about her," Hébert reminded her.

His own fury had subsided, and he threw himself into a chair. Thérèse made an abrupt movement.

"There is nothing more to find out. I have it all."

"You 've been long enough getting it," said Hébert, sitting up.

"Well, I have it now, and I told you all along that Rosalie was more obstinate than a mule. She has been in one of her silent moods; she would go to all the executions, and then, instead of being a pleasant companion, there she would sit quite mum, or muttering to herself. Yesterday, however, she seemed excited. There was a large batch told off, three women amongst them, and one of them shrieked when Sanson took her kerchief off. That seemed to wake Rosalie up. She got quite red, and began to talk as if she had a fever."

"It is one you have caught from her, then," said Hébert impatiently. "The news, my girl, the news! What do I care for your cousin and her tantrums?"

Thérèse looked dangerous.

"Am I your cat's-paw, Hébert?" she said. "Pah! do your own dirty work-you 'll get no more from me."

Hébert cursed his impatience-fool that he was not to remember Thérèse's temper!

He forced an ugly smile.

"Oh, well, as you please," he said. "Let the girl go. There are other fish in the sea. Best let Cléry go too, and then they can make a match of it, unless she should prefer Dangeau."

His intent eyes saw the girl's face change at that. "A thousand devils!" she burst out. "Why do you plague me, Hébert? Be civil and play fair, and you 'll get what you want."

"Come, come, Thérèse," he said soothingly. "We both want the same thing-to teach a stuck-up baggage of an aristocrat a lesson. Let's be friends again, and give me the news. Is it any good?"

"Good enough," said Thérèse, with a sulky look—"good enough to take her out of my way, if I say the word. Why, she 's a cousin of the ci-devant Montargis, who got so prettily served on the third of September."

"What?" exclaimed Hébert.

"Ah! you never guessed that, and you 'd never have got it out of Rosalie; for she 's as close as the devil, and I believe has a sneaking fondness for the girl."

"The Montargis!" repeated Hébert, rubbing his hands, slowly. This was better than he expected. No wonder the girl went in terror! He had heard the Paris mob howl for the blood of the Austrian spy, and he knew that a word now would seal her fate.

"Her name?" he demanded.

"Rochambeau-Aline de Rochambeau. She only clipped the tail off, you see, and with a taste that way, she should have no objection to a head clipping-eh, my friend?" said Thérèse, with a short laugh.

Hébert went off with his plans made ready to his hand. It pleased him to be able to ruin Cléry, since Cléry had crossed his path; and besides, it would terrify the girl, and annoy Dangeau, who had a liking for the boy. It was inconceivable that he should have been so imprudent as to trust a woman like Thérèse, but since he had been such a fool he must just pay for it with his head.

The truth was that Cléry during his service at the Temple had been strangely impressed, like many another, by the bearing of the unfortunate Royal Family, and had conceived a young, whole-hearted adoration for the Queen, which did not, unfortunately for himself, interfere with his wholly mundane passion for Thérèse Marcel. In a moment of extraordinary imprudence he made the latter his confidante, never doubting that her love for himself would make her a perfectly safe one. Poor lad! he was to pay a heavy price for his trust.

On the day following Hébert's interview with Thérèse he was arrested, and after a short preliminary examination, which revealed to him her treachery and his dangerous position, he was lodged in the Abbaye.

His arrest made some little stir in his own small world. Thérèse herself brought the news of it to the rue des Lanternes. Her eyes were very bright and hard as she glanced round the shop, and she laughed louder than usual, as she threw out broad hints as to her own share in the matter, for she liked Rosalie to know her power.

"I think you are a devil, Thérèse," said the fat woman gloomily.

"So others have said," returned Thérèse, with a wicked smile.

Mlle. de Rochambeau took the blow in deadly silence. Hope was dead in her heart, and she prayed earnestly that she alone might suffer, and not have the wretchedness of feeling she had drawn another into the net which was closing around her.

Hébert dallied yet a day or two, and then struck home. Aline was hurrying homewards, her ears strained for the step she had grown to expect, when all in a minute he was there by her side.

She turned on him with a sudden resolve.

"Citizen," she said earnestly, "why do you persecute me? What have I done to you-to any one? Surely by now you realise that this pursuit is useless?"

"The day that I realise that will be a bad day for you," said Hébert, with malignant emphasis.

The threat brought her head up, with one of those movements of mingled pride and grace which made him hate and covet her.

"I have done no wrong-what harm can you do me?" she said steadily.

"I have interest with the Revolutionary Tribunal-you may have heard of the arrest of our young friend Cléry? Ah! I thought so,"—as her colour faded under his cruel gaze.

She shrank a little, but forced her voice to composure. "And does the Revolutionary Tribunal concern itself with the affairs of a poor girl who only asks to be allowed to earn her living honestly?"

Hébert smiled—a smile so wicked that she realised an impending blow, and on the instant it fell.

"It would concern itself with the affairs of Mlle. de Rochambeau, cousin of the ci-devant Marquise de Montargis, who, if my memory serves me right, was arrested on a charge of treasonable correspondence with Austria, and who met a well-deserved fate at the hands of an indignant people." He leaned closer as he spoke, and marked the instant stiffening of each muscle in the white face.

For a moment her heart had stopped. Then it raced on again at a deadly speed. She turned her head away that he might not see the terror in her eyes, and a keen wind met her full, clearing the faintness from her brain.

She walked on as steadily as she might, but the smooth voice was still at her ear.

"You are in danger. My friendship alone can save you. What do you hope for? The return of your lover Dangeau? I don't think I should count on that if I were you, my angel. Once upon a time there was a young man of the name of Cléry-Edmond Cléry to be quite correct-yes, I see you know the story. No, I don't think your Dangeau will be of any assistance to you when I denounce you, and denounce you I most certainly shall, unless you ask me not to, prettily, with your arms round my neck, shall we say-eh, Citoyenne Marie?"

As he spoke there was a rumble of wheels, and a rough cart came round the corner towards them. He touched her arm, and she looked up mechanically, to see that it held from eight to ten persons, all pinioned, and through her own dull misery she was aware of pity stirring at her heart, for these were prisoners on their way to the Place de la Revolution.

One was an old man, very white and thin, his scanty hair straggling above a stained, uncared-for coat, his misty blue eyes looking out at the world with the unseeing stare of the blind or dying. Beside him leaned a youth of about fifteen, whose laboured breath spoke of the effort by which he preserved an appearance of calm. Beyond them was a woman, very handsome and upright. Her hair, just cut, floated in short, ragged wisps about her pale, set face. Her lips moved constantly, her eyes looked down. Hébert laughed and pointed as the cart went by.

"That is where you 'll be if I give the word," he whispered. "Choose, then—a place there, or a place here,"—and he made as if to encircle her with his arm—"choose, ma mie."

Aline closed her eyes. All her young life ran hotly in her veins, but the force of its recoil from the man beside her was stronger than the force of its recoil from death.

"The Citizen insults me when he assumes there is a choice," she said, with cold lips.

"The prison is so attractive then? The embraces of the Guillotine so preferable to mine-hein?"

"The Citizen has expressed my views."

Hébert cursed and flung away, but as she moved on he was by her side again.

"After all," he said, "you may change your mind again. Until to-morrow, I can save you."

"Citizen, I shall never change my mind. There is no choice; it is simply that."

An inexorable decision looked from her face, and carried conviction even to him.

"One cannot save imbeciles," he muttered as he left her.

Mademoiselle walked home with an odd sense of relief. Now that the first shock was over, and the danger so long anticipated was actually upon her, she was calm. At least Hébert would be gone from her life. Death was clean and final; there would be no dishonour, no soiling of her ears by that sensual voice, nor of her eyes by those evil glances.

She knelt and prayed for a while, and sat down to her work with hands that moved as skilfully as before.

That night she slept more peacefully than she had done for weeks. In her dreams she walked along a green and leafy lane, birds sang, and the sky burned blue in the rising sun. She walked, and breathed blissful air, and was happy.

Out of such dreams one awakes with a sense of the unreality of everyday life. Some of the glamour clings about us, and we see a mirage of happiness instead of the sands of the Desert of Desolation. Is it only mirage, or some sense sealed, except at rarest intervals?—a sense before whose awakened exercise the veil wears thin, and from behind we catch the voices of the withdrawn, we feel the presence of peace, and garner a little of the light of Eternity to shed a glow on Time.

Aline woke happily to a soft May dawn. Her dream lay warm against her heart and cherished it.

In the evening she was arrested and taken to the prison of the Abbaye.

## CHAPTER XV

In after days Aline de Rochambeau looked back upon her time in prison as a not unpeaceful interlude between two periods of stress and terror. After loneliness unspeakable, broken only by companionship with the coarse, the dull, the cruel, she found herself in the politest society of France, and in daily, hourly contact with all that was graceful, exquisite, and refined in her own sex-gallant, witty, and courteous in the other.

When she joined the other prisoners on the morning after her arrest, the scene surprised her by its resemblance to that ill-fated reception which had witnessed at once her debut and her farewell to society. The dresses were a good deal shabbier, the ladies' coiffures not quite so well arranged, but there was the same gay, light talk, the same bowing and curtsying, the same air of high-bred indifference to all that did not concern the polite arts.

All at once she became very acutely conscious of her bourgeoise dress and unpowdered hair. She felt the roughness of her pricked fingers, and experienced that painful sense of inferiority which sometimes afflicts young girls who are unaccustomed to the world. The sensation passed in a flash, but the memory of it stung her not a little, and she crossed the room with her head held high.

The old Comtesse de Matigny eyed her through a tortoise-shell lorgnette which bore a Queen's cipher in brilliants, and had been a gift from Marie Antoinette.

"Who is that?" she demanded, in her deep, imperious tones.

"Some little bourgeoise, accused of Heaven knows what," shrugged M. de Lancy.

The old lady allowed hazel eyes which were still piercing to rest for a moment longer on Aline. Then they flashed mockingly on M. le Marquis.

"My friend, you are not as intelligent as usual. Did you see the girl's colour change when she came in? When a bourgeoise is embarrassed, she hangs her head and walks awkwardly. If she had an apron on, she would bite the corner. This girl looked round, and flushed-it showed the fine grain of her skin-then up went her head, and she walked like a princess. Besides, I know the face."

A slight, fair woman, with tired eyes which looked as if the colour had been washed from them by much weeping, leaned forward. She was Mme. de Créspigny, and her husband had been guillotined a fortnight before.

"I have seen her too, Madame," she said in an uninterested sort of way, "but I cannot recall where it was."

Mme. la Comtesse rapped her knee impatiently with a much-beringed hand.

"It is some one she reminds me of," she said at last —"some one long ago, when I was younger. I never forget a face, I always prided myself on that. It was at Court-long ago-those were gay days, my friends. Ah! I have it. La belle Irlandaise, Mlle. Desmond, who married-Now, who did Mlle. Desmond marry? It is I who am stupid to-day. It is the cold, I think."

"Was it Henri de Rochambeau?" said De Lancy.

She nodded vivaciously.

"It was-yes, that was it, and I danced at their wedding, and dreamed on a piece of the wedding-cake. I shall not say of whom I dreamed, but it was not of feu M. le Comte, for I had never seen him then. Yes, yes, Henri de Rochambeau, and la belle Irlandaise. They were a very personable couple, and why they saw fit to go and exist in the country, Heaven alone knows-and perhaps his late Majesty, who did Mme. de Rochambeau the honour of a very particular admiration."

"And she objected, chère Comtesse?" De Lancy's tone was one of pained incredulity.

Chère Comtesse shrugged her shoulders delicately.

"What would you?" she observed. "She was as beautiful as a picture, and as virtuous as if Our Lady had sat for it. It even fatigued one a little, her virtue."

Her own had bored no one-she had not permitted it any such social solecism.

"I remember," said De Lancy; "they went down to Rochambeau, and expired there of dulness and each other's unrelieved society."

Mme. de Créspigny had been looking attentively at Aline. "Now I know who the girl is," she said. "It is the girl who disappeared, who was supposed to have been massacred. I saw her at Laure de Montargis' reception the day of the arrests, and I remember her now. Ah! that poor Laure — —"

She shuddered faintly. De Lancy became interested.

"But she accompanied her cousin to La Force and perished there."

"She must have escaped. I am sure it is she. She had that way of holding her head-like a stag-proud and timid."

"It was one of her mother's attractions," said the Comtesse. "Mlle. Desmond was, however, a great deal more beautiful. Her daughter, if this girl is her daughter, has only that trick, and the eyes-yes, she has the lovely eyes," as Aline turned her head and looked in their direction. "M. de Lancy, do me the favour of conducting her here, and presenting her to me."

The little old dandy clicked away on his high heels, and in a moment Mademoiselle was aware of a truly courtly bow, whilst a thin, shaky voice said gallantly:

"We rejoice to welcome Mademoiselle to our society."

She curtsied —a graceful action-and Madame de Matigny watching, nodded twice complacently. "Bourgeoise indeed!" she murmured, and pressed her lips together.

"You are too good, Monsieur," said Mademoiselle.

Only four words, but the voice-the composure.

"Madame la Comtesse is right, as always; she is certainly one of us," thought De Lancy.

"Madame la Comtesse de Matigny begs the honour of your acquaintance," he pursued; "she had the pleasure of knowing your parents."

"Monsieur?"

"Do I not address Mlle. de Rochambeau?"

Surprise, and a sense of terror at hearing her name, so long concealed, brought the colour to her face.

"That is my name," she murmured.

"She is always right-she is wonderful," repeated the Marquis to himself, as he piloted his charge across the room.

He made the presentation in form.

"Madame la Comtesse, permit that I present to you Mademoiselle de Rochambeau."

Aline bent to the white, wrinkled hand, but was raised and embraced.

"You resemble your mother too closely to be mistaken by any one who had the happiness of her acquaintance," said a gracious voice, and thereon ensued a whole series of introductions. "M. le Marquis de Lancy, who also knew your parents."

"Mme. de Créspigny, my granddaughter Mlle. Marguerite de Matigny."

A delightful sensation of having come home to a place of safety and shelter came over Aline as she smiled and curtsied, forgetting her poor dress and hard-worked fingers in the pleasure of being restored to the society of her equals.

"Sit down here, beside me," commanded Mme. de Matigny. She had been a great beauty as well as a great lady in her day, and she spoke with an imperious air that fitted either part. "Marguerite, give Mademoiselle your stool."

Aline protested civilly, but Mlle. Marguerite, a little dark-eyed creature, with a baby mouth, dropped a soft whisper in her ear as she rose:

"Grandmamma is always obeyed-but on the instant," and Aline sat down submissively.

"And now, racontez donc, mon enfant, racontez," said the old lady, "where have you been all these months, and how did you escape?"

Embarrassing questions these, but to hesitate was out of the question. That would at once point to necessity for concealment. She began, therefore, and told her story quite simply, and truly, only omitting mention of her work with Dangeau.

Mme. de Matigny tapped her knee.

"But, enfin, I do not understand. What is all this? Why did you not appeal to your cousin's friends, to Mme. de St. Aignan, or Mme. de Rabutin, for example?"

"I knew only the names, Madame," said Aline, lifting her truthful eyes. "And at first I thought all had perished. I dared not ask, and there was no one to tell me."

"Poor child," the hand stopped tapping, and patted her shoulder kindly. "And this Rosalie you speak of, what was she?"

"Sometimes she was kind. I do not think she meant me any harm, and at least she saved my life once."

When she came to the story of her arrest, she faltered a little. The old eyes were so keen.

"What do they accuse you of? You have done nothing?"

"Oh, chère Comtesse, is it then necessary that one should have done anything?" broke in Adèle de Créspigny, a little bitter colour in that faded voice of hers. "Have you done anything, or I, or little Marguerite here?"

Madame fanned herself, her manner slightly distant. She was not accustomed to be interrupted.

"They say I wrote letters to emigrés, to my son Charles, in fact. Marguerite also. It is a crime, it appears, to indulge in family feeling. But, you, you, Mademoiselle, did not even do that."

"No," said Aline, blushing. "It was... it was that the Citizen Hébert found out my real name — I do not know how-and denounced me."

Her downcast looks filled in enough of the story for those penetrating eyes.

"Canaille!" said the old lady under her breath, and then aloud:

"You are better here, with us. It is more convenable," and once more she patted the shoulder, and that odd sense of being at home brought sudden tears to Aline's eyes.

A few days later a piece of news reached her. She and Marguerite de Matigny sat embroidering the same long strip of silk. They had become close friends in the enforced daily intimacy of prison life, and the luxury of possessing a friend with whom she could revive the old, innocent, free talk of convent times was delightful in the extreme to the lonely girl, forced too soon into a self-reliance beyond her years.

Mlle. Marguerite looked up from the brilliant half-set stitch, and glanced warily round.

"Tiens, Aline," she said, putting her small head on one side, "I heard something this morning, something that concerns you."

Aline grew paler. That all news was bad news was one axiom which the events of the last few months had graved deeply on her heart. Marguerite saw the tremor that passed over her, and made haste to be reassuring.

"No, no, ma belle, it is nothing bad. Stupid that I am! It is that these wretches outside have been fighting amongst themselves, and your M. Hébert has been sent to prison. I hope he likes it," and she took a little vicious stitch which knotted her yellow thread, and confused the symmetrical centre of a most gorgeous flower. "There, I have tangled my thread again, and grandmamma will scold me. I shall say it was the fault of your M. Hébert."

"Please don't call him *my* M. Hébert," said Aline proudly. Marguerite laid down her needle.

"Aline, why did he denounce you?"

"Ah, Marguerite, don't talk of him. You don't know what a wretch —" and she broke off shuddering.

"No, but I should like to know. I can see you could tell tales-oh, but most exciting ones! Why did he do it? He must have had some reason; or did he just see you, and hate you, like love at first sight, only the other way round?"

Mlle. de Rochambeau assumed an air of prudence and reproof.

"Fi donc, Mlle. de Matigny, what would your grandmother say to such talk?"

Marguerite made a little, wicked *moue*.

"She would say-it was not convenable," she mimicked, and laid a coaxing hand on her friend's knee. "But tell me then, Aline, tell me what I want to know-tell me all about it, all there is to tell. I shall tease and tease until you do," she declared.

"Oh, Marguerite, it is too dreadful to laugh about."

"If one never laughed, because of dreadful things, why, then, we should all forget how to do it nowadays," pouted Marguerite. "But, see then, already I cry —" and she lifted an infinitesimal scrap of cambric to her dancing eyes.

Mlle. de Rochambeau laughed, but she shook her head, and Marguerite gave her a little pinch.

"Wicked one," she said; "but I shall find out all the same. All my life I have found out what I wanted to, yes, even secrets of grandmamma's," and she nodded mischievously; but Aline turned back to the original subject of the conversation.

"Are you sure he is in prison?" she asked anxiously.

"Yes, yes, quite sure. The Abbé Loisel said so when he came this morning. I heard him say to grand-mamma, 'The wolves begin to tear each other. It is a just retribution.' And then he said, 'Hébert, who edits that disgrace to the civilised world, the *Père Duchesne*, is in prison.' Oh, Aline, would n't it have been fun if he had been sent here?"

Aline's hand went to her heart.

"Oh, mon Dieu!" she said quickly.

Marguerite made round baby eyes of wonder.

"You *are* frightened of him," she cried. "He must have done, or said, something very bad to make you look like that. If you would tell me what it was, I should not have to go on worrying you about him, but as it is, I shall have to make you simply hate me. I know I shall," she concluded mournfully.

"Oh, child, child, you don't understand," cried Mlle. de Rochambeau, feeling suddenly that her two years of greater age were twenty of bitter experience. Her eyes filled as she bent her burning face over the embroidery, whilst two large tears fell from them and lay on the petals of her golden flower like points of glittering dew.

Marguerite coloured, and looked first down at the floor and then up at her friend's flushed face.

"Oh, Aline!" she breathed, "was it really that? Oh, the wretch! And when you wouldn't look at him he revenged himself? Ouf, it makes me creep. No wonder you feel badly about it. The villain!" she stamped a childish foot, and knotted her thread again.

"Oh dear, it will have to be cut," she declared, "and what grandmamma will say, the saints alone know."

Aline took the work out of the too vehement hands, and spent five minutes in bringing order out of a sad confusion. "Now it is better," she said, handing it back again; "you are too impatient, little one."

"Ah, 'twas not my fault, but that villain's. How could I be calm when I thought of him? But you are an angel of patience, ma mie. How can you be so quiet and still when things go wrong?"

"Ah," said Mademoiselle with half a sigh, "for eight months I earned my living by my work, you know, and if I had lost patience when my thread knotted I should have had nothing to eat next day, so you see I was obliged to learn."

Mme. de Matigny came by as she ended, and both girls rose and curtsied. She glanced at the work, nodded her head, and passed on, on M. de Lancy's arm. For the moment chattering Marguerite became decorous Mlle. de Matigny —a *jeune fille, bien élevée.* In her grandmother's presence only the demurest of glances shot from the soft brown eyes, only the most dutiful and conventional remarks dropped from the pretty, prudish lips-but with Aline, what a difference! Now, the stately passage over, she leaned close again above the neglected needle.

"Dis donc, Aline! You were betrothed, were you not, to that poor M. de Sélincourt? Were you inconsolable when he was killed? Did you like him?"

The ambiguous "aimer" fell from her lips with a teasing inflection.

"He is dead," reproved Mlle. de Rochambeau.

"Tiens, I did not say he was alive! But did you; tell me? What did it feel like to be betrothed?"

"Ask Mme. de Matigny what is the correct feeling for a young girl to have for her betrothed," said Aline, a hint of bitterness behind her smile.

"De grêce!" and Marguerite's plump hands went up in horror. "See then, Aline, I think it would be nice to love-really to love-do you not think so?"

Mlle. de Rochambeau shook her head with decision. Something in the light words had stabbed her, and she felt an inward pain.

"I do not see why one should not love one's husband," pursued Marguerite reflectively. "If one has to live with some one always, it would be far more agreeable to love him. But it appears that that is a very bourgeoise idea, and that it is more convenable to love some one else."

"Oh, Marguerite!"

"Yes, yes, I tell you it is so! Here one hears everything. They cannot send one out of the room when the conversation begins to grow interesting. There is Mme. de Créspigny-she is in our room-she weeps much in the night, but it is not because of her husband, oh no; it is for M. le Chevalier de St. Armand, who was guillotined on the same day."

"Hush, Marguerite, you should not say such things."

"But if they are true, and this is really true, for when they brought her the news she cried out 'Etienne' very loud, and fainted. M. de Créspigny was our cousin, so I know all his names. There is no Etienne amongst them," and she nodded wisely.

"Oh, Marguerite!"

"So you see it is true. I find that odious, for my part, though, to be sure, what could she do if she loved him? One cannot make oneself love or not love. It comes or it goes, and you can only weep like Mme. de Créspigny, unless, to be sure, one could make shift to laugh, as I think I shall try to do when my time comes."

Mlle. de Rochambeau looked up with a sudden flame in her eyes.

"It is not true that one cannot help loving," she said quickly. "One can-one can. If it is a wrong love it can be crushed, and one forgets. Oh, you do not know what you are talking about, Marguerite."

Marguerite embraced her.

"And do you?" she whispered slyly.

Girls' talk-strange talk for a prison, and one where Death stood by the entrance, beckoning one and another.

One day it was M. de Lancy who was called away in the midst of a compliment to his "Chère Comtesse," called to appear at Fouquier Tinville's bar, and later, at that of another and more merciful Judge.

The next, Mme. de Créspigny's tired eyes rested for the last time upon prison walls, and she went out smiling wistful good-byes, to follow husband and lover to a world where there is neither marrying nor giving in marriage.

As each departed, the groups would close their ranks, and after a moment's pause would talk the faster and more lightly, until once more the summons came, and again one would be taken and one left.

This was one side of prison society. On the other a group of devout persons kept up the forms of convent life, just as the coterie of Mme. de Matigny did those of the salon. The Abbé de Nérac, the Abbé Constantin, and half a dozen nuns were the nucleus of this second group, but not all were ecclesiastics or religious. M. de Maurepas, the young soldier, with the ugly rugged face and good brown eyes, was of their number, and devout ladies not a few, who spent their time between encouraging one another in the holy life, and hours of silent prayer for those in the peril of trial and the agony of death.

Their conversations may still be read, and breathe a piety as exquisite as it is natural and touching. To both these groups came daily the Abbé Loisel, bringing to the one news of the outside world, and to the other the consolations of religion. Mass was said furtively, the Host elevated, the faithful communicated, and Loisel would pass out again to his life of hourly peril, moving from hiding-place to hiding-place, and from plot to plot, risking his safety by day to comfort the prisoners, or to bless the condemned on their way to the scaffold, and by night to give encouragement to some little band of aristocrats who thought they could fight the Revolution.

Singular mixture of conspirator and saint, his courage was undoubted. The recorded heroisms of the times are many, those unrecorded more, and his strange adventures have never found an historian.

Outside the Gironde rocked, tottered, and fell. Imprisoned Hébert was loose again. Danton struck for the Mountain, and struck right home. First arrest, then prison, and lastly death came upon the men who had dreamed of ruling France. The strong man armed had kept the house, until there came one stronger than he.

So passed the Girondins, first of the Revolution's children to fall beneath the Juggernaut car they had reared and set in motion.

## CHAPTER XVI
## AN UNWELCOME VISITOR

Mlle. de Rochambeau shared a small, unwholesome cell with three other women. One of them, Mme. de Coigny, a young widow, had lately given birth to a child, a poor, fretful little creature whose wailings added to the general discomfort.

Mme. Renard, the linen draper's wife, tossed her head, and complained volubly to whoever would listen, that she got no sleep at nights, since the brat came. She had been a great man's mistress, and was under arrest because he had emigrated. Terrified to death, she bewailed her lot continually, was sometimes fawning, sometimes insolent to her aristocratic companions, and always very disdainful of the fourth inmate, a stout Breton peasant, with a wooden manner which concealed an enormous respect for the company in which she found herself. She told her rosary incessantly, when not occupied with the baby, who was less ill at ease in her accustomed arms than with its frail, young mother.

One night Mademoiselle awoke with a start. She thought she was being called, and listened intently. A little light came through the grated window-moonlight, but sallow, and impure, as if the rays were infected by the heaviness of the atmosphere. It served, however, to show the heavy immobility of Marie Kérac's form as she lay, emitting unmistakable snores, the baby caught in her left arm and sleeping too. A dingy beam fell right across Mme. Renard's face. It had been pretty enough, in a round dimpled way, but now it looked heavy and leaden, showing lines of fretful fear, even in sleep.

Out of the darkness in the corner there came a long-drawn sigh, and then a very low voice just breathed the words, "Mademoiselle de Rochambeau, are you awake?" Aline sat up.

"Is it you, Madame de Coigny?" she asked, a little startled, for both sigh and voice had a vague unearthliness that seemed to make the night darker. The Bretonne's honest breathing was a reassuring sound.

"Yes!" said the low voice.

"Are you ill-can I do anything for you?"

There was a rustling movement and a dim shape emerged from the shadow.

"If I might lie down beside you for a while. The little one went so peacefully to sleep with that good soul, that I had not the heart to take her back, and it is lonely-mon Dieu, it is lonely!"

Aline made room on the straw pallet, and put an arm round the cold, shrinking figure.

"Why, you are chilled," she said gently, "and the night is quite warm."

"To-morrow I shall be colder," said Mme. de Coigny in a strange whisper.

"My dear, what do you mean?"

Something like a shiver made the straw rustle.

"I am not afraid. It is only that I cannot get warm"; then turning her face to Aline she whispered, "they will come for me to-morrow."

"No, no; why should you think so? How can you know?"

"Ah, I know—I know quite well-and I am glad, really. I should have been glad to die before the little one came, for then she would have been safe too. Now she has this business of life before her, and, see you, I find life too sad, at all events for us women."

"Life is not always sad," said Aline soothingly.

"Mine has been sad," said Mme. de Coigny. "May I talk to you a little? We are of the same age, and to-night—to-night I feel so strange, as if I were quite alone in some great empty place."

"Yes, talk to me, and I will put my arms round you. There! Now you will be warmer."

Another shiver shook the bed, and then the low voice began again.

"I wanted to be a nun, you know. When I was a child they called me the little nun, and always I said I would be one. Then when I was eighteen, my elder sister died, and I was an heiress, and they married me to M. de Coigny."

"Did you not want to marry him?"

"Nobody thought of asking me, and, mon Dieu, how I cried, and wept, and tortured myself. I thought I was a martyr, no less, and prayed that I might die. It was terrible! By the time the wedding-day came, M. de Coigny must have wondered at his bride, for my face was swollen with weeping, and my eyes red and sore," and she gave a little ghost of a laugh.

"Was he kind to you?"

"Yes, he was kind"—there was a queer inflection in the low tone—"and almost at once he was called away for six months, and I went back to my prayers, and tried to fancy myself a nun again. Then he came back, and all at once, I don't know how, something seemed to break in my heart, and I loved him. Mon Dieu, how I loved him! And he loved me-that was what was so wonderful."

"Then you were happy?"

"For a month-one little month-only one little month—" she broke off on a sob, and clung to Aline in the dark. "They arrested us, took us to prison, and when I would have gone to the scaffold with him, they tore me away, yes, though I went on my knees and prayed to them. 'The Republic does not kill her unborn citizens,' they said; and they sent me here to wait."

"You will live for the poor little baby," whispered Aline, her eyes full of tears, but Mme. de Coigny shook her head.

"No," she said quietly; "it is over now. To-morrow they will take me away."

She lay a little longer, but did not talk much, and after a while she slipped away to her own mattress, and Aline, listening, could hear that she slept.

In the morning she made no reference to what had passed, but when Aline left the cell to go to Mme. de Matigny's room she thought as she passed out that she heard a whispered "Adieu," though on looking round she saw that Mme. de Coigny's face was bent over the child, whom she was rocking on her knee.

She went on her way, walking fast, and lifting her skirts carefully, for the passages of the Abbaye were places of indescribable noisomeness. About half-way down, the open door of an empty cell let a little light in upon the filth and confusion, and showed the bestial, empurpled face of a drunken turnkey, who lay all along a bench, sleeping off the previous night's excesses. As Aline hastened, she saw a man come down the corridor, holding feebly to the wall. Opposite the empty cell he paused, catching at the jamb with shaking fingers, and lifting a face which Mademoiselle de Rochambeau recognised with a little cry of shocked surprise.

"M. Cléry!" she exclaimed.

Edmond Cléry could hardly stand, but he forced a pitiful parody of his old, gay laugh and bow.

"Myself," he said, "or at least as much of me as the ague has left."

Just inside the cell was a rough stool, and Aline drew it quickly forward. He sank down gratefully, leaning against the door-post, and closing his eyes for a moment.

"Oh," said Mademoiselle, "how ill you look; you are not fit to walk alone."

He gave her a whimsical glance.

"So it appears," he murmured, "since De Maurepas, you, and my own legs are all of the same story. Well, he will be after me in a few moments, that good Maurepas, and then I shall get to my room again."

"I think I know M. de Maurepas a little," said Aline; "he is very religious."

Cléry gave a faint laugh.

"Yes, we are strange room-mates, he and I. He prays all the time and I not at all, since I never could imagine that le bon Dieu could possibly be interested in my banal conversation; but he is a good comrade, that Maurepas, in spite of his prayers."

"But, Monsieur, how come you to be so ill? If you knew how I have reproached myself, and now to see you like this-oh, you cannot tell how I feel."

Cléry found the pity in her eyes very agreeable.

"And why reproach yourself, Citoyenne; it is not your fault that my cell is damp."

"No, no, but your arrest; to think that I should have brought that upon you. Had I known, I would have done anything rather than ask your help."

"Ah, then you would have deprived me of a pleasure. Indeed, Citoyenne, my arrest need not trouble you; it was due, not to your affairs, but my own."

"Ah, M. Cléry, is that true?" and her voice spoke her relief.

"I should be able to think better of myself if it were not," said Cléry a little bitterly. "I was a fool, and I am being punished for my folly. Dangeau warned me too. When you see him again, Citoyenne, you may tell him that he was right about Thérèse."

"Thérèse-Thérèse Marcel?" asked Aline, shrinking a little.

"Ah-you know her! Well, I trusted her, and she betrayed me, and here I am. Dangeau always said that she was dangerous-the devil's imitation of a woman, he called her once, and you can tell him that he was quite right."

Aline averted her eyes, and her colour rose a shade. For a moment her heart felt warm. Then she looked back at Cléry, and fell quickly upon her knees beside him, for he was gasping for breath, and falling sideways from the stool. She managed to support him for the moment, but her heart beat violently, and at the sound of footsteps she called out. To her relief, M. de Maurepas came up quickly. If he felt any surprise at finding her in such a situation, he was too well-bred to show it.

"Do not be alarmed," he said hastily. "He has been very ill, but this is only a swoon; he should not have walked." Then, "Mademoiselle, move your arm, and let me put mine around him, so-now I can manage."

He lifted Cléry as he spoke, and carried him the length of the corridor.

"Now, if Mademoiselle will have the goodness to push the door a little wider," and he passed in and laid Cléry gently down.

Mademoiselle hesitated by the door for a minute.

"He looks so ill, will he die?" she said.

"Not of this," returned M. de Maurepas; then, after a moment's pause, and with a grave smile, "Nor at all till it is God's will, Mademoiselle."

Mlle. de Rochambeau spent the morning with Marguerite. On her return to her own cell she found an empty place. Mme. de Coigny was gone, and the little infant wailed on the peasant woman's lap.

Cléry was better next day. On the third Aline met M. de Maurepas in the corridor. He was accompanied by a rough-looking turnkey, and she was about to pass without speaking, but their eyes met, and on the impulse she stopped and asked:

"How is M. Cléry to-day?"

The young soldier looked at her steadily.

"He has-he has moved on, Mademoiselle," he returned, something of distress in his tone.

The turnkey burst into a loud, brutal laugh.

"Eh, that was the citizen with the ague? At the last he shook and shook so much that he shook his head off-yes-right out of the little window, where his friend is now going to look for it," and he clapped De Maurepas on the shoulder with a dingy, jocular hand.

Aline drew a sharp breath.

"Oh, no," she said involuntarily, but De Maurepas bent his head in grave assent.

"Is this so pleasant a camp that you grudge me my marching orders?" he asked; and as they passed he looked back a moment and said, "Adieu, Mademoiselle."

She gave him back the word very low, and he smiled again, a smile that irradiated his rough features and steady brown eyes. "Indeed, I think I go to 'Him,'" he said, and was gone.

Aline steadied herself against the wall, and closed her eyes for a moment. She had conceived a sincere liking for the young soldier; Cléry had done her a service, and now both were gone, and she still left. And yet she knew that Hébert was loose again. When she had first heard of his release she spent days of shuddering apprehension, but as the time went on she began to entertain a trembling hope that she was forgotten, as happened to more than one prisoner in those days.

Hébert was loose again, but, for a time at least, with hands too full of public matters, and brain too occupied with the struggle for existence, to concern himself with matters of private pleasure or revenge.

It was the middle of June before he thought seriously of Mlle. de Rochambeau.

"Dangeau is returning," said Danton one morning, and Hébert's dormant spite woke again into full activity.

At the Abbaye, the hot afternoon waned; a drowsy stillness fell upon its inmates. Mme. de Matigny dozed a little. She had grown older in the past few weeks, but her glance was still piercing, and she woke at intervals with a start, and let it rest sharply upon her little circle, as if forbidding them to be aware of Juno nodding.

Marguerite and Aline sat together: Aline half asleep with her head in her friend's lap, for Mme. de Coigny's baby had died at dawn, and she had been up all night tending it, and now fatigue had its way with her.

Suddenly a turnkey stumbled in. He had been drinking, and stood blinking a moment as, coming from the dark corridor, he met the level sunlight full. Then he called Mlle. de Rochambeau's name, and as she awoke with a sense of startled amazement Marguerite flung soft arms about her.

"Ah, ma mie, ma belle, ma bien aimée!" she cried, sobbing.

"Chut!" said the man, with a leer. "She 'd rather hear that from some one else, I take it, my little Citoyenne. If I 'm not mistaken there 's some one ready enough. There 's no need to cry this time, since it is only to see a visitor that I want the Citoyenne. There 's a Citizen Deputy below with an order to see her, so less noise, please, and march."

The blood ran back to Aline's cheek. Only two days back the Abbé had mentioned Dangeau's name, and had said he was returning. If it should be he? The thought flashed, and was checked even as it flashed, but she followed the man with a step that was buoyant in spite of her fatigue. Then in the gaoler's room-Hébert!

Just a moment's pause, and she came forward with a composure that hid God knows what of shrinking, maidenly disgust.

Hébert was not attractive to look at. His garments were dusty and wine-stained, his creased, yellow linen revealing a frowsy and unshaven chin, where the reddish hair showed unpleasantly upon the fat, unwholesome flesh. He laughed, disclosing broken teeth.

"It was not I whom you expected, hein Citoyenne," he said, with diabolical intuition. "He gets tired easily, you see, our good Jacques Dangeau, and lips that have been kissed too often don't tempt him any more."

His leer pointed the insult, and an intolerable burning invaded every limb, but she steadied herself against the wall, and leaned there, her head still up, facing him.

"Did you think I had forgotten you too?" he pursued, smiling odiously. "Ah! I see you did me that injustice, but you do not know me, ma belle. Mine is such a faithful heart. It never forgets, never; and it always gets what it wants in the end. I have been in prison too, as you may have heard-yes, you did? And grieved for me, pretty one, that I am sure of. A few rascals crossed my path and annoyed me for the moment. Where are they now? Trembling under arrest. Had they not detained me, I should have flown to you long ago; but I trust that now you acquit me of the discourtesy of keeping a lady waiting. I am really the soul of politeness."

There was a pause. Mademoiselle held to the wall, and kept her eyes away from his face.

"Your affair comes on to-morrow," he said, with a brisk change of tone.

For the moment she really felt a sense of thankfulness. So she was delivered from the unbearable affront of this man's presence what did death matter?

Hébert guessed her thoughts.

"Rather death than me, hein?" he said, leaning closer. "Is that what you are thinking, Ma'mselle White-face?"

Her eyes spoke for her.

"I can save you yet," he cried, angered by her silence. "A word from me and your patriotism is above reproach. Come, you 've made a good fight, and I won't say that has n't made me like you all the better. I always admire spirit; but now it's time the play was over. Down with the curtain, and let's kiss and make friends behind it."

Mademoiselle stood silent, a helpless thing at bay.

"You won't, eh?" and his tone changed suddenly. "Very well, my pretty piece of innocence; it's Fouquier Tinville to-morrow, and then the guillotine-but"—his voice sank savagely—"my turn first."

She quivered in a sick horror. "What did he mean; what could he do? Oh, Mary Virgin!"

His face came very close with its pale, hideous smile.

"Come to me willingly, and I 'll save your life and set you free when I 've had enough of you. Remain the obstinate pig you are, and you shall come all the same, but the guillotine shall have you next day."

Her white lips moved.

"You cannot—" she breathed almost inaudibly. Her senses were clouding and reeling, but she clutched desperately at that one thought. Some things were impossible. This was one of them. Death-yes, and oh, quickly, quickly; no more of this torture. But this new, monstrous threat-no, no, dear God! no, such a thing could not, could not happen!

The room was all mist, swirling, rolling mist out of which looked Hébert's eyes. Through it sounded his voice, his laugh.

"Cannot, cannot-fine words, my pretty, fine words. When one has friends, good friends, one can do a good deal more than you think, and instead of finding yourself in the Conciergerie between sentence and execution, I can arrange quite nicely that you should be in these loving arms of mine. Aha, my dear! What do you say now? Will you hear reason, or no?"

The mist covered everything now, and the wall she leaned against seemed to rock and give. She spread out her hands, and with a gasp fell waveringly, first to her knees, and then sideways upon the stones in a dead faint.

## CHAPTER XVII
## DISTRESSING NEWS

Dangeau entered Paris next morning. His mission had dragged itself out to an interminable length. Even now he returned alone, his colleague, Bonnet, having been ordered to remain at Lyons for the present, whilst Dangeau made report at headquarters. The cities of the South smouldered ominously, and were ready at a breath to break into roaring flame. Even as Dangeau rode the first tongues of fire ran up, and a general conflagration threatened. Of this he rode to give earnest warning, and his face was troubled and anxious, though the outdoor life had given it a brown vigour which had been lacking before.

He put up his horse at an inn and walked to his old quarters with a warm glow rising in his breast; a glow before which all misgivings and preoccupations grew faint.

He had not been able to forget the pale, proud aristocrat, who had claimed his love so much against his will and hers; but in his days of absence he had set her image as far apart as might be, involving himself in the press of public business, to the exclusion of his thoughts of her. But now-now that he was about to see her again, the curtain at the back of his mind lifted, and showed her standing-an image in a shrine-unapproachably radiant, unforgettably enchanting, unalterably dear, and all the love in him fell on its knees and adored with hidden face.

He passed up the Rue des Lanternes and beheld its familiar features transfigured. Here she had walked all the months of his absence, and here perhaps she had thought of him; there in the little room had mingled his name with her sweet prayers. He remembered hotly the night he had asked her if she prayed for him, and her low, exquisitely tremulous, "Yes, Citizen."

He drew a long, deep breath and entered the small shop.

It was dark coming in from the glare, but he made out Rosalie in her accustomed seat, only it seemed to him that she was huddled forward in an unusual manner.

"Why, Citoyenne!" he cried cheerfully, "I am back, you see."

Rosalie raised her head and stared at him, and she seemed to be coming back with difficulty from a great distance. As his eyes grew used to the change from the outer day he looked curiously at her face. There was something strange, it seemed to him, about the sunken eyes; they had lost the old shrewd look, and were dull and wavering. For a moment it occurred to him that she had been drinking; then the heavy glance changed, brightening into recognition.

"You, Citizen?" she said, with a sort of dull surprise.

"Myself, and very glad to be back."

"You are well, Citizen?"

"And you, I fear, suffering?"

Rosalie pulled herself together.

"No, no," she protested, "I am well too, quite well. It is only that the days are dull when there is no spectacle, and I sit there and think, and count the heads, and wonder if it hurt them much; and then it makes my own head ache, and I become stupid."

Dangeau shuddered lightly. A gruesome welcome this.

"I would not go and see such things," he said.

"Sometimes I wish—" began Rosalie, and then paused; a red patch came on either sallow cheek. "It is too ennuyant when there is nothing to excite one, voyez-vous? Yesterday there were five, and one of them struggled. Ah, that gave me a palpitation! They say it was n't an aristocrat. *They* all die alike, with a little stretched smile and steady eyes-no crying out—I find that tiresome at the last."

"Why, Rosalie," said Dangeau, "you should stay at home as you used to. Since when have you become a gadabout? You will finish by having bad dreams and losing your appetite."

Rosalie looked up with a sort of horrid animation.

"Ah, j'y suis déjà," she said quickly. "Already I see them in the night. A week ago I wake, cold, wet-and there stands the Citizen Cléry with his head under his arm like any St. Denis. Could I eat next day?—Ma foi, no! And why should he come to me, that Cléry? Was it I who had a hand in his death? These revenants have not common-sense. It is my cousin Thérèse whose nights should be disturbed, not mine."

Dangeau looked at her steadily.

"Come, come, Rosalie," he said, "enough of this-Edmond Cléry's head is safe enough."

"Yes, yes," nodded Rosalie, "safe enough in the great trench. Safe enough till Judgment day, and then it is Thérèse who must answer, and not I. It was none of my doing."

"But, Rosalie-mon Dieu! what are you saying-Edmond——?"

"Why, did you not know?"

"Woman!—what?"

"Ask Thérèse," said Rosalie with a sullen look, and fell to plaiting the border of her coarse apron.

"Rosalie!"

His voice startled her, and her mood shifted.

"Yes, to be sure, he was a friend of yours, and it is bad news. Ah, he 's dead, there 's no doubt of that. I saw it with my own eyes. He had been ill, and could hardly mount the steps; but in the end he smiled and waved his hand, and went off as bravely as the best of them. It is a pity, but he offended Thérèse, and she is a devil. I told her so; I said to her, 'Thérèse, I think you are a devil,' and she only laughed."

Dangeau could see that laugh-red, red lips, and white, even teeth, and all the while lips that had kissed hers livid, dabbled with blood. Oh, horrible! Poor Cléry, poor Edmond!

He gave a great shudder and forced his thoughts away from the vision they had evoked, but he sought voice twice before he could say:

"All else are well?"

She looked sullen again, and shrugged her shoulders.

"Ma foi, Citizen, Paris does not stand still."

He bit his lip.

"But here, in this house?"

"I am well, I have said so before."

He turned as if to go.

"And the Citoyenne Roche?" He had his voice in hand now, and the question had a careless ring.

"Gone," said Rosalie curtly.

In a flash that veil of carelessness had dropped. His hand fell heavily upon her shoulder.

"Gone-where?" he asked tensely.

"Where every one goes these days, these fine days. To prison, to the guillotine. They all go there."

For a moment Dangeau's heart stood still, then laboured so that his voice was beyond control. It came in husky gasps. "Dead-she is dead. Oh, mon Dieu, mon Dieu!"

Rosalie was rocking to and fro, counting on her fingers. His emotion seemed to please her, for she gave a foolish smile.

"She has a little white neck, very smooth and soft," she muttered.

A terrible sound broke from Dangeau's ghastly lips; a sound that steadied for a moment the woman's tottering mind. She looked up curiously, as if recalling something, smoothed the hair from her forehead, and touched the rigid hand which lay upon her shoulder.

"Tiens, Citizen," she said in a different tone, "she is not dead yet"; and the immense relief gave Dangeau's anger rein.

"Woman!" he said violently, "what has happened? Where is she? At once——"

Rosalie twitched away her shoulder, shrinking back against the wall. This blaze of anger kept her sane for the moment.

"She is in prison, at the Abbaye," she said. Under the excitement her brain cleared, and she was thinking now, debating how much she should tell him.

"Since when?"

"A month-six weeks-what do I know?"

"How came she to be arrested?"

"How should I know, Citizen?"

"Did you betray her? You knew who she was. Take care and do not lie to me."

"I lie, I—Citizen! But I was her best friend, and when that beast Hébert came hanging round——"

"Hébert?"

"She took his fancy, Heaven knows why, and you know her proud ways. Any other girl would have played with him a little, given a smile or two, and kept him off; but she, with her nose in the air, and her eyes looking past him, as if he was n't fit for her to see-why, she made him feel as if he were the mud under her feet, and what could any one expect? He got her clapped into the Abbaye, to repent at leisure."

Dangeau was a man of clean lips, but now he called down damnation upon Hébert's black soul with an earnestness that frightened Rosalie.

"What more do you know? Tell me at once!"

She turned uneasily from the look in his eyes.

"She will be tried to-day."

"You are sure?"

"Thérèse told me, and she and Hébert are thick as thieves again."

"What hour? Dieu! what hour? It is ten o'clock now."

"Before noon, I think she said, but I can't be sure of that."

"You are lying?"

"No, no, Citizen—I do not know-indeed I do not."

He saw that she was speaking the truth, and turned from her with a despairing gesture. As he stumbled out of the shop he knocked over a great basket of potatoes, and Rosalie, with a sort of groan of relief, went down on her knees and began to gather them up. As the excitement of the scene she had been through subsided her eyes took that dull glaze again. Her movements became slower, and she stared oddly at the brown potatoes as she handled them.

"One-two-three," she counted in a monotonous voice, dropping them into the basket. At each little thud she started slightly, then went on counting.

"Four-five-six-seven-eight—" Suddenly she stared at them heavily. "There's no blood," she muttered, "no blood."

Half an hour later Thérèse found her with a phlegmatic smile upon her face and idle hands folded over something that lay beneath her coarse apron.

"Come along then, Rosalie," she called out impatiently. "Have you forgotten the trial?—we've not too much time."

"Ah!" said Rosalie, nodding slowly; "ah, the trial."

Thérèse tapped impatiently with her foot.

"Come then, for Heaven's sake! or we shall not get places."

"Places," said Rosalie suddenly; "what for?"

"Ma foi, if you are not stupid to-day. The trial, I tell you, that Rochambeau girl's trial-white-faced little fool. Ciel! if I could not play my cards better than that," and she laughed.

Rosalie's hands were hidden by her apron. One of them clutched something. The fingers lifted one by one, and in her mind she counted, "One-two-three-four-five"—and then back again—"One-two-three-four-five—" Thérèse was staring at her.

"What's the matter with you to-day?" she said. "Are you coming or no? It will be amusing, Hébert says; but if you prefer to sit here and sulk, do so by all means. For me, I go."

She turned to do so, but Rosalie was already getting out of her chair.

"Wait then, Thérèse," she grumbled. "Is no one to have any amusement but you? There, give me your arm, come close. Now tell me what's going to happen?"

"Oh, just the trial, but I thought you wanted to see it. For me, I always think it makes the execution more interesting if one has seen the trial also."

"Dangeau is back," said Rosalie irrelevantly.

Thérèse laughed loud.

"He has a fine welcome home," she said. "Well, are you coming, for I 've no mind to wait?"

"It is only the trial," said Rosalie vaguely. "Just a trial-and what is that? I do not care for a trial, there is no blood."

She laughed a little and rocked, cuddling what lay beneath her apron.

"Just a trial," she muttered; "but whose trial did you say?"

Thérèse lost patience. She stamped on the floor.

"What, again? What the devil is the matter with you to-day? Are you drunk?"

Rosalie turned her big head and looked at her cousin. They were standing close together, and her left hand, with its strong, stumpy fingers, closed like a vice upon the girl's arm.

"No, I 'm not drunk, not drunk, Thérèse," she said in a thick voice.

Thérèse tried to shake her off.

"Well, you sound like it, and behave like it, you old fool," she said furiously. "Drunk or crazy, it's all one. Let go of me, I shall be late."

"Yes," said Rosalie, nodding her head—"yes, you will be late, Thérèse."

"Va, imbécile!" cried the girl in a passion.

As she spoke she hit the nodding face sharply, twitching violently to one side in the effort to free her arm.

The ponderous hand closed tighter, and Thérèse, turning again with a curse, saw that upon Rosalie's heavily flushed face that stopped the words half-way, and changed them to a shriek.

"Oh, Mary Virgin!" she screamed, and saw the hidden right hand come swinging into sight, holding a long, sharp knife such as butchers use at their work. Her eyes were all black, dilated pupil, and she choked on the breath she tried to draw in order to scream again. Oh, the hand! the knife!

It flashed and fell, wrenched free and fell again, and Thérèse went down, horribly mute, her hands grasping in the air, and catching at the basket across which she fell.

She would scream no more now. The knife clattered to the floor from Rosalie's suddenly opened hand, and, as if the sound were a signal, Thérèse gave one convulsive shudder, which passed with a gush of crimson.

Rosalie went down on her knees, and gathered a handful of the brown tubers from the piled basket. She had to push the corpse aside to get at them, and she did it without a glance.

Then she threw the potatoes back into the basket one by one. She wore a complacent smile. Her eyes were intent.

"Now, there is blood," she said, nodding as if satisfied. "Now, there is blood."

## CHAPTER XVIII
## A TRIAL AND A WEDDING

Of the hours that passed after that death-like swoon of hers Mlle. de Rochambeau never spoke. Never again could she open the door behind which lurked madness, and an agony such as women have had to bear, time and again, but of which no woman whom it has threatened can speak. Hébert had given his orders, and she was thrust into an empty cell, where she lay cowering, with hidden face, and lips that trembled too much to pray.

Hébert's threat lay in her mind like a poison in the body. Soon it would kill-but not in time, not soon enough. She could not think, or reason, and hope was dead. Something else had come in its place, a thing unformulated and dreadful, not to be thought of, unbelievable, and yet unbearably, irrevocably present.

Oh, the long, shuddering hours, and yet, by a twist of the tortured brain, how short-how brief-for now she saw them as barriers between her and hell, and each as it fell away left her a thing more utterly unhelped.

When they brought her out in the morning, and she stepped from the dark prison into the warm, sunny daylight, she raised her head and looked about her a little wonderingly.

Still a sun in the sky! Still summer shine and breath, and beautiful calm space of blue ethereal light above. A sort of stunned bewilderment fell upon her, and she sat very still and quiet all the way.

Inside the hall citizens crowded and jostled one another for a place; plump, respectable mothers of families, cheek by jowl with draggled wrecks of the slums, moneyed shopkeepers, tattered loafers, a wild-eyed Jacobin or two, and everywhere women, women, women. Women with their children, lifting a round-eyed starer high to see the white-faced aristocrat go past; women with their work, whose chattering tongues kept pace with the clattering needles; women fiercer and more cruel than men, to whom death and blood and anguish were become a stimulant more fatally potent than any alcohol.

There were men there too, gaping, yawning, telling horrible tales, men whose hands had dripped innocent blood in September. There was a reek of garlic, the air was abominably hot and close, and wherever citizens could get an elbow free one saw a mopping of greasy faces going forward.

As Mademoiselle de Rochambeau was brought in, a sort of growling murmur went round. The crowd was in a dangerous mood: on the verge of ennui, it wanted something fresh—a sauce piquante to its daily dish-and here was only another cursed aristocrat with nothing very remarkable about her.

She looked round, not curiously, but in some vague, helpless fashion, which might have struck pity from hearts less inured to suffering. On the raised stage to which they had brought her there were a couple of rough tables. At the nearest of the two sat a number of men, very dirty and evil-eyed—Fouquier Tinville's carefully packed jury; and at the farther one, Herman, the great tow-haired Judge President, with his heavy air of being half asleep; and Tinville himself, the Public Prosecutor, low-browed, with retreating chin-Renard the Fox, as a contemporary squib has it, the perpetrator of which lost his head for his pains. Behind him lounged Hébert, hands in pockets, light eyes roving here and there. She saw him and turned her head away with the wince of a trapped animal, looking through a haze of misery to the sea of faces below.

There is a peculiar effluence from any large body of people. Their encouragement, or their hostility, radiates from them, and has an overwhelming influence upon the mind. When the crowd cheers how quickly enthusiasm spreads, until, like a rising tide, it covers its myriad human grains of sand! And a multitude in anger?—No one who has heard it can forget!

Imagine, then, one bruised, tormented human speck, girl in years, gently nurtured, set high in face of a packed assemblage, every upturned face in which looked at her with appraising lust, bloodthirsty cruelty, or inhuman curiosity. A wild panic unknown before swept in upon her soul. She had not thought it could feel again, but between Hébert's glance, which struck her like a shameful blow, and all these eyes staring with hatred, her reason rocked, and she felt a scream rise shuddering from the very centre of her being.

Those watching saw both slender hands catch suddenly at the white throat, whilst for a minute the darkened eyes stared wildly round; then, with a supreme effort, she drew herself up, and stood quietly, and if the blood beat a mad tune on heart and brain, there was no outward sign, except a pallor more complete, and a tightening of the clasped, fallen hands that left the knuckles white.

It was thus, after months of absence, that Dangeau saw her again, and the rage and love and pity in his heart boiled up until it challenged his utmost self-control to keep his hands from Hébert's throat.

Hébert smiled, but uneasily. This was what he had planned-wished for-and yet-Face to face with Dangeau again, he felt the old desire to slink past, and get out of the range of the white, hot anger in the eyes that for a moment seemed to scorch his face.

Dangeau had come in quietly enough, and stood first at the edge of the crowd, by the steps which led to the raised platform on which accused and judges were placed. He had shot his bolt, had made a vain effort to see Danton, and was now come here to do he knew not what.

Mademoiselle looking straight before her, with eyes that now saw nothing, was not aware of his presence, as in a strained, far-away voice she answered the questions Fouquier Tinville put to her.

"Your name?"

"Aline Marie de Rochambeau."

"You are a cousin of the late ci-devant and conspirator Montargis?"

"Yes."

A sort of howl went up from the back of the room, where a knot of filthy men stood gesticulating.

"And you were betrothed to that other traitor Sélincourt?"

"Yes."

The answers dropped almost indifferently from the scarcely parted lips, but she shrank and swayed a little, as a second shout followed her reply, and she caught curses, cries for her death, and a woman's scream of, "Down with Sélincourt's mistress! Give her to us! Throw her down!"

Tinville waved for silence and gradually the noise lessened, the audience settling down with the reflection that perhaps it would be a pity to cut the play short in its first act.

"You have conspired against the Republic?"

"No."

"But I say yes," said Tinville loudly. "Citizen Hébert discovered you under an assumed name. Why did you take a name that was not your own if you had no intention of plotting? Are honest citizens ashamed of their names?"

Dangeau swung himself on to the platform and came forward.

"Citizen President," he said quietly. "I claim to represent the accused, who has, I see, no counsel."

Herman looked up stupidly, a vague smile on his broad, blond face.

"We have done away with counsel for the defence," he observed, with a large, explanatory wave of the hand. "It took too much time. The Revolutionary Tribunal now has increased powers, and requires only to hear and to be convinced of the prisoners' crimes. We have simplified the forms since you went south, Citizen."

Fouquier Tinville glanced at him with venomous intention. "And the Citizen delays us," he said politely.

Aline had let one only sign of feeling escape her —a soft, quick gasp as Dangeau came within the contracting circle of her consciousness-but the sound reached him and came sweetly to his ears.

He turned again to Herman.

"But you still hear witnesses, or whence the conviction?" he said in a carefully controlled voice.

"It is Dangeau, our Dangeau!" shouted a woman near the front. "Let him speak if he wants to: what does he know of the girl?"

He recognised little Louison, hanging to her big husband's arm, and sent her a smiling nod of thanks.

"Witnesses, by all means," shrugged Tinville, to whom Hébert had been whispering. "Only be quick, Citizen, and remember it is a serious thing to try to justify a conspirator." He turned and whispered back, "He 'll talk his head off if we give him the chance-devil speed him!" then leaned across the table and inquired:

"What do you know of the accused?"

"I know her motive for changing her name."

"Oh, you know her motive-eh?"

Dangeau raised his voice.

"A patriotic one. She came to Paris, she witnessed the corruption and vice of aristocrats, and she determined to come out from among them and throw in her lot with the people."

Mademoiselle turned slowly and faced him. Now if she spoke, if she demurred, if she even looked a contradiction of his words, they were both lost-both.

His eyes implored, commanded her, but her lips were already opening, and he could see denial shaping there, denial which would be a warrant of death, when of a sudden she met Hébert's dull, anxious gaze, and, shuddering, closed her lips, and looked down again at the uneven, dusty floor. Dangeau let out his breath with a gasp of relief, and spoke once more.

"She called herself Marie Roche because her former name was hateful to her. She worked hard, and went hungry. I call on Louison Michel to corroborate my words."

Hébert raised a careless hand, and instantly there was a clamour of voices from the back. He congratulated himself in having had the forethought to install a claque, as they listened to the cries of, "Death to the aristocrat! Down with the conspirator! Death! Death!"

Dangeau turned from the bar to the people.

"Citizens," he cried, "I turn to you for justice. What did they say in the bad old days? —'The King's voice is God's voice,' and I say it still." The clamour rose again, but his voice dominated it.

"I say it still, for, though the King is dead, a new king lives whose reign will never end-the Sovereign People-and at their bar I know there will be equal justice shown, and no consideration of persons. Why did Capet fall? Why did I vote for his death? Because of oppression and injustice. Because there was no protection for the weak-no hearing for the poor. But shall not the People do justice? Citizens, I appeal to you —I am confident in your integrity."

A confused uproar followed, some shouting, "Hear him!" and others still at their old parrot-cry of, "Death! Death!"

Above it all rang Louison's shrill cry:

"A speech, a speech! Let Dangeau speak!" and by degrees it was taken up by others.

"The girl is innocent. Will you, just Citizens, punish her for a name which she has discarded, for parents who are dead, and relations from whom she shrank in horror? I vouch for her, I tell you —I, Jacques Dangeau. Does any one accuse me? Does any one cast a slur upon my patriotism? I tell you I would cut off my right hand if it offended those principles which I hold dearer than my life; and saying that, I say again, I vouch for her."

"All very fine that," called a man's voice, "but what right have you to speak for her, Citizen? Has n't the girl a tongue of her own?"

"Yes, yes!" shouted a big brewer who had swung himself to the edge of the platform, and sat there kicking his heels noisily. "Yes, yes! it 's all very well to say 'I vouch for her,' but there 's only one woman any man can vouch for, and that's his wife."

"What, Robinot, can you vouch for yours?" screamed Louison; and a roar of laughter went up, spiced by the brewer's very evident discomfort.

"Yes, what's she to you after all?" said another woman.

"A hussy!" shrieked a third.

"An aristocrat!"

"What do you know of her, and how do you know it?"

"Explain, explain!"

"Death, death to the aristocrat!"

Dangeau sent his voice ringing through the hall:

"She is my betrothed!"

A momentary hush fell upon the assembly. Hébert sprang forward with a curse, but Tinville plucked him back, whispering, "Let him go on; that 'll damn him, and is n't that what you want?"

Again Aline's lips moved, but instead of speaking she put both hands to her heart, and stood pressing them there silently. In the strength of that silence Dangeau turned upon the murmuring crowd.

"She is my betrothed, and I answer for her. You all know me. She is an aristocrat no longer, but the Daughter of the Revolution, for it has borne her into a new life. All the years before she has discarded. From its mighty heart she has drawn the principles of freedom, and at its guiding hand learned her first trembling steps towards Liberty. In trial of poverty, loneliness, and hunger she has proved her loyalty to the other children of our great Mother. Sons and Daughters of the Republic, protect this child who claims to be of your line, who holds out her hands to you and cries: 'Am I not one of you? Will you not acknowledge me? brothers before whom I have walked blamelessly, sisters amongst whom I have lived in poverty and humility.'"

He caught Mademoiselle's hand, and held it up.

"See the fingers pricked and worn, as many of yours are pricked and worn. See the thin face-thin as your daughters' faces are thin when there is not food for all, and the elder must go without that the younger may have more. Look at her. Look well, and remember she comes to you for justice. Citizens, will you kill your converts? She gives her life and all its hopes to the Republic, and will the Republic destroy the gift? Keep the knife to cut away the alien and the enemy. Is my betrothed an alien? Shall my wife be an enemy? I swear to you that, if I believed it, my own hand would strike her down! If there is a citizen here who does not believe that I would shed the last drop of my heart's blood before I would connive at the danger of the Republic, let him come forward and accuse me!"

"Stop him!" gasped Hébert.

Fouquier Tinville shrugged his shoulders, as he and Herman exchanged glances.

"No, thanks, Hébert," he said coolly. "He's got them now, and I 've no fancy for a snug position between the upper and the nether millstone. After all, what does it matter? There are a hundred other girls" and he spat on the dirty floor.

Undoubtedly Dangeau had them, for in that pause no one spoke, and his voice rang out again at its full strength:

"Come forward then. Do any accuse me?"

There was a prolonged hush. The jury growled amongst themselves, but no one coveted the part of spokesman.

Once Hébert started forward, cleared his throat, then reflected for a moment on Danton and his ways-reflected, too, that this transaction would hardly bear the light of day, cursed the universe at large, and fell back into his chair choking with rage.

It appeared that no one accused Dangeau. Far in the crowd a pretty gipsy of a girl laughed loudly.

"Handsome Dangeau for me!" she cried. "Vive Dangeau!"

In a minute the whole hall took it up, and the roof rang with the shouting. The girl who had laughed had been lifted to her lover's shoulders, and stood there, flushed and exuberant, leading the cheers with her wild, shrill voice.

When the noise fell a little, she waved her arms, crying, with a peal of laughter:

"Let's have a wedding, a wedding, mes amis! If she 's the Daughter of the Revolution, let the Revolution give away the bride, and we 'll all say Amen!"

The crowd's changed mood tossed the new suggestion into instant popularity. The girl's cry was taken up on all sides, there was bustling to and fro, laughter, gossip, whispering, shouting, and general jubilation. A fête, a spectacle-something new-oh, but quite new. A trial that ended in the bridal of the victim, to be sure one did not see that every day. That was romantic. That made one's heart beat. Well, well, she was in luck to get a handsome lover instead of having her head sliced off.

"Vive Dangeau! Vive Dangeau and the Daughter of the Revolution!"

Up on to the platform swarmed the crowd, laughing, gesticulating, pressing upon the jury, and even jostling Fouquier Tinville himself.

Hébert bent to his ear in a last effort, but got only a curse and a shrug for his pains.

"I tell you, he 's got them, and no human power can thwart them now."

"You should have shut his mouth! Why in the devil's name did you let him speak?"

"You wanted him to compromise himself, and it seemed the easiest way. He has the devil's own luck. Hark to the fools with their 'Vive Dangeau!' A while ago it was 'Death to the aristocrat!' and now it 's 'Dangeau and the Daughter of the Revolution!' "

"Speak to them-do something," insisted Hébert.

"Try it yourself, and get torn to pieces," retorted the other. "The girl 's not my fancy. Burn your own fingers if you want to."

Dangeau was at the table now.

"We await the decision of the Tribunal," he said, with a hint of sarcasm in the quiet tones.

Fouquier Tinville's eyes rested insolently upon him.

"Our Sovereign has decided, it seems," he said. "For me —I throw up the prosecution."

Hébert flung away with an oath, and Herman bent stolidly and wrote against the interrogatory the one word, "Acquitted."

It stood out black and bold in his gross scrawl, and as he threw the sand on it, Dangeau turned away with a bow.

Some one was being pushed through the crowd —a dark man in civil dress, but with the priest's look on his sallow, nervous face. Dangeau recognised the odd, cleft chin and restless eyes of Latour, the Constitutional curé of St. Jean.

"A wedding, a wedding!" shouted the whole assembly, those at the back crying the more loudly, as if to make up by their own noise for not being able to hear what was passing on the platform.

"A wedding, a wedding!" shrieked the same women who, not half an hour ago, had raised the howl for the aristocrat's blood.

"Bride, bridegroom, and priest," laughed the gipsy-eyed girl. "What more do we want? The Citizen President can give away the bride, and I 'll be brides-maid. Set me down then, Réné, and let 's to work."

Her lover pushed a way to the front and lifted her on to the stage. She ran to Mademoiselle and began to touch her hair and settle the kerchief at her throat, whilst Aline stood quite, quite still, and let her do what she would.

She had not stirred since Dangeau had released her hand, and within her every feeling and emotion lay swooning. It was as if a black tide had risen, covering all within. Upon its dark mirror floated the reflection of Hébert's cruel eyes, and loose lips that smiled upon a girl's shamed agony. If those waters rose any higher they would flood her brain and send her mad with horror, Dangeau's voice seemed to arrest the tide, and whilst he spoke the reflection wavered and grew faint. She listened, knowing what he said, as one knows the contents of a book read long ago; but it was the voice itself, not the words carried on it, that reached her reeling brain and steadied it.

All at once a hand on her hair, at her breast; a girl's eyes shining with excitement, whilst a shrill voice whispered, "Saints! how pale you are! What! not a blush for the bridegroom?" Then loud laughter all around, and she felt herself pushed forward into an open space.

A ring had been formed around one of the tables; men and women jostled at its outskirts, pushed one another aside, and stood on tiptoe, peeping and applauding. In the centre, Dangeau with his tricolour sash; Mademoiselle, upon whose head some one had thrust the scarlet cap of Liberty; and the priest, whose eyes looked back and forth like those of a nervous horse. He cleared his throat, moistened his dry lips, and began the Office. After a second's pause, Dangeau took the bride's hand and did his part. Cold as no living thing should be, it lay in his, unresisting and unresponsive, whilst his was like his mood-hotly masterful. After one glance he dared not trust himself to look at her. Her white features showed no trace of emotion, her eyes looked straight before her in a calm stare, her voice made due response without tremor or hesitation. "Ego conjugo vos," rang the tremendous words, and they rose from their knees before that strange assembly, man and wife in the sight of God and the Republic.

"Kiss her then, Citizen," laughed the bridesmaid, slipping her arm through Dangeau's, and he touched the marble forehead with his lips. The first kiss of his strong love, and given and taken so. Fire and ice met, thrust into contact of all contacts the most intimate. How strange, how unbearable! Fraught with what presage of disaster.

"Now you may kiss me," said the bridesmaid, pouting. "Réné isn't looking; but be quick, Citizen, for he 's jealous, and a broken head would n't be a pleasant marriage gift."

Like a man in a dream he brushed the glowing cheek, and felt its warmth.

Yes, so the living felt; but his bride was cold, as the week-old dead are cold.

## CHAPTER XIX
## THE BARRIER

After the wedding, what a home-coming! Dangeau had led his pale bride through the cheering, applauding crowd, which followed them to their very door, and on the threshold horror met them-for the floor was dabbled with blood. Thérèse's corpse lay yet in the house, and a voluble neighbour told how Rosalie had murdered her cousin, and had been taken, raving, to the cells of the Salpêtrière. The crowd was all agog for details, and, taking advantage of the diversion, Dangeau cleared a path for himself and Aline. He took her to her old room and closed the door. The silence fell strangely.

"My dearest, you are safe. Thank God you are safe," he said in broken tones.

She looked straight before her with an expression deeper than that which is usually called unconscious, her eyes wide and piteous, like those of a child too badly frightened to cry out. He took her cold hands and held them to his breast, chafing them gently, trying to revive their warmth, and she let him do it, still with that far-away, unreal look.

"My dear, I must go," he said after a moment. "For both our sakes I must see Danton at once, before any garbled tale reaches his ear. I will see that there is some one in the house. Louison Michel would come I think. There is my report to make, letters of the first importance to be delivered; a good deal of work before me, in fact. But you will not be afraid now? You are safer than any woman in Paris to-day. You will not be nervous?"

She shook her head slightly, and drew one hand away in order to push the hair from her forehead. The gesture was a very weary one, and Dangeau would have given the world to catch her in his arms.

"So tired, my heart," he said in a low voice; and as a little quiver took her, he continued quickly: "I will find Louison; she came here with us, and is sure not to be far away. She will look after you, and bring you food, and then you should sleep. I dare not stay."

He kissed the hand which still lay passively in his and went out hurriedly, not trusting himself to turn and look at her again lest he should lose his careful self-control and startle her by some wild outpouring of love, triumph, and thankfulness.

Aline heard his footsteps die away, listening with strained attention until the last sound melted into a tense silence. Then she looked wildly round, her breast heaved distressfully, and tottering to the bed she fell on it face downwards, and lay there in a stunned fatigue of mind and body that left no place for thought or tears. Presently came Louison, all voluble eagerness to talk of the wedding and the murder, especially the latter.

"And to think that it was Jean's knife! Holy Virgin, if I had known what she came for! There she sat, and stared, and stared, until I told her she had best be going, since I, at least, had no time to waste. Yesterday, that was; and this morning when Jean seeks his knife it is gone-and the noise, and the fuss. 'My friend,' I said, 'do I eat knives?' and with that I turned him out, and all the while Rosalie had it. Ugh! that makes one shudder. Not that that baggage Thérèse was any loss, but it might as well have been you, or me. When one is mad they do not distinguish. For me, I have said for a long time that Rosalie's mind was going, and now it is seen who is right. Well, well, now Charlotte will come round. Mark my words, Charlotte will be here bright and early to-morrow, if not to-night. It will be the first time she has set foot here in ten years. She hated Rosalie like poison —a stepmother, only a dozen years older than herself, and when the old man died she cleared out, and has never spoken to Rosalie since the funeral. But she 'll be round now, mark my words."

Aline lay quite still. She was just conscious that Louison was there, talking a great deal, and that presently she brought her some hot soup, which it was strangely comfortable to swallow. The little woman was not ungentle with her, and did not leave her until the half-swoon of fatigue had passed into deep sleep. She herself was to sleep in the house. Dangeau had asked her to, saying he might be late, and she had promised, pleased to be on the spot where such exciting events had taken place, and convinced that it would be for the health of her husband's soul to have the charge of the children for once.

It was very late before Dangeau came home. If the French language holds no such word, his heart supplied it, for the first time in all the long years during which there had been no one to miss him going, or look for him returning. Now the little room under the roof held the long-loved, the despaired-of, the unattainably-distant—and she was his, his wife, caught by his hands from insult and from death. Outside her door he hesitated a moment, then lifted the latch with a gentle touch, and went in reverently. The moon was shining into the room, and one long beam trembled mistily just above the bed, throwing upon the motionless form below a light like that of the land wherein we walk in dreams. Aline was asleep. She lay on her side, with one hand under her cheek, and her loosened hair in a great swathe across the bosom that scarcely seemed to lift beneath it, so deep the tranced fatigue that held her.

The moon was still rising, and the beam slid lower, lower; now it silvered her brow-now showed the dark, curled lashes lying upon a cheek white with that translucent pallor-sleep's gift to youth. Her chin was a little lifted, the soft mouth relaxed, and its tender curve had taken a look at once pitiful and pure, like that of a child drowsing after pain. Her eyelids were only half-closed, and he was aware of the sleeping blue within, of the deeper stain below; and all his heart went out to her in a tremulous rapture of adoration which caught his breath, and ran in fire through every vein. How tired she was, and how deeply asleep-how young, and pure.

A thought of Hébert rose upon his shuddering mind, and involuntarily words broke from him—"Ah, mon Dieu!" he said, with heaving chest.

Aline stirred a little; a slow, fluttering sigh interrupted her breathing, as she withdrew the hand beneath her cheek and put it out gropingly. Then she sighed again and turned from the light, nestling into the pillow with a movement that hid her face. If Dangeau had gone to her then, knelt by the bed, and put his arms about her, she might have turned to his protecting love as instinctively as ever child to its mother. But that very love withheld him. That, and the thought of Hébert. If she should think him such another! Oh, God forbid!

He looked once more, blessed her in his soul, and turned away.

In the morning he was afoot betimes. Danton had set an early hour for the conclusion of the business between them, and it was noon past before he returned.

In the shop he found a pale, dark, thin-lipped woman, engaged in an extremely thorough scrubbing and tidying of the premises. She stopped him at once, with a grin—

"I 'll have no loafing or gossiping here, Citizen"; and received his explanation with perfect indifference.

"I am Charlotte Leboeuf. I take everything over. Bah! the state the house is in! Fitter for pigs than Christians. For the time you may stay on. You have two rooms, you say?"

"Yes, two, Citoyenne."

"And you wish to keep them? Well, I have no objection. Later on I shall dispose of the business, but these are bad times for selling; and now, if the Citizen will kindly not hinder me at my work any more for the present." She shrugged her shoulders expressively, adding, as she seized the broom again, "Half the quarter has been here already, but they got nothing out of me."

Aline had risen and dressed herself. Rosalie had left her room just as it was on the day of her arrest, and the dust stood thick on table, floor, and window-sill. Mechanically she began to set things straight; to dust and arrange her few possessions, which lay just as they had been left after the usual rummage for treasonable papers.

Presently she found the work she had been doing, a stitch half taken, the needle rusty. She cleaned it carefully, running it backwards and forwards through the stuff of her skirt, and taking the work, she began to sew, quickly, and without thought of anything except the neat, fine stitches.

At Dangeau's knock, followed almost immediately by his entrance, her hands dropped into her lap, and she looked up in a scared panic of realisation. All that she had kept at bay rushed in upon her; the little tasks which she had set as barriers between her and thought fell away into the past, leaving her face to face with her husband and the future.

He crossed the floor to her quickly, and took her hands. He felt them tremble, and put them to his lips.

"Aline, my dearest!" he said in a low, vibrating voice.

With a quick-caught breath she drew away from him, sore trouble in her eyes.

"Wait!" she panted. Oh, where was her courage? Why had she not thought, planned? What could she say? "Oh, please wait!"

There was a long pause, whilst he held her hands and looked into her face.

"There is something-something I must tell you," she murmured at last, her colour coming and going.

The pressure upon her hands became suddenly agonising.

"Ah, mon Dieu! he has not harmed you? Aline, Aline-for God's sake — —"

She said, "No, no," hastily, relieved to have something to answer, wondering that he should be so moved, frightened by the great sob that shook him. Then —

"How do you know about-him?" and the words came hardly from her.

"Rosalie," he said, catching at his self-control —"Rosalie told me-curse him-curse him! Thank God you are safe. He cannot touch you now. What is it, then, my dear?" and the voice that had cursed Hébert seemed to caress her.

"If you know-that" —the word came on a shudder —"you know why I did-what I did-yesterday. But no —I forget; no one knew it all, no one knew the worst. I could n't say it, but now I must —I must."

"My dear, leave it-leave it. Why should you say anything?"

But she took a long breath and went on, speaking very low, and hurriedly, with bent head, and cheeks that flamed with a shamed, crimson patch.

"He is a devil, I think; and when I said I would die, he said-oh, mon Dieu! —he said his turn came first, he had friends, he could get me into his power after I was condemned."

Dangeau's arm went up-the arm with which he would have killed Hébert had he stood before him-and then fell protectingly about her shoulders.

"Aline, let him go-don't think of him again. You are safe-Death has given you back to me." But she shrank away.

"Oh, Monsieur," she said, with a quick gasp, "it was not death that I feared-indeed it was not death. I could have died, I should have died, before I betrayed-everything-as I did yesterday. I should have died, but there are some things too hard to bear. Oh, I do not think God can expect a woman to bear-that!" Again the deep shudder shook her. "Then you came, and I took the one way out, or let you take it."

"Aline!"

"No, no," she cried —"no, no, you must understand-surely you understand that there is too much between us-we can never be-never be-oh, don't you understand?"

Dangeau's face hardened. The tenderness went out of it, and his eyes were cold as steel. How cruelly she was stabbing him she did not know. Her mind held dazed to its one idea. She had betrayed the honour of her race, to save her own. That red river of which she had spoken long months before, it lay between them still, only now she had stained her very soul with it. But not for profit of safety, not for pleasure of love, not even for life, bare life, but to escape the last, worst insult life holds-insult of which it is no disgrace to be afraid. She must make that clear to him, but it was so hard, so hard to find words, and she was so tired, so bruised, she hungered so for peace. How easy to yield, to take life's sweetness with the bitterness, love's promise with love's pain! But no, it were too base; the bitterness and the pain were her portion. His part escaped her.

When he spoke his changed voice startled her ears.

"So it comes to this," he said, with a short, bitter laugh; "having to choose between me and Hébert, you chose me. Had the choice lain between me and death, you would have gone to the guillotine without soiling your fingers by touching me."

She looked at him—a bewildered, frightened look.

Pain spurred him on.

"Oh, you make it very clear, my wife. Ah! that makes you wince? Yes, you are my wife, and you have just told me that you would rather have died than have married me. Yesterday I kissed your forehead. Is there a stain there? Suppose I were to kiss you now? Suppose I were to claim what is mine? What then, Aline, what then?"

A look she had never seen before was in his eyes, as he bent them upon her. His breath came fast, and for a moment her mind was terrified by the realisation that her power to hold, to check him, was gone. This was a new Dangeau-one she had never seen. She had been so sure of him. All her fears had been for herself, for that rebel in her own heart; but she had thought her self-control could give the law to his, and had never for a moment dreamed that his could break down thus, leaving her face to face with-what? Was it the brute?

She shrank, waiting.

"I am your husband, Aline," he said in a strange voice. "I could compel your kisses. If I bade you come to me now, what then? Does your Church not order wives to obey their husbands?"

She looked at him piteously.

"Yes, Monsieur."

"Yes, Monsieur? Very well, then, since I order it, and the Church tells you to obey me, come here and kiss me, my wife."

That drew a shiver from her, but she came slowly and stood before him with such a look of appeal as smote him through all his bitter anger.

"You will obey?"

She spoke, agonised.

"You can compel me. Ah! you have been good to me—I have thought you good-you will not——"

He laid his hands heavily upon her shoulders and felt her shrink. Oh death-the pain of it! He thought of her lying in the moonlight, and the confiding innocence of her face. How changed now!—all drawn and terrified. Hébert had seen it so. He spoke his thought roughly.

"Is that how you looked at him?" he said, bending over her, and she felt her whole body quiver as he spoke. She half closed her eyes, and looked about to swoon.

"Yes, I can compel you," he said again, low and bitterly. "I can compel you, but I 'm not Hébert, Aline, and I shan't ask you to choose between me and death." He took his hands away and stepped back from her, breathing hard.

"I kissed you once, but I shall never kiss you again. I shall never touch you against your will, you need not be afraid. That I have loved you will not harm you-you can forget it. That you must call yourself Dangeau, instead of Roche, need not matter to you so greatly. I shall not trouble you again, so you need not wish you had chosen my rival, Death. Child, child! don't look at me like that!"

As he spoke Aline sank into a chair, and laying her arms upon the table, she put her head down on them with a sharp, broken cry:

"Oh God, what have I done-what have I done?"

Dangeau looked at her with a sort of strained pity. Then he laughed again that short, hard laugh, which comes to some men instead of a sob.

"Mlle. de Rochambeau has married out of her order, but since her plebeian husband quite understands his place, quite understands that a touch from him would be worse than death, and since he is fool enough to accept this proud position, there is not so much harm done, and you may console yourself, poor child."

Every word stabbed deep, and deeper. How she had hurt him-oh, how she had hurt him! She pressed her burning forehead against her trembling hands, and felt the tears run hot, as if they came from her very heart.

Dangeau had reached the door when he turned suddenly, came back and laid his hand for a moment on her shoulder. Even at that moment, to touch her was a poignant and wonderful thing, but he drew back instantly, and spoke in a harsh tone.

"One thing I have a right to ask-that you remember that you bear my name, that you bear in mind that I have pledged my honour for you. You have been at the Abbaye; I hear the place is honeycombed with plots. My wife must not plot. If I have saved your honour, remember you hold mine. I pledged it to the people yesterday, I pledged it to Danton to-day."

Aline raised her head proudly. Her eyes were steady behind the brimming tears.

"Monsieur, your honour is safe," she said, with a thrill in her voice.

Dangeau gazed long at her-something of the look upon his face with which a man takes his farewell of the beloved dead. Then his whole face set cool and hard, and without another word he turned and strode out, his dreamed-of home in ruins-love's ashes heaped and dusty on the cold and broken hearth.

## CHAPTER XX
## A ROYALIST PLOT

Charlotte Leboeuf was one of the people who would certainly have set cleanliness above godliness, and she sacrificed comfort to it with a certain ruthless pleasure. The house she declared to be a sty, impossible to cleanse, but she would do her best, and her best apparently involved a perpetual steam of hot water, and a continual reek of soap-suds. Dangeau put up more than one sigh at the shrine of the absent Rosalie as he stumbled over pails and brooms, or slipped on the damp floor. For the rest, the old life had begun again, but with a dead, dreary weight upon it.

Dangeau at his busy writing, at his nightly pacings, and Aline at her old task of embroidering, felt the burden of life press heavily, chafed at it for a moment, perhaps, and turned again with a sigh to toil, unsweetened by that nameless something which is the salt of life. Once he ventured on a half-angry remonstrance on the long hours of stitching, which left her face so pale and her eyes so tired. It was not necessary for his wife, he began, but at the first word so painful a colour stained her cheek, eyes so proudly distressed looked at him between imploring and defiance, that he stammered, drew a long breath, and turned away with a sound, half groan, half curse. Aline wept bitterly when he was gone, worked harder than before, and life went drearily enough for a week or so.

Then one day in July Dangeau received orders to go South again. He had known they would come, and the call to action was what he craved, and yet what to do with the girl who bore his name he could not tell.

He was walking homewards, revolving a plan in his mind, when to his surprise he saw Aline before him, and not alone. Beside her walked a man in workman's dress, and they were in close conversation. As he caught sight of them they turned down a small side street, and after a moment's amazed hesitation he took the same direction, walking slowly, but ready to interfere if he saw cause.

Earlier in the afternoon, Aline having finished her work, had tied it up neatly and gone out. The streets were a horror to her, but she was obliged to take her embroidery to the woman who disposed of it, and on these hot days she craved for air. She accomplished her business, and started homewards, walking slowly, and enjoying the cool breeze which had sprung up. As she turned out of the more frequented thoroughfares, a man, roughly dressed, passed her, hung on his footsteps a little, and as she came up to him, looked sharply at her, and said in a low voice, "Mlle. de Rochambeau?"

She started, her heart beating violently, and was about to walk on, when coming still nearer her, he glanced all round and rapidly made the sign of the cross in the air. With a sudden shock she recognised the Abbé Loisel.

"It is M. l'Abbé?" she said in a voice as low as his own.

"Yes, it is I. Walk on quietly, and do not appear to be specially attentive. I saw you last at the Abbaye, how is it that I meet you here?"

A slight colour rose to Aline's cheek. Her tone became distant.

"I think you are too well informed as to what passes in Paris not to know, M. l'Abbé," she said.

They came out into a little crowd of people as she spoke, and he walked on without replying, his thoughts busy.

Part saint, part conspirator, he had enough of the busybody in his composition to make his position as arch manipulator of Royalist plots a thoroughly congenial one. In Mlle. de Rochambeau he saw a ravelled thread, and hastened to pick it up, with the laudable intention of working it into his network of intrigue. They came clear of the press, and he turned to her, his pale face austerely plump, his restless eyes hard.

"I heard what I could hardly believe," he returned. "I heard that Henri de Rochambeau's daughter had bought her life by accepting marriage with an atheist and a regicide, a Republican Deputy of the name of Dangeau."

Aline bit her lip, her eyes stung. She would not justify herself to this man. There was only one man alive who mattered enough for that, but it was bitter enough to hear, for this was what all would say. She had known it all along, but realisation was keen, and she shrank from the pictured scorn of Mme. de Matigny's eyes and from Marguerite's imagined recoil. She walked on a little way before she could say quietly:

"It is true that I am married to M. Dangeau."

But the Abbé had seen her face quiver, and drew his own conclusions. He was versed in reading between the lines.

"Mme. de Matigny suffered yesterday," he said with intentional abruptness, and Aline gave a low cry.

"Marguerite-not Marguerite!" she cried out, and he touched her arm warningly.

"Not quite so loud, if you please, Madame, and control your features better. Yes, that is not so bad. And now allow me to ask you a question. Why should Mlle. de Matigny's fate interest the wife of the regicide Dangeau?"

"M. l'Abbé, for pity's sake, tell me, she is not dead-little Marguerite?"

"Not this time, Madame, but who knows when the blow will fall? But there, it can matter very little to you."

"To me?" She sighed heavily. "It matters greatly. M. l'Abbé; I do not forget my friends. I have not so many that I can forget them."

"You remember?"

"Oh, M. l'Abbé!"

"And you would help them?"

"If I could."

He paused, scrutinising her earnest face. Then he said slowly:

"You bought your life at a great price, and something is due to those whom you left behind you in peril whilst you went out to safety. I knew your father. It is well that he is dead-yes, I say that it is well; but there is an atonement possible. In that you are happy. From where you are, you can hold out a hand to those who are in danger; you may do more, if you have the courage, and-if we can trust you."

His keen look dwelt on her, and saw her face change suddenly, the eager light go out of it.

"M. l'Abbé, you must not tell me anything," she said quickly, catching her breath; for Dangeau's voice had sounded suddenly in her memory:

"I have pledged my honour"; and she heard the ring of her own response —"Monsieur, your honour is safe." She had answered so confidently, and now, whatever she did, dishonour seemed imminent, unavoidable.

"You have indeed gone far," he said. "You must not hear —I must not tell. What does it mean? Who forbids?"

Aline turned to him desperately.

"M. l'Abbé, my hands are tied. You spoke just now of M. Dangeau, but you do not know him. He is a good man-an honourable man. He has protected me from worse than death, and in order to do this he risked his own life, and he pledged his honour for me that I would engage in no plots-do nothing against the Republic. When I let him make that pledge, and what drove me to do so, lies between me and my own conscience. I accepted a trust, and I cannot betray it."

"Fine words," said Loisel curtly. "Fine words. Dutiful words from a daughter of the Church. Let me remind you that an oath taken under compulsion is not binding."

"He said that he had pledged his honour, and I told him that his honour was safe. I do not break a pledge, M. l'Abbé."

"So for a word spoken in haste to this atheist, to this traitor stained with your King's blood, you will allow your friends to perish, you will throw away their lives and your own chance of atoning for the scandal of your marriage —" he began; but she lifted her head with a quick, proud gesture.

"M. l'Abbé, I cannot hear such words."

"You only have to raise your voice a little more and you will hear no more words of mine. See, there is a municipal guard. Tell him that this is the Abbé Loisel, non-juring priest, and you will be rid of me easily enough. You will find it harder to stifle the voice of your own conscience. Remember, Madame, that there is a worse thing even than dishonour of the body, and that is damnation of the soul. If you have been preserved from the one, take care how you fall into the other. What do you owe to this man who has seduced you from your duty? Nothing, I tell you. And what do you owe to your Church and to your order? Can you doubt? Your obedience, your help, your repentance."

The Abbé had raised his voice a little as he spoke. The street before them was empty, and he was unaware that they were being followed. A portion of what he said reached Dangeau's ears, for the prolonged conversation had made him uneasy, and he had hastened his steps. Up to now he had caught no word of what was passing, but Aline's gestures were familiar to him, and he recognised that lift of the head which was always with her a signal of distress. Now he had caught enough, and more than enough, and a couple of strides brought him level with them. Aline started violently, and looked quickly from Dangeau to the priest, and back again at Dangeau. He was very stern, and wore an expression of indignant contempt which was new to her.

"Good-day, Citizen," he said, with a sarcastic inflexion. "I will relieve you of the trouble of escorting my wife any farther."

Loisel was wondering how much had been overheard, and wished himself well out of the situation. He was not in the least afraid of going to prison or to the guillotine, but there were reasons enough and to spare why his liberty at the present juncture was imperative. One of the many plots for releasing the Queen was in progress, and he carried upon him papers of the first importance. It was to serve this plot that he had made a bid for Aline's help. In her unique position she might have rendered priceless services, but it was not to be, and he hastened to extricate himself from a position which threatened disaster to his central scheme.

"Good-day," he returned with composure, and was moving off, when Dangeau detained him with a gesture.

"One moment, Citizen. I neither know your name nor do I wish to know it, but it seemed to me that your conversation was distressing to my wife. I very earnestly deprecate any renewal of it, and should my wishes in the matter be disregarded I should conceive it my duty to inform myself more fully-but I think you understand me, Citizen?"

So this was the husband? A strong man, not the type to be hoodwinked, best to let the girl go; but as the thoughts flashed on his mind, he was aware of her at his elbow.

"M. l'Abbé," she said very low, "tell Marguerite-tell her-oh! ask her not to think hardly of me. I pray for her always, I hope to see her again, and I will do what I can."

She ran back again, without waiting for a reply, and walked in silence by Dangeau's side until they reached the house. He made no attempt to speak, but on the landing he hesitated a moment, and then followed her into her room.

"Danton spoke to me this morning," he said, moving to the window, where he stood looking out. "They want me to go South again. Lyons is in revolt, and is to be reduced by arms. Dubois-Crancy commands, but Bonnet has fallen sick, and I am to take his place."

Aline had seated herself, and picked up a strip of muslin. Under its cover her hands clasped each other very tightly. When he paused she said: "Yes, Monsieur."

"I am to start immediately."

"Yes, Monsieur."

He swung round, looked at her angrily for a moment, and then stared again into the dirty street.

"It is a question of what you are to do," he said impatiently.

"I? But I shall stay here. What else is there for me to do?"

"I cannot leave you alone in Paris again."

"Monsieur?"

"What!" he cried. "Have you forgotten?" and she bent to hide her sudden pallor.

"What am I to do, then?" she asked very low. Her submission at once touched and angered him. It allured by its resemblance to a wife's obedience, and repelled because the resemblance was only mirage, and not reality.

"I cannot have you here, I cannot take you with me, and there is only one place I can send you to —a little place called Rancy-les-Bois, about thirty miles from Paris. My mother's sisters live there, and I should ask them to receive you."

"I will do as you think best," murmured Aline.

"They are unmarried, one is an invalid, and they are good women. It is some years since I have seen them, but I remember my Aunt Ange was greatly beloved in Rancy. I think you would be safe with her."

A vision of safety and a woman's protection rose persuasively before Aline, and she looked up with a quick, confiding glance that moved Dangeau strangely. She was at once so rigid and so soft, so made for love and trusting happiness, and yet so resolute to repel it. He bit his lip as he stood looking at her, and a sort of rage against life and fate rose hotly, unsubdued within him. He turned to leave her, but she called him back, in a soft, hesitating tone that brought back the days of their first intercourse. When he looked round he saw that she was pale and agitated.

"Monsieur!" she stammered, and seemed afraid of her own voice; and all at once a wild stirring of hope set his heart beating.

"What is it? Won't you tell me?" he said; and again she tried to speak and broke off, then caught her courage and went on.

"Oh, Monsieur, if you would do something!"

"Why, what is it you want me to do, child?"

That was almost his old kind look, and it emboldened her. She rose and leaned towards him, clasping her hands.

"Oh, Monsieur, you have influence —" and at that his brow darkened.

"What is it?" he said.

"I heard —I heard —" She stopped in confusion. "Oh! it is my friend, Marguerite de Matigny. Her grandmother is dead, and she is alone. Monsieur, she is only seventeen, and such a pretty child, so gay, and she has done no harm to any one. It is impossible that she could do any harm."

"I thought you had no friends?"

"No, I had none; but in the prison they were good to me-all of them. Old Madame de Matigny knew my parents, and welcomed me for their sakes; but Marguerite I loved. She was like a kitten, all soft and caressing. Monsieur, if you could see her, so little, and pretty-just a child!" Her eyes implored him, but his were shadowed by frowning brows.

"Is that what the priest told you to say?" he asked harshly.

"The priest — —"

"You 'd lie to me," he broke out, and stopped himself. "Do you think I didn't recognise the look, the tone? Did he put words into your mouth?"

Her eyes filled.

"He told me about Marguerite," she said simply. "He told me she was alone, and it came into my heart to ask you to help her. I have no one to ask but you."

The voice, the child's look would have disarmed him, but the words he had overheard came back, and made his torment.

"If it came into your heart, I know who put it there," he said. "And what else came with it? What else were you to do? Do you forget I overheard? If I thought you had lent yourself to be a tool, to influence, to bribe-mon Dieu, if I thought that — —"

"Monsieur!" but the soft, agitated protest fell unheard.

"I should kill you-yes, I think that I should kill you," he said in a cold, level voice.

She moved a step towards him then, and if her voice had trembled, her eyes were clear and untroubled as they met his full.

"You shall not need to," she said quietly, and there was a long pause.

It was he who looked away at last, and then she spoke.

"I asked you at no one's prompting," she said softly. "See, Monsieur, let there be truth between us. That at least I can give, and will-yes, always. He, the man you saw, asked me to help him, to help others, and I told him no, my hands were tied. If he had asked for ever, I must still have said the same thing; and if it had cut my heart in two, I would still have said it. But about Marguerite, that was different. She knows nothing of any plots, she is no conspirator. I would not ask, if it touched your honour. I would not indeed."

"Are you sure?" he asked in a strange voice, and she answered his question with another.

"Would you have pledged your honour if you had not been sure?"

He gave a short, hard laugh.

"Upon my soul, child, I think so," he said, and the colour ran blazing to her face.

"Oh, Monsieur, I keep faith!" she cried in a voice that came from her heart.

Her outstretched hands came near to touching him, and he turned away with a sudden wrench of his whole body.

"And it is hard-yes, hard enough," he said bitterly, and went out with a mist before his eyes.

## CHAPTER XXI
## A NEW ENVIRONMENT

Madelon Pinel stood by the window of the inn parlour, and looked out with round shining eyes. She was in a state of pleasing excitement, and her comely cheeks vied in colour with the carnation riband in her cap, for this was her first jaunt with her husband since their marriage, and an expedition from quiet Rancy to the eight-miles-distant market-town was a dissipation of the most agreeable nature. The inn looked out on the small, crowded Place, where a great traffic of buying and selling, of cheapening and haggling was in process, and she chafed with impatience for her husband to finish his wine, and take her out into the thick of it again. He, good man, miller by the flour on his broad shoulders, stood at his ease beside her, smiling broadly. No one, he considered, could behold him without envy; for Madelon was the acknowledged belle of the countryside, and well dowered into the bargain. Altogether, a man very pleased with life, and full of pride in his married state, as he lounged beside his pretty wife, and drank his wine, one arm round her neat waist.

With a roll and a flourish the diligence drew up, and Madelon's excitement grew.

"Ah, my friend, look-look!" she cried. "There will be passengers from Paris. Oh! I hope it is full. No-what a pity! There are only four. See then, Jean Jacques, the fat old man with the nose. It is redder than Gargoulet's and one would have said that was impossible. And the little man like a rat. Fie! he has a wicked eye, that one—I declare he winked at me"; and she drew back, darting a virtuously coquettish glance at the unperturbed Jean Jacques.

"Not he," he observed with complete tranquillity. "Calm thyself, Madelon. Thou art no longer the prettiest girl in Rancy, but a sober matron. Thy winking days are over."

"My winking days!" exclaimed Madelon—"my winking days indeed!" She tossed her head with feigned displeasure and leaned out again, wide-eyed.

A third passenger had just alighted, and stood by the door of the diligence holding out a hand to some one yet unseen.

"Seigneur!" cried Madelon maliciously; "look there, Jean Jacques, if that is not a fine man!"

"What, the rat?" grinned the miller.

"No, stupid!—the handsome man by the door there, he with the tricolour sash. Ciel! what a sash! What can he be, then—a Deputy, thinkest thou? Oh, I hope he is a Deputy. There, now there is a woman getting out-he helps her down, and now he turns this way. They are coming in. Eh! what blue eyes he has! Well, I would not have him angry with me, that one; I should think his eyes would scorch like lightning."

"Eh, Madelon, how you talk!"

"There, they are on the step. Hold me then, Jean Jacques, or I shall fall. Do you think the woman is his wife? How white she is!—but quite young, not older than I. And her hair-oh, but that is pretty! I wish I had hair like that-all gold in the sun."

"Thy hair is well enough," said the enamoured Jean Jacques. "There, come back a little, Madelon, or thou wilt fall out. They are coming in."

Madelon turned from the window to watch the door, and in a minute Dangeau and Aline came in. For a moment Aline looked timidly round, then seeing the pleasant face and shining brown eyes of the miller's wife, she made her way gratefully towards her, and sat down on the rough bench which ran along the wall. Madelon disengaged herself from her husband's arm, gave him a little push in Dangeau's direction, and sat down too, asking at once, with a stare of frank curiosity:

"You are from Paris? All the way from Paris?"

"Yes, from Paris," said Aline rather wearily.

"Ciel! That is a distance to come. Are you not tired?"

"Just a little, perhaps."

"Paris is a big place, is it not? I have never been there, but my father has. He left the inn for a month last year, and went to Paris, and saw all the sights. Yes, he went to the Convention

Hall, and heard the Deputies speak. Would any one believe there were so many of them? Four hundred and more, he said. Every one did not believe him-Gargoulet even laughed, and spat on the floor-but my father is a very truthful man, and not at all boastful. He would not say such a thing unless he had seen it, for he does not believe everything that he is told-oh no! For my part, I believed him, and Jean Jacques too. But imagine then, four hundred Deputies all making speeches!"

Aline could not help laughing.

"Yes, I believe there are quite as many as that. My husband is one of them, you know."

"Seigneur!" exclaimed Madelon. "I said so. Where is that great stupid of mine? I said the Citizen was a Deputy-at once I said it!"

"Why, how did you guess?"

"Oh, by the fine tricolour sash," said Madelon naively; "and then there is a look about him, is there not? Do you not think he has the air of being a Deputy?"

"I do not know," said Aline, smiling.

"Well, I think so. And now I will tell you another thing I said. I said that he could be angry, and that then I should not like to meet his eyes, they would be like blue fire. Is that true too?"

Aline was amused by the girl's confiding chatter.

"I do not think he is often angry," she said.

"Ah, but when he is," and Madelon nodded airily. "Those that are angry often-oh, well, one gets used to it, and in the end one takes no notice. It is like a kettle that goes on boiling until at last the water is all boiled away. But when one is like the Citizen Deputy, not angry often-oh, then that can be terrible, when it comes! I should think he was like that."

"Perhaps," said Aline, still smiling, but with a little contraction of the heart, as she remembered anger she had roused and faced. It did not frighten her, but it made her heart beat fast, and had a strange fascination for her now. Sometimes she even surprised a longing to heap fuel on the fire, to make it blaze high-high enough to melt the ice in which she had encased herself.

Then her own thought startled her, and she turned quickly to her companion.

"Is that your husband?" she asked, for the sake of saying something.

"Yes, indeed," said Madelon. "He is a fine man, is he not? He and the Citizen Deputy are talking together. They seem to have plenty to say-one would say they were old friends. Yes, that is my Jean Jacques; he is the miller of Rancy-les-Bois. We have travelled too, for Rancy is eight miles from here, and a road to break your heart."

"From Rancy-you come from Rancy?" said Aline, with a little, soft, surprised sound.

"Yes, from Rancy. Did I not say my father kept the inn there? But I have been married two months now"; and she twisted her wedding ring proudly.

"I am going to Rancy," said Aline on the impulse.

"You, Citoyenne?" and Madelon's brown eyes became completely round with surprise.

Aline nodded. She liked this girl with the light tongue and honest red cheeks. It was pleasant to talk to her after four hours of tense silence, during the most part of which she had feigned sleep, and even then had been aware of Dangeau's eyes upon her face.

"Yes," she said. "Does that surprise you so much? My husband goes South on mission, and I am to stay with his aunts at Rancy. They have written to say that I am welcome."

"Oh!" cried Madelon quickly. "Then I know who you are. Stupid that I am, not to have guessed before! All the world knows that the Citoyennes Desaix have a nephew who is a Deputy, and you must be his wife-you must be the Citoyenne Dangeau."

"Yes," said Aline.

"To be sure, if I had seen the Citoyenne Ange, she would have told me you were coming; but it is ten days since I saw her to speak to-there has been so much to do in the house. She will be pleased to have you. Both of them will be pleased. If they are proud of the nephew who is a Deputy-Seigneur!" and Madelon's plump brown hands were waved high and wide to express the pride of Dangeau's aunts.

"Yes?" said Aline again.

"But of course. It is a fine thing nowadays, a very fine thing indeed. All the world would turn out to look at him if he came to Rancy. What a pity he must go South! Have you been married long?"

Aline was vexed to feel the colour rise to her cheeks as she answered:

"No-not long."

"And already he must leave you! That is hard-yes, I find that very hard. If Jean Jacques were to go away, I should certainly be inconsolable. Before one is married it is different; one has a light heart, one is quick to forget. If a man goes, one does not care-there are always plenty more. But when one is married, then it is another story; then there is something that hurts one at the heart when they are not there—n'est-ce pas?"

Aline turned a tell-tale face away, and Madelon edged a little nearer.

"Later on, again, they say one does not mind so much. There are the children, you see, and that makes all the difference. For me, I hope for a boy—a strong, fat boy like Marie my sister-in-law had last year. Ah! that was a boy! and I hope mine will be just such another. If one has a girl, one feels as if one had committed a bêtise, do you not think so?—or"—with a polite glance at the averted face—"perhaps you desire a girl, Citoyenne?"

Aline felt an unbearable heat assail her, for suddenly her old dream flashed into her mind, and she saw herself with a child in her arms—a wailing, starving child with sad blue eyes. With an indistinct murmur she started up and moved a step or two towards the door, and as she did so, Dangeau nodded briefly to the miller, and came to meet her.

"We are fortunate," he said—"really very fortunate. These worthy people are the miller of Rancy and his wife, as no doubt she has told you. I saw you were talking together."

"Yes, it is strange," said Aline.

"Nothing could have been more convenient, since they will be able to take you to my aunt's very door. I have spoken to the miller, and he is very willing. Nothing could have fallen out better."

"And you?" faltered Aline, her eyes on the ground.

"I go on at once. You know my orders—'to lose no time.' If it had been necessary, I should have taken you to Rancy, but as it turns out I have no excuse for not going on at once."

"At once?" she repeated in a little voice like a child's.

He nodded, and walked to the window, where he stood looking out for a moment.

"The horses are in," he said, turning again. "It is time I took my seat."

He passed out, saluting Pinel and Madelon, who was much elated by his bow.

Aline followed him into the square, and saw that the other two passengers were in their places. Her heart had begun to beat so violently that she thought it impossible that he should not hear it, but he only threw her a grave, cold look.

"You will like perhaps to know that your friend's case came on yesterday and that she was set free. There was nothing against her," he said, with some constraint.

"Marguerite?"

"Yes, the Citoyenne Matigny. She is free. I thought you would be glad to know."

"Yes-yes-oh, thank you! I am glad!"

"You will tell my aunts that my business was pressing, or I should have visited them. Give them my greetings. They will be good to you."

"Yes-the letter was kind."

"They are good women." He handed her a folded paper. "This is my direction. Keep it carefully, and if you need anything, or are in any trouble, you will write." His voice made it an order, not a request, and she winced.

"Yes," she said, with stiff lips.

Dangeau's face grew harder. If it were only over, this parting! He craved for action-longed to be away-to be quit of this intolerable strain. He had kept his word, he had assured her safety, let him be gone out of her life, into such a life as a man might make for himself, in the tumult and flame of war.

"Seigneur!" said Madelon, at the window. "See, Jean Jacques," —and she nudged that patient man —"see how he looks at her! Ma foi, I am glad it is not I! And with a face as if it had been cut out of stone, and there he gets in without so much as a touch of the hand, let alone a kiss! Is this the way of it in Paris?"

"Thou must still be talking, Madelon," said Jean Jacques, complacently.

"Well, I should not like it," shrugged Madelon pettishly.

"No, I 'll warrant you wouldn't," said the miller, with a grin and a hearty kiss.

At four o'clock the business and pleasure of the market-day were over, and the folk began to jog home again. Aline sat beside Madelon on the empty meal-sacks, and looked about her with a vague curiosity as they made their way through the poplar-bordered lanes, bumping prodigiously every now and then, in a manner that testified to the truth of Madelon's description of the road.

It was one of the days that seems to have drawn out all summer's beauty, whilst keeping yet faint memories of spring, and hinting in its breadth of evening shade at autumn's mellowness.

Madelon chattered all the way, but Aline's thoughts were too busy to be distracted. She thought continually of the smouldering South and its dangers, of the thousand perils that menaced Dangeau, and of the bitter hardness of his face as he turned from her at the last.

Jean Jacques let the reins fall loose after a while, and turning at his ease, slipped his arm about his wife's waist and drew her head to his shoulder. Aline's eyes smarted with sudden tears. Here were two happy people, here was love and home, and she out in the cold, barred out by a barrier of her own raising. Oh! if he had only looked kindly at the last! —if he had smiled, or taken her hand!

They came over the brow of a little hill, and dipped towards the wooded pocket where Rancy lay, among its trees, watched from half-way up the hill by an old grey stone château, on the windows of which the setting sun shone full, showing them broken and dusty.

"Who lives in the château?" asked Aline suddenly.

"No one-now," returned Jean Jacques; and Madelon broke in quickly.

"It was the château of the Montenay but a year ago. —Now why dost thou nudge me, Jean Jacques? —A year ago, I say, it was pillaged. Not by our own people, but by a mob from the town. They broke the windows and the furniture, and hunted high and low for traitors, and then went back again to where they came from. There was nobody there, so not much harm done."

"De Montenay?" said Aline in a low voice. How strange! So this was why the name of Rancy had seemed familiar from the first. They were of her kin, the De Montenay.

"Yes, the De Montenay," said Madelon, nodding. "They were great folk once, and now there is only the old Marquise left, and she has emigrated. She is very old now, but do you know they say the De Montenay can only die here? However ill they are in a foreign place, the spirit cannot pass, and I always wonder will the old Marquise come back, for she is a Montenay by birth as well as by marriage?"

"Eh, Madelon, how you talk!" said Jean Jacques, with an uneasy lift of his floury shoulders. He picked up the reins and flicked the mare's plump sides with a "Come up, Suzette; it grows late."

Madelon tossed her head.

"It is true, all the same," she protested. "Why, there was M. Réné-all the world knows how she brought M. Réné here to die."

"Chut then, Madelon!" said the miller, in a decided tone this time; and, as she pouted, he spoke over his shoulder in a low voice, and Aline caught the words, "Ma'mselle Ange," whereon Madelon promptly echoed "Ma'mselle" with a teasing inflexion.

Jean Jacques became angry, and the back of his neck seemed to well over the collar of his blouse, turning very red as it did so.

"Tiens, Citoyenne Ange, then. Can a man remember all the time?" he growled, and flicked Suzette again. Madelon looked penitent.

"No, no, my friend," she said soothingly; "and the Citoyenne here understands well enough, I am sure. It is that my father is so good a patriot," she explained, "and he grows angry if one says Monsieur, Madame, or Mademoiselle any more. It must be Citizen and Citoyenne to please him, because we are all equal now. And Jean Jacques is quite as good a patriot as my father-oh, quite; but it is, see you, a little hard to remember always, for after all he has been saying the other for nearly forty years."

"Yes, it is hard always to remember," Aline agreed.

They came down into the shadow under the hill, and turned into the village street. The little houses lay all a-straggle along it, with the inn about half-way down. Madelon pointed out this cottage and that, named the neighbours, and informed Aline how many children they had. Jean Jacques did not make any contribution to the talk until they were clear of the houses, when he raised his whip, and pointing ahead, said:

"Now we are almost there-see, that is the house, the white one amongst those trees"; and in a moment Aline realised that she was nervous, and would be very thankful when the meeting with Dangeau's aunts should be over. Even as she tried to summon her courage, the cart drew up at the little white gate, and she found herself being helped down, whilst Madelon pressed her hands and promised to come and see her soon.

"The Citoyenne Ange knows me well enough," she said, laughing. "She taught me to read, and tried to make me wise, but it was too hard."

"There, there, come, Madelon. It is late," said the miller. "Good evening, Citoyenne. Come up, Suzette"; and in a moment Aline was alone, with her modest bundle by her side. She opened the gate, and found herself in a very pretty garden. The evening light slanted across the roof of the small white house, which stood back from the road with a modest air. It had green shutters to every window, and green creepers pushed aspiring tendrils everywhere. The garden was all aflash with summer, and the air fragrant with lavender, a tall hedge of which presented a surface of dim, sweet greenery, and dimmer, sweeter bloom. Behind the lavender was a double row of tall dark-eyed sunflowers, and in front blazed rose and purple phlox, carnations white and red, late larkspur, and gilly-flowers.

Such a feast of colour had not been spread before Aline's town-wearied eyes for many and many a long month, and the beauty of it came into her heart like the breath of some strong cordial. At the open door of the house were two large myrtle trees in tubs. The white flowers stood thick amongst the smooth dark leaves, and scented all the air with their sweetness. Aline set down her bundle, and went in, hesitating, and a murmur of voices directing her, she turned to the right.

It was dark after the evening glow outside, but the light shone through an open door, and she made her way to it, and stood looking in, upon a small narrow room, very barely furnished as to tables and chairs, but most completely filled with children of all ages.

They sat in rows, some on the few chairs, some on the floor, and some on the laps of the elder ones. Here and there a tiny baby dozed in the lap of an older girl, but for the most part they were from three years old and upwards.

All had clean, shining faces, and on the front of each child's dress was pinned a tricolour bow, whilst on the large corner table stood a coarse pottery jar stuffed full of white Margaret daisies, scarlet poppies, and bright blue cornflowers. Aline frowned a little impatiently and tapped with her foot on the floor, but no one took any notice. A tall lady with her back to the door was apparently concluding a tale to which all the children listened spellbound.

"Yes, indeed," Aline heard her say, in a full pleasant voice —"yes, indeed, children, the dragon was most dreadfully fierce and wicked. His eyes shot out sparks, hot like the sparks at the forge, and flames ran out of his mouth so that all the ground was scorched, and the grass died. —Jeanne Marie, thou little foolish one, there is no need to cry. Have courage, and take Amelie's hand. The brave youth will not be harmed, because of the magic sword. —It was all very well for the dragon to spit fire at him, but he could not make him afraid. No, indeed! He raised the great sword in both hands, and struck at the monster. At the first blow the earth shook, and the sea roared. At the second blow the clouds fell down out of the sky, and all the wild beasts of the woods roared horribly, but at the third blow the dragon's head was cut clean off, and he fell down dead at the hero's feet. Then the chains that were on the wrists and ankles of the lovely lady vanished away, and she ran into the hero's arms, free and beautiful."

A long sigh went up from the rows of children, and one said regretfully:

"Is that all, Citoyenne?"

"That is all the story, my children; but now I shall ask questions. Félicité, say then, who is the young hero?"

A big, sharp-eyed girl looked up, and said in a quick sing-song, "He is the glorious Revolution and the dragon."

"Chut then —I asked only for the hero. It is Candide who shall tell us who is the dragon."

Every one looked at Candide, who, for her part, looked at the ceiling, as if seeking inspiration there.

"The dragon is-is —

"Come then, my child, thou knowest."

"Is he not a dragon, then?" said Candide, opening eyes as blue as the sky, and quite as devoid of intelligence.

"Little stupid one-and the times I have told thee! What is it, then, that the glorious Revolution has destroyed?"

She paused, and half a dozen arms went up eagerly, whilst as many voices clamoured:

"I know!" —"No, ask me!" —"No, me, Citoyenne!" —"No, me!" —"Me!"

"What! Jeanne knows? Little Jeanne Marie, who cried? She shall say. Tell us, then, my child-who is the dragon?"

Jeanne looked wonderfully serious.

"It is the tyranny of kings, is it not, chère Citoyenne?"

"Very good, little one. And the lovely lady, who is the lovely lady?"

"France-our beautiful France!" cried all the children together.

Aline pushed the door quite wide and stepped forward, and as she came into view all the children became as quiet as mice, staring, and nudging one another.

At this, and the slight rustle of Aline's dress, Ange Desaix turned round, and uttered a cry of surprise. She was a tall woman, soft and ample of arm and bosom, with dark, silvered hair laid in classic fashion about a very nobly shaped head. Her skin was very white and soft, and her hazel eyes had a curious misty look, like the hollows of a hill brimmed with a weeping haze that never quite falls in rain. They were brooding eyes, and very peaceful, and they seemed to look right through Aline and away to some place of dreams beyond. All this was the impression of a moment-this, and the fact that the tall figure was all in white, with a large breast-knot of the same three-coloured flowers as stood in the jar. Then the motherly arms were round Aline, at once comfortable and appealing, and Mlle. Desaix' voice said caressingly, "My dear niece, a thousand welcomes!"

After a moment she was quietly released, and Ange Desaix turned to the children.

"Away with you, little ones, and come again to-morrow. Louise and Marthe must give up their bows, but the rest can keep them."

The indescribable hubbub of a party of children preparing for departure arose, and Ange said smilingly, "We are late to-day, but on market-day some are from home, and like to know the children are safe with me."

As she spoke a little procession formed itself. Each child passed before Mlle. Desaix, and received a kiss and a smile. Two little girls looked very downcast. They sniffed loudly as they unpinned their ribbon bows and gave them up.

"Another time you will be wise," said Ange consolingly; and Louise and Marthe went out hanging their heads.

"They chattered, instead of listening," explained Mlle. Desaix. "I do not like punishments, but what will you? If children do not learn self-control, they grow up so unhappy."

There was an alluring simplicity in voice and manner that touched the child in Aline. To her own surprise she felt her eyes fill with tears-not the hot drops which burn and sting, but the pleasant water of sympathy, which refreshes the tired soul. On the impulse she said:

"It is good of you to let me come here. I—I am very grateful, chère Mademoiselle."

Ange put a hand on her arm.

"You will say 'ma tante,' will you not, dear child? Our nephew is dear to us, and we welcome his wife. Come then and see Marthe. She suffers much, my poor Marthe, and the children's chatter is too much for her, so I do not take them into her room, except now and then. She likes to see little Jeanne sometimes, and Candide, the little blue-eyed one. Marthe says she is like Nature-unconsciously stupid-and she finds that refreshing, since like Nature she is so beautiful. But there, the child is well enough-we cannot all be clever."

Mlle. Desaix led the way through the hall and up a narrow stair as she spoke. Outside a door on the landing above she paused.

"But where, then, is Jacques-the dear Jacques?"

"After all he could not come," said Aline. "His orders were so strict—'to press on without any delay,'—and if he had lost the diligence, it would have kept him twenty-four hours. He charged me with many messages."

"Ah," said Mlle. Ange, "it will be a grief to Marthe. I told her all the time that perhaps he would not be able to come, but she counted on it. But of course, my dear, we understand that his duty must come first-only," with a sigh, "it will disappoint my poor Marthe."

She opened the door as she spoke, and they came into a room all in the dark except for the afterglow which filled the wide, square window. A bed or couch was drawn up to the open casement, and Aline took a quick breath, for the profile which was relieved against the light was startlingly like Dangeau's as she had seen it at the coach window that morning.

Ange drew her forward.

"See then, Marthe," she said, "our new niece is come, but alas, Jacques was not able to spare the time. Business of the Republic that could not wait."

Marthe Desaix turned her head with a sharp movement—a movement of restless pain.

"How do you do, my dear niece," she said, in a voice that distinctly indicated quotation marks. "As to seeing, it is too dark to see anything but the sky."

"Yes, truly," said Ange; "I will get the lamp. We are late to-night, but the tale was a long one, and I knew the market folk would be late on such a fine evening."

She went out quickly, and Aline, coming nearer to the window, uttered a little exclamation of pleasure.

"Ah, how lovely!" she said, just above her breath.

The window looked west through the open end of the hollow where Rancy lay, and a level wash of gold held the horizon. Wing-like clouds of grey and purple rested brooding above it, and between them shone the evening star. On either side the massed trees stood black against the glow, and the scent of the lavender came up like the incense of peace.

Marthe Desaix looked curiously at her, but all she could see was a slim form, in the dusk.

"You find that better than lamplight?" she asked.

"I find it very beautiful," said Aline. "It is so long since I saw trees and flowers, and the sun going down amongst the hills. My window in Paris looked into a street like a gutter, and one could only see, oh, such a little piece of sky."

As she spoke Ange came in with a lamp, which she set beside the bed; and immediately the glowing sky seemed to fade and recede to an immeasurable distance. In the lamplight the likeness which had startled Aline almost disappeared. Marthe Desaix' strong, handsome features were in their original cast almost identical with those of her nephew, but seen full face, they were so blanched and lined with pain that the resemblance was blurred, and the big dark eyes, like pools of ink, had nothing in common with Dangeau's.

Aline herself was conscious of being looked up and down. Then Marthe Desaix said, with a queer twist of the mouth:

"You did not live long in Paris, then?"

"It seemed a long time," said Aline. "It seems years when I try to look back, but it really is n't a year yet."

"You like the country?"

"Yes, I think so," faltered Aline, conscious of having said too much.

"Poor child," said Ange. "It is sad for you this separation. I know what you must feel. You have been married so short a time, and he has to leave you. It is very hard, but the time will pass, and we will try and make you happy."

"You are very good," said Aline in a low voice. Then she looked and saw Mlle. Marthe's eyes gazing at her between perplexity and sarcasm.

When Aline was in bed, Ange heard her sister's views at length.

"A still tongue 's best, my Ange, but between you and me" —she shrugged her shoulders, and then bit her lip, as the movement jarred her—"there is certainly something strange about 'our new niece,' as you call her."

"Well, she is our nephew's wife," said Ange.

"Our nephew's wife, but no wife for our nephew, if I'm not much mistaken," returned Marthe sharply.

"I thought she looked sweet, and good."

"Good, good-yes, we 're all good at that age! Bless my soul, Ange, if goodness made a happy marriage, the devil would soon have more holidays than working days."

"Ma chérie, if any one heard you!"

"Well, they don't, and I should n't mind if they did. What I do mind is that Jacques should have made a marriage which will probably break his heart."

"But why, why?"

"Oh, my Angel, if you saw things under your nose as clearly as you do those that are a hundred years away, you would n't have to ask why."

"I saw nothing wrong," said Ange in a voice of distress.

"I did not say the girl was a thief, or a murderess," returned Marthe quickly. "No, I 'll not tell you what I mean-not if you were to ask me on your knees-not if you were to beg it with your last breath."

Ange laughed a little.

"Well, well, dearest, perhaps I shall guess. Good-night, and sleep well."

"As if I ever slept well!"

"Poor darling! Poor dearest! Is it so bad to-night? Let me turn the pillow. Is it a little better so?"

"Perhaps." Then as Ange reached the door:

"Angel!"

"What is it then, chérie?"

Mlle. Marthe put a thin arm about her sister's neck and drew her close.

"After all, I will tell you."

"Though I did not beg it on my knees?"

"Chut!"

"Or with my last breath?"

"Very well, then; if you do not wish to hear——"

"No, no; tell me."

"Well then, Ange, she is noble-that girl."

"Oh no!"

"I am sure of it. The mystery, her coming here. Why has she no relations, no friends? And then her look, her manner. Why, the first tone of her voice made me start."

"Oh no, he would not——"

"Would not?" scoffed Marthe. "He 's a fool in love, and I suppose she was in danger. I tell you, I suspected it at once when his letter came. There, go to bed, and dream of our connection with the aristocracy. My faith, how times change! It is an edifying world."

She pushed Ange away, and lay a long time watching the stars.

## CHAPTER XXII
## AT HOME AND AFIELD

Aline slept late in the morning after her arrival. Everything was so fresh, and sweet, and clean that it was a pleasure just to lie between the lavender-scented sheets, and smell the softness of the summer air which came in at the open casement. She had meant to rise early, but whilst she thought of it, she slept again, drawn into the pleasant peace of the hour.

When she did awake the sun was quite high, and she dressed hastily and went down into the garden. Here she was aware of Mlle. Ange, basket on arm, busily snipping, cutting, and choosing amongst the low herbs which filled this part of the enclosure. She straightened herself, and turned with a kind smile and kiss, which called about her the atmosphere of home. The look and touch seemed things at once familiar and comfortable, found again after many days of loss.

"Are you rested then, my dear?" asked the pleasant voice. "Yesterday you looked so tired, and pale. We must bring some roses into those cheeks, or Jacques will surely chide us when he comes."

On the instant the roses were there, and Aline stood transfigured; but they faded almost at once, and left her paler than before.

Mlle. Ange opened her basket, and showed neat bunches of green herbs disposed within.

"I make ointments and tinctures," she said, "and to-day I must be busy, for some of the herbs I use are at their best just now, and if they are not picked, will spoil. All the village comes to me for simples and salves, so that between them, and the children, and my poor Marthe, I am not idle."

"May I help?" asked Aline eagerly; and Mlle. Ange nodded a pleased "Yes, yes."

That was a pleasant morning. The buzz of the bees, the scent of the flowers, the warm freshness of the day-all were delightful; and presently, to watch Ange boiling one mysterious compound, straining another, distilling a third, had all the charm of a child's new game. Life's complications fell back, leaving a little space of peace like a fairy ring amongst new-dried grass. Mlle. Marthe lay on her couch knitting, and watching. Every now and again she flashed a remark into the breathless silence, on which Ange would look up with her sweet smile, and then turn absently to her work again.

"There is then to be no food to-day?" said Marthe at last, her voice calmly sarcastic.

Ange finished counting the drops she was transferring from one mysterious vessel to another.

"Eight, nine, ten, eleven, twelve-what was that you said, chérie?"

"Nothing, my dear. Angels, of course, are not dependent on food, and Jacques is too far away to prosecute us if we starve his wife."

"Oh, tres chère, is it so late? Why did you not say? And after such a night, too-my poor dearest. See, I fly. Oh, I am vexed, and to-day too, when I told Jeanne I would make the omelette."

Marthe's eyebrows went up, and Ange turned in smiling distress to Aline.

"She will be so cross, our old Jeanne! She loves punctuality, and she adores making omelettes; but then, see you, she has no gift for making an omelette-it is just sheer waste of my good eggs-so to-day I said I would do it myself, in your honour."

"And mine," observed Marthe, with a click of the needles. "Jeanne's omelettes I will not eat."

"Oh, tres chère, be careful. She has such ears, she heard what you said about the last one, and she was so angry. Aline must come with me now, or I dare not face her."

They went down together and into the immaculate kitchen, where Jeanne, busily compounding a pie, turned a little cross, sallow face upon them, and rose, grumbling audibly, to fetch eggs and the pan.

"That good Jeanne," said Ange in an undertone, "she has all the virtues except a good temper. Marthe says she is like food without salt-all very good and wholesome, but so nasty; but she is really attached to us and after twenty years thinks she has a right to her temper."

Here, the returning Jeanne banged down a dish, and clattered with a small pile of spoons and forks.

Ange Desaix broke an egg delicately, and watched the white drip from the splintered shell.

"Things are beautiful, are they not, little niece? Just see this gold and white, and the speckled shell of this one, and the pink glow shining here. One could swear one saw the life brooding within, and here I break it, and its little embryo miracle, in order to please a taste which Jeanne considers the direct temptation of some imp who delights to plague her."

She laughed softly, and putting the egg-shells on one side, began to chop up a little bunch of herbs.

"An omelette is very much like a life, I think," she said after a moment. "No two are alike, though all are made with eggs. One puts in too many herbs, and the dish is bitter; another too few, and it is tasteless. Or we are impatient, and snatch at life in the raw; or idle, and burn our mixture. It is only one here and there who gets both matter and circumstance right."

Jeanne was hovering like an angry bird, and as Mlle. Desaix' voice became more dreamy, and her eyes looked farther and farther away into space, she twitched out a small, vicious claw of a hand, and stealthily drew away the bowl that held the eggs.

"One must just make the most of what one has," Ange was saying. Was she thinking of that sudden blush and pallor of a few hours back, or of her sister's words the night before?

"If one's lot is tasteless, one must flavour it with cheerfulness; and if it is bitter, drink clear water after it, and forget."

Aline shivered a little, and then, in spite of herself, she smiled. Jeanne had her pan on the fire, and a sudden raw smell of burning rose up, almost palpably. The mistress of the house came back from her dreams with a start, looked wildly round, and missed her eggs, her herbs, her every ingredient. "Jeanne! but truly, Jeanne!" she cried hotly; and as she spoke the little figure at the fire whisked round and precipitated a burnt, sodden substance on to the waiting dish.

"Ma'mselle is served," she said snappishly, but there was a glint of triumph in her eye.

"No, Jeanne, it is too much," said Ange, flushing; whereat Jeanne merely picked up the dish and observed:

"If Ma'mselle will proceed into the other room, I will serve the dejeuner. Ma'mselle has perhaps not remarked that it grows late."

After which speech Mlle. Desaix walked out of the room with a fine dignity, and the smell of the burnt omelette followed her.

Then began a time of household peace and quiet healing, in which at first Aline rested happily. In this small backwater, life went on very uneventfully-birth and death in the village being the only happenings of note-the state of Jeanne's temper the most pressing anxiety, since Mlle. Marthe's suffering condition was a thing of such long standing as to be accepted as a matter of course, even by her devoted sister.

Of France beyond the hills-of Paris, only thirty miles away-they heard very little. The news of the Queen's trial and death did penetrate, and fell into the quiet like a stone into a sleeping pond. All the village rippled with it-broke into waves of discussion, splashes of lamentation, froth of approval, and then settled again into its wonted placidity.

Aline felt a pang of awakening. Whilst she was dreaming here amongst the peace of herby scents and the drowse of harvesting bees, tragedy still moved on Fate's highways, and she felt sudden terror and the sting of a sharp self-reproach. She shrank from Mlle. Ange's kind eyes of pity, touched-just touched-with an unfaltering faith in the necessity for the appalling judgment. The misty hazel eyes wept bitterly, but the will behind them bowed loyally to the decrees of the Revolution.

"There 's no great cause without its victim, no new faith without bloodshed," she said to Marthe, with a kindling glance.

"I said nothing, my dear," was the dry reply.

Ange paced the room, brushing away hot tears.

"It is for the future, for the new generations, that we make these sacrifices, these terrible sacrifices," she cried.

"Oh, my dear!" said Marthe quickly, and then added with a shrug: "For me, I never felt any vocation for reforming the world; and if I were you, my Angel, I would let it alone. The devil has too much to do with things in general, that is my opinion."

"There is nothing I can do," said Ange, at her saddest.

"Thank Heaven for that!" observed her sister piously. "But I will tell you one thing-you need not talk of noble sacrifices and such-like toys in front of Jacques's wife."

"I would not hurt her," said Ange; "but, chérie, she is a Republican's wife-she must know his views, his aims. Why, he voted for the King's death!"

"Just so," nodded Marthe: "he voted for the King's death. I should keep a still tongue, if I were you."

"You still think——?"

"Think?" with scorn. "I am sure."

A few days later there was a letter from Dangeau, just a few lines. He was well. Lyons still held out, but they hoped that any day might end the siege. He begged to be commended to his aunts. Aline read the letter aloud, in a faltering voice, then laid it in her lap, and sat staring at it with eyes that suddenly filled, and saw the letters now blurred, now unnaturally black and large. Mlle. Ange went out of the room, leaving her alone under Marthe's intent regard; but for once she was too absorbed to heed it, and sat there looking into her lap and twisting her wedding-ring round and round. Marthe's voice broke crisply in upon her thoughts.

"So he married you with his mother's ring?"

She started, covering it quickly with her other hand.

"Is it? No, I didn't know," she murmured confusedly. Then, with an effort at defence: "How do you know, Mademoiselle Marthe?"

"How does one know anything, child? By using one's eyes, and putting two and two together. Sometimes they make four, and sometimes they don't, but it 's worth trying. The ring is plainly old, and my sister wore just such another; and after her death Jacques wore it too, on his little finger. He adored his mother."

The scene of her wedding flashed before Aline. At the time she had not seemed to be aware of anything, but now she distinctly saw the priest's hand stretched out for the ring, and Dangeau's little pause of hesitation before he took it off and gave it.

Marthe's brows were drawn together.

"Now, did he give it her for love, or because there was need for haste?" she was thinking, and decided: "No, not for love, or he would have told her it was his mother's." And aloud she said calmly: "You see, you were married in such a hurry that there was no time to get a new one."

Aline looked up and spoke on impulse.

"What did he tell you about our marriage?" she asked.

"My dear, what was there to tell? He wrote a few lines-he does not love writing letters, it appears-he had married a young girl. Her name was Marie Aline Roche, and he commended her to our protection."

"Was that all?"

"Certainly."

"Then do you think I had better tell you more?" said Aline unsteadily.

Marthe looked at her with a certain pity in her glance.

"You did not learn prudence in an easy school," she said slowly, and then added: "No, better not; and besides, there 's not much need-it's all plain enough to any one who has eyes."

Dangeau's letter of about this date to Danton contained a little more information than that he sent his wife.

"The scoundrels have thrown off the mask at last," he wrote in a vigorous hand, which showed anger. "Yesterday Précy fought under the fleur-de-lys. Well, better an open enemy, an avowed Royalist, than a Girondist aping of Republican principles, and treachery under the surface. France may now guess at what she has been saved by the fall of the Gironde. They hope for reinforcements here. Our latest advices are that Sardinia will not move. As to Autichamp, he promises help, and instigates plots from a judicious distance; but he and his master, Artois, feel safer on any soil but that of France, and I gather that he will not leave Switzerland at present. Losses on both sides are considerable. To give the devil his due, Précy has the courage of ten, and we never know when he will be at our throats. Very brilliant work, those sallies of his. I wish we had half a dozen like him."

On the ninth of October Lyons fell, and the fiat of the Republic went forth. "Lyons has no longer a name among cities. Down with her to the dust from which she rose, and on the bloodstained site let build a pillar bearing these warning words: 'Lyons rebelled against the Republic: Lyons is no more.'"

Forthwith terror was let loose, and the town ran blood, till the shriek of its torment went up night and day unceasingly, and things were done which may not be written.

At this time Dangeau's letters ceased, and it was not until Christmas that news of him came again to Rancy. Then he wrote shortly, saying he had been wounded on the last day of the siege, and had lain ill for weeks, but was now recovered, and had received orders to join Dugommier, the Victor of Toulon, on his march against Spain. The letter was short enough, but something of the writer's longing to be up and away from reeking Lyons was discernible in the stiff, curt sentences.

In truth the tide of disgust rose high about him, and raise what barriers he would, it threatened to break in upon his convictions and drown them. News from Paris was worse and worse. The Queen's trial sickened, the Feast of Reason revolted him.

Down with tyrants, but for liberty's sake with decency! Away with superstition and all the network of priests' intrigues; but, in the outraged name of reason, no more of these drunken orgies, these feasts which defied public morality, whilst a light woman postured half naked on the altar where his mother had worshipped. This nauseated him, and drew from his pen an imprudently indignant letter, which Danton frowned over and consigned to the flames. He wrote back, however, scarcely less emphatically, though he recommended prudence and a still tongue.

"Mad times these, my friend, but decency I will have, though all Paris runs raving. It's a fool business, but you 'd best not say so. Take my advice and hold your tongue, though I 've not held mine."

Dangeau made haste to be gone from blood-drenched Lyons, and to wipe out his recollections of her punishment in the success which from the first attended Dugommier's arms.

Spain receded to the Pyrenees; and over the passes in wild wet weather, stung by the cold, and tormented by a wind that cut like a sword of ice, the French army followed.

Here, heroism was the order of the day. If in Paris, where Terror stalked, men were less than men and worse than brutes, because possessed by some devil soul, damned, and dancing, here they were more than men, animated by a superhuman courage and persistence. Yet, terrible puzzle of human life, the men were of the same breed, the same stuff, the same kin.

Antoine, shouting lewd songs about a desecrated altar, or watching with red, cruel eyes the death-agony of innocent women and young boys, was own brother to Jean, whose straw-shod feet carried his brave, starving body over the blood-stained Pyrenean passes, and who shared his last crust cheerfully with an unprovided comrade. One mother bore and nursed them both, and both were the spiritual children of that great Revolution who bore twin sons to France-Licence and Liberty. Nothing gives one so vivid a picture of France under the Terror as the realisation that to find relief from the prevailing horror and inhumanity one must turn to the battlefields.

The army fought with an empty stomach, bare back, and bleeding feet, and Dangeau found enough work to his hand to occupy the energies of ten men. The commissariat was disgraceful, supplies scant, and the men lacking of every necessary.

Having made inquiries, he turned back to France, and ranged the South like a flame, gathering stores, ammunition, arms, shoes-everything, in fact, of which that famished but indomitable army stood in such dire need. Summary enough the methods of those days, and Dangeau's way was as short a one as most, and more successful than many.

He would ride into a town, establish himself at the inn, and send for the Mayor, who, according as his nature were bold or timid, came blustering or trembling. France had no king, but the tricoloured feathers on her Commissioner's hat were a sign of power quite as autocratic as the obsolete fleur-de-lys.

Dangeau sat at a table spread with papers, wrote on for a space, and then —

"Citizen Mayor, I require, on behalf of the National Army, five hundred (or it might be a thousand) pairs of boots, so many beds, such and such provisions."

"But, Citizen Commissioner, we have them not."

Dangeau consulted a notebook.

"I can give you twenty-four hours to produce them, not more."

"But, Citizen, these are impossibilities. We cannot produce what we have not got."

"And neither can our armies save your throats from being cut if they are unprovided. Twenty-four hours, Citizen Mayor."

According to his nature, the Mayor swore or cringed.

"It is impossible."

Dangeau drew out a list. The principal towns of the South figured on it legibly. Setting a thick mark against one name, he fixed his eyes upon the man before him.

"Have you considered, Citizen," he said sternly, "that what is grudged to France will be taken by Spain? Also, it were wiser to yield to my demands than to those of such an embassy as the Republic sent to Lyons. My report goes in to-night."

"Your report?"

"Non-compliance with requisitions is to be reported to the Convention without delay. I have my orders, and you, Citizen Mayor, have yours."

"But, Citizen, where am I to get the things?"

Dangeau shrugged his shoulders.

"Is it my business? But I see you wear an excellent pair of shoes, I see well-shod citizens in your streets-you neither starve nor lie on the ground. Our soldiers do both. If any must go without, let it be the idle. Twenty-four hours, Citizen Mayor."

And in twenty-four hours boots, beds, and provisions were forthcoming. Lyons had not been rased for nothing, and with the smell of her burning yet upon the air, the shriek of her victims still in the wintry wind, no town had the courage to refuse what was asked for. Protestingly they gave; the army was provided, and Dangeau, shutting his ears to Paris and her madness, pressed forward with it into Spain.

## CHAPTER XXIII
## RETURN OF TWO FUGITIVES

"Aline, dear child!"

"Yes, dear aunt."

"I do not think I will leave Marthe to-day, the pain is so bad; but I do not like to disappoint old Mère Leroux. No one's hens are laying but mine, and I promised her an egg for her fête day. She is old, and old people are like children, and very little pleases or makes them unhappy."

Aline folded her work.

"Do you mean you would like me to go? But of course, dear aunt."

"If you will, my child. Take your warm cloak, and be back before sundown; and-Aline — —"

"Yes," said Aline at the door.

"If you see Mathieu Leroux, stop and bid him 'Good-day.' Just say a word or two."

"I do not like Mathieu Leroux," observed Aline, with the old lift of the head.

Mlle. Ange flushed a little.

"He has a good heart, I 'm sure he has a good heart, but he is suspicious by nature. Lately Madelon has let fall a hint or two. It does not do, my child, to let people think one is proud, or-or-in any way different."

Aline's eyes were a little startled.

"What, what do you mean?" she asked.

"Child, need you ask me that?"

"Oh!" she said quickly. "What did Madelon say?"

"Very little. You know she is afraid of her father, and so is Jean Jacques. It was to Marthe she spoke, and Marthe says Mathieu Leroux is a dangerous man; but then you know Marthe's way. Only, if I were you, I should bid him 'Good-day,' and say a friendly word or two as you pass."

As Aline walked down to the village at a pace suited to the sharpness of the February day, Mlle. Ange's words kept ringing in her head. Had Mlle. Marthe warned her far more emphatically, it would have made a slighter impression; but when Ange, who saw good in all, was aware of impending trouble, it seemed to Aline that the prospect was threatening indeed. All at once the pleasant monotony of her life at Rancy appeared to be at an end, and she looked into a cloudy and uncertain future, full of the perils from which she had had so short a respite.

When she came to the inn door and found it filled by the stout form of Mathieu Leroux she did her best to smile in neighbourly fashion; but her eyes sank before his, and her voice sounded forced as she murmured, "Bonjour, Citizen."

Leroux' black eyes looked over his heavy red cheeks at her. They were full of a desire to discover something discreditable about this stranger who had dropped into their little village, and who, though a patriot's wife, displayed none of the signs by which he, Leroux, estimated patriotism.

"Bonjour," he returned, without removing his pipe.

Aline struggled with her annoyance.

"How is your mother to-day?" she inquired. "My aunt has sent her a new-laid egg. May I go in?"

"Eh, she 's well enough," he grumbled. "There is too much fuss made over her. She 'll live this twenty years, and never do another stroke of work. That's my luck. A strong, economical, handy wife must needs die, whilst an old woman, who, you 'd think, would be glad enough to rest in her grave, hangs on and on. Oh, yes, go in, go in; she 'll be glad enough to have some one to complain to."

Aline slipped past him, frightened. He had evidently been drinking, and she knew from Madelon that he was liable to sudden outbursts of passion when this was the case.

In a small back room she found old Mère Leroux crouched by the fire, groaning a little as she rocked herself to and fro. When she saw that Aline was alone, she gave a little cry of disappointment.

"And Mlle. Ange?" she cried in her cracked old voice.

"My aunt Marthe is bad to-day; she could not leave her," explained Aline.

"Oh, poor Ma'mselle Marthe-and I remember her straight and strong and handsome; not a beauty like Ma'mselle Ange, but well enough, well enough. Then she falls down a bank with a great stone on top of her, and there she is, no better than an old woman like me, who has had her life, and whom no one cares for any more."

"Oh, Mère Leroux, you should n't say that!"

"It's true, my dear, true enough. Mathieu is a bad son, a bad son. Some day he 'll turn me out, and I shall go to Madelon. She 's a good girl, Madelon; but when a girl has got a husband, what does she care for an old grandmother? Now Charles was a good son. Yes, if Charles had lived-but then it is always the best who go."

"You had another son, then?" said Aline, bringing a wooden stool to the old woman's side.

"Yes, my son Charles. Ah, a fine lad that, and handsome. He was M. Réné's body servant, and you should have seen him in his livery—a fine, straight man, handsomer than M. Réné. Ah, well, he fretted after his master, and then he took a fever and died of it, and Mathieu has never been a good son to me."

"M. Réné died?" asked Aline quickly, for the old woman had begun to cry.

Mère Leroux dried her eyes.

"Ah, yes; there 's no one who knows more about that than I. He was in Paris, and as he came out of M. le duc de Noailles's Hôtel, he met M. de Brézé, and M. de Brézé said to him, 'Well, Réné, we have been hearing of you,' and M. Réné said, 'How so?' 'Why,' says M. de Brézé (my son Charles was with M. Réné, and he heard it all), 'Why,' says M. de Brézé, 'I hear you have found a guardian angel of quite surpassing beauty. May I not be presented to her?' Then, Charles said, M. Réné looked straight at him and answered, 'When I bring Mme. Réné de Montenay to Paris, I will present you.' M. de Brézé shrugged his shoulders, and slapped M. Réné on the arm. 'Oho,' said he, 'you are very sly, my friend. I was not talking of your marriage, but of your mistress.'

"Then M. Réné put his hand on his sword, and said, still very quietly, 'You have been misinformed; it is a question of my marriage.' Charles said that M. de Brézé was flushed with wine, or he would not have laughed as he did then. Well, well, well, it's a great many years ago, but it was a pity, a sad pity. M. de Brézé was the better swordsman, and he ran M. Réné through the body."

"And he died?" said Aline.

"Not then; no, not then. It would have been better like that-yes, much better."

"Oh, what happened?"

"Charles heard it all. The surgeon attended to the wound, and said that with care it would do well, only there must be perfect quiet, perfect rest. With his own ears he heard that said, and the old Marquise went straight from the surgeon to M. Réné's bedside, and sat down, and took his hand. Charles was in the next room, but the door was ajar, and he could hear and see.

"'Réné, my son,' she said, 'I hear your duel was about Ange Desaix.' M. Réné said, 'Yes, ma mere.' Then she said very scornfully, 'I have undoubtedly been misinformed, for I was told that you fought because-but no, it is too absurd.'

"M. Réné moved his hand. He was all strapped up, but his hand could move, and he jerked it, thus, to stop his mother; and she stopped and looked at him. Then he said, 'I fought M. de Brézé because he spoke disrespectfully of my future wife.' Yes, just like that he said it; and what it must have been to Madame to hear it, Lucifer alone knows, for her pride was like his. There was a long silence, and they looked hard at each other, and then Madame said, 'No!'—only that, but Charles said her face was dreadful, and M. Réné said 'Yes!' almost in a whisper, for he was weak, and then again there was silence. After a long time Madame got up and went out of the room, and M. Réné gave a long sigh, and called Charles, and asked for something to drink. Next day Madame came back. She did not sit down this time, but stood and stared at M. Réné. Big black eyes she had then, and her face all white, as white as his. 'Réné,' she said, 'are you still mad?' and M. Réné smiled and said, 'I am not mad at all.' She put her hand on his forehead. 'You would really do this thing?' she said. 'Lower our name, take as wife what you might have for the asking as mistress?' M. Réné turned in bed at that, and between pain and anger his voice sounded strong and loud. 'Whilst I am alive, there 's no man living shall say that,' he cried. 'On my soul I swear I shall marry her, and on my soul I swear she is fit to be a king's wife.'

"Madame took her hand away, and looked at it for a moment. Afterwards, when Charles told me, I thought, did she wonder if she should see blood on it? And then without another word she went out of the room, and gave orders that her carriages were to be got ready, for she was taking M. Réné to Rancy."

"Oh, no!" said Aline.

"Yes, my dear, yes; and she did it too, and he died of the journey-died calling for Mlle. Ange."

"Oh, did she come?"

"Charles fetched her, and for that Madame never forgave him."

"Oh, how dreadful!"

"Yes, yes, it is sad; but it would have been a terrible mésalliance. A Montenay and his steward's daughter! No, no, it would not have done; one does not do such things."

Aline got up abruptly.

"Oh, I must go," she said. "I promised I would not be long. See, here is the egg."

"You are in such a hurry," mumbled the old woman, confused. She was still in the past, and the sudden change of subject bewildered her.

"I will come again," said Aline gently.

When she was clear of the inn she walked very fast for a few moments, and then stopped. She did not want to go home at once-the story she had just heard had taken possession of her, and she wanted to be alone to adjust her thoughts, to grow accustomed to kind placid Mlle. Ange as the central figure of such a tragedy. After a moment's pause she took the path that led to the château, but stopped short at the high iron gates. Beyond them the avenue looked black and eerie. Her desire to go farther left her, and she leaned against the gates, taking breath after the climb.

The early dusk was settling fast upon the bare woods, and the hollow where the village lay below was already dark and flecked with a light or two. Above, a little yellowish glow lurked behind the low, sullen clouds.

It was very still, and Aline could hear the drip, drip of the moisture which last night had coated all the trees with white, and which to-night would surely freeze again. It was turning very cold; she would not wait. It was foolish to have come, more than foolish to let an old woman's words sting her so sharply—"One does not do such things." Was it her fancy that the dim eyes had been turned curiously upon her for a moment just then? Yes, of course, it was only fancy, for what could Mère Leroux know or suspect? She drew her cloak closer, and was about to turn away when a sound startled her. Close by the gate a stick cracked as if it had been trodden on, and there was a faint brushing sound as of a dress trailing against the bark of a tree. Aline peered into the shadows with a beating heart, and thought she saw some one move. Frightened and unnerved, she caught at the scroll-work of the gate and stared open-eyed, unable to stir; and again something rustled and moved within. This time it was plainly a woman's shape that flitted from one tree to the next—a woman who hid a moment, then leaned and looked, and at last came lightly down the avenue to the gate. Here the last of the light fell on Marguerite de Matigny's face, showing it very white and hollow-eyed. Aline's heart stood still. Could this be flesh and blood? Marguerite here? Not in the flesh, then.

"Marguerite," she breathed.

Marguerite's hand came through the wrought-work and caught at her. It was cold, but human, and Aline recovered herself with a gasp.

"Marguerite, you?"

"And Aline, you? I looked, and looked, and thought 't was you, and at last I thought, well, I 'll risk it. Oh, my dear!"

"But I don't understand. Oh, Marguerite, I thought you were a ghost."

"And wondered why I should come here? Well, I 've some right to, for my mother was a Montenay. Did you not know it?"

"No. But what brings you here, since you are not a ghost, but your very own self?"

"Tiens, Aline, I have wished myself any one or anything but myself this last fortnight! You must know that when I was set free-and oh, ma chérie, I heard it was your husband who saved me, and of course that means you — —"

"Not me," said Aline quickly. "He did it. Who told you?"

"The Abbé Loisel. He knows everything-too much, I think! I don't like him, which is ungrateful, since he got me out of Paris."

"Did he? Where did you go then?"

"Why, to Switzerland, to Bâle, where I joined my father; and then, then-oh, Aline, do you know I am betrothed?"

"My dear, and you are happy?"

Marguerite screwed up her face in an unavailing attempt to keep grave, but after a moment burst out laughing.

"Why, Aline, he is so droll, and a countryman of your own. Indeed, I believe he is a cousin, for his name is Desmond."

"And you like him?"

"Oh, I adore him," said Mlle. Marguerite calmly. "Aline, if you could see him! His hair-well, it's rather red; and he has freckles just like the dear little frogs we used to find by the ponds, Jean and I, when we were children; and his eyes are green and droll-oh, but to make you die of laughing — —"

"He is not handsome, then?" said Aline, laughing too.

"Oh no, ugly-but most adorably ugly, and tall, and broad; and oh, Aline, he is nice, and he says that in Ireland I may love him as much as I please, and no one will think it a breach of decorum."

"Marguerite, you are just the same, you funny child!"

"Well, why not-it's not so long since we saw each other, is it? Only a few months."

"I feel as if it were centuries," said Aline, pressing her hands together.

"Ah, that's because you are married. Ciel! that was a sensation, your marriage. They talked-yes, they talked to split your ears. The things they said — —"

"And you?"

"You are my friend," said Mlle. de Matigny with decision. "But I must go on with my story. Well, I was at Bâle and betrothed, and then my father and Monsieur my fiancé set off to join the Princes, leaving me with Mme. de Montenay, my great-aunt, who is ever so old, and quite, quite mad!"

"Oh, Marguerite!"

"Yes, but she is. Imagine being safe in Bâle, and then coming back here, all across France, just because she could not die anywhere but at the Château de Montenay in Rancy-les-Bois."

"She has come back?"

"Should I be here otherwise?" demanded Marguerite pathetically. "And the journey! —What I endured! —for I saw guillotines round every corner, and suspicious patriots on every doorstep. It is a miracle that we are here; and now that we have come, it is all very well for Madame my aunt, who has come here to die, and requires no food to accomplish that end; but for me, I do not fancy starving, and we have nothing to eat in the house."

"Oh, my poor dear! What made you come?"

"Could I let her come alone? She is too old and too weak; but I ought to have locked the door and kept the key-only, old as she is, she can still make every one do as she wants."

"You are not alone?"

"Jean and Louise, her old servants, started with us; but Jean got himself arrested. Poor Jean, he could not pretend well enough."

"And Louise?"

"Oh, Louise is there, but she is nearly as old as Madame."

"You must have food," said Aline decidedly. "I will bring you some."

"Oh, you angel!" exclaimed Marguerite, kissing her through the bars. "When you came I was standing here trying to screw up my courage to go down to the inn and ask for some."

"Oh, not the inn," said Aline quickly; "that's the last place to go. I 'm afraid there 's danger everywhere, but I 'll do what I can. Go back to the château, and I 'll come as soon as possible."

"Yes, as soon as possible, please, for I am hungry enough to eat you, my dear. See, have n't I got thin-yes, and pale too? I assure you that I have a most interesting air."

"Does M. my cousin find pallor interesting?" inquired Aline teasingly.

"No, my dear; he has a bourgeois's taste for colour. He compared me once to a carnation, but I punished him well for that. I stole the vinegar, and drank enough to make me feel shockingly ill. Then I powdered my cheeks, and then-then I talked all the evening to M. de Maillé!"

"And my cousin, M. le Chevalier, what did he do?"

Marguerite gave an irrepressible giggle.

"He went away, and I was just beginning to feel that perhaps he had been punished enough, when back he came, very easy and smiling, with a sweet large and beautiful bouquet of white carnations, and with an elegant bow he begged me to accept them, since white was my preference, though for his part he preferred the beauteous red that blushed like happy love!"

"And then?"

Marguerite's voice became very demure.

"Poor grandmamma used to say life was compromise, so I compromised; next morning I did not drink vinegar, and I wore a blush pink bud in my hair. M. le Chevalier was pleased to admire it extravagantly."

Aline ran off laughing, but she was grave enough before she had gone very far, for certainly the situation was not an easy one. She racked her brains for a plan, but could find none; and when she came in, Mlle. Marthe's quick eyes at once discerned that something was wrong.

"What is it, child?" she said hastily. "Was Mathieu rude?"

"My dear, how late you are," said Mlle. Ange, looking up from her needlework.

"Not Mathieu?" continued Marthe. "What has happened, Aline? You have not bad news? It is not Jacques?" and her lips grew paler.

"No, no, ma tante."

"What is it, then? Speak, or-or-why, you have been to the château!" she said abruptly, as Aline came into the lamplight.

"Why, Marthe, what makes you say that?" said Ange, in a startled voice.

"The rust on her cloak-see, it is all stained. She has been leaning against the iron gates. What took you there, and what has alarmed you?"

"I—I saw——"

"A ghost?" inquired Marthe with sharp sarcasm.

Ange rose up, trembling.

"Oh, she has come back! I know it, I have felt it! She has come back," she cried.

"Ange, don't be a fool," said Marthe, but her eyes were anxious.

"Speak then, Aline, and tell us what you saw."

"It is true, she has come back," said Aline, looking away from Mlle. Ange, who put her hands before her eyes with a little cry and stood so a full minute, whilst Marthe gave a harsh laugh, and then bit her lip as if in pain.

"Come back to die?" Ange said at last, very low. "Alone?"—and she turned on Aline.

"No, a niece is with her. It was she whom I saw. I knew her in Paris-in prison; and, ma tante, they have no food in the house, and I said I would take them some."

"No food goes from this house to that," said Marthe loudly, but Ange caught her hand.

"Oh, we can't let them starve."

"And why not, Angel, why not? The old devil! She has done enough mischief in the world, and now that her time has come, let her go. Does she expect us, us, to weep for her?"

"No, no; but I can't let her starve-you know I can't."

Marthe laughed again.

"No, perhaps not, but I could, and I would." She paused. "So you 'd heap coals of fire-feed her, save her, eh, Angel?"

"Oh, Marthe, don't! For the love of God, don't speak to me like that-when you know-when you know!"

Marthe pulled her down with an impulsive gesture that drew a groan from her.

"Ah, Ange," she said in a queer, broken voice; and Ange kissed her passionately and ran out of the room.

There was a long, heavy pause. Then Marthe said:

"So you've heard the story? Who told you?"

"Mère Leroux, to-night."

"And a very suitable occasion. Who says life is not dramatic? So Mère Leroux told you, and you went up to the château to see if it was haunted, and it was. Ciel, if those stones could speak! But there 's enough without that-quite enough."

She was silent again, and after awhile Mlle. Ange came back, wrapped in a thick cloak and carrying a basket.

Aline started forward.

"Ma tante, I may come too? It is so dark."

"And the dark is full of ghosts?" said Ange Desaix, under her breath. "Well, then, child, you may come. Indeed, the basket is heavy, and I shall be glad of your help."

Outside, the night had settled heavily, and without the small lantern which Mlle. Ange produced from under her cloak, it would have been impossible to see the path. A little breeze had risen and seemed to follow them, moaning among the leafless boughs, and rustling the dead leaves below. They walked in silence, each with a hand on the heavy basket. It was very cold, and yet oppressive, as if snow were about to fall or a storm to break. Mlle. Ange led the way up a bridle-path, and when the grey pile of the château loomed before them she turned sharply to the left, and Aline felt her hand taken. "This way," whispered Ange; and they stumbled up a broken step or two, and passed through a long, shattered window. "This way," said Ange again. "Mon Dieu, how long since I came here! Ah, mon Dieu!"

The empty room echoed to their steps and to that low-voiced exclamation, and the lantern light fell waveringly upon the shadows, driving them into the corners, where they crowded like ghosts out of that past of which the room seemed full.

It was a small room, and had been exquisite. Here and there a moulded cupid still smiled its dimpled smile, and clutched with plump, engaging fingers at the falling garland of white, heavy-bloomed roses which served it for girdle and plaything. In one corner a tattered rag of brocade still showed that the hangings had been green. Ange looked round mournfully.

"It was Madame's boudoir," she said slowly, with pauses between the sentences. "Madame sat here, by the window, because she liked to look out at the terrace, and the garden her Italian mother had made. Madame was beautiful then-like a picture, though her hair was too white to need powder. She had little hands, soft like a child's hands; but her eyes looked through you, and at once you thought of all the bad things you had ever done or thought. It was worse than confession, for there was no absolution afterwards." She paused and moved a step or two.

"I sat here. The hours I have read to her, or worked whilst she was busy with her letters!"

"You!" said Aline, surprised.

"Yes, I, her godchild, and a pet until-come then, child, until I forgot I was on the same footing as cat or dog, petted for their looks, and presumed to find a common humanity in myself and her. Ah, Marraine, it was you who made me a Republican. Oh, my child, pride is an evil god to serve! Don't sacrifice your life to him as mine was sacrificed."

She crossed hastily to the door as she spoke, and they came through a corridor to the great stairs, where the darkness seemed to lie in solid blocks, and the faint lantern light showed just one narrow path on which to set their feet. And on that path the dust lay thick; here drifted into mounds, and there spread desert-smooth along the broad, shallow steps, eloquent of desolation indescribable. But on the centre of the grey smoothness was a footmark-very small and lonely-looking. It seemed to make the gloom more eerie, the stillness more terrible, and the two women kept close together as they went up the stair.

At the top another corridor, and then a door in front of which Ange hesitated long. Twice she put out her hand, and twice drew back, until at last it was Aline who lifted the latch and drew her through the doorway. Darkness and silence.

Across that room, and to another. Darkness and silence still. At the third door Ange came forward again.

"It is past," she said, half to herself, and went in before Aline.

Whilst the west was all in darkness, this long east room fronted the rising moon, and the shimmer of it lay full across the chamber, making it light as day. Here the dust had been lately disturbed, for it hung like a mist in the air, and its shining particles floated all a-glitter in the broad wash of silver. Full in the moonlight stood a great canopied bed, its crimson hangings all wrenched away, and trailing to the dusty floor, where they lay like some ineffaceable stain of rusting blood. On the dark hearth a handful of sticks burned to a dull red ash, and between fire and moon there was a chair. It stood in to the hearth, as if for warmth, but aslant so that the moon shaft lay across it.

Ange set down the lantern and took a quick step forward, crying, "Madame!" Something stirred in the tattered chair, something grey amongst the grey of the shadows. It was like the movement of the roused spider, for here was the web, all dust and moonshine, and here, secret and fierce, grey and elusive, lurked the weaver. The shape in the chair leaned forward, and the oldest woman's face she had ever seen looked at Aline across the moted moonlight. The face was all grey; the bony ridge above the deep eye-pits, the wrinkled skin that lay beneath, the shrivelled, discoloured lips-plainly this was a woman not only old, but dying. Then the lids lifted, and Aline could have screamed, for the movement showed eyes as smoulderingly bright as the sudden sparks which fly up from grey ash that should be cold, but has still a heart of flame if stirred. They spoke of the indomitable will which had dragged this old, frail woman here to die.

Through the silence came a mere thread of a voice —

"Who is it?"

"I am Ange Desaix."

The shrivelled fingers picked at the shrouding shawl. Aline, watching uneasily, saw the pinched face fall into a new arrangement of wrinkles. The mouth opened like a pit, and from it came an attenuated sound. With creeping flesh she realised that this was a laugh-Madame was laughing.

"Ange Desaix, Ange Desaix-Réné's Angel. Oh, la belle comédie!"

"Madame!" the sound came like a sob, and in a flash Aline guessed how long it was since any one had named Réné de Montenay before this woman who had loved him. After the silence of nearly forty years it stabbed her like a sword thrust.

Again that faint sound like the echo of laughter long dead:

"My compliments, Mlle. Desaix. Will you not be seated, and let me know to what I owe the pleasure of this visit? But you are not alone. Who is that with you? Come here!"

Aline crossed the room obediently.

"Who are you?" said the faint voice again, and the burning eyes looked searchingly into her face.

Something stirred in Aline. This old wreck of womanhood was not only of her order, but of her kin. Before she knew it she heard her own voice say:

"I am Aline de Rochambeau."

Ange Desaix gave a great start. She had guessed-but this was certainty, and the shock took her breath. From the chair a minute, tiny hand was beckoning.

"Rochambeau, Rochambeau. I know all the Rochambeau-Réné de Rochambeau was my first cousin, for I was a Montenay born, you know. He and his brother were the talk of the town when I was young. They married the twin heiresses of old M. de Vivonne, and every one sang the catch which M. de Coulanges made —

> Fiers et beaux, les Rochambeau;
>
> Fiere et bonnes, les belles Vivonne.'

Whose daughter are you?"

Aline knelt by the chair and kissed the little claw where a diamond shone from the gold circlet which was so much too loose.

"Réné de Rochambeau was my grandfather," she said.

"Well, he would have thought you a pretty girl. Beauty never came amiss to a Rochambeau, and you have your share. We are kinsfolk, Mademoiselle, and in other circumstances, I should have wished-have wished —" she drew her hand away impatiently and put it to her head. "Who said that Ange Desaix was here? Why does she come now? Réné is dead, and I have no more sons; I am really a little at a loss."

The words which should have sounded pathetic came in staccato mockery, and Aline sprang up in indignation, but even as she moved Mlle. Ange spoke.

"Let the past alone, Madame," she said slowly. "Believe, if you can, that I have come to help you. You are not alone?"

"I have Louise, but she-really, I forget where she is at present, but she is not cooking, for we have nothing to cook. It is as well that I have come here to die, since for that there are always conveniences. One dies more comfortably chez soi. In fact, unless one had the honour of dying on the field of battle, there is to my mind something bourgeois about dying in a strange place. At least, it has never been our habit. Now I recollect when Réné was dying-dear me, how many years ago it is now?"

"It is thirty-seven years ago," said Ange Desaix in low muffled tones.

"Thank you, Mademoiselle, you are quite correct. Well, thirty-seven years ago, you, with that excellent memory of yours, will recall how I brought my son Réné here, that he might die at home."

"Yes," said Ange. "You brought him home that he might die."

The slight change of words was an accusation, and there was a moment's silence, broken by an almost inaudible whisper from Mlle. Ange.

"Thirty-seven years. Oh, mon Dieu!"

The tremulous grey head moved a little, bent forward, and was propped by a shaking hand, but Madame's eyes shone unalterably amused.

"Yes, my dear Ange, he died-unmarried, and I had the consolations of religion, and also of knowing that a mésalliance is not possible in the grave."

Ange Desaix started forward with a sob.

"And have you never repented, Madame, have you never repented? Never thought that you might have had his children about your knees? That night, when I saw him die, I said, 'God will punish,' and are you not punished? You have neither son nor grandson; you are childless as I am childless; you are alone and the last of your line!"

The sudden fire transfigured her, and she looked like a prophetess. Madame de Montenay stared at her and fell to fidgeting with her shawl.

"I am too old for scenes," she said fretfully. "Réné was a fool —a fool. I never interfered with his amusements, but marriage-that is not an affair for oneself alone. Did he think I should permit? But it is enough, he is dead, and I think you forget yourself, Ange Desaix, when you come to my house and talk to me in such a strain. I should like to be alone."

The old imperious note swelled the thin voice; the old imperious gesture raised the trembling hand. Even in her recoil Aline felt a faint thrill of admiration as for something indomitable, indestructible.

Ange swept through the door.

"Ah!" she said with a long shuddering breath, "ah, mon Dieu! mon Dieu!" All her beautiful dreamy expression was gone. "Ah! what a coward I am; even now, even now she frightens me, cows me," and she leaned panting against the wall, whilst Aline closed the door.

Out of the darkness Marguerite came trembling.

"Aline, what is it?" she whispered. "I heard you, and came as far as the door, and then, Holy Virgin, is n't she terrible? She makes me cold like ice, and her laugh, it 's—oh, one does not know how to bear it!"

Mlle. Ange turned, collecting herself.

"Is it Louise?" she asked.

"No, I am Marguerite de Matigny. Louise is in the corridor."

"Let us come away from here," said Aline, taking the lantern, and they hastened through the two dark rooms, meeting Louise at the farthest door. She was a tall, haggard woman, with loose grey hair and restless, terrified eyes. Mlle. Ange drew her aside, whispering, and after a moment the fear went out of her face, leaving a sallow exhaustion in its place.

"It is a miracle," she was saying as Aline and Marguerite joined them. "The saints know how we got here. I remember nothing, I am too tired; and Madame-how she is not dead! Nothing would hold her, when the doctor told her she had a mortal complaint. If you know Madame, you will know that she laughed. 'Mon Dieu,' she said to me, 'I have had one mortal complaint for ten years now, and that is old age, but since he says I have another, no doubt he is right, and the two together will kill me.' Then she said, 'Pack my mail, Louise, for I do not choose to die here, where no one has ever heard of the Montenay.' 'But, Mademoiselle,' I said, and Madame shrugged her shoulders. 'But the Terror,' I said, and indeed, Ma'mselle, I went on my knees to her, but if you think she cared! Not the least in the world, and here we are, and God knows what comes next! I am afraid, very much afraid, Ma'mselle."

"Yes, and so am I," whispered Marguerite, pinching Aline's arm. "It is really dreadful here. La tante mad, and this old house all ghosts and horrors, and nothing to eat, it is triste-yes, I can tell you it is triste."

"We will come again," said Aline, kissing her, "and at least there is food here."

"Yes, take the basket, Louise," said Mlle. Ange, "and now we must go."

"Oh, no, don't go," cried Marguerite. "Stay just a little —" but Louise broke in — —

"No, no, Ma'mselle, let them go. Madame would not be pleased. I thought I heard her call just now." She shrugged her shoulders expressively, and Marguerite released her friend with a little sobbing kiss.

"Come, Aline," said Mlle. Ange with dignity, and they went down the echoing stair in silence.

Neither spoke for a long while. Then amongst the deeper shadows of the wood Aline heard a curiously strained voice say:

"So you are Rochambeau, and noble?"

"Yes."

"Marthe said so from the first; she is always right."

"Yes."

A little pause, and then Ange said passionately:

"What made you give that name? Are you ashamed to be called Dangeau?"

"She was so old, and of my kin; I said the name that she would know. Oh, I do not know why I said it," faltered Aline.

"Does he know it, Jacques?"

"Yes, oh yes!"

"He knew before you were married?"

"Yes, always; he has been so good."

"So good, and you his wife, and could deny his name! I do not understand you, Aline de Rochambeau."

Aline flushed scarlet in the darkness. Her own name spoken thus seemed to set a bruise upon her heart.

"It was not that," she cried: "I do not know why I said it, but it was not to deny-him."

Her voice sank very low, and something in it made Ange halt a moment and say:

"Aline, do you love Jacques?"

Aline's hand went to her breast.

"Yes," she said under her breath, and thought the whole wood echoed with the one soft word.

"And does he know that too?" The questioning voice had sunk again to gentleness.

"No, no-oh, no."

"Poor child," said Agnes Desaix, and after that they spoke no more.

## CHAPTER XXIV
## BURNING OF THE CHÂTEAU

Mlle. Marthe lay in the dusk frowning and knitting her brows until they made a straight dark line over her restless eyes. A sense of angry impotence possessed her and found expression in a continual sharp movement of head and hand; the stabbing physical pain evoked was sheer relief to the strained mind. Two days had now passed since the first expedition to the château, and every hour of them had seemed more heavily weighted with impending danger. Nothing would persuade Mme. de Montenay to move, or Ange to leave her to her fate. Louise was tearful, and useless; Marguerite, a lonely child, terrified of the great shadowed rooms, and clinging eagerly to her friend;—a complication, in fact, which roused Mlle. Marthe's anger more than all the rest, since even her resolution recoiled from the abandonment of a young girl, who had no share in Mme. de Montenay's obstinacy. Marthe fretted, turned a little, groaned, and bit her lip.

As the door opened she looked up sharply, but it was only Jeanne, who came to ask her if she should light the lamp, and got a snappish "No!" for answer.

"It is dark, Ma'mselle," she said.

"I will wait till they come in."

"Eh-it 's queer weather, and a queer time of day to be out," muttered Jeanne sulkily.

"Madame is young; she needs exercise," said Marthe, prompted by something in the woman's tone.

"Ah, yes, exercise," said Jeanne in a queer voice, and she went out, shutting the door sharply. Mlle. Marthe's thoughts kept tone with the darkening sky. Her eyes watched the door with an anxious stare. When at last Ange and Aline came in snow-sprinkled and warm, her temper was fretted to a sharp edge, and she spoke with quick impatience.

"Mon Dieu, how long you have been! If you must go, you must, but there is no occasion to stay and stay, until I am beside myself with wondering what has happened!"

Ange threw off her wet cloak and bent to kiss her sister. "Oh, my dearest, has it been so long?" she said. "Why, I thought we were being so quick, and that you would commend us. We did not wait at all, only gave the food to Louise and came straight back. Has the pain been bad then, my poor darling? Have you wanted anything?"

Marthe pushed her away with an angry jerk.

"What I want is a way out of this abominable situation," she exclaimed. "If you had any common-sense, Ange-the slightest instinct of self-preservation—but no, you will sacrifice all our lives to that wicked old woman, and then flatter yourself that you have done something to be proud of. Come here to die, has she? Heavens, she 'll outlive us all, and then go happy in the thought that she has contrived to do a little more mischief before the end!"

Ange winced, but only said gently:

"Dearest, don't."

"There, Ange, I 've no patience! I tell you we are all on the brink of ruin. Madelon has been here."

"Madelon? Ah, the dear child. It is so long since I have really seen her. I am sorry to have missed her. Was she well?"

Mlle. Marthe caught her sister's hand and pressed it until she cried out, "Marthe, you are hurting me!"

"Ange! Sometimes I could swear at you! For Heaven's sake think of yourself for a few moments, or if that is asking too much, think of Aline, think of me. Madelon came here because her father sent her!"

"Her father sent her! Marthe, dearest, don't—that hurts."

"I mean it to. Yes, her father——"

"But why. I don't understand."

Aline had been lighting the lamp. She looked up now, and the yellow flare showed the trouble in her face.

"Oh, ma tante," she breathed.

"Yes, child. Ange, wake up; don't you realise?"

"Mathieu suspects?" asked Aline quickly. "But how?"

"He saw you take the path to the château the other day. Saw, or thought he saw, a light in the west wing last night, and sent Madelon to find out how much we knew. A mischief-maker Mathieu, and a bad man-devil take him."

"Oh, Marthe, don't. Madelon-Madelon is as true as steel."

"Oh, yes, but mightily afraid of her father. She sat here with her round cheeks as white as curds, and cried, and begged me not to tell her anything; —as if I should be such a fool."

"Ah, poor Madelon," said Ange, "she must not distress herself like that, it is so bad for her just now."

Marthe ground her teeth.

"Ange, I won't have it—I won't. I tell you all our lives are at stake, and you discuss Madelon's health."

"My dearest, don't be vexed; indeed, I am trying to think what can be done."

"Now, Ange, listen to me. If you will go on with this mad business, there is only one thing to be done. I have thought it all out. They must do with as little as possible, and you must not go there oftener than once in four days. You will go at eleven o'clock at night when there is no one abroad, and Louise will meet you half-way and take the basket on. There must be no other communication of any sort: you hear me, Aline?"

"Yes," said Aline, "I think you are quite right."

"That is always a consolation." Marthe's voice took a sarcastic tone. "Now, Ange, do you agree?"

"If you really think——"

"Why, yes, I do. Ange, I 'm a cross animal, but I can't see you throw your life away and not say a word. I 'm a useless cripple enough, but I have the use of my tongue. Will you promise?"

"Well-yes."

"That's right. Now for goodness let's talk about something else. If there 's going to be trouble it will come, and we need n't go over and over it all before it does come. Aline, do, for the love of heaven, remember that I cannot bear the light in my eyes like that. Put the lamp over here, behind me, and then you can take a book and read aloud so as to give us all a chance of composing our minds."

Aline waked late that night. All the surface calm in her had been broken up by the events of the last few days. The slight sprinkling of snow had ceased, but there was a high wind abroad, and as it complained amongst the stripped and creaking woods, it seemed to voice the yearning that strained the very fibres of her being.

She stood at midnight and looked out. Very high and pale rode the moon, and the driving cloud wrack swept like shallow, eddying water across the one clear space of sky in which she queened it. All below was dense, dull, cloud mass, darkening to the hill slope, and the black sighing woodland. Thoughts drove in her brain, like the driving cloud. Sadness of life, imminence of death, shortness of love. She had seen an ugly side of ancestral pride in these two days, and suddenly she glimpsed a vision of herself grown old and grey, looking back along the interminable years to the time when she had sacrificed youth and love. Then it would be too late. Life was irrevocable; but now-now? She threw open her window and leaned far out, drawing the strong air into her lungs, whilst the wind caught her hair and spread it all abroad. The spirit of life, of youth, cried to her, and she stretched her arms wide and mingled her voice with its voice. "Jacques!" she called under her breath, "Jacques!" and then as suddenly she drew back trembling and hid her face in her cold hands.

She did not know how the time passed after that, but when she looked up again there was a faint glow in the sky. She watched it curiously, thinking for a moment that it was the dawn, and then aware that morning must still be far away.

A tinge of rose brightened the cloud bank over the hill, and at its edge the ether showed blue. Then quite suddenly a tongue of fire flared above the trees and sank again. As the flames rose a second time Ange Desaix was in the room.

"Aline! The château! It is on fire!" she cried. "Oh, mon Dieu, what shall we do?"

They ran out, wrapped hastily in muffling cloaks, and as they climbed the hill Ange spoke in gasps.

"They must have seen it in the village before we did. All the world will be there. Oh, that poor child! God help us all!"

"Oh, come quickly!" cried Aline, and they took hands and ran. The slope once mounted, the path so dark a few hours back was illuminated. A red, unnatural dusk filled the wood, and against it the trees stretched great black groping arms. The sky was like the reflection from some huge furnace, and all the way the fire roared in the rising wind.

"How could it have happened? Do you think-oh, do you suppose this is what she meant to do?" Aline asked once, and Ange gave a sort of sob as she answered:

"Oh, my dear, God knows-but I 'm afraid so," and then they pushed on again in silence.

They came out of the bridle-path into the cypress walk that led to Madame's Italian garden. At a turn the flaming building came into view for the first time. South and east it burned furiously, but the west front, that which faced them, was still intact, though the smoke eddied about it, and a dull glare from the windows spoke of rooms beyond that were already in the grip of the flames. Between low hedges of box the two pressed on, and climbed the terrace steps.

Here the heat drove to meet them full of stinging particles of grit. The hot blast dried the skin and stung the eyes. The wind blew strongly from the east, but every now and then it veered, and then the fire lapped round the corner and was blown out in long dreadful tongues, which licked the walls as if tasting them, and threw a crimson glare along the dark west wing. Great sparks like flashes of flame flew high and far, and the dense reek made breathing painful.

"Look!" said Aline, catching her companion by the arm, and pointing. From where they stood the broad south terrace was full in view, and the fire lighted it brilliantly. Below it, where the avenue ceased, was a small crowd of dark gesticulating figures, intent on the blazing pile.

"They can't see us," said Ange; "but come this way, here, where the statue screens us."

They paused a moment, leaning against the pedestal where a white Diana lifted an arrow against the glare. Then both cried out simultaneously, for driven by a sudden gust the smoke wreaths parted, and for a moment they saw at a window above them a moving whiteness-an arm thrust out, only to fall again, and hang with fatal limpness across the sill.

"Ah, it was Marguerite," cried Aline with catching breath. "I saw her face. Marguerite! Marguerite!"

"Hush!" said Mlle. Ange. "It is no use calling. She has fainted. Thank God she came this way. There is a stair if I could only find it. Once I knew it well enough."

As she spoke she hurried into the smoke, and Aline followed, gasping.

"Your cloak over your face, child, and remember you must not faint."

How they gained the boudoir, Aline hardly knew, but she found herself there with the smoke all round, pressing on her like a solid thing, blinding, stinging, choking. Ahead of her Mlle. Ange groped along the wall. Once she staggered, but with a great effort kept on, and at last stopped and pressed with all her strength.

In the darkness appeared a darker patch, and then, just as Aline's throbbing senses seemed about to fail her, she felt her hand caught, she was pulled through a narrow opening, her feet felt steps, mounted instinctively, and her lungs drew in a long, long breath of relief, for here the smoke had hardly penetrated, and the air, though heavy, was quite fit to breathe. For a moment they halted and then climbed on. The stair went steeply up, wound to the left, and ceased. Then again Ange stood feeling for the catch with fingers that had known it well enough in the dead days. Now they hesitated, tried here and there, failed of the secret, and went groping to and fro, until Aline's blood beat in her throat, and she could have cried out with fear and impatience. The moment seemed interminable, and the smoke mounted behind them in ever-thickening whirls.

"It was here, mon Dieu, what has become of it? So many years ago, but I thought I could have found it blindfold. Réné showing me-his hand on mine-ah, at last," and with that the murmuring voice ceased, and the panelling slipped smoothly back, letting in more smoke, to press like a nightmare upon their already labouring lungs. Through it the window showed a red square, against which was outlined a white, huddled shape. It was Marguerite, who lay just as she had fallen, head bowed, one hand thrust out, the other at her throat. Ange and Aline stood by her for a moment leaning from the window, and taking in what air they might, and then the confusion and the stumbling began once more, only this time they had a weight to carry, and could shield neither eyes nor lungs from the pervading smoke. Twice they stopped, and twice that dreadful roar of the fire, a roar that drowned even the heavy beat of their burdened pulses, drove them on again, until at last they stumbled out upon the terrace, and there halted, gasping terribly. The intolerable heat dripped from them in a black sweat, and for a while they crouched trembling in every limb. Then Ange whispered with dry lips:

"We must go on. This is not safe."

They staggered forward once more, and even as they did so there was a most appalling crash, and the flames rushed up like a pyramid to heaven, making all the countryside light with a red travesty of day. Urged by terror, and with a final effort, they dragged Marguerite down the steps, and on, until they sank at last exhausted under a cypress which watched the pool where the fountain played no more.

In a minute or two Aline recovered sufficiently to wet the hem of her cloak and bathe Marguerite's face. This and the cold air brought her to with a shudder and a cry. She sat up coughing, and clung to Aline.

"Oh, save me, save me!"

"Chérie, you are saved."

"And they are burnt. Oh, Holy Virgin, I shall see it always."

"Don't talk of it, my dear!"

"Oh, I must. I saw it, Aline; I saw it! There was a little thread of fire that ran up Louise's skirt, like a gold wire. Oh, mon Dieu! They are burnt."

"Madame?" asked Ange, very low.

"Yes, yes; and Louise, poor Louise! I was so cross with her last night; but I did n't know. I would n't have been if I had known. Oh, poor Louise!"

"Tell us what happened, my dear, if you can."

"Oh, I don't know." Marguerite hid her face a moment, and then spoke excitedly, pushing back her dishevelled hair. "I woke up with the smoke in my throat, and ran in to la tante's room. She had n't gone to bed at all. There she was in her big chair, sitting up straight, Louise on her knees begging her to get up, and all between the boards of the floor there was smoke coming up, as if there were a great fire underneath."

"Underneath! It began below, then?"

"Yes, Aline, she did it herself! She must have crept down and set light in ever so many places. Yes, it is true, for she boasted of it. 'Ange Desaix says I am the last of the Montenay. Very well, then; she shall see, and the world shall see, how Montenay and I will go together!' That is what she said, and Louise screamed, 'Save yourself, Ma'mselle!' But la tante nodded and said, 'Yes, if you have wings, use them, by all means.' It was like some perfectly horrid dream. I ran through the rooms to see if I could get down the stairs, but they were all in a blaze. Then I ran back again; but when I was still some way from the door I saw that the fire was coming up through the floor. Louise gave one great scream, but la tante just sat and smiled, and then the floor gave way, and they went down with a crash. Oh, Aline-Aline!"

"Oh, Marguerite, my dear-and you?"

Marguerite shuddered.

"I ran across the corridor and into the farthest room, and the smoke came after me, and I fainted, and then you came and saved me."

"Hush! there is some one coming," said Mlle. Ange in a quick whisper.

They crouched down and waited breathlessly. Then, after an agonised struggle, Marguerite coughed, and at once a dark figure bore down on them.

"Thank the Saints I have found you," said Madelon's voice.

Aline sprang up.

"Madelon-you? How did you know?"

"Ah! Bah—I saw you when you crossed the terrace. I saw you were carrying some one. Is it Madame?"

"No, no; a girl-younger than we are. Oh, Madelon, you will help us?"

"Well, at least I won't harm you-you know that; but you are safe enough, so far, for no one else saw you. They were all watching to see the roof fall in over there to the right, and I should have been watching too, only that my cousin Anne had just been scolding me so for being there at all. She said my baby would have St. John's fire right across his face. She herself has a red patch over one eye, and only because her mother would sit staring at the embers. Well, I thought I would be prudent, so I bade Jean Jacques look instead of me, and turned my head the other way, and, just as the flames shot up, I saw you cross the terrace and go down the steps. And now, what are you going to do with Mademoiselle?"

This most pertinent question took them all aback, and Marguerite looked up with round, bewildered eyes; she certainly had no suggestions to make. At last Mlle. Ange said slowly:

"She must come home with us."

"Impossible! No, no, that would never do, dear Ma'mselle."

"But there is nothing else to be done."

"Oh, there must be. Why, you could not hide an infant in your house. Everything is known in the village-and—I should not trust Jeanne overmuch."

"Madelon! Jeanne? She has been with us a life-time."

"Maybe, but she hates the Montenay more than she loves you and Mlle. Marthe. Also, she is jealous of Madame here-and-in fact, she has talked too much already."

"Then what is to be done?" asked Ange distractedly. She was trembling and unnerved. That a man's foes could be they of his own household, was one of those horrible truths which now came home to her for the first time. "Jeanne," she kept repeating; "no, it is not possible that Jeanne would do anything to harm us."

Madelon drew Aline aside.

"Jeanne is an old beast," she said frankly. "I always said so; but until the other day I did not think she was unfaithful. Now-well, I only tell you that my father said she had given him 'valuable information.' What do you make of that, eh?"

"What you do," said Aline calmly.

"Well, then, what next?"

"What do you advise?"

"Seigneur! Don't put it on me. What is there to advise?"

As she spoke, with a shrug of her plump shoulders, Marguerite came forward. In her white undergarment, with her brown hair loose and curling, and her brown eyes brimmed with tears, she looked like a punished child. Even the smuts on her face seemed to add somehow to the youth and pathos of her appearance.

"Oh, Aline," she said, with a half sob, "where am I to go? What am I to do?" And in a moment the mother in Madelon melted in her.

"There, there, little Ma'mselle," she said quickly, "there 's nothing to cry about. You shall come along with me, and if I can't give you as fine a bed as you had in this old gloomy place, at any rate it will be a safer one, and, please the Saints, you 'll not be burnt out of it."

"No, no, Madelon, you mustn't," said Mlle. Ange.

"And why not, chère Ma'mselle?"

"The danger-your father-your good husband. It would not be fair. I will not let you do what you have just said would be so dangerous."

"Dangerous for you, but not for me. Who is going to suspect me? As to Jean Jacques, you need n't be afraid of him. Thank God he is no meddler, and what I do is right in his eyes."

"Dear child, he is a good husband; but-but just now you should not have anxiety or run any risks."

Madelon laughed, and then grew suddenly grave.

"Ah, you mean my baby. Why, you are just like Anne; but there, Ma'mselle, do you really think le bon Dieu would let my baby suffer because I tried to help poor little Ma'mselle here, who does n't look much more than a baby herself?"

Ange kissed her impulsively.

"God bless you, my dear," she said. "You are a good woman, Madelon."

"Well, then, it is settled. Here, take my cloak, Ma'mselle. What is your name? Ma'mselle Marguerite, then-no, not yours; it is much better that you should not come into the matter any more, Ma'mselle Ange, nor you, Madame. Ma'mselle Marguerite will put on my cloak and come along with me, and as quickly as possible, since Jean Jacques will be getting impatient."

"Where is he, then?" asked Aline.

"Oh, yonder behind the big cypress. I left him there to keep a look-out and tell us if any one came this way. He has probably gone to sleep, my poor Jean Jacques. It took me a quarter of an hour to wake him, the great sleepy head. He had no desire to come, not he, and will be only too thankful to be allowed to go back to bed again."

"Now, Ma'mselle, are you ready?"

They went off together into the shadows, and Ange and Aline took their way home to remove the smoke and grime, and to tell Mlle. Marthe the events of the night.

## CHAPTER XXV
## ESCAPE OF TWO MADCAPS

"Well, it is a mercy, only what's to happen next?" said Mlle. Marthe in the morning.

"I don't know," said Aline doubtfully.

Marthe caught her sister's hand.

"Now, Ange, promise me to keep out of it, and you, Aline, I require you to do the same. Madelon is a most capable young woman, and if she and Jean Jacques can't contrive something, yes, and run next to no risk in doing so, you may be sure that you won't do any better. The sooner the girl is got out of the place the better, and while she 's here, for Heaven's sake act with prudence, and don't go sniffing round the secret, like a dog with a hidden bone, until every one knows it's there."

"My dearest, you forget we can't desert Madelon."

"My dear Ange, you may be a good woman, but sometimes I think you 're a bit of a fool. Don't you see that Madelon is not in the least danger as long as you keep well away from her? Who does Mathieu suspect? Us. Well, and if you and Aline are always in Madelon's pocket, do you think he will put it all down to an interest in that impending infant of hers? He 's not such a fool-and I wish to Heaven you weren't."

This adjuration produced sufficient effect to make Mlle. Ange pass Madelon on the road that very afternoon with no more than a dozen words on either side.

"Approve of me," she said laughingly on her return. "It was really very, very good of me, for there were a hundred things I was simply dying to say."

Mlle. Marthe was pleased to smile.

"Oh, you can be very angelic when you like, my Angel. Kindly remember that goodness is your rôle, and stick to this particular version of it."

"Madelon says the poor child is rested. She has put her in the loft where she stored her winter apples."

"Sensible girl. Now you would have given her the best bed, if it meant everybody's arrest next moment."

"Oh, if it pleases you to say so, you may, but I 'm not really quite so foolish as you try to make me out. Mathieu thinks everyone was burnt."

"Well, one hoped he would. For Heaven's sake keep out of the whole matter, and he 'll continue to think so."

"Yes, I will. I see you are right, dearest. Jean Jacques has a plan. After a few days he thinks he could get her out of the place. Madelon would not tell me more."

"Oho, Mademoiselle Virtue, then it was Madelon who was good, not you."

"We were both good," asserted Ange demurely.

After that there were no further confidences between Madelon and the ladies of the white house. If they met on the road, they nodded, passed a friendly greeting, and went each on her own way without further words.

Ten days went by and brought them to the first week of March. It came in like the proverbial lamb, with dewy nights which sparkled into tender sunny days. The brushwood tangles reddened with innumerable buds; here and there in the hedgerow a white violet appeared like a belated snowflake, and in the undergrowth primrose leaves showed fresh and green. Aline gave herself up to these first prophecies of spring. She roamed the woods and lanes for hours, finding in every budded tree, in every promised flower, not only the sweetest memories of her childhood, but also, God knows what, of elusive beckoning hopes that played on the spring stirring in her blood, as softly as the Lent breeze, which brought a new blush to her cheek. One exquisite afternoon found her still miles from home. So many birds were singing that no one could have felt the loneliness of the countryside. She turned with regret to make her way towards Rancy, taking here a well-known and there an unfamiliar path. Nearer home she struck into the woods by a new and interesting track. It wandered a good deal, winding this way and that until she lost her bearings and had no longer any clear notion of what direction she was taking. Presently a sweetness met her, and with a little exclamation of pleasure she went on her knees before the first purple violets of the year. It seemed a shame to pick, but impossible to leave them, and by searching carefully she obtained quite a bunch, salving her conscience with the thought of what pleasure they would give Mlle. Marthe, who seemed so much more suffering of late.

"It is the spring-it will pass," Ange said repeatedly.

Aline walked on, violets in hand, wondering why the spring, which brought new life to all Nature, should bring-she caught herself up with a shiver-Death? Of course there was no question of death. How foolish of her to think of it, but having thought, the thought clung until she dwelt painfully upon it, and every moment it needed a stronger effort to turn her mind away. So immersed was she that she did not notice at all where she was going. The little path climbed on, pursued a tortuous way, and suddenly brought her out to the east of the château, and in full view of its ruined pile, where the blackened mass of it still smoked faintly, and one high skeleton wall towered gaunt and bare, its empty window spaces like the eyeless stare of a skull.

The sun was behind it, throwing it into strong relief, and the sight brought back the sort of terror which the place had always had for Aline. She walked on quickly, skirting the ruins and keeping to the outer edge of the wide terraces, on her way to the familiar bridle-path, which was her quickest way home. When she came into the Italian garden she paused, remembering the nightmare of that struggle for Marguerite's life. The pool with its low stone rim reflected nothing more terrible than sunset clouds now, but she still shuddered as she thought how the smoke and flame had woven strange spirals on its clear, passive mirror. She stooped now, and dipped her violets in the water to keep them fresh. Her own eyes looked back at her, very bright and clear, and she smiled a little as she put up a hand to smooth a straying curl. Then, of a sudden she saw her own eyes change, grow frightened. A step sounded on the path behind her, and another face appeared in the pool—a man's face-and a stranger's.

Aline got up quickly and turned to see a tall young man in a riding-dress, who slapped his boot with a silver-headed cane and exclaimed gallantly:

"Venus her mirror, no less! Faith, my lady Venus, can you tell me where I have the good fortune to find myself?"

His voice was a deep, pleasant one, but it carried Aline back oddly to her convent days, and it seemed to her that she had heard Sister Marie Séraphine say, "Attention, then, my child."

Then she remembered that Sister Marie Séraphine in religion was Nora O'Connor in the world, and realised that it was the kindly Irish touch upon French consonants and vowels which she had in common with this young man, who was surely as unlike a nun as he could be. She looked at him with great attention, and saw red unpowdered hair cut to a soldier's (or a Republican's) length, a face all freckles, and queer twinkling eyes, a great deal too light for his skin.

"Monsieur my cousin, or I 'm much mistaken," she said to herself, but aloud she answered:

"And do you not know where you are then, Citizen?"

"I know where I want to be, but I hope I have n't got there," said the young man, coming closer.

"And why is that, Citizen?"

He made a quick impatient gesture.

"Oh, a little less of the Citizen, my dear. I know I 'm an ugly devil, but do I look like a Jacobin?"

Aline was amazed at his recklessness.

"Monsieur is a very imprudent person," she said warningly.

"Monsieur would like to know where he is," responded the young man, laughing.

She fixed her eyes on him.

"You are at Rancy-les-Bois, Monsieur."

He bit his lip, made a half turn, and indicated the blackened ruins above them.

"And this?"

"This is, or was, the Château de Montenay."

In a minute all the freckles seemed to be accentuated by the pallor of the skin below. The hand that held the cane gripped it until the knuckles whitened. He stared a minute or two at the faintly rising vapour that told of heat not yet exhausted, and then said sharply:

"When was it burned?"

"Ten days ago."

"Any-lives-lost?"

"It is believed so," said Aline, watching him.

He put his hand to his face a moment, then let it fall, and stood rigid, his queer eyes suddenly tragic, and Aline could not forbear any longer.

"Marguerite is safe," she cried quickly and saw him colour to the roots of his hair.

"Marguerite-mon Dieu! I thought she was gone!" and with that he sat down on the coping, put his head down upon his arms, and a long sobbing breath or two heaved his broad shoulders in a fashion that at once touched and embarrassed Aline.

She drew nearer and watched uneasily, her own breathing a little quicker than usual. A woman's tears are of small account to a woman, but when a man sobs, it stirs in her the strangest mixture of pity, repulsion, gentleness, and contempt.

"She is quite safe," she repeated nervously, whereupon the young man raised his head, exclaiming in impulsive tones:

"And a thousand blessings on you for saying it, my dear," whilst in the same moment he slipped an arm about her waist, pulled her a little down, and before she could draw back, had kissed her very heartily upon the cheek.

It had hardly happened before she was free, and a yard away, with her head up, and a look in her eyes that brought him to his feet, flushing and bowing.

"I ask a thousand pardons," he stammered. "Indeed if it had been the blessed Saint Bridget herself that gave me that news, I 'd have kissed her, and meant no disrespect. For it was out of hell you took me, with the best word I ever heard spoken. You see, when I found Marguerite gone with that old mad lady, her aunt, I was ready to cut my throat, only I thought I 'd do more good by following her. Then when I saw these ruins, my heart went cold, till it was all I could do to ask the name. And when you said it, and I pictured her there under all these hot cinders-well, if you 've a heart in you, you 'll know what I felt, and the blessed relief of hearing she was safe. Would n't you have kissed the first person handy yourself, now?"

He regarded her with such complete earnestness that Aline could hardly refrain from smiling. She bent her head a little and said:

"I can understand that Monsieur le Chevalier did not know what he was doing."

He stared.

"What, you know me?"

"And do you perhaps think that I go about volunteering information about Mlle. de Matigny to every stranger I come across? Every one is not so imprudent as M. Desmond."

"I 'll not deny my name, but that I 'm imprudent-yes, with my last breath."

Aline could not repress a smile.

"Do you talk to all strangers as you did to me?" she inquired.

"Come, now, how do you think I got here?" he returned.

"I am wondering," she said drily.

"Well, it 's a simple plan, and all my own. When I see an honest face I let myself go, and tell the whole truth. Not a woman has failed me yet, and if I 've told the moving tale of my pursuit of Marguerite to one between this and Bâle, I 've told it to half a dozen."

Aline gasped.

"Oh, it 's a jewel of a plan," he said easily, "and much simpler than telling lies. There are some who can manage their lies, but mine have a way of disagreeing amongst themselves that beats cock-fighting. No, no, it 's the truth for me, and see how well it 's served me. So now you know all about me, but I 've no notion who you are."

"I am a friend of Marguerite's, fortunately," she said, "and, I believe, M. le Chevalier, that I am a cousin of yours."

Mr. Desmond looked disappointed.

"My dear lady, it would be so much more wonderful if you were n't. You see my great-grandfather had sixteen daughters, besides sons to the number of eight or so, and between them they married into every family in Europe, or nearly every one. Marguerite is n't a cousin, bless her. Now, I wonder, would you be a grand-daughter of my Aunt Elizabeth, who ran away with her French dancing-master, in the year of grace 1740?"

The blood of the Rochambeau rose to Aline's cheeks in a becoming blush, as she answered with rather an indignant negative.

"No?" said Mr. Desmond regretfully. "Well, then, a pity it is too, for never a one of my Aunt Elizabeth's descendants have I met with yet, and I 'm beginning to be afraid that she was so lost to all sense of the family traditions as to die without leaving any."

"If she so far forgot," Aline began a little haughtily, and then, remembering, blushed a very vivid crimson, and was silent.

"Well, well, I 'm afraid she did," sighed Mr. Desmond; "and now I come to think of it you 'll be Conor Desmond's granddaughter, he that was proscribed, and racketed all over Europe. His daughter married a M. de-Roche-Roche — —"

"Rochambeau, Monsieur. Yes, I was Aline de Rochambeau."

"Was?" said Mr. Desmond curiously, and then fell to whistling.

"Oh, my faith, yes, I remember-Marguerite told me," and there was a slight embarrassed pause which Desmond broke into with a laugh.

"After all, now, that kiss was not so out of place," he said, with a twinkle in his green eyes. "Cousins may kiss all the world over."

His glance was too frank to warrant offence, and Aline answered it with a smile.

"With Monsieur's permission I shall wait until I can kiss Madame ma cousine," she said, and dropped him a little curtsey.

Mr. Desmond sighed.

"I wish we were all well out of this," he said gloomily; "but how in the devil's name, or the saints' names, or any one else's name, we are to get out of it, I don't know. Well, well, the sooner it's tried the better; so where is Marguerite, Madame my cousin?"

Aline considered.

"I can't take you to her without asking leave of the friend she is with," she said at last; "but if you will wait here I will go and speak to her, and come back again when we have talked things over. We shall have to wait till it is quite dark, and you 'll be careful, won't you?"

"I will," said Mr. Desmond, without hesitation. He kissed his hand to Aline as she went off, and she frowned at him, then smiled to herself, and disappeared amongst the trees, walking quickly and wondering what was to come next.

At eleven o'clock that night a council of four sat in the apple loft at the mill. Marguerite, perched on a pile of hay, was leaning against Aline, who sat beside her. Every now and then she let one hand fall within reach of Mr. Desmond, who, reclining at her feet, invariably kissed it, and was invariably scolded for doing so. Madelon sat on the edge of the trap-door, her feet supported by the top rungs of the ladder which led to the barn below. She and Aline were grave, Marguerite pouting, and Mr. Desmond very much at his ease.

"But what plan have you?" Aline was asking.

"Oh, a hundred," he said carelessly.

Marguerite pulled her hand away with a jerk.

"Then you might at least tell us one," she said.

"Ah, now I 'd tell you anything when you look at me like that," he said with fervour.

"Then, tell me. No, now-at once."

He sat up and extracted a paper from his waistcoat pocket. It set forth that the Citizen Lemoine and his wife were at liberty to travel in France at their pleasure.

"In France," said Aline.

"Why, yes, one can't advertise oneself as an emigré. Once on the frontier, one must make a dash for it-it's done every day."

"But it says his wife," objected Marguerite, "and I 'm not your wife."

"And I 'm not Lemoine, but it does n't hurt my conscience to say I am-not in the least," returned Mr. Desmond.

"But I can't go with you like that," she protested. "What would grandmamma have said?"

Mr. Desmond gave an ironical laugh. "Your sainted grandmamma is past knowing what we do, and we 're past the conventions, my dear," he observed, but she only sat up the straighter.

"Indeed, Monsieur, you may be, but I 'm not. Why, there was Julie de Lérac, who escaped with her brother's friend. It was when I was in prison, and I heard what grandmamma and the other ladies said of her. Nothing would induce me to be spoken of like that."

"But your life depends on it. Marguerite, don't you trust me?"

"Why, of course; but that has nothing to do with it."

"But, my dearest child, what is to be done? You can't stay here, and we can't be married here, so the only thing to be done is to get away, and then we 'll be married as soon as your father will allow it. My aunt Judith's money has come in the very nick of time, for now we 'll be able to go back to the old place. Ah, you 'll love Ireland."

Marguerite tapped with her foot.

"Why can't we be married now?" she said quickly.

Madelon, who had been listening in silence, started and looked up, but did not speak.

"Impossible," said Mr. Desmond; and Aline whispered:

"My dear, you could n't."

"Why not? There is a priest here."

"You could n't trust him. He has taken the oath to the Convention," said Aline.

"Well but-Madelon, you told me of him; tell them what you said. Do you think he would betray us?"

"How do I know?" said Madelon, with a frown. "I do not think so, but one never knows. It is a risk."

"I don't mind the risk."

"To us all," continued Madelon bluntly. "I am thinking of more than you, little Ma'mselle."

"Who is this priest?" asked Desmond. "What do you know of him?"

"What I know is from my husband's cousin, Anne Pinel, who is his housekeeper. He took the oath, and ever since he has a trouble on his mind, and walks at night, sometimes all night long. At first Anne would get up and listen, and then she would hear groans and prayers, and once he called out: 'Judas! Judas! Judas!' so that she was frightened, and went back to her bed and put her hands over her ears. Now she takes no notice, she is so used to it."

"There!" cried Marguerite. "Poor man, if he can torment himself in such a way he would not put a fresh burden on his conscience by betraying us. Besides, why should he? I have a beautiful plan."

"Well?"

"We shall start at night; and first we will go to the priest's house, and I shall throw pebbles at his window. He will open, and I shall say, 'Mon père, here are two people who wish to be married.'

"Yes! and he 'd want to know why?"

"Of course, and I shall say, 'Mon père, we are escaping for our lives, and we wish to be married because I am a jeune fille bien élevée, and my grandmamma would turn in her grave at the thought of my crossing France alone with ma fiancé; and then he will marry us, and we shall walk away again, and go on walking until we can't walk any more."

"Marguerite, what folly!" cried Aline, and Madelon nodded her head.

"It's a beautiful plan!" exclaimed Mr. Desmond. He had his betrothed's hand in his once more, and was kissing it unrebuked. "My dear, we were made for each other, for it's a scheme after my own heart! Madame, my cousin, will you come with us?"

"Oh, yes, as chaperon, and then we needn't bother about getting married," said Marguerite, kissing her.

"That's not what I meant at all," observed Mr. Desmond reproachfully, and Aline was obliged to laugh.

"No, no, ma mie; not even to keep you out of so mad a scrape," she said, and Madelon nodded again.

"No, no," she echoed. "That would be a pretty state of affairs. There is Citizen Dangeau to be thought of. Deputies' wives must not emigrate."

Aline drew away from Marguerite, and caught Madelon by the arm.

"What's to be done?" she asked.

"Why, let them go."

"But the plan 's sheer folly."

Madelon shrugged.

"Madame Aline," she said in a low voice, "look at them. Is it any use talking? and we waste time. Once I saw a man at a fair. There was a rope stretched between two booths, and he walked on it. Then a woman in the crowd screamed out, 'Oh, he will fall!' and he looked down at her, went giddy, and fell. He broke his leg; but if no one had called out he would not have fallen."

"You mean?"

"It will be like walking on the rope for Monsieur and little Ma'mselle Marguerite, all the way until they get out of France. If they think they can do it-well, they say God helps those who cannot help themselves, and perhaps they will get across safely; but if they get frightened, if they think of the danger, they will be like the man who looked down and grew giddy, and pouf! —it will be all over."

"But this added risk — —"

"I do not think there is much risk. The curé is timid; for his own sake he will say nothing. If Anne hears anything, she will shut her ears; and, Madame Aline, the great thing is for them to get away. I tell you, I am afraid of my father. He watches us. I do not like his eyes."

She broke off, looking troubled; and Desmond stopped whispering to Marguerite and turned to them.

"Well, you good Madelon, we shall be off your mind to-morrow. Tell us where this curé lives; set us in the way, and we 'll be off as soon as may be. My dear cousin, believe me that frown will bring you lines ten years before they are due. Do force a smile, and wish us joy."

"To-night!" exclaimed Aline.

"Yes, that's best," said Madelon decidedly. "Little Ma'mselle knows that she has been a welcome guest, but she 's best away, and that 's the truth. If we had n't been watched, Jean Jacques would have driven her out in the cart a week ago."

"Watched! By whom?" Desmond's eyes were alert.

"By my father, Mathieu Leroux, the inn-keeper."

"Ah! well, we 'll be away by morning-in fact we 'll be moving now. Marguerite is ready. Faith, now I 've found the comfort of travelling without mails, I 'm ready to swear I 'll never take them again."

"I 'm not," said Marguerite, with a whimsical glance at her costume, which consisted of an old brown skirt of Madelon's, a rough print bodice, and a dark, patched cloak, which covered her from head to foot. They stole out noiselessly, Madelon calling under her breath to the yard dog, who sniffed at them in the darkness, and then lay down again with a rustle of straw.

Afterwards Aline thought of the scene which followed as the most dreamlike of all her queer experiences. The things which she remembered most vividly were Marguerite's soft ripple of laughter, half-childish, half-nervous, as she threw a handful of pebbles at the curé's window, and the moonlight glinting on the pane as the casement opened. What followed was like the inconsequent and fantastic dramas of sleep.

The explanations-the protests, the curé's voice ashake with timidity, until at last his fear of immediate discovery overbore his terror of future consequences, and he began to murmur the words which Aline had heard last in circumstances as strange, and far more terrifying. For days she wondered to herself over the odd scene: Desmond with his head bent towards his betrothed, and his deep voice muffled; and Marguerite pledging herself childishly-taking the great vows, and smiling all the time. Only at the very end she turned and threw her arms round Aline, holding her as if she would never leave go, and straining against her with a choked sob or two.

"No, no, I can't go —I can't!" she murmured, but Aline wrenched herself away.

"Marguerite, for God's sake!" she said. "It is too late-you must go"; and as Desmond stepped between them Marguerite caught his arm and held it in a wild grip.

"Oh, you'll save me!" And for once Aline was thankful for his tone of careless ease — —

"My jewel, what a question! Why, we 're off on our honeymoon. 'T is a most original one. Well, we must go. Good-bye, my cousin," and he took Aline's hand in a grip that surprised her.

"I'll not forget what you've done," he said, and kissed it; and so, without more ado, they were gone, and Aline was alone in the chequered moonlight before the priest's house, where the closed window spoke of the haste with which M. le Curé withdrew himself from participation in so perilous an affair.

## CHAPTER XXVI
## A DYING WOMAN

Next day brought it home to Madelon how true her forebodings had been. Noon brought her a visit from her father, and nothing would serve him but to go into every hole and corner. He alleged a wish to admire her housewifery, but the dark brow with which he accompanied her, and the quick, suspicious glances which he cast all round, made Madelon thank every saint in the calendar that the fugitives were well on the road, and that she had removed every trace of their presence betimes.

"Mon Dieu, Madame Aline!" she said afterwards, "when he came to the apple loft he seemed to know something. There he stood, not speaking, but just staring at me, like a dog at a rat-hole. I tell you, I thanked Saint Perpetua, whose day it was, that the rats were away!" In the end he went away, frowning, and swearing a little to himself, and quiet days set in.

No news was good news, and no news came; presently Aline stopped being terrified at every meeting with the inn-keeper, or the curé, and then Mlle. Marthe became so ill that all interests centred in her sick-room. Her malady, which had remained stationary for so long, began to gain ground quickly, and nights and days of agony consumed her strength, and made even the sister to whom she was everything look upon Death as the Angel not of the Sword, but of Peace.

One day the pain ebbed with the light, and at sunset she was more comfortable than she had been for a long while. Aline persuaded Mlle. Ange to go and lie down for a little, and she and Marthe were alone.

"The day is a long time going," said Marthe after a silence of some minutes.

"Yes, the days are lengthening."

"And mine are shortening-only I 'm an unreasonable time over my dying. It's a trial to me, for I liked to do things quickly. I suppose no one has ever known what it has been to me to see Jeanne pottering about her work, or Ange moving a chair, or a book, in her slow, deliberate way; and now that it's come to my turn I 'm having my revenge, and inflicting the same kind of annoyance on you."

She spoke in a quick, toneless voice, that sounded very feeble-almost as if the life going from her had left it behind as a stranded wreck of sound.

Aline turned with a sob.

"Heavens, child! did you think I did n't know I was going, or that I expected you to cry over me? You 've been a butt for my sharp tongue too often to be heart-broken when there 's a chance of your being left in peace."

"Oh, don't!" said Aline, choking; and something in voice and face brought a queer look to the black, mocking eyes.

"What, you really care a little? My dear, it's too amiable of you. Why, Aline,"—as the girl buried her face in her hands—"why, Aline!"

There was a pause, and then the weak voice went on again:

"If you do care at all-if I mean anything at all in your life-then I will ask you one thing. What are you doing to Jacques?"

"Was that why you hated me?" said Aline quickly.

"Oh, hate? Well, I never hated you, but-Yes, that was it. He and Ange are the two things I 've had to love, and though I don't suppose he thinks about me twice a year, still his happiness means more to me than it does-well, to you."

"Oh, that's not true!" cried Aline on a quick breath.

Marthe Desaix looked sharply at her.

"Aline," she said, "how long are you going to break his heart and your own?"

"I don't know," whispered the girl. "There's so much between us. Too much for honour."

"Too much for pride, Aline de Rochambeau," said Marthe with cruel emphasis, and her own name made Aline wince. It seemed a thing of hard, unyielding pride; a thing her heart shrank from.

"Listen to me. When he is dead over there in Spain, what good will your pride do you? Women who live without love, or natural ties, what do they become? Hard, and sour, and bitter, like me; or foolish, and spiteful, and soft, and petty. I tell you, I could have shed the last drop of my blood, worked my fingers to the raw stump, for the man I loved. I 'd have borne his children by the roadside, followed him footsore through the world, slept by his side in the snow, and thought myself blessed. But to me there came neither love nor lover. Aline, can you live in other people's lives, love with other women's hearts, rear and foster other mothers' children as Ange does? That is the only road for a barren woman, that does not lead to desert places and a land dry as her heart. Can you take my sister's road? Is there nothing in you that calls out for the man who loves you, for the children that might be yours? Is your pride more to you than all this?"

Aline looked up steadily.

"No," she said, "it is nothing. I would do as you say you would have done, but there was one thing I thought I could not do. May I tell you the whole story now? I have wished to often, but it is hard to begin."

"Tell me," said Marthe; and Aline told her all, from the beginning.

When she had finished she saw that Marthe's eyes were closed, and moved a little to rise, thinking that she had dropped asleep. But as she did so the eyes opened again, and Marthe said fretfully, "No, I heard it all. It is very hard to judge, very hard."

Aline looked at her in alarm, for she seemed all at once to have grown very old.

"Yes, it is hard. Life is so difficult," she went on slowly-weakly, "I 'm glad to be going out of it-out into the dark."

Aline kissed her hand, and spoke wistfully:

"Is it all so dark to you?"

"Why yes, dark enough-cold enough-lonely enough. Is n't it so to you?"

"Not altogether, ma tante."

"What, because of those old tales which you believe? Well, if they comfort you, take comfort from them. I can't."

"But Mlle. Ange-believes?"

Marthe frowned impatiently.

"Who knows what Ange believes? Not she herself. She is a saint to be sure, but orthodox? A hundred years ago she would have been lucky if she had escaped Purgatory fire in this life. She is content to wander in vague, beautiful imaginings. She abstracts her mind, and calls it prayer; confuses it, and says she has been meditating. I am not like that. I like things clear and settled, with a good hard edge to them. I should have been the worker and Ange the invalid-no, no! what am I saying? God forgive me, I don't mean that."

"You would not like to see M. le Curé?" said Aline timidly. The question had been on her lips a hundred times, but she had not had the courage to let it pass them.

Mlle. Marthe was too weak for anger, but she raised her eyebrows in the old sarcastic way.

"Poor man," she said, "he needs absolution a great deal more than I do. He thinks he has sold his soul, and can't even enjoy the price of it. After all, those are the people to pity-the ones who have courage for neither good nor evil."

She lay silent for a long while then, and watched the sunset colours burn to flame, and fade to cold ash-grey.

Suddenly Aline said:

"Ma tante."

"Well?"

"Ma tante, do you think he loves me still?"

"Why should he?"

The girl took her breath sharply, and Mlle. Marthe moved her head with an impatient jerk.

"There, there, I 'm too near my end to lie. Jacques is like his mother, he has n't the talent of forgetfulness."

"He looked so hard when he went away."

"Little fool, if he had smiled he would have forgotten easily enough."

Aline turned her head aside.

"Listen to me," said Mlle. Marthe insistently. "What kind of a man do you take your husband to be, good or bad?"

"Oh, he is good-don't I know that! What would have become of me if he had been a bad man?" said the girl in a tense whisper.

"Then would you not have him follow his conscience? In all that is between you has he not acted as a man should do? Would you have him do what is right in your eyes and not in his own; follow your lead, take the law from you? Do you, or does any woman, desire a husband like that?"

Aline did not answer, only stared out of the window. She was recalling the King's death, Dangeau's vote, and her passion of loyalty and pain. It seemed to her now a thing incredibly old and far away, like a tale read of in history a hundred years ago. Something seemed to touch her heart and shrivel it, as she wondered if in years to come she would look back as remotely upon the love, and longing, which rent her now.

There was a long, long silence, and in the end Mlle. Marthe dozed a little. When Ange came in, she found her lying easily, and so free from pain that she took heart and was quite cheerful over the little sick-room offices. But at midnight there was a change —a greyness of face, a labouring of failing lungs-and with the dawn she sighed heavily once or twice and died, leaving the white house a house of mourning.

Mlle. Ange took the blow quietly, too quietly to satisfy Aline, who would rather have seen her weep. Her cold, dreamy composure was somehow very alarming, and the few tears she shed on the day they buried Marthe in the little windy graveyard were dried almost as they fell. After that she took up all her daily tasks at once, but went about them abstractedly.

Even the children could not make her smile, or a visit to the grave draw tears. The sad monotony of grief settled down upon the household, the days were heavy, work without zest, and a wet April splashed the window-panes with torrents of warm, unceasing rain.

## CHAPTER XXVII
## BETRAYAL

In the early days of April the wind-swept, ice-tormented Pyrenees had been exchanged for the Spanish lowlands, vexed by the drought and heat of those spring days. If the army had suffered from frostbite and pneumonia before, it groaned now under a plague of dysentery, but it was still, and increasingly, victorious. An approving Convention sent congratulatory messages to Dugommier, who enjoyed the distinction-somewhat unusual for a general in those days-of having been neither superseded nor recalled to suffer an insulting trial and an ignoble death.

France had a short way with her public servants just then. Was an army in retreat? To Paris with the traitor who commanded it. Was an advantage insufficiently followed up? To the guillotine with the officer responsible. Dumouriez saved his head by going to Austria with young Égalité at his heels, but many and many a general who had led the troops of France looked out of the little window, and was flung into the common trench, to be dust in dust with nobles, great ladies, common murderers, and the poor Queen herself. Closer and closer shaved the national razor, heavier and heavier fell the pall upon blood-soaked Paris. Marat, long since assassinated, and canonised as first Saint of the New Calendar, with rites of an impiety quite indescribable, would, had he lived, have seen his prophecy fulfilled. Paris had drunk and was athirst again, and always with that drunkard's craving which cannot be allayed-no, not by all the floods of the infernal lake. Men were no longer men, but victims of a horrible dementia. Listen to Hébert demanding the Queen's blood.

"Do you think that any of us will be able to save ourselves?" he cries. "I tell you we are all damned already, but if my blood must flow, it shall not flow alone. I tell you that if we pass, our passing shall devastate France, and leave her ruined and bloody, a spectacle for the nations!" And this at the beginning of the Terror!

A curious thought comes to one. Are these words, instinct with pure, fate-driven tragedy, the fruit of Hébert's mind-Hébert gross with Paris slime, sensual, self-seeking, flushed with evil living? or is he, too, unwillingly amongst the prophets, mouthpiece only of an immutable law, which, outraged by him and his like, pronounces thus an irrevocable doom?

Well might Danton write—"This is chaos, and the worlds are a-shaping. One cannot see one's way for the red vapour. I am sick of it-sick. There is nothing but blood, blood, blood. Camille says that the infernal gods are athirst. If they are not glutted soon there will be no blood left to flow. They may have mine before long. Maximilian eyes my head as if it irked him to see it higher than his own. If it were off he would seem the taller. I am going home to Arles-with my wife. The spring is beautiful there, and the Aube runs clean from blood. It were better to fish its waters than to meddle with the governing of men."

Dangeau sighed heavily as he destroyed the letter. Surely the strong hand would be able to steer the ship to calmer waters, and yet there was a deep sense of approaching fatality upon him.

His fellow-Commissioner was of Robespierre's party—a tall man, wonderfully thin, with grizzled hair, and a nose where the bony ridge showed yellow under the tight skin. He had a cold, suspicious eye, light grey, with a green under-tinge, and was, as Dangeau knew beyond a doubt, a spy both on himself and on Dugommier. There came an April day full of heat, and sullen with brooding thunder. Dangeau in his tent, writing his report, found the pen heavy in his hand, and for once was glad of the interruption, when Vibert's shadow fell across the entrance, and his long form bent to enter at the low door.

"Ah, come in," he said, pushing his inkstand away; and Vibert, who had not waited for the invitation, sat down and looked at him curiously for a moment. Then he said:

"A courier from Paris came in an hour ago."

Dangeau stretched out his hand, but the other held his papers close.

"There is news-weighty news," he continued; and Dangeau felt his courage leap to meet an impending blow.

"What news?" he asked, quite quietly, hand still held out.

"You are Danton's friend?"

"As you very well know, Citizen."

Vibert flung all his papers on the table.

"You 'll be less ready to claim his friendship in the future, I take it," he said, with a sudden twang of steel in his voice. Dangeau turned frightfully pale, but the hand that reached for the letters was controlled.

"Your meaning, Citizen?"

Vibert's strident laugh rang out.

"Danton was-somebody, and your friend. Danton is—a name and nothing more. Once the knife has fallen there is not a penny to choose between him and any other carrion. A good riddance to France, and all good patriots will say 'Amen' to that."

"Patriots!" muttered Dangeau, and then fell to reading the papers with bent head and eyes resolutely calm. When he looked up no one would have guessed that he was moved, and the sneering look which dwelt upon his face glanced off again. He met Vibert's eyes full, his own steady with a cold composure, and after a moment or two the thin man shuffled with his feet, and spat noisily.

"Well," he said, "Robespierre for my money; but, of course, Danton was backing you, and you stand to lose by his fall."

"Ah," said Dangeau softly, "you think so?"

He looked to the open door of the tent as he spoke. The flap was rolled high to let in the air, and showed a slope, planted with vines in stiff rows, and, above, a space of sky. This seemed to consist of one low, bulging cloud, dark with suppressed thunder, and in the heavy bosom of it a pulse of lightning throbbed continually. With each throb the play of light grew more vivid, whilst out of the distance came a low, answering boom, the far-off heart-beat of the storm. Dangeau's eyes rested on the prospect with a strange, sardonic expression. Danton was dead, and dead with him all hopes that he might lead a France, purged terribly, and regenerate by fire and blood, to her place as the first, because the freest, of nations. Danton was dead, and Paris adrift, unrestrained, upon a sea of blood. Danton was dead, and the last, lingering, constructive purpose had departed from a confederacy given over to a mere drunken orgy of destruction-slaves to an ignoble passion for self-preservation. To Dangeau's thought death became suddenly a thing honourable and to be desired. From the public services of those days it was the only resignation, and he saw it now before him, inevitable, more dignified than life beneath a squalid yoke. All the ideals withered, all the idols shattered, youth worn through, patriotism chilled, disenchantment, disintegration, decay-these he saw in sombre retrospect, and nausea, long repressed, broke upon him like a flood.

A flash brighter than any before shot in a vicious fork across the blackening sky, and the thunder followed it close, with a crash that startled Vibert to his feet.

Dangeau sat motionless, but when the reverberations had died away, he leaned across the table, still with that slight smile, and said:

"And what do you say of me in your report, Vibert?"

Still dazed with the noise, the man stared nervously.

"My report, Citizen?"

"Your report, Vibert."

"My report to the Convention?"

Dangeau laughed, with the air of a man who is enjoying himself. After the dissimulation, the hateful necessity for repression and evasion, frankness was a luxury.

"Oh, no, my good Vibert, not your report to the Convention. It is your report to Robespierre that I mean. I have a curiosity to know how you mean to put the thing. 'Emotion at hearing of Danton's death,' is that your line, eh?"

"Citizen——"

"What, protestations? Really, Vibert, you underrate my intelligence. Shall I tell you what you said about me last time?"

Vibert shifted his eyes to the door, and seemed to measure his distance from it.

"What I said last time, Citizen?" he stammered. Once out of the tent he knew he could break Dangeau easily enough, but at present, alone with a man who he was aware must be desperate, he felt a creeping in his bones, and a strong desire to be elsewhere.

Dangeau's lip lifted.

"Be reassured, my friend. I am not a spy, and I really have no idea what it was that you said, though now that you have been so obligingly transparent I think I might hazard a guess. It would be a pity if this week's report were to contain nothing fresh. Robespierre might even be bored-in the intervals of killing his betters."

Vibert's lips closed with a snap. Here was recklessness, here was matter enough to condemn a man who stood firmer than Dangeau.

Dangeau leaned back in his chair and crossed his legs.

"You agree with me that that would be a pity? Very well then, you may get out your notebook and write the truth for once. Tell the incorruptible Maximilian that he is making the world too unpleasant a place for any self-respecting Frenchman to care about remaining in it, and, if that is not enough, you can inform him that Danton's blood will yet call loud enough to bid him down to hell."

There was no emotion at all in his voice. He spoke drily, as one stating facts too obvious to require any stress of tone, or emphasis.

Vibert was puzzled, but his nerves were recovering, and he wrote defiantly, looking up with a half-start at every other word as if he expected to see Dangeau's arm above him, poised to strike.

Dangeau shrugged his shoulders.

"You needn't be afraid," he said, with hard contempt. "You are too obviously suited to the present débâcle for me to wish to remove you from it. No doubt your time will come, but I have no desire to play Sanson's part."

Vibert winced. Perhaps he saw the red-edged axe of the Revolution poised above him. When, four months later, he was indeed waiting for it to fall, they say he cursed Dangeau very heartily.

The lightning stabbed with a blinding flame, the thunder crashed scarce a heart-beat behind, and with that the rain began. It fell in great gouts and splashes, with here and there a big hailstone, and for a minute or two the air seemed full of water, pierced now by a sudden flare of blue, and shattered again by the roar that followed. Then, as it had come, so it went, and in a moment the whirl of the wind swept the sky clear again.

Vibert pulled himself together. His long limbs had stiffened into a curious rigidity whilst the storm was at its height, but now they came out of it with a jerk. He thrust his notebook into the pocket which bulged against his thin form, and under his drooping lids he sent a queer, inquisitive glance at his companion. Dangeau was leaning back in his chair, one arm thrown carelessly over the back of it, his attitude one of acquiescence, his expression that of a man released from some distasteful task. Vibert had seen many a man under sentence of death, but this phase piqued him, and he turned in the doorway.

"Come then, Dangeau," he said, with a would-be familiar air, "what made you do it? Between colleagues now? I may tell you, you had fairly puzzled me. When you read those papers, I could have sworn you did not care a jot, that it was all one to you who was at the top of the tree so you kept your own particular branch; and then, just as I was thinking you had bested me, and betrayed nothing, out you come with your 'To hell with Robespierre.' What the devil took you?"

Dangeau looked at him with a strange gleam in his eyes. The impulse to speak, to confide, attacks us at curious moments; years may pass, a man may be set in all circumstances that invite betrayal, he may be closeted with some surgeon skilled in the soul's hurts, and the impulse may not wake-and then, quite suddenly, at an untoward time, and to a listener the most unlikely, his soul breaks bounds and displays its secret springs.

Such an hour was upon Dangeau now, and he experienced its intoxication to the full.

"My reason?" he said slowly. "My good Vibert, is one a creature of reason? For me, I doubt it —I doubt it. Look at our reasonable town of Paris, our reasonable Maximilian, our reasonable guillotine. Heavens! how the infernal powers must laugh at us and our reason."

Then of a sudden the sneer dropped out of his tone, and a ring almost forgotten came to it, and brought each word distinctly to Vibert's ear, though the voice itself fell lower and lower, as he spoke less and less to the man in the tent-door and more and more to his own crystallising thoughts.

"My reason? Impulse-just the sheer animal desire to strike at what hurts. What was reason not to do for us? and in the end we come back to impulse again. A vicious circle everywhere. The wheel turns, and we rise, fancying the stars are within our grasp. The wheel turns on, and we fall-lose the stars and have our wage —a handful of bloody dust. Louis was a tyrant, and he fell. I had a hand in that, and said, 'Tyranny is dead.' Dead? Just Heaven! and in Paris to-day every man is a tyrant who is not a victim. Tyranny has the Hydra's gift of multiplying in death. Better one tyrant than a hundred. Perhaps Robespierre thinks that, but God knows it is better a people should be oppressed than that they should become oppressors." Here his head came up with a jerk, and his manner changed abruptly. "And then," he continued, with a little bow, "and then, you see, I am so intolerably bored with your society, my good Vibert."

Vibert scowled, cursed, and went out. Half an hour afterwards he thought of several things he might have said, and felt an additional rancour against Dangeau because they had not come to him at the time. A mean creature, Vibert, and not quick, but very apt for dirty work, and therefore worth his price to the Incorruptible Robespierre.

Dangeau, left alone, fell to thinking. His strange elation was still upon him, and he felt an unwonted lightness of spirit. He began to consider whether he should wait to be arrested, or end now in the Roman way. Suicide was much in vogue at the time, and was gilded with a strong halo of heroics. The doctrine of a purpose in the individual existence being rejected, the Stoic argument that life was a thing to be laid down at will seemed reasonable enough. It appealed to the dramatic sense, a thing very inherent in man, and the records of the times set down almost as many suicides as executions. Dangeau had often enough maintained man's right to relinquish that which he had not asked to receive, but at this crisis in his life there came up in him old teachings, those which are imperishable, because they have their roots in an imperishable affection. His mother, whom he adored, had lived and died a devout Catholic, and there came back to him now a strange, faint sense of the dignity and purpose of the soul, of life as a trial, life as a trust. It seemed suddenly nobler to endure than to relinquish. An image of the deserter flitted through his brain, to be followed by another of the child that pettishly casts away a broken toy, and from that his mind went back, back through the years. For a moment his mother's eyes looked quite clearly into his, and he heard her voice say, "Jacques, you do not listen."

Ah, those tricks of the brain! How at a touch, a turn of the head, a breath, a scent, the past rises quick, and the brain, phonograph and photograph in one, shows us our dead again, and brings their voices to our ears. Dangeau saw the chimney corner, and a crooked log on the fire. The resin in it boiled up, and ran down all ablaze. He watched it with wondering, childish eyes, and heard the gentle voice at his ears say, "Jacques, you do not listen."

It was there and gone between one breath and the next, but it took with it the dust of years, and left the old love very fresh and tender. Ah-the dear woman, the dear mother. "Que Dieu te bénisse," he said under his breath.

The current of thought veered to Aline, and at that life woke in him, the desire to live, the desire of her, the desire to love. Then on a tide of bitterness, "She will be free." Quickly came the answer, "Free and defenceless."

He sank his head in his hands, and, for the first time for months, deliberately evoked her image.

It seemed as if Fate were concerning herself with Dangeau's affairs, for she sent a bullet Vibert's way next morning. It ripped his scalp, and sent him bleeding and delirious to a sick-bed from which he did not rise for several weeks. It was, therefore, not until late in June that Robespierre stretched out his long arm, and haled Dangeau from his post in Spain to Paris and the prison of La Force.

Meanwhile there was trouble at Rancy-les-Bois. Mr. and Mrs. Desmond, after a series of most adventurous adventures, had arrived at Bâle, and there, with characteristic imprudence, proceeded to narrate to a much interested circle of friends and relatives the full and particular details of their escape. Rancy was mentioned, Mlle. Ange described and praised, Aline's story brought in, Madelon's part in the drama given its full value. Such imprudence may seem inconceivable, but it had more than one parallel.

In this instance trouble was not long in breeding. Three years previously Joseph Pichon of Bâle had gone Paris-wards to seek his fortune. Circumstances had sent him as apprentice to M. Bompard, the watchmaker of Rancy's market-town. Here he stayed two years, years which were enlivened by tender passages between him and Marie, old Bompard's only child. At the end of two years M. Pichon senior died, having lost his elder son about six months before. Joseph, therefore, came in for his father's business, and immediately made proposals for the hand of Mlle. Marie. Bompard liked the young man, Marie declared she loved him; but the times were ticklish. It was not the moment for giving one's heiress to a foreigner. Such an action might be unfavourably construed, deemed unpatriotic; so Joseph departed unbetrothed, but with as much hope as it is good for a young man to nourish. His views were Republican, his sentiments ardent. By the time his own affairs were settled it was to be hoped that public matters would also be quieter, and then-why, then Marie Bompard might become Marie Pichon, no one forbidding. Imagine, then, the story of the Desmonds' escape coming to the ears of Joseph the Republican. He burned with interest, and, having more than a touch of the busybody, sat down and wrote Bompard a full account of the whole affair. Bompard was annoyed. He crackled the pages angrily, and stigmatised Joseph as a fool and a meddler. Bompard was fat, and a good, kind, easy man; he desired to live peaceably, and really the times made it very difficult. His first impulse was to put the paper in the fire and hold his tongue. Then he reflected that he was not Joseph's only acquaintance in the place. If the young man were to write to Jean Dumont, the Mayor's son, for instance, and then it was to come out that the facts had been known to Bompard, and concealed by him. "Seigneur!" exclaimed Bompard, mopping his brow, which had become suddenly moist. Men's heads had come off for less than that. He read the letter again, drumming on his counter the while, with a stubby, black-nailed hand; at any rate, risk or no risk, Madelon must not be mentioned. He had known her from a child; there was, in fact, some very distant connection between the families, and she was a good, pretty girl. Bompard was a fatherly man. He liked to chuck a pretty girl under the chin, and see her blush, and Madelon had a pleasant trick of it; and then, just now, all the world knew she was expecting the birth of her first child. No, certainly he would hold his tongue about Madelon. He burnt the letter, feeling like a conspirator, and it was just as he was blowing away the last compromising bit of ash that Mathieu Leroux walked in upon him.

They talked of the weather first, and then of the prospects of a good apple year. Then Mathieu harked back to the old story of the fire, worked himself into a passion over it, noted Bompard's confusion, and in ten minutes had the whole story out-all, that is, except his own daughter's share in it, and at that he guessed with an inward fury which fairly frightened poor fat Bompard.

"Those Desaix!" he exclaimed with an oath. "If I 'd had your tale six weeks ago! Now there 's only Ange and the niece. It's like Marthe to cheat one in the end!"

Bompard looked curiously at him. He did not know the secret of Mathieu's hostility to the Desaix family. Old Mère Anne could have told him that when Marthe was a handsome, black-eyed girl, Mathieu Leroux had lifted his eyes high, and conceived a sullen passion for one as much above him as Réné de Montenay was above her sister Ange. The village talked, Marthe noted the looks that followed her everywhere, and boiled with pride and anger. Then one day Mme. de Montenay, coldly ignoring all differences in the ranks below her own, said:

"So, Marthe, you are to make a match of it with young Leroux"; and at that the girl flamed up.

"If we 're not high enough for the Château, at least we 're too high for the gutter," she said, with a furiously pointed glance at Réné de Montenay, whose eyes were on her sister.

Ange turned deadly pale, Réné flushed to the roots of his hair, Madame bit her lip, and Charles Leroux, who was listening at the door, took note of the bitter words, and next time he was angry with his brother flung them at him tauntingly. Mathieu neither forgot nor forgave them. After forty years his resentment still festered, and was to break at last into an open poison.

His trip to Paris had furnished him with the names and style of patriots whose measures could be trusted not to err on the side of leniency, and to one of these he wrote a hot denunciation of Ange Desaix and Aline Dangeau, whom he accused of being enemies to the Republic, and traitors to Liberty, inasmuch as they had assisted proscribed persons to emigrate. No greater crime existed. The denunciation did its work, and in a trice down came Commissioner Brutus Carré to set up his tribunal amongst the frightened villagers, and institute a little terror within the Terror at quiet Rancy-les-Bois.

The village buzzed like a startled hive, women bent white faces over their household tasks, men shuffled embarrassed feet at the inn, glancing suspiciously at one another, and all avoiding Mathieu's hard black eyes. At the white house Commissioner Brutus Carré occupied Mlle. Marthe's sunny room, whilst Ange and Aline sat under lock and key, and heard wild oaths and viler songs defile the peaceful precincts.

Up at the mill, Madelon lay abed with her newborn son at her breast. Strange how the softness and the warmth of him stirred her heart, braced it, and gave her a courage which amazed Jean Jacques. She lay, a little pale, but quite composed, and fixed her round brown eyes upon her father's scowling face. In the background Jean Jacques stood stolidly. He was quite ready to strangle Mathieu with those strong hands of his, but had sufficient wit to realise that such a proceeding would probably not help Madelon.

"They were here!" vociferated Mathieu loudly. "You took them in, you concealed them, you helped them to get away. You thought you had cheated me finely, you and that oaf who stands there; and you thought me a good, easy man, one who would cover your fault because you were his daughter. I tell you I am a patriot, I! If my daughter betrays the Republic shall I shield her? I say no, a thousand times no!"

Madelon's clear gaze never wavered. Her arm held her baby tight, and if her heart beat heavily no one heard it except the child, who whimpered a little and put groping hands against her breast.

"Then you mean to denounce me?" she said quite low.

"Denounce you! Yes, you 're no daughter of mine! Every one shall know that you are a traitress."

"And my baby?" asked Madelon.

Leroux cursed it aloud, and the child, frightened by the harsh voice, burst into a lusty wailing that took all its mother's tender hushing to still.

When she looked at her father again there was something very bright and intent in her expression.

"Very well, my father," she said; "it is understood that you denounce me. Do you perhaps suppose that I shall hold my tongue?"

"Say what you like, and be damned to you!" shouted Mathieu.

Jean Jacques clenched his hands and took a step forward, but his wife's expression checked him.

"I may say what I like?" she observed.

"The more the better. Why, see here, Madelon, if you will give evidence against Ange Desaix and her niece, I 'll do my best to get you off."

"Why, what has Mlle. Ange to do with it?" said Madelon, open-eyed.

Leroux became speechless for a moment. Then he swore volubly, and cursed Madelon for a liar.

"A liar, and a damned fool!" he spluttered. "For now I 'll not lift a finger for you, my girl, and when you see the guillotine ready for you, perhaps you 'll wish you 'd kept a civil tongue in your head."

"Enough!" said Madelon sharply. "Let us understand each other. If you speak, I speak too. If you accuse me, I accuse you."

"Accuse me, accuse me-and of what?"

Madelon's eyes flashed.

"You have a short memory," she said; "others will not believe it is so short. When I say, as I shall say, that it was you that arranged Mlle. Marguerite's flight there will be plenty of people who will believe me." She paused, panting a little, and Mathieu, white with passion, stared helplessly at her.

Jean Jacques, in the background, looked from one to the other, amazed to the point of wondering whether he were asleep or awake. Was this Madelon, who had been afraid of raising her voice in her father's presence? And what was all this about Leroux and the escape? It was beyond him, but he opened ears and eyes to their widest.

"There is no proof!" shouted Mathieu.

"Ah, but yes," said Madelon at once; "you forget that Mlle. Marguerite gave you her diamond shoe-buckles as a reward for helping her and M. le Chevalier to get away."

"Shoe-buckles!" exclaimed Mathieu Leroux, his eyes almost starting from his head.

"Yes, indeed, shoe-buckles with diamonds in them, fit for a princess; and they are hidden in your garden, my father, and when I tell the Commissioner that, and show him where they are buried, do you think that your patriotism will save you?"

"It is not true," gasped Mathieu, putting one hand to his head, where the hair clung suddenly damp.

"Citizen Brutus Carré will believe it," returned Madelon steadily.

"Hell-cat! She-devil! You would not dare — —"

"Yes, I would dare. I will dare anything if you push me too far, but if you hold your tongue I will hold mine," said Madelon, looking at him over her baby's head. She laid her free arm across the child as she spoke, and Leroux saw truth and determination in her eyes.

Jean Jacques began to understand. Eh, but Madelon was clever. A smile came slowly into his broad face, and his hands unclenched. After all, there would be no strangling. It was much better so. Quarrels in families were a mistake. He conceived that the moment had arrived when he might usefully intervene.

"It is a mistake to quarrel," he observed in his deep, slow voice.

Mathieu swung round, glaring, and Madelon closed her eyes for a moment. There was a slight pause, during which Jean Jacques met his father-in-law's furious gaze with placidity.

Then he said again:

"Quarrels in families are a mistake. It is better to live peaceably. Madelon and I are quiet people."

Leroux gave a short, enraged grunt, and looked again at his daughter. As he moved she opened her eyes, and he read in them an unchanged resolve.

"I don't want to quarrel, I 'm sure," he said sulkily.

"We don't," observed Jean Jacques with simplicity.

"Then it is understood. Madelon will tell no lies about me?"

"I say nothing unless I am arrested. If that happens, I tell what I know."

"But you know nothing," exploded Leroux.

"The shoe-buckles," said Madelon.

Leroux stared at her silently for a full minute. Then, with an angrily-muttered oath, he flung out of the room, shutting the door behind him with violence.

Jean Jacques stood scratching his head.

"Eh, Madelon," he said, "you faced him grandly. But when did he get those shoe-buckles, and how did you know about them?"

Madelon began to laugh faintly, with catching breath.

"Oh, thou great stupid," she panted; "did'st thou not understand? There never, never, never were any buckles at all, but he thought they were there in his garden, and it did just as well," and with that she buried her face in the pillow and broke into passionate weeping.

Mathieu Leroux held his tongue about his daughter and walked softly for a day or two. Also he took much exercise in his garden, where he dug to the depth of three feet, but without finding anything.

Meanwhile Brutus Carré was occupied with the forms of republican justice. His prisoners were to be taken to Paris, since Justice lacked implements here, and Rancy owned no convenient stream where one might drown the accused in pairs, or sink them by the boat-load.

Ange Desaix faced him with a high look. If her ideals were tottering, their nobility still clung about her, wrapping her from this man's rude gaze.

"I was a Republican before the Revolution," she said, and her look drew from Citizen Carré an outburst of venom.

"You are suspect, gravely suspect," he bellowed.

"But, Citizen—" and the frank gaze grew a little bewildered.

"But, Citoyenne!—but, Aristocrat! What! you answer me, you bandy words? Is treason so bold in Rancy-les-Bois? Truly it's time the wasp's nest was smoked out. Take her away!" and Mlle. Ange went out, still with that bewildered look.

M. le Curé came next. There was a high flush on his thin cheeks, and his fingers laced and interlaced continually.

When Carré blustered at him he started, leaned forward, and tapped the table sharply.

"I wish to speak, to make a statement," he said in a high, trembling voice.

There was a surprised silence, whilst the priest stretched out his hand and spoke as from the pulpit.

"My children, I have been as Judas amongst you, as Judas who betrayed his Lord. I desire to ask pardon of the souls I have offended, before I go to answer for my sin."

Carré stared at him.

"Is he mad?" he asked, with a brutal laugh.

"No, not mad," said M. le Curé quietly.

"Not that it matters having a crack in a head that's so soon to come off," continued the Commissioner. "Take him away. When I want to hear a sermon I 'll send for him"; and out went the curé.

On the road to Paris he was very quiet, sitting for the most part with his head in his hands. After they reached Paris, Mlle. Ange and Aline saw him no more. No doubt he perished amongst the hundreds who died and left no sign. As for the women, they were sent to the Abbaye, and there waited for the end.

## CHAPTER XXVIII
## INMATES OF THE PRISON

It was the first week in July, and heat fetid and airless brooded over the crowded prison. Mlle. Ange drooped daily. To all consoling words she made but one reply—"C'est fini"—and at last Aline gave up all attempt at rousing her. After all, what did it matter since they were all upon the edge of death?

There were six people in the small, crowded cell, and they changed continually. No one ever returned, no one was ever released now.

Little Madame de Verdier, stumbling in half blind with tears, sat with them through one long night unsleeping. In her hand she held always the blotted, ill-spelled letter written at the scaffold's foot by her only child, a lad of thirteen. In the morning she was fetched away, taking to her own death a lighter heart than she could have borne towards liberty. In her place came Jeanne Verdier, ex-mistress of Philippe Égalité, she who had leaned on the rail and laughed as the votes went up for the King's death. Her laughing days were over now, tears blistered her raddled skin, and she wrung her hands continually and moaned for a priest. When the gaoler came for her, she reeled against him, fainting, and he had to catch her round the waist, and use a hard word before he could get her across the threshold. That evening the door opened, and an old man was pushed in.

"He is a hundred at least, so there need be no scandal," said the gaoler with a wink, and indeed the old gentleman tottered to a corner and lay there peaceably enough, without so much as a word or look for his companions.

In a day or two, however, he revived. The heat which oppressed the others seemed to suit him, and after a while he even began to talk a little, throwing out mysterious hints of great powers, strange influences, and what not.

Mme. de Labédoyère, inveterate chatterbox, was much interested.

"He is somebody," she assured Aline, aside. "An astrologer, perhaps. Who knows? He may be able to tell the future."

"I have no future," said the melancholy Mme. de Vieuxmesnil with a deep sigh. "No one can bring back the past, not even le bon Dieu Himself, and that is all I care for now."

The little Labédoyère shrugged her plump shoulders, and old Mme. de Breteuil struck into the conversation.

"He reminds me of some one," she said, turning her bright dark eyes upon the old man's face. He was leaning against the wall, dozing, his fine-cut features pallid with a clear yellowish pallor like dead ivory. As she looked his eyes opened, very blue, through the mist which age and drowsiness hung over them. He smiled a little and sat up, rubbing his thin hands slowly, as if they felt a chill even on that stifling afternoon.

"The ladies do me the honour of discussing me," he said in his queer, level voice, from which all the living quality seemed to have drained away, leaving it steadily passionless.

"I was thinking I had seen you somewhere," said Mme. de Breteuil, "and perhaps if Monsieur were to tell me his name, I should remember."

He smiled again.

"My name is Aristide," he said, and seemed to be waiting for a sensation. The ladies looked at one another puzzled. Only Mme. de Breteuil frowned a moment, and then clapped her hands.

"I have it-ah, Monsieur Aristide, it is so many years ago. I think we won't say how many, but all Paris talked about you then. They called you the Sorcerer, and one's priest scolded one soundly if one so much as mentioned your name."

"Yes," said the old man with a nod.

"Well, you have forgotten it, I daresay, but I came to see you then, I and my sister-in-law, Jeanne de Breteuil. In those days the future interested me enormously, but when I got into the room, and thought that perhaps I should see the devil, I was scared to death; and as to Jeanne, she pinched me black and blue. There was a pool of ink, and a child who saw pictures in it."

"Oh, but how delightful," exclaimed Julie de Labédoyère.

"Not at all, my dear, it was most alarming."

"But what did he tell you?"

The old lady bridled a little.

"Oh, a number of things that would interest nobody now, though at the time they were extremely absorbing. But one thing you told me, Monsieur, and that was that I should die in a foreign land, and I assure you I find it a vastly consoling prophecy at present."

"It is true," said Aristide, fixing his blue eyes upon her.

"To be sure," she continued, "you told Jeanne she would have three husbands, and a child by each of them, all of which came most punctually to pass; but, Monsieur, I fear now that Jeanne will have my prophecy as well as her own, since she had the sense to leave France two years ago when it was still possible, and I was foolish enough to stay here."

The old man shook his head and leaned back again, closing his eyes.

"What is the future to us now?" said Mme. de Vieuxmesnil in a low voice. "It holds nothing."

"Are you so sure?" asked Aristide, and she started, turning a little paler, but Mme. de Labédoyère turned on him with vivacity.

"Oh, but can you really tell the future?" she asked.

"When there is a future to tell," he said, stroking his white beard with a thin transparent hand, and his eyes rested curiously upon her as he spoke. Something in their expression made old Mme. de Breteuil shiver a little.

"Even now he frightens me," she whispered to Aline, but Julie de Labédoyère had clasped her hands.

"Oh, but how ravishing," she exclaimed. "Tell us then, Monsieur, tell us all our futures. I am ready to die of dulness, and so I am sure are these ladies. It will really be a deed of charity if you will amuse us for an hour."

"The future is not always amusing," said Aristide with a slight chilly smile. "Also," he added after a pause, "there is no child here. I need one to read the visions in the pool of ink."

"The gaoler has a tribe of children," said Mme. de Labédoyère eagerly. "I have a little money. If I made him a present he would send us one."

"It must be a young child, under seven years old."

"But why?"

"The eyes, Madame, must be clear. With conscious sin, with the first touch of sorrow, the first breath of passion, there comes a mist, and the visions are read no longer."

"Well, there are children enough," she answered with a shrug. "I have seen a little girl of about five-Marie, I think she is called: we will ask for her."

Almost as she spoke the door was thrown open and the gaoler entered. He brought another prisoner to share the already crowded room. If Paris streets were silent and empty, her prisons were full enough. This was a pale slip of a girl, with a pitiful hacking cough. She entered listlessly, and sank down in a corner as if she had not strength to stand.

"The end of the journey," said Aristide under his breath, but Mme. de Labédoyère was by the gaoler's side talking volubly.

"It is only for an hour-and see —" here something slipped from her hand to his. "It will be a diversion for the child, and for us, mon Dieu, it may save our lives! How would you feel if you were to find us all dead one morning just from sheer ennui?"

"I don't know that I should fret," said the man with a grin, and Mme. de Labédoyère bit her lip.

"But you will lend us Marie," she said insistently.

"Oh, if you like, and if she will come. It is nothing to me, and she is not of an age to have her principles corrupted," said the man, laughing at his own wit.

He went out with a jingle of keys, and in a few minutes the door opened once more, and a serious-eyed person of about five years old staggered in, carrying a very fat, heavy baby, whose sleepy head nodded across her shoulder.

She hesitated a moment and then came in, closed the door, and finally sat down between Aline and Mlle. Ange, disposing the baby upon her diminutive lap.

"This is Mutius Scaevola," she volunteered; "my mother washes and I am in charge. He is very sleepy, but one is never sure. He is a wicked baby. Sometimes he roars so that the roof comes off one's head. Then my mother says it is my fault, and slaps me."

"Give him to me," said Mlle. Ange suddenly.

The serious Marie regarded her for a moment, and then allowed her charge to be transferred to the stranger's lap, where he promptly fell fast asleep.

"Come here, my child," said the old gentleman in the corner, and Marie went to him obediently.

He had poured ink into his palm, and now held it under her eyes, putting his other arm gently round the child.

"Look now, little one. Look and tell us what you see, and you, Madame," he said, beckoning to Mme. de Labédoyère, "come nearer and put your hand upon her head."

"Do you see anything, child?"

"I see ink," said Marie sedately. "It will make your hand very dirty, sir. Once I got some on my frock, and it never came out. I was beaten for that."

"Hush, then, little one, and look into the ink. Presently there will be pictures there. Then you may speak and tell us what you see."

Silence fell on the small hot room. Ange Desaix rocked softly with the sleeping child. She was the only one who never even glanced at the astrologer and his pupil.

Presently Marie said:

"Monsieur, there is a picture."

"What then, say?"

"A boy, with a broom, sweeping."

He nodded gravely.

"Yes, yes. Watch well; the pictures come."

"He has made a clean place," said the child, "and on the clean place there is a shadow. Ah, now it turns into a lady-into this lady whose hand is on my head. She stands and looks at me, and a man comes and catches her by the neck and cuts off her hair. That is a pity, for her hair is very long and fine. Why does he cut it?"

"Mon Dieu!" said Mme. de Labédoyère with a sob. She released the child and sat down by the wall, leaning against it, her eyes wide with fear.

"You asked to see the future, Madame," said the old man impassively.

"Can you show the past?" asked Mme. de Vieuxmesnil, half hesitatingly.

"Assuredly. You must touch the child, and think of what you wish to see."

She came forward and put out her hand, but drew it quickly back again.

"No," she murmured; "it is perhaps a sin. I am too near the end for that, and when one cannot even confess."

"As you will," said the old man.

"And you, Madame," he turned to Aline, "is there nothing you would know; no one for whose welfare you are anxious?"

She started, for he had read her thoughts, which were full of Dangeau. It was months now since any word had come from him, and she longed inexpressibly for tidings. Lawful or unlawful, she would try this way, since there was no other. She laid her hand lightly on the little girl's head, and once more the child looked into the dark pool.

"There are so many people," she said at last. "They run to and fro, and wave their arms. That makes one's head ache."

"Go on looking," said Aristide.

"There is a lady there now. It is this lady. She looks very frightened. Some one has put a red cap on her head. Ah-now a gentleman comes. He takes her hand and puts a ring on it. Now he kisses her."

Aline drew away. The clamour and the crowd, the hasty wedding, the cold first kiss, all swam together in her mind.

"That is the past," she said in a low, strained voice. "Tell me where he is now. Is he alive? Where is he? Shall I see him again?"

She had forgotten her surroundings, the listeners, Mme. de Breteuil's sharp eyes. She only looked eagerly at Aristide, and he nodded once or twice, and laid her hand again on the child's head.

"She shall look," he said, but Marie lifted weary eyes.

"Monsieur, I am tired," she said.

"Just this once more, little one. Then you shall sleep," and she turned obediently and bent again over his hand.

"I do not like this picture," she said fretfully.

"What is it?"

"I do not know. There is a platform, with a ladder that goes up. I cannot see the top. Ah-there is the lady again. She goes up the ladder. Her hair is cut off, close to the head. That is not at all pretty, but it is the same lady, and the gentleman is there too."

"What gentleman?" asked Aline, in a clear voice.

"The same who was in the other picture, who put the ring upon your finger and kissed your forehead. It is he, a tall monsieur with blue eyes. He has no hat on, and his arms are tied behind him. Oh, I do not like this picture. Need I look any more?" and her voice took a wailing sound.

"No, it is enough," said Aline gently.

She drew the child away and sat down by Mlle. Ange, who still rocked the sleeping baby. Marie leaned her head beside her brother's and shut her eyes. Ange Desaix put an arm about her too, and she slept.

But Aristide was still looking at Aline.

"I do not understand," he said under his breath. "You have none of the signs, none of them. Now she,"—he indicated Mme. de Labédoyère, "one can see it at a glance. A short life, and a death of violence, but with you it is different. Give me your hand."

He was within reach, and she put it out half mechanically. He looked at it long, and then laid it back in her lap.

"You have a long life still," he said, "a long, prosperous life. The child was tired, she read amiss. The sign was not for you."

Aline shook her head. It did not seem to matter very much now. She was so tired. What was death? At least, if the vision were true, she would see her husband again. They would forgive one another, and she would be able to forget his bitter farewell look.

Meanwhile Dangeau waited for death in La Force. His cell contained only one inmate, a man who seemed to have sustained some serious injury to the head, since he lay swathed in bandages and moaned continually.

"Who is he?" he asked Defarge, the gaoler, and the man shrugged his shoulders.

"One there is enough coil about for ten," he grumbled. "One pays that he should have a cell to himself, and another sends him milk. It seems he is wanted to live, since this morning I get orders to admit a surgeon to him. Bah! If he knew when he was well off, he would make haste and die. For me, I would prefer that to sneezing into Sanson's basket; but what would you? No one is ever contented."

That afternoon the surgeon came, a brisk, round-bodied person with a light roving hazel eye, and quick, clever hands. He fell to his work, and after loitering a moment Defarge went out, leaving the door open, and passing occasionally, when he would pop his head in, grumble a little, and pass on again.

Dangeau watched idly. Something in the little man's appearance seemed familiar, but for the moment he could not place him. Suddenly, however, the busy hands ceased their work for a moment, and the surgeon glanced sharply over his shoulder. "Here, can you hold this for me?" and as Dangeau knelt opposite to him and put his finger to steady the bandage, he said:

"I know your face. Where have I seen you, eh?"

"And I know yours. My name is Dangeau."

"Aha—I thought so. You were Edmond's friend. Poor Edmond! But what would you? He was too imprudent."

"Yes, I was Edmond Cléry's friend," said Dangeau; "and you are his uncle. I met you with him once. Citizen Goyot, is it not?"

"At your service. There, that's finished."

"Who is he; will he live?" asked Dangeau, as the patient twitched and groaned.

Goyot shrugged.

"He has friends who want him to live, and enemies who are almost as anxious that he should n't die."

"A riddle, Citizen?"

"Oh, I don't know. You may conceive, if you will, that his friends desire his assistance, and that his enemies desire him to compromise his friends."

"Ah, it is that way?"

"I did not say so," said Goyot. "Good-day, Citizen," and he departed, leaving Dangeau something to think about, and a new interest in his fellow-prisoner.

Next day behold Goyot back again. He enlisted Dangeau's services at once, and Defarge having left them, shutting the door this time, he observed with a keen look:

"I 've been refreshing my memory about you, Citizen Dangeau."

"Indeed."

"Yes; you still have a friend or two. Who says the days of miracles are over? You have been away a year and are not quite forgotten."

"And what did my friends say?" asked Dangeau, smiling a little.

"They said you were an honest man. I said there were n't two in Paris. They declared you were one of them."

"Ciel, Citizen, you are a pessimist."

"Optimists lose their heads these days," said Goyot with a grimace. "But after all one must trust some one, or one gets no further."

"Certainly."

"Well, we want to get further, that is all."

"Your meaning, Citizen?"

"Mon Dieu, must I dot all the i's?"

"Well, one or two perhaps."

"I have a patient sicker than this," said Goyot abruptly.

"Yes?"

"France," he said in a low voice.

Dangeau gave a deep sigh.

"You are right," he said.

"Of course, it's my trade. The patient is very ill. Too much blood-letting—you understand? There 's a gangrene which is eating away the flesh, poisoning the whole body. It must be cut out."

"Robespierre."

"Mon Dieu, Citizen, no names! Though, to be sure, that one 's in the air. A queer thing human nature. I knew him well years ago. You 'd have said he could n't hurt a fly; would turn pale at the mention of an execution; and now-well, they say the appetite comes with eating, and life is a queer comedy."

"Comedy?" said Dangeau bitterly. "It's tragedy that fills the boards for most of us to-day."

"Ah! that depends on how you take it. Keep an eye on the ridiculous: foster it, play for it, and you have farce. Take things lightly, with a turn of wit and a playful way, and it is comedy. Tragedy demands less effort, I 'll admit, but for me-Vive la Comédie. We are discussing the ethics of the drama," he explained to Defarge, who poked his head in at this juncture.

"Will that mend his head?" inquired the gaoler with a scowl.

"Ah, my dear Defarge, that, I fear, is past praying for; but I have better hopes of my other patient."

"Who 's that?" asked the man, staring.

"A lady, my friend, in whom Citizen Dangeau is interested. A surgical case-but I have great hopes, great hopes of curing her," and with that he went out, smiling and talking all the way down the corridor.

Dangeau grew to look for his coming. Sometimes he merely got through his work as quickly as possible, but occasionally he would drop some hint of a plot-of plans to overthrow Robespierre.

"The patient's friends are willing now," he said one day. "It is a matter of seizing the favourable moment. Meanwhile one must have patience."

Dangeau smiled a trifle grimly. Patience, when one's head is under the axe, may be a desirable, but it is not an easily cultivated, virtue.

Life had begun to look sweet to him once more. The mood in which he had suddenly flung defiance at Robespierre was past, and if the old, vivid dreams came back no more, yet the dark horizon began to show a sober gleam of hope.

Every sign proclaimed the approaching fall of Robespierre, and Dangeau looked past the Nation's temporary delirium to a time of convalescence, when the State, restored to sanity, might be built up, if not towards perfection, at least in the direction of sober statesmanship and peaceful government.

## CHAPTER XXIX
## THROUGH DARKNESS TO LIGHT

So dawned the morning of the twenty-seventh of July, the 9th Thermidor in the new Calendar of the Revolution. A very hot, still day, with a veiled sky dreaming of thunder. Dangeau had passed a very disturbed night, for his fellow-prisoner was worse. The long unconsciousness yielded at last, and slid through vague mutterings into a high delirium, which tasked his utmost strength to control. Goyot was to come early, since this development was not entirely unexpected; but the morning passed, and still he did not appear. By two o'clock the patient was in a stupour again, and visibly within an hour or two of the end. No skill could avail him now.

Suddenly the door was thrown open, and Dangeau heard himself summoned.

"Your time at last," said Defarge, and he followed the man without a word. In the corridor they met Goyot, his hair much rumpled, his eyes bright and restless with excitement.

"You? Where are you going?" he panted.

"Where does one go nowadays?" returned Dangeau, with a slight shrug.

"No, no," exclaimed Goyot. "It's not possible. We had arranged-your name was to be kept back."

"Bah," said Defarge, spitting on the ground. "You need not look at me like that, Citizen. It is not my fault. You know that well enough. Orders come, and must be obeyed. I 'm neither blind nor deaf. Things are changing out there, I 'm told, but orders are orders, and a plain man looks no further."

Goyot caught at Dangeau's arm.

"We'll save you yet," he said. "Robespierre is down. Accused this morning in Convention. They 're all at his throat now. Keep a good heart, my friend; his time has come at last."

"And mine," returned Dangeau.

"No, no —I tell you there is hope. It is only a matter of hours."

"Just so."

Defarge interposed.

"Ciel, Citizens, are we to stand here all day? Citizen Goyot, your patient is dying, and you had better see to him. This citizen and I have an engagement-yes, and a pressing one."

An hour later Dangeau passed in to take his trial. His predecessor's case had taken a scant five minutes, so simple a matter had the death penalty become.

Fouquier Tinville seated himself, his sharp features more like the fox's mask than ever, only now it was the fox who hears the hounds so close upon his heels that he dares not look behind to see how close they are. Fear does not improve the temper, and he nodded maliciously at his former colleague.

"Name," he rapped out, voice and eye alike vicious.

With smooth indifference Dangeau repeated his names, and added with a touch of amusement:

"You know me and my names well enough, or did once, my good Tinville."

The thin lips lifted in a snarl.

"That, my friend, was when you were higher in the world than you are now. Place of abode?"

Dangeau's gaze went past him. He shrugged his shoulders with a faintly whimsical effect.

"Shall we say the edges of the world?" he suggested.

Fouquier Tinville spat on the floor and leaned over the table with a yellow glitter in his eyes.

"How does it feel?" he sneered. "The edges of the world. Ma foi, how does it feel to look over them into annihilation?"

Dangeau returned his look with composure.

"I imagine you may soon have an opportunity of judging," he observed.

At Tinville's right hand a man sat drumming on the table. Now he looked up sharply, exhibiting a dead white face, where the lips hung loose, and the eyes showed wildly bloodshot.

"But if one could know first," he said in a shaking voice. "When one is so close and looks over, one should see more than others. I have asked so many what they saw. I asked Danton. He said 'The void.' Do you think it is that? As man to man now, Dangeau, do you think there is anything beyond or not?"

Dangeau recognised him with a movement of half-contemptuous pity. It was Duval, the actor who had taken to politics and drink, and sold his soul for a bribe of Robespierre's.

Tinville plucked him down with a curse.

"Tiens, Duval, you grow too mad," he said angrily. "You and your beyond. What should there be?"

"If there were-Hell," muttered Duval, with shaking lips. Tinville banged the table.

"Am I to have all the Salpêtrière here?" he shouted. "Have n't we cut off enough priests' heads yet? I tell you we have abolished Heaven, and Purgatory, and Hell, and all the rest of those child's tales."

A murmur of applause ran round. Duval's hand went to his breast, and drew out a flask. He drank furtively, and leaned back again.

Dangeau was moving away, but he turned for a moment, the old sparkle in his eyes.

"My felicitations, Tinville," he observed with a casual air.

"On what?"

Dangeau smiled politely.

"The convenience for you of having abolished Hell! It is a masterstroke. It only remains for me to wish you an early opportunity of verifying your statements."

"Take him out," said Tinville, stamping his foot, and Dangeau went down the steps, and into the long adjoining room where the prisoners waited for the tumbrils. It was too much trouble now to take them back again to prison, so the Justice Hall was itself the ante-chamber of the guillotine. It was hot, and Dangeau felt the lassitude which succeeds a strain. Of what use to bandy words with Fouquier Tinville, of what use anything, since the last word lay with the strongest, and this hour was the hour of his death? It is very difficult for a strong man, with his youth still vigorous in every vein, to realise that for him hope and fear, joy and pain, struggle and endurance, are all at an end, and that the next step is that final one into the blind and unknown pathways of the infinite.

He thought of Robespierre, out there in the tideway fighting for his life against the inexorable waves of Fate. Even now the water crept salt and sickly about his mouth. Well, if it drowned him, and swept France clean again, what did it matter if the swirl of the tide swept Dangeau from his foothold too?

Absorbed in thought, he took no note of his companions in misfortune. There was a small crowd of them at the farther end of the room, a gendarme or two stood gossiping by, and there was a harsh clipping sound now and again, for the prisoners' hair was a perquisite of the concierge's wife, and it was cut off here, before they went to the scaffold.

The woman stood by to-day and watched it done. The perquisite was a valuable one, and on the previous day she had been much annoyed by the careless cutting which had ruined a magnificent head of auburn hair. To-day she had noted that one of the women had a valuable crop, and she was instant in her directions for its cutting. Presently she pushed past Dangeau and lifted the lid of a basket which hung against the wall. His glance followed her idly, and saw that the basket was piled high with human hair. The woman muttered to herself as her eye rested on the ruined auburn locks. Then she took to-day's spoil, tress by tress, from her apron, knotting the hair roughly together, and dropping it into the open basket. Dangeau watched her with a curious sick sensation. The contrast between the woman's unsexed face and the pitiful relics she handled affected him disagreeably, but beyond this he experienced a strange, tingling sensation unlike anything in his recollection.

The auburn hair was hidden now by a bunch of gay black curls. A long, straight, flaxen mass fell next, and then a thick waving tress, gold in the light, and brown in the shade, catching the sun that crossed it for a moment, as Aline's hair had always done.

He shuddered through all his frame, and turned away. Thank God, thank God she was safe at Rancy! And with that a sudden movement parted the crowd at the other side of the room, and he looked across and saw her.

He had heard of visions in the hour of death, but as he gazed, a cold sweat broke upon his brow, and he knew it was she herself, Aline, his wife, cast for death as he was cast. Her profile was towards him, cut sharply against the blackened wall. Her face was lifted. Her eyes dwelt on the patch of sky which an open window gave to view. How changed, O God, how changed she was! How visibly upon the threshold. The beauty had fallen away from her face, leaving it a mere frail mask, but out of her eyes looked a spirit serenely touched with immortality. It is the look worn only by those who are about to die, and look past death into the Presence.

It was a look that drove the blood from Dangeau's heart; a wave of intolerable anger against Fate, of intolerable anguish for the wife so found again, swept it back again. He moved to go to her, and as he did so, saw a man approach and begin to pinion her arms, whilst the opening of a door and the roll of wheels outside proclaimed the arrival of the tumbrils. In the same moment Dangeau accosted the man, his last coin in his hand.

"This for you if you will get me into the same cart as this lady, and see, friend, let it be the last one."

What desperate relic of spent hope prompted his last words he hardly knew, for after all what miracle could Goyot work? but at least he would have a few more minutes to gaze at Aline before the darkness blotted out her face.

Jean Legros, stupid and red-faced, stared a moment at the coin, then pocketed it with a nod and grunt, and fell to tying Dangeau's arms. At the touch of the cord an exclamation escaped him, and it was at this moment that Aline, roused from her state of abstraction by something in the voice behind her, turned her head and saw him.

They were so close together that her movement brought them into contact, and at the touch, and as their eyes met, anguish was blotted out, and for one wonderful instant they leaned together whilst each heart felt the other's throb.

"My heart!" he said, and then before either could speak again they were being pushed forward towards the open door.

The last tumbril waited; Dangeau was thrust into it, roughly enough, and as he pitched forward he saw that Aline behind him had stumbled, and would have fallen but for fat Jean's arm about her waist. She shrank a little, and the fellow gave a stupid laugh.

"What, have you never had a man's arm round you before?" he said loudly, and gave her a push that sent her swaying against Dangeau's shoulder. The knot of idlers about the door broke into coarse jesting, and the bound man's hands writhed against his bonds until the cords cut deep into the flesh of his wrist, and the blood oozed against the twisted rope.

Aline leaned nearer. She was conscious only that here was rest. Since Mlle. Ange died of the prison fever two days ago, she had not slept or wept. She had thought perhaps she might die too, and be saved the knife, but now nothing mattered any more. He was here; he loved her. They would die together. God was very good.

His voice sounded from far, far away.

"I thought you safe; I thought you at Rancy, oh, God!" and she roused a little to the agony in his tone, and looked at him with those clear eyes of hers. Through all the dreamlike strangeness she felt still the woman's impulse to comfort the beloved.

"God, who holds us in the hollow of His hand, knows that we are safe," she said, and at that he groaned "Safe!" so that she fought against the weariness that made her long just to put her head upon his shoulder and be at peace.

"There was too much between us," she said very low. "We could not be together here, but we could not be happy apart. I do not think God will take us away from one another. It is better like this, my dear!—it is better."

Her voice fell on a low, contented note, and he felt her lean more closely yet. An agony of rebellion rent his very soul. To love one woman only, to renounce her, to find her after long months of pain, to hear her say what he had hoped for only in his dreams, and then to know that he must watch her die. What vision of Paradise could blot this torture out? Powerless, powerless, powerless! In the height of his strength, and not able even to strike down the brute whose coarse hand touched her, and that other brute who would presently butcher her before his very eyes.

Then, whilst his straining senses reeled, he felt a jolt and the cart stopped. All about them surged an excited crowd.

There was a confused noise, women screamed. One high, clear voice called out, "Murderers! Assassins!" and the crowd took up the cry with angry insistence.

"See the old man! and the girl! ma foi, she has an angel's face. Is the guillotine to eat up every one?"

The muttering rose to a growl, and the growl to a roar. To and fro surged the growing crowd, the horses began to back, the car tilted. Dangeau looked round him, his heart beating to suffocation, but Aline appeared neither to know nor care what passed. For her the world was empty save for they two, and for them the gate of Heaven stood wide. She heard the song of the morning stars; she caught a glimpse of the glory unutterable, unthinkable.

As the shouting grew, the driver of their cart cast anxious glances over his shoulder. All at once he stood up, waving his red cap, calling, gesticulating.

A cry went up, "The gendarmerie, Henriot! Henriot and the gendarmes!" and the press was driven apart by the charge of armed horsemen. At their head rode Henriot, just freed from prison, flushed with strong drink, savage with his own impending doom.

The crowd scattered, but a man sprang for an instant to the wheels of the cart, and whispered one swift sentence in Dangeau's ear:

"Robespierre falls; nothing can save him."

It was Goyot in a workman's blouse, and as he dropped off again Dangeau made curt answer.

"In time for France, if not for me. Good-bye, my friend," and then Goyot was gone and the lumbering wheels rolled on.

On the other side of the cart, the Abbé Delacroix prayed audibly, and the smooth Latin made a familiar cadence, like running water heard in childhood, and kept in some secret cell of the memory. Beside the priest sat old General de Loiserolles, grey and soldierly, hugging the thought that he had saved his boy; how entirely he was not to know. Answering his son's name, leaving that son sleeping, he was giving him, not the doubtful reprieve of a day, but all the years of his natural life, since young De Loiserolles was amongst those set free by the death of Robespierre.

As the cart stopped by the scaffold foot, he crossed himself, and followed the Abbé to the axe, with a simple dignity that drew a strange murmur from the crowd. For the heart of Paris was melting fast, and the bloodshed was become a weariness. Prisoner after prisoner went up the steps, and after each dull thud announced the fallen axe, that long ominous "ah" of the crowd went up.

Dangeau and Aline were the last, and when they came to the steps he moved to go before her, then cursed himself for a coward, and stood aside to let her pass. She looked sweetly at him for a moment and passed on, climbing with feet that never faltered. She did not note the splashed and slippery boards, nor Sanson and his assistants all grimed and daubed from their butcher's work, but her eye was caught by the sea of upturned faces, all white, all eyeing her, and her head turned giddy. Then some one touched her, held her, pulled away the kerchief at her breast, and as the sun struck hot upon her uncovered shoulders, a burning blush rose to her very brow, and the dream in which she had walked was gone. Her brain reeled with the awakening, heaven clouded, and the stars were lost. She was aware only of Sanson's hot hand at her throat, and all those eyes astare to see her death.

The hand pushed her, her foot felt the slime of blood beneath it, she saw the dripping knife, and all at once she felt herself naked to the abyss. In Sanson's grip she turned wide terror-stricken eyes on Dangeau, making a little, piteous, instinctive movement towards him, her protector, and at that and his own impotence he felt each pulse in his strong body thud like a hammered drum, and with one last violent effort of the will he wrenched his eyelids down, lest he should look upon the end. All through the journey there had been as it were a sword in his heart, but at her look and gesture-her frightened look, her imploring gesture-the sword was turned and still he was alive, alive to watch her die. In those moments his soul left time and space, and hung a tortured point, infinitely lonely, infinitely agonised, in some illimitable region of never-ending pain. There was no past, no future, only Eternity and his undying soul in anguish. The thousand years were as a day, and the day as a thousand years. There was no beginning and no end. O God, no end!

He did not hear the crowd stir a little, and drift hither and thither as it was pressed upon from one side; he did not see the gendarmes press against the drift, only to be driven back again, hustled, surrounded so that their horses were too hampered to answer to the spur. Suddenly a woman went down screaming under the horses' feet, and on the instant the crowd flamed into fury before the agonised shriek had died away. In a moment all was a seething, shouting, cursing welter of struggling humanity. The noise of it reached even Dangeau's stunned brain, and he said within himself, "It is over. She is dead," and opened his eyes.

The scaffold stood like an island in a sea grown suddenly wild with tempest, and even as he looked, the human waves of it broke in a fierce swirl which welled up and overflowed it on every side.

Sanson, his hand on the machinery, was whirled aside, jostled, pushed, cursed. A fat woman, with bare, mottled arms, Heaven knows how she came on the platform, dealt him a resounding smack on the face, and shrieked voluble abuse, which was freely echoed.

Dangeau was surrounded, embraced, cheered, lifted off his feet, the cord that bound his arms slashed through, and of a sudden Goyot had him round the neck, and he found voice and clamoured Aline's name. The little surgeon, after one glance at his wild eyes, pushed with him through the surging press; they had to fight their way, and the place was slippery, but they were through at last, through and down on their knees by the woman who lay bound beneath the knife that Sanson's hand was freeing when the tumult caught him. A dozen hands snatched her back again now, the cords were cut, and Dangeau's shaking voice called in her ears, called loudly, and in vain.

"Air, give her air and room," he cried, and some pushed forwards and others back. The fat woman took the girl's head upon her lap, whilst tears rained down her crimson cheeks.

"Eh, the poor pretty one," she sobbed hysterically, and pulled off her own ample kerchief to cover Aline's thin bosom. Dangeau leaned over her calling, calling still, unaware of Goyot at his side, and of Goyot's voice saying insistently, "Tiens, my friend, that was a near shave, eh?"

"My wife," he muttered, "my wife-my wife is dead," and with that he gazed round wildly, cried "No, no!" in a sharp voice, and fell to calling her again.

Goyot knelt on the reeking boards, caught the frail wrist in that brown skilful hand of his, shifted his grasp once, twice, a third time, shook his head, and took another grip. "No, she 's alive," he said at last, and had to say it more than once, for Dangeau took no heed.

"Aline! Aline! Aline!" he called in hoarse, trembling tones, and Goyot dropped the girl's wrist and took him harshly by the shoulder.

"Rouse, man, rouse!" he cried. "She's alive. I tell you. I swear it. For the love of Heaven, wake up, and help me to get her away. It's touch and go for all of us these next few hours. At any moment Henriot may have the upper hand, and half an hour would do our business, with this pretty toy so handy." He grimaced at the red axe above them, "Come, Dangeau, play the man!"

Dangeau stared at him.

"What am I to do?" he asked irritably.

Goyot pressed his shoulder with a firm hand.

"Lift your wife, and bring her along after me. Can you manage? She looks light enough."

It was no easy matter to come through the excited crowd, but Dangeau's height told, and with Aline's head against his shoulder he pushed doggedly in the wake of Goyot, who made his way through the press with a wonderful agility. Down the steps now, and inch by inch forward through the jostling excited people. Up a by way at last, and then sharp to the left where a carriage waited, and with that Goyot gave a gasp of relief, and mopped a dripping brow.

"Eh, mon Dieu!" he said; "get in, get in!"

The carriage had mouldy straw on the floor, and the musty odour of it mounted in the hot air.

Dangeau complained of it sharply.

"A devil of a smell, this, Goyot!" and the little surgeon fixed him with keen, watchful eyes, as he nodded acquiescence.

What house they came to, or how they came to it, Dangeau knew no more than his unconscious wife. She lay across his breast, white and still as the dead, and when he laid her down on the bed in the upper room they reached at last, she fell limply from his grasp, and he turned to Goyot with a groan.

A soft, white-haired woman, dark-eyed and placid-afterwards he knew her for Goyot's housekeeper-tried to turn him out of the room, but he would go no farther than the window, where he sat staring, staring at the houses across the way, watching them darken in the gathering dusk, and mechanically counting the lights that presently sprang into view.

Behind him Marie Carlier came and went, at Goyot's shortly worded orders, until at last Dangeau's straining ears caught the sound of a faint, fluttering sigh. He turned then, the lights in the room dancing before his burning eyes. For a moment the room seemed full of the small tongues of flame, and then beyond them he saw his wife's eyes open again, whilst her hand moved in feeble protest against the draught which Goyot himself was holding to her lips.

Dangeau got up, stood a moment gazing, and then stumbled from the room and broke into heavy sobbing. Presently Goyot brought him something in a glass, which he drank obediently.

"Now you will sleep," said the little man in cheerful accents, and sleep he did, and never stirred until the high sun struck across his face and waked him to France's new day, and his.

For in that night fell Robespierre, cast down by the Convention he had dominated so long. The dawn that found him shattered, praying for the death he had vainly sought, awakened Paris from the long nightmare which had been the marriage gift of her nuptials with this incubus.

At four o'clock on the afternoon of the 10th Thermidor, Robespierre's head fell under the bloody axe of the Terror, and with his last gasp the life went out of the greatest tyranny of modern times.

When Goyot came home with the news, Dangeau's face flamed, and he put his hand before his eyes for a moment.

Then he went up to Aline. She had lain in a deep sleep for many, many hours, but towards the afternoon she had wakened, taken food, and dressed herself, all in a strange, mechanical fashion. She was neither to be gainsaid nor persuaded, and Dangeau, reasonable once more, had left her to the kind and unexciting ministrations of Marie Carlier. Now he could keep away no longer; Goyot followed him and the housekeeper met them by the door.

"She is strange, Monsieur," she whispered.

"She has not roused at all?" inquired Goyot rather anxiously.

Marie shook her head.

"She just sits and stares at the sky. God knows what she sees there, poor lamb. If she would weep — —"

"Just so, just so," Goyot nodded once or twice. Then he turned a penetrating look on Dangeau.

"Ha, you are all right again. A near thing, my friend, eh? Small wonder you were upset by it."

"Oh, I!" said Dangeau, with an impatient gesture. "It is my wife we are speaking of."

"Yes, yes, of course —a little patience, my dear Dangeau-yes, your wife. Marie here, without being scientific, is a sensible woman, and it's a wonderful thing how common-sense comes to the same conclusions as science. A fascinating subject that, but, as you are about to observe, this is not the time to pursue it. What I mean to say is, that your wife is suffering from severe shock; her brain is overcharged, and Marie is quite right when she suggests that tears would relieve it. Now, my good Dangeau, do you think you can make your wife cry?"

"I don't know—I must go to her."

"Well, well, go. Don't excite her, but-dear me, Marie, how impatient people are. When one has saved a man's life, he might at least let one finish a sentence, instead of breaking away in the middle of it. Get me something to eat, for, parbleu, I 've earned it."

Dangeau had closed the door, and stood looking at his wife.

"Aline," he said, "have they told you? We are safe-Robespierre is dead."

Then he threw back his head, took a long, deep breath, and cried:

"It is new life-new life for France, new work for those who love her-new life for us-for us, Aline."

Aline stood by the window, very still. At the sound of Dangeau's voice she turned her head. He saw that she was smiling, and his heart contracted as he looked at her.

Death had come so close to her, so very close, that it seemed to him the shadow of it lay cold and still above that strange unchanging smile; and he called to her abruptly, with a rough tenderness.

"Aline! Aline!"

She looked up then, and he saw then the same smile lie deep within her eyes. Unfathomably peaceful they were, but not with the peace of the living.

"Won't you come to me, my dear," he said gently, and with the simplicity he would have used to a child.

A little shiver just stirred the stillness of her form, and she came slowly, very slowly, across the room, and then stood waiting, and with a sudden passion Dangeau laid both hands upon her shoulders insistently, heavily.

He wondered had she lost the memory of the last time he had touched and held her thus. Then he had fought with pride and been defeated. Now he must fight again, fight for her very soul and reason, and this time he must win, or the whole world would be lost. He paused, gathering all the forces of his soul, then looked at her with passionate uneasiness.

If she would tremble, if she would even shrink from him-anything but that calm which was there, and shone serenely fixed, like the smile upon the faces of the dead.

It hinted of the final secret known.

"Mon Dieu! Aline, don't look like that!" he cried, and in strong protest his arms slipped lower, and drew her close to his heart that beat, and beat, as if it would supply the life hers lacked. She came passively at his touch, and stood in his embrace unresisting and unresponsive.

Remembering how she had flushed at a look and quivered at a touch, his fears redoubled, and he caught her close, and closer, kissing her, at first gently, but in the end with all the force of a passion so long restrained. For now at last the dam was down, and they stood together in love's full flowing tide.

When he drew back, the smile was gone, and the lips that it had left trembled piteously, as her colour came and went to each quickened breath.

"Aline," he said, very low, "Aline, my heart! It is new life-new life together."

She pushed him back a pace then, and raised her eyes with a look he never forgot. The peace had left them now, and they were troubled to the depths, and brimmed with tears. Her lips quivered more and more, the breath came from them in a great sob, and suddenly she fell upon his breast in a passion of weeping.

www.ingramcontent.com/pod-product-compliance
Lightning Source LLC
Chambersburg PA
CBHW071013030425
24551CB00022B/216
* 9 7 8 8 0 2 7 3 4 0 0 4 0 *